The CHILDREN OF BERLIN

BOOKS BY SHARON MAAS

SHARON MAAS

The CHILDREN OF BERLIN

bookouture

Published by Bookouture in 2023

An imprint of Storyfire Ltd.
Carmelite House
50 Victoria Embankment
London EC4Y 0DZ

www.bookouture.com

ISBN: 978-1-83790-511-9
eBook ISBN: 978-1-83790-510-2

This book is a work of fiction. Whilst some characters and circumstances portrayed by the author are based on real people and historical fact, references to real people, events, establishments, organizations or locales are intended only to provide a sense of authenticity and are used fictitiously. All other characters and all incidents and dialogue are drawn from the author's imagination and are not to be construed as real.

In memory of the three women who inspired this novel: Uschi, Trudel, M.

PROLOGUE: BEFORE

LEAH

The letter sat in my postbox, bulky and intriguing and all innocent, amid the usual wad of bills and invoices. The Bundesrepublik Deutschland stamp gave me my first shock. It had been years since I'd had a letter from West Germany. Not since Tante Helga's death, in fact. Just a few official letters, which wrapped up all my German affairs. I'd washed my hands of Germany, that evil state.

I frowned as I regarded the fat envelope, as yet so innocent. My name and address, handwritten in a large scrawl that was somehow familiar. I didn't receive many personal letters. I turned the envelope over and there on the back flap was the name and address of the sender. A name that sent chills down my spine. An address that I knew all too well:

Magdalena Bosch
Kaiserkorso Eins
Berlin
West Germany

That name! A stab through my heart. I had not even thought of it in over a decade. Or rather, when memories arose uninvited, I pushed them away again. I had effectively wiped that name from my memory. I wanted never to hear it again, or read it. Or even think it. There was no need to. She was in the past, along with the darkness her name evoked. We had moved on, Naomi and I. Twenty years and more had passed since her birth in 1940, years of agony and pain and bereavement and struggle and displacement and relocation and everything in between. Here I was, now, with my new life. Why was *she* intruding?

It was the Easter holidays, and I'd hoped for a lovely time of freedom from the boisterous children in my primary school class – I loved them all, but a respite to gather my forces was always good. Naomi, now in her first year at university, had gone to stay with a friend in Scotland. Jörg was also not at home; he was in Norway, attending a course in ecological loghouse construction. I'd be alone for a while, with this letter and all it contained.

A private letter was usually inviting, a chance to reconnect with an old friend, delve into their lives, hear their news, repair severed lines. But not this letter. Not this... I couldn't call her a *friend*. Magda had long lost the right to that word. Yet – a letter. What could she possibly have to say? And why should I ever want to read her duplicitous words?

My first instinct was to chuck the unopened letter in the rubbish bin. But no, that would be too tempting. Curiosity would see me rummaging to retrieve it. I had to destroy it. Tear it up. No – too much temptation to put the pieces together again, a jigsaw puzzle. Burn it then, obliterate it from existence. Burn it whole.

I leaned down to the fireplace and placed the envelope on the grate. I reached for the box of matches on the mantelpiece, removed one match. Struck it, once, twice. A little flame flickered. I leaned forward to put flame to paper. And then I hesitated. I don't know why. I just couldn't. Just as the past cannot be deleted, so too I knew that turning this last piece of evidence that such a past even existed into ashes would not undo the years. Those years were still there. And though I had spent many more years doing my best to bury it all beneath the new life I'd built for myself, somehow they still existed. And that single question – what could she possibly have to say to me? – still burned within me.

Instead of burning it, I placed the letter on the kitchen table, leaning against the salt-and-pepper cruet. I stared at it. Looked away. Stared at it again. It sat there for days, and for days, I tried to ignore it. In vain. It seemed to have some kind of magical power. Memory after memory began to rise up in my mind, uninvited, forcing their way to the fore, evoked by the sight of that envelope, that so-familiar handwriting. Events I had tried so hard to forget. Pains that I had thought healed. Wounds that had grown healthy scabs. There it was again, a mass of unresolved, unnerving chaos. All the turmoil, all the anguish, all the fear and the agony and the unmitigated fury. All released at the sight of an envelope sitting in the middle of my table, staring at me as I ate my breakfast in the morning and my dinner in the evening. It was dangerous. More so than a grenade, an unexploded bomb. I had to defuse it, somehow. Make it safe. But how?

An envelope is in itself innocent, free of blame. It simply sat there, waiting. The most powerful thing in my kitchen. Eventually I picked it up. It felt hot, dangerous. Yes: I had to destroy it. I took it into the living room and once again laid it in the hearth, this time determined to do the necessary. But my hands trembled as I tried to put a match to a corner of the envelope and I dropped it and instead collapsed right there, dissolved in tears. Weeping and wailing because it all came back to me and I knew there was no way out but to face it.

I removed the envelope from the grate, slit the envelope's flap carefully open with a knife. A photograph immediately fell out. I picked it up and could not suppress the sob that rose in my throat. The photo was of four youths: two girls, two boys. The girls were about thirteen, the boys about three years older. The girls were me and Magda. The boys were our brothers, Markus and Aaron.

Our arms linked round each other's shoulders, bookended by the boys, Magda and me with our heads slightly touching, and all grinning cheek to cheek as if we'd just won the lottery and had booked our tickets to America.

America! The richest country in the world! Flowing with milk and honey, unlike our home country, Germany, still recovering from the Great War. America was the big dream, back then, for all four of us. The big adventure! We'd seen the Hollywood movies; Markus and Aaron dreamed of owning one of those fashionable Model T Fords and driving across the country, and we girls, just as we were becoming women – well, we'd wear sun hats and fancy shoes and we'd go to all the latest movies and fall in love with the stars and do the Charleston and the Shimmy and it would all be one big long holiday, and it would all happen in a few years' time, once we'd grown up. And we'd stick together. I already had a crush on Markus, but it was never meant to be. You made sure of that, didn't you, Magda? I suspected Magda was sweet on Aaron, though she'd never admit it in a thousand years.

In the photo, we are all on ice skates; I remembered that day, when we'd all gone to the ice rink in Kreuzberg. Politics didn't interest us. The adults were all so boring and depressing, always going on about reparations and the unfairness of the Versailles Treaty, and rations and hardships. Our response was to ignore boring reality and look ahead, forward, into a brilliant future in Technicolour. We were young, we were optimistic, we knew we'd live forever and life would scatter roses on our paths.

A memory now popped up of Magda, at the upright piano in her home, plonking out the accompaniment as she sang, at the top of her voice, 'Und der Haifisch, der hat Zähne', while we all danced, with exaggerated mimicry, as we sang along. 'The Shark has Teeth'. Indeed. Magda loved Brecht's *Die Dreigroschenoper, The Threepenny Opera*, just as she loved everything musical and cultural but, most especially, fun. Her taste was eclectic. Chorales and cabaret, Wolfgang Amadeus Mozart as well as Marlene Dietrich.

We all had hobbies. Mine was art; I loved sketching, and I became quite adept at drawing facial likenesses in charcoal. Aaron's hobby was chess; he was once crowned Berlin's youth chess champion. Markus was a born actor. He joined a youth theatre group and had already played many a leading role in public performances: which of course the rest of us always attended, rising up at the fall of the curtain to lead the cheers and the standing ovations.

And we all loved ice skating, as evidenced by this photo in my hand.

But that was then. They say photos don't lie. This one did.

The sentimental moment of reminiscence ended in a cold shudder as the aftermath burst through the veil of nostalgia. I removed the thick wad of papers from the envelope, plumped myself down into my favourite armchair and unfolded the wad.

The first thing I noticed was the actual typing. I recognised it at once: the letter 't' slightly raised, the bottom half of the capital letter 'S' missing, the missing letter 'd', which she'd always meticulously add in ink.

So, then. Magda was not only back at home: she was using her old typewriter, her precious Olympia. The heavy one that had once sat in a corner of her room at home, not the small portable one she'd taken with her when she went off on her mysterious missions.

I remembered that typewriter. At one point, she must have

been twelve or so, she'd been determined to become a novelist. To write stories. The three of us – she, Markus, me – were great readers, and it was convenient that Mother was a librarian, as she brought home a living stream of our favourite books. Markus loved the Karl May books, the German author who wrote countless stories set in the Wild West of America's pioneer days; stories of the cowboy Old Shatterhand, Winnetou, the fictional chief of the Mescalero tribe of the Apache.

I preferred stories of love and human drama, preferably set in foreign countries, especially England; a foretaste, perhaps, of my future: Jane Austen, Charlotte Brontë, Thomas Hardy, Dickens. Magda loved the German classics, the novels, poetry and plays of Goethe, Mann, Brecht, Schiller, Rilke. She also loved Shakespeare, which she read in the original English.

Magda would give her own overdramatic short stories to me to read and critique (or rather, admire): *'I'm going to be a writer, Leah! One day, my books will be in the shops and libraries! And I'll give you free signed copies and thank you publicly for being my first reader!'*

Now, the first page of her letter in hand, I grunted at the memory and almost, once again, chucked the whole thing in the fire. I knew her so well. Knowing Magda, she'd written it in duplicate, making two piles, the original for me, the carbon copy for herself, to be filed away. Magda was meticulous, organised.

I shook my head to free it from those cobwebs of the past and began to read.

MAGDA

Kaiserkorso 1
Berlin

Dear Leah,

You'll be surprised – shocked, actually – to be hearing from me after all these years. So many terrible and unforgiveable things have transpired in that time. You know now that I am not a good person. But this letter is not to ask forgiveness. I have no right to ask you for that.

In case you're wondering: I've known your address in England for many years, but never had the courage to write until now. I've been living in Mama's house ever since she died, and of course I found the letters you once wrote her, and your address. And of course I read them, so I am quite up to date on your situation, at least up to Mama's death. Did you wonder, at the time, who had sent you that death announcement, without a further word? Well, that was me. I just did not dare add a personal message to the announcement. That might have scared you.

Perhaps this is just a letter to myself, because I do not understand myself, and perhaps, through writing, I can gain a little comprehension. I am trying to make head or tail of the process that turned a thoroughly decent, caring German girl into – well, you know what I became. I was always given to ruminations. Perhaps a little too much; I tend to overthink things, analyse them, and that's not always a good thing. And perhaps that very idiosyncrasy is what led me down the path I took, a path that eventually tore us apart. Be that as it may, the time has come to render an account; I owe it to myself, and, perhaps, to you.

There is, or was, great evil in me and I must find the strength to face it.

I have reached the end of the road, and writing this is the only way forward for me. To truly and honestly face up to my past, without excuses or justifications or defences. This is not an attempt to assuage my guilt, which will always stand. It is an attempt to expose it. It might not be fair of me to burden you with my own unburdening but you are the only person I *can confess to, and I do think confession is important if there is ever to be healing. The Catholics have got that one right, at least.*

But perhaps I do not deserve healing. Once I have written this, I will know. Can there ever be healing from the evil that exists in one's own soul? I'm going to try and find out. Does evil deserve healing; can perpetrators ever find redemption? Of course, the victims of great injustice need healing and closure. What about the culprits? Can evil be completely scrubbed from such a heart? And again and again, I come back to the fact that it is not fair to turn to you, you of all people, in this my tortured need to rise, healed, from the wrong I have committed.

But now, you are reading this. At least this far. You will have seen my name and address on the envelope before you opened it. Thank you for having done so. You might have chosen not to open and read it at all, and I could not blame you for that decision. That is your prerogative. Maybe I'll receive a 'Return to Sender' and I will understand. It is what I deserve. But you are reading, and I am so very grateful and hope you will read on. I think it will be a long letter.

Thank you for giving me this one chance. I was never a humble person, as you well know, but even in these opening sentences I've found that the self-humiliation has done me good and is even healing. It's like beginning to breathe again after years of suffocation. Perhaps that is enough. Perhaps I will never send it. Perhaps I don't even deserve to breathe again.

But again: perhaps your rejection of this letter, the anger you will demonstrate by returning it unopened – perhaps that is exactly what I need, the next phase in my journey of complete and utter mortification. I dare not even think that you might reply.

What I want to say first will make you chuckle, but not in mirth, in mockery. If I were to stand before you and say it to your face you would slap me. I would deserve that slap. But I will say it nevertheless: you were my best friend. All through my childhood, you were there and I loved you. I never stopped loving you. I always loved you as the closest, dearest friend I had. That never stopped, even for a second. And yet, I did what I did. Not just to you and your family but to your entire community. My guilt is colossal.

And I love you still. Make of that what you will. I know you loved me, too. Love is precious, and I destroyed it, willingly and consciously. There is no pardon. You were my dearest friend, and our childhood was precious.

A lump rose in my throat and I let the letter drop to my lap as the memories came flooding back, uninvited.

PART ONE: KAISERKORSO EINS

1

LEAH – BERLIN

We always wrote it out in full: Eins, not the boring digit 1. Kaiserkorso Eins: home.

Kaiserkorso Eins was a massive corner building close to what would later become the Tempelhof Airport, Berlin. Five storeys high, full of ordinary families, Magda's and mine and at least eighteen others, Jews and gentiles. Among the Jews, us, the Gottliebs. And them, Magda's family, the Boschs.

Our families lived along the first-floor corridor, Magda's flat overlooking the street, mine the courtyard. Both flats had three bedrooms. There were two other flats further down the hallway, but we had little contact with those neighbours beyond the obligatory *'Guten Tag, Frau Weber!'* or *'Gute Nacht, Herr Mühlhause!'*

There were other Jewish families higher up in the building: the Levy family, two floors above us, had three children, all much older than us, the youngest in the final year of university, the elder two already working and starting families of their own. On the top floor lived Herr and Frau Bienstock, who had four adult children and several grandchildren who all lived nearby and often came to play. Everyone else in the building was a gentile . It didn't matter. Everyone got on well with everyone else. In those early days there was no sense of a difference between us, of a hierarchy.

Our family was better off than the Bosch parents. My father was a doctor, after all, Magda's 'only' a teacher, and we had a few more luxuries as a result: a telephone, for example, which they were always welcome to use. We even had a television set, and that, too, we shared, the Bosch parents often coming over to watch the evening news.

When you opened the massive front door of our building, just off the Kaiserkorso junction with what we called Red Baron Street, you came into a massive lobby, two rows of postboxes fixed to the left-hand wall, and several bicycles parked along the right-hand wall, hers and mine among them. At the back, the lift in its iron cage, a little wood-panelled box that rattled and rumbled its way up and down the shaft.

Magda and I, the best of friends, closer even than sisters. Neither of us had a real sister of our own, just several brothers between us, and we naturally drifted together. We'd been close from the start. There were many other children in the building, but we girls were the closest in age, and even as toddlers in the sandbox we'd found mutual interests. Our mothers, too, were friends; we called them Tante Helga and Tante Hannah respectively.

The courtyard, wedged between tall buildings and accessible only through the hallway, containing several metal rubbish bins serving the entire building, was our playground, even though its only playground apparatus was a sandbox. Doors in the walls gave access to coal cellars, storage rooms, and to the neighbouring buildings. At the end of each day, the ground would be littered with forgotten toys, balls rolled into corners, maybe a skipping rope, bits of chalk, and it was Magda's and my job to go down and clear up, placing stray toys in a wooden box under the stairs, making sure all was swept and tidy, leaving behind only fading hopscotch grids. The sandbox had to be covered over with a tarpaulin for the night, to prevent the various housecats using it as a toilet.

We kids of Kaiserkorso Eins played the usual childhood games in that little courtyard: blind man's buff, hit-the pot, cat-and-mouse. It was always Magda who reinforced the rules and made sure we all played fairly. Magda loved children, the smaller the better. A few mothers would leave their babies in prams in the courtyard for fresh air and their own peace and quiet, knowing well that Magda would pick them up and comfort them if they cried, or make sure they were well covered in winter and protected from the sun in summer; she'd lift those babies up and rock them and sing to them, and they responded with smiles and gurgles. Or else she'd run up to call the mothers down if the child needed maternal care. This was the Magda I knew and loved.

All of the windows in our flat overlooked that playground, and, even when closed, the shrill happy sound of children at play penetrated the glass and filled our home. In summer, when we opened the windows for air, childhood laughter was our constant backdrop, as pleasant as a splashing brook. The court-yard might be bleak and mostly sunless, with not so much as a blade of grass to evoke nature, but we were as happy as can be because all children want and need is a loving family and loyal friends, and that we had in spades, Magda and I.

Once, a little Jewish girl called Anna fell rather badly while running away, shrieking, from a blindfolded bigger boy. She sprawled onto the rough concrete ground and scraped her knee. It bled profusely; possibly the blood was scarier than the pain. Magda did not hesitate. She picked up the screaming Anna, pulled a (clean) handkerchief out of her pocket. I watched with interest as she tied it to the wound with a ribbon from her hair, blood dripping all over her own clothes as she did so.

'Hush, Anna!' she said to the little girl. 'It's not as bad as it looks! It's just a scratch!'

But Anna continued to howl.

'Come with me, Leah!' Magda said as she picked the little girl up in her arms. All the other children stood around watching as Magda carried that squalling, wriggling child into the lobby. I helped by carrying Anna's favourite doll, Lottie, the doll she always clung to and had dropped in falling.

We took the lift; Anna was a Bienstock grandchild from the top floor. We clanked our way all the way to the top of the building, where Magda finally set her down as she pulled open the lift doors. Anna ran screaming down the hall to her flat, with us following, and hammered on the door as if she'd been half-murdered. The door opened and Anna fell into her granny's arms.

'It's all right, Frau Bienstock. It's just a scratch, nothing serious. But it needs to be cleaned and dressed. I know how to do it; Mama's a nurse, you know!'

Frau Bienstock chuckled. 'I know your mama,' she said. 'And I can take care of this. But you can help if you want.'

'Helping' turned out to be watching, with Magda commenting all the time and offering her advice. Frau Bienstock took it all with great humour and later, when Anna was all cleaned up and very proud of her freshly bandaged knee, invited us both to sit down and have a glass of cold mint tea and a slice of cake.

'Thank you, Magda. That was very kind of you,' she said between all the action; and that is the most potent memory I have of what kind of a person Magda was back then. Bossy, yes; but kind. THAT was the Magda I knew and loved.

2

LEAH – BERLIN

There were two children in the Bosch family, Magda and her older brother, Markus. Magda was six months older than me and, while we'd attended the same kindergarten and then primary school, hand in hand on the walk to school, she, an April-born child, went off to secondary school a year before me, a September-born child. Markus became close friends with my older brother, Aaron. They were of similar age, Aaron two years older than us, Markus three.

My brother Samuel, meanwhile, was three years younger than me, while Mosche, the eldest, was six years older. There were many other girls and boys in the building, but the four of us, Magda, Markus, Aaron and I, went in and out of each other's homes as if we shared parents. Magda and me: we were 'Herzensschwester' – sisters of the heart. In German, one word, capitalised, making it so much more intimate than the English translation. And yes, it was true: we shared a heart.

That year, 1933, the year it all began, Markus was to start university in the autumn to study engineering. Aaron was due to start the following year. But of course, in his case, nothing went to plan.

Magda, I knew, longed to go to university herself. She was very clever; she loved literature and philosophy, and could talk for hours on such matters; but what she really wanted to be was a vet. She adored animals, big and small, and, though her parents wouldn't allow her to have either a dog or a cat, she would bring home stray animals she found in the neighbourhood, hoard them in the building's cellar storeroom, and keep them secretly for a while; any wounded animal she found, she would nurse back to health.

But only one of the Bosch children could go to university, due to the family's financial constraints, and that was Markus, the elder and the boy. And only the eldest Gottlieb child, our Mosche, went to university. The others? Not possible, after the watershed date: 30 January 1933.

Engineering, most people thought, was Germany's great strength. Magda disagreed. She considered culture to be Germany's strength. Germany was the land of great *'Dichter und Denker'* – poets and thinkers. She revelled in Germany's great works of literature. She also loved music; Bach's St Matthew Passion and the Brandenburg Concertos, Beethoven's Pastoral.

She played the piano well, but the violin was her favourite instrument, and she envied me because I played it reasonably well. This was Magda as she really was: sensitive, caring, cultured. A girl who tried to get to the bottom of things, to understand.

And understand she did. Until she didn't.

Magda, at the piano in her living room. Playing 'The Blue Danube', Aaron watching, Markus teaching me to waltz, all three of us laughing our heads off because I was so clumsy on my feet, always stepping on Markus's toes.

'Sorry!' I said, deeply embarrassed. My cheeks burned; they must have been beetroot red.

'It's fine!' he replied, looking down at me with that beautiful smile of his. 'I'll survive.'

I think that was the moment. I never told anyone, least of all him, of course. But even back then, when I was only fourteen, I had a huge crush on Markus. He was so tall, towering above me. So handsome. So very kind. His eyes, with that half-amused, half-understanding softness in them. And that moment when he looked down and forgave me for treading on his toes – that was the moment it all began. I've never been able to hear 'The Blue Danube' without remembering, without an emotional swelling I have to push away. Back then it was just a schoolgirl crush, of course. But we all know how those crushes live on. Tendrils of sentiment, with the power to pull us back to relive those so very tender moments.

Magda was the model student, good in every subject, especially German. Later, when we both progressed to the Lyceum – she again a year before me – foreign languages were her forte: English, French, Latin. We both loved the classics, and our philosophical discussions could last hours; even when we argued it was always amiably, never contentiously.

Magda also excelled in scientific subjects, which weren't encouraged in women. Given the opportunity, she'd have chosen to study veterinary medicine, to follow her childhood dream and her love of animals.

One day she brought upstairs a stray cat; a ginger cat with a kink near the end of its tail, skinny and bedraggled and homeless and, as a result, not the prettiest of cats, but very loving and hungry for affection. He got that from Magda. She had been smuggling food down from her kitchen to the courtyard for him for weeks, and had made firm friends with him. She called him Ingo, a male name from the word 'Ingwer', meaning ginger. But one day she looked at me with concern written all over her face.

'Poor little Ingo's got a lame paw,' she said. 'I think it's broken – he won't even let me touch it. He needs to see a vet!'

That was of course a problem, because vets cost money and her parents weren't rich and, even if they'd been rich, they wouldn't have wasted money on a stray cat. But both of us had been saving up to go and see a performance of *Die Dreigroschenoper* in the coming winter, and Magda announced that her savings would instead go towards the vet.

'Well, I won't go without you anyway, so you can have my savings too,' I said, and we'd have taken poor Ingo to the vet if Father hadn't got wind of the story, and, being a doctor and moving in certain circles, recruited one of his friends, a vet, to treat Ingo for free. It turned out that the leg wasn't broken after all. But the care and feeding of Ingo, restoring his scrawny appearance, turning him into a handsome, well-groomed cat, became for that summer Magda's mission in life. She was still determined to be a vet herself. But it was never to be. Life had other plans for her.

Our personalities complemented each other. I was shy, soft-spoken, a listener. She was outgoing, extraverted, a talker. Fun, and funny. Yes, funny. It seems strange to say that now. In fact, it pricks my heart. No one made me laugh the way Magda did. And how we laughed!

One winter when we were about ten the circus came to Berlin and our parents treated us to a performance; again, it was Father who footed the bill. And of course we both developed starry eyes and made up our minds to run away and join the circus. I was going to be a trapeze artiste, dancing high above the crowds, and Magda would be a clown. She practised her skills on me and all the kids in the courtyard. She pieced together a costume out of coloured scraps of cloth given to her by her horrible Tante Gundhilde, set a date, sent out formal invitations, and organised us in rows from smallest to biggest.

There we all sat cross-legged on the concrete ground,

eagerly awaiting the star performer; Magda came tumbling in, falling over her own legs, a big red rubber ball on her nose, turning cartwheels and juggling apples from her grandmother's farm – an act she must have been practising in secret. We laughed ourselves silly, and I felt so proud of her, proud to know her as my friend. She was so gifted.

Although we lived in the city, you could in many ways call our childhood idyllic. But sometimes the Bosch parents took me and Aaron with them on holiday to Bavaria, to the farm close to the Chiemsee lake, where Tante Helga, Magda's mother, had grown up; and those holidays were the real idyll. We'd take the train to Traunstein station, where Magda's grandfather, Opa Otto, would pick us up and drive us to that charming old wooden house with the geraniums hanging from the balconies and the orchards at the back and the ducks and geese and chickens waddling about the place. Magda of course was in seventh heaven, and so was I.

One particular day is seared into my memory, that Sunday when Herr Bosch borrowed his father-in-law's truck and drove us into the mountains beyond Garmisch-Partenkirchen. It was a brilliantly sunny day, the cloudless sky a radiant cobalt blue. The four of us kids sat in the flatbed of the lorry. Herr Bosch deposited us somewhere in the foothills of the Zugspitze, Germany's highest mountain, and returned to Garmisch, where he was meeting a few friends for their own day off.

Magda and I were about twelve at the time, the boys around fifteen. Markus was our leader – after all, he was experienced in these mountains, having hiked in them with Opa Otto since he was a little boy. He looked so smart, so different, in his lederhosen shorts and long socks and hiking boots, a leather cap at a jaunty angle on his head. He held a walking stick, and a water bottle was strapped across his back, and he wore a small knapsack.

'This way!' he called, making a sweeping upward gesture with his arm, and up we went, following a narrow path between rocks and bushes, upwards. We had no intention, of course, of reaching the summit – that was an overnight excursion of at least two days – but Markus, apparently, knew of a hut about two hours' hike up the path, where we could have a picnic and enjoy a spectacular view.

Up and up we went, Markus leading the way. The path was definitely off the beaten track, and quite steep. Soon I was panting as I tried to keep up with the boys; their long legs seemed to swallow the mountain. I fell behind, and called to Magda, a few metres ahead of me. She looked back, called to the boys, and returned to sit next to me on a boulder while I caught my breath, completely unprepared as I was by the streets and pavements of Berlin.

Markus and Aaron, about ten metres ahead, turned round and walked back to join us.

'Sorry, Leah,' said Markus. 'I shouldn't have raced ahead like that. When I'm here, it's as if the sky's calling me up!'

He handed me the water bottle and I took a few sips and passed it round. We sat there for a while, Markus telling us stories of the mountains and various adventures he and Magda had had there as children. Then we walked on again, and by midday we had reached the hut, a simple wooden thing perched on a sort of flat shoulder, a meadow of tall grass of a green so brilliant it took my breath away.

The door to the cabin was unlocked. It was a tiny structure, just one room, and in it was a simple cot shoved into a corner, a table and two chairs.

'It's for people like us,' Markus said. 'A shelter for hikers to take a rest. There are lots of them in the mountains; this one is the Glockenhütte. The Bell Hut. Look, there's a little stream over there, next to the rocks. And just look at that view!'

He waved his arm again over the landscape stretched out before us. I hadn't really looked down before, so intent had I been on the strenuous climb. But now I stopped and looked – and gasped aloud. I had never seen anything like it. Below us, beyond the mountainside, lay a spectacular panorama of undulating hills, stretching into the horizon, the saturated green of the grass merging there with the radiant blue of the sky. Villages and isolated farms dotted the landscape. Church towers ranged up between the red tiles of roofs. The fields were speckled black and white by grazing cows. Thickets of trees here and there, and dense woods of a darker green than the grass. It was, quite literally, breathtaking. For the first time in my life I became aware of the sheer beauty of my homeland. My Germany. This was my land. This was our land. This beauty, this magnificence, was my heritage.

A glance to the left revealed a different landscape. There in the distance, the snow-capped mountains of the Alps, jutting into the brilliant blue of the sky. Small fluffy clouds floated by leisurely. Time itself stood still.

'This is IT,' said Markus, and I knew exactly what he meant.

In Markus's backpack was a picnic his mother has prepared for us, and a thin blanket. We sat down on the soft grass and ate and drank, Wurst-and-cucumber sandwiches, apples. We drank from the stream, water purer and sweeter than I'd ever tasted in my life. The stream gurgled and splashed in the background. Magda began to tell her own stories, some quite amusing, but all I could listen to really was that stream, all I felt was this delicious sense of home.

Indeed, as Markus had said, this was it. IT: that incredible sense of pure, unspoiled serenity and peace. Of being one with the landscape, the mountains and the sky and the green of the grass and the gurgling of the stream and the people I shared this moment with. I was so moved tears came to my eyes, tears of sheer happiness, and a sense of this is what it's supposed to be, for ever and ever.

After the picnic Magda and I lay flat out on the grass for a little nap while the boys, clearly restless, wandered off. There was a promontory of stone behind the cabin, about three metres high, that looked as if a giant had just carelessly let a handful of boulders tumble to the slope. I must have been snoozing for no more than ten minutes when I heard Magda calling my name. I sat up; there she was, on the highest rock.

'Come on up, Leah!' she called.

So I got up and walked over and began to climb. Soon I reached the highest rock, where Magda was sitting. I sat next to her and she put her arm round me, and there we sat in silence, arms on each other's shoulders, simply breathing in the perfection.

Aaron and Markus returned from their exploration. 'It's time to go back,' Markus said, looking at his watch. His father had arranged to pick us up at around two. So Magda and I got up and made our way down, climbing from boulder to boulder. I was about halfway down when my foot slipped and twisted, and I found myself tumbling to the ground. I cried out in pain.

Aaron and Markus were with me in an instant, while Magda called up from above: 'Are you all right?'

Aaron helped me to my feet, but I couldn't stand on my left foot, and when I tried, I cried out again: 'I can't walk! Maybe it's broken!' and slipped back down to the grass.

'Hopefully it's just a sprain,' said Markus. He held the foot ever so tenderly. It rested in the palm of his hand and he moved it gently.

I didn't want to be a baby, so I held back from making any further noises, but Markus noticed that I was biting my lip, trying not to cry out.

'I'll have to carry you back,' he said.

'We both will,' said Aaron.

They helped me back up so that I stood on one foot and then they both made a kind of seat with their joined hands between them, and we started on our way back down. But it was soon obvious that it wouldn't work; not only was the path too narrow, but Markus was by far the taller of the two and he had to bend over uncomfortably to make that human chair.

Markus was also by far the stronger. 'Lift her on to my back,' he said to Aaron. No sooner said than done. And that's how the expedition ended, with me piggyback astride Markus. Herr Bosch was waiting for us where he had left us.

My injury turned out to be no more than a sprain. A very sore end to a wonderful day, one that I would never forget, one that sealed us all together in what seemed an eternal bond. A bond that could never break. Until it did.

A cloud was waiting for us, a dark, ugly cloud just waiting to obscure the sheer joy that that day had brought. Not just the four of us. It was a cloud that filled every single German heart. For some of us, it was a cloud of fear, of terror, even. But for many others, too many others, it was a cloud of unimaginable evil. And it was waiting on the horizon, and none of the four of us had an inkling.

It was a cloud that ushered in the end of friendship, the end of glorious lakes and mountains and combined family outings. The end of Germany as we knew it. It came slowly, imperceptibly at first.

I certainly had no inkling of what was going on. My parents must have known but they kept it all from me, at least in the beginning I was coddled in innocence. Until it was too late. As for Magda – something was growing within her, and of that too I had no inkling.

.   .   .

Magda had always been protective of me. There was a gang of rough boys who lived round the corner from us. They never bothered us when we walked back and forth from school, arms as ever linked. But one day Magda was ill, and I walked home alone, and that's when they came for me. I must have been about thirteen; it was definitely after that Zugspitze outing. As I walked down the pavement towards Kaiserkorso, they pounced. Four of them, several years older than me.

One of them grabbed my satchel. 'What you got in here, Jew-girl?' he taunted. He opened the satchel and spilled its contents on the pavement. Books, pens, an empty sandwich box, a small glass bottle that had contained water, all lay on the ground. The bottle shattered, the books scattered.

The boys laughed and mocked and kicked the items around. Stepped on my books. Crunched the shattered bottle into the pavement with their boots.

I tried to ignore them and stooped to gather my books, but they wouldn't let me; they kept kicking the books from my hand, or grabbing them and throwing them around like a ball, guffawing and taunting as they sprang around.

'Stop it! Just stop!' I cried in vain, and eventually they all spat on me and ran away.

Of course I told Magda. She was furious. 'I will always protect you, Leah,' she promised as she hugged me. 'They're scared of me. They won't dare tease you if you're with me.'

So yes, I felt safe with her. She was the confident, assertive one, never afraid of confrontation, while I was the reticent, soft-spoken one, who avoided confrontation if at all possible. And so we complemented each other. Where did it all change? When, and why?

I still don't know when Magda changed, or what brought that change about. There was no precise moment, as far as I could tell. It happened slowly, gradually. Growing within her long before the watershed day when Hitler came to power. She thought more deeply about things than I did, though, so perhaps that is why she went off at a tangent. More deeply about everyday matters, and about deep, inexplicable things like death, which I accepted as a matter of course, an everyday given, a part of life we had to accept.

My family had a cat, Mitzi, who like most cats liked to lay dead mice on our doorstep. Once, though, Mitzi brought home a sparrow that wasn't yet quite dead, and Magda happened to see as she dropped it on the doormat. She let out a fierce scream and chased off poor Mitzi – who, after all, was only following her instinct. Then she, Magda, picked up the little wounded bird, fluttering uselessly, and stroked its broken wing and wept.

'It's so hard to understand!' she said as the bird finally stopped moving and lay still and dead in her hand. 'Just a few minutes ago it was alive and happy and now it's just a dead body. Just a little lump of flesh and bones and feathers. What happened?'

There was nowhere in our courtyard where we could bury the dead sparrow, now cold and stiff like a stone, but Magda insisted that it should have a decent burial and so we found some loose earth in a flower bed in the nearby park and there we buried it, and Magda said a Christian prayer. I was so moved by her caring. I would not have had that impulse. But it just goes to show. Magda had all the right instincts, but somewhere along the line it all went awry. Something cracked, and poison oozed into her soul.

MAGDA

I was always shocked by the finality of death. Do you remember, Leah, little Eduard from upstairs? How old were we – maybe eight, and he six? It was awful. A playmate, a boy who had laughed and run with us, right there, living, warm, funny, with his shock of blond hair that always fell into his eyes. Suddenly dead, never coming back from hospital. You and I were flabbergasted. It was impossible to think that he would never return to play with us. And then the ginger cat with the crooked tail – do you remember? Poor little Ingo. The porter killed Ingo just because he knocked over the rubbish bin and made a mess in the courtyard.

And then the photo I kept in my treasure box. The photo of the dead soldier. Do you remember, Leah? That photo had been, for me, such a catalyst for my thoughts on death, the final mystery.

It was a photo Markus had torn from a magazine, a photo of a German soldier lying dead in a field, and another soldier standing above him, looking down, a rifle strapped across his chest, looking down on his dead comrade with his hands wide open, open hands that cried WHY? His back was to the camera so his face was not visible. It was those wide-open hands that cried to the heavens. WHY. WHY. WHY. Those open hands spoke of the agony of those of us left behind to confront the abyss.

'He died for Germany!' I said to you. 'Can you imagine? He gave up his life for his Fatherland. How brave of him! What a hero!'

I'm sure I bored you to tears when I plunged into a long and tortured lament on the wastefulness of war and the finality of death, and what it meant to die young, and why it should not be, and how precious was life, and how we humans could never pierce the tragedy of death, never ever accept or understand it. That photo hit hard. But one thought remained uppermost in my mind.

He died for Germany. How grand, how heroic, to sacrifice one's most precious possession, life itself, for one's country!

That photo planted a seed into my consciousness. That

there was a reason and a meaning to death. Death wasn't just the end. Death could grant nobility to a person, if that death was part of a noble cause. If there was something more than an individual life. A greater and higher good, for which the price of death is worth paying.

I inundated you with such observations, and I knew they left you cold, and wondering if I was off my head. For you, life itself was precious and you had no time for melodrama or mawkish interpretations of death, and you let me know in no uncertain words.

'Get a grip, Magda!' you scolded me. 'We all want to live. Every creature on Earth wants to live, and wants just to be happy, here and now.'

I dismissed you as too shallow, unable to grasp the profundity of my observations. Now I know that I was the fool.

3

MAGDA

What is it that drew me to the path I took, the decisions I made, Leah? You must have asked yourself a million times how I could have been drawn into that evil sphere. I will try to explain to you – not in order to vindicate myself, but for me to understand myself. Linking to those thoughts on death I'd been mulling, I think it was a yearning for something greater than myself. Something grand, something beyond the confines of our narrow childhood, that bleak little courtyard-cum-playground at Kaiserkorso Eins. Beyond the mundane realities of daily life. I wanted to escape.

Perhaps that is a fundamental human urge. Perhaps it is the basic urge that is in its essence our need for religion, for God, something beyond ourselves. Because yes, in spite of the superficial joys of childhood, I did have that yearning. It's a yearning to grow out of myself, to grow into something bigger, grander, more noble. It's a good urge in and of itself, the urge that perhaps inspires the great works of our cultural heritage. That might be why I so love the great works of literature, and, even more than that, the grand works of music.

Who can listen to the sheer grandeur of Beethoven's

*Emperor Concerto, or the deep serenity of his Pastoral; or
Bach's Toccata and Fugue, played on the organ, sitting in the
magnificent space of a grand cathedral, without being swept
up into glorious spheres far above our little mundane lives of
eating and sleeping and waking up to another day just like the
last? Without yearning for more, or to be a part of it, swept
away from the little boxed-in 'me'? Only death jolts us out of
such mundanity. Mozart's Requiem! What magnificence!*

*Yes, I yearned for such splendour in my life. And then I
was swept away by a single thought: That greatness was
Germany. Germany, not as a geographical entity, but as a
concept. A philosophical reality. Something grand and great
and worth living and dying for. I did not think this on my own.
I was taught this. Do you remember Tante Gundhilde? She
had lent me a book on German history, and I wanted to return
it. I had so many questions for her. She lived not far from us,
and so one afternoon we walked over together. We were both
fifteen at the time. Do you remember what she said, Leah? For
that was the turning point:* 30 January 1933.

LEAH – BERLIN

Magda and I walked, arms linked, down the pavement to the
block in Kreuzberg where Tante Gundhilde lived in a pokey
little ground-floor flat. I even remember how the curtain
twitched as Magda rang the bell, and a ghostly face appeared
behind the windowpane. Instinctively, I flinched. I had never
met Tante Gundhilde before, but I knew she was Magda's
godmother as well as her aunt, a person she held in high respect.

She opened the door and in we went, into that gloomy little
front room with the heavy oak furniture and the dark green
worn-down carpet, frayed at the edges. She led us through into
the even gloomier kitchen at the back of the flat, frowning as she
glanced my way.

She lived alone. It seemed she worked as a seamstress. In a corner of her kitchen stood the sewing machine with the pedal, and a small chest of drawers with a pile of fabrics on top of it. But that look she threw me – it sent shivers down my spine. Magda didn't notice. She chatted gaily, about her school work and schoolmates and about the book she was reading. At first, Tante Gundhilde just listened. But I took note that she kept glancing my way.

The woman gave me the creeps. Her beady eyes, the tensed lips, the hardly perceptible sniff she gave as I sat down at her kitchen table. She went back to whatever she was sewing – hemming a dress, I think – because now she had pins sticking out of her pinched lips and as she sat there, with those spikes jutting out, she looked like a witch from a Grimms' fairy tale, wickedness personified.

Magda chattered away, oblivious to the oppressive atmosphere, doing all the talking as usual, still going on and on about the book. And Tante Gundhilde was throwing me these nasty looks, her eyes flicking over to me as if wishing me to dissolve. Putting a curse on me. I shuddered inwardly. I saw in her eyes pure malevolence. Magda, meanwhile, was too involved in her own matters to pay attention to those evil glances, rattling on in her usual ebullient manner.

In the end I could bear it no longer. I excused myself and left. And as I left, I noticed the brooch Tante Gundhilde wore on her lapel.

The brooch was a swastika.

I knew what a swastika was, what it signified. Aaron kept me well informed, as did my parents; yet, not wanting to scare me, they always comforted me by taking the positive slant that it would all blow over soon. But on that January day in 1933 it was clear that something was brewing. And though I didn't quite understand, I knew that change was in the air.

MAGDA

I'd had glimpses before of the swastika Tante Gundhilde wore on the lapel of her dress. I'd seen it whenever she came to visit. She made sure I saw it. Tante Gundhilde was Father's unmarried sister, the poor relative Mama thought she had to be kind to, portly and ungainly while Mama was beautiful. Nevertheless, Mama couldn't stand her, for some reason I didn't understand. She never explained.

Tante Gundhilde was my godmother and had always taken a particular interest in me. I never understood why, before that day. I knew later that she had seen my rebellion against the Catholic Church and thought it her duty to educate me, show me a greater world than the conventional and narrow beliefs of my parents. To turn me away from Christian teaching and lead me into her own beliefs and convictions. Some godmother! She must have seen the fertile earth within me, into which she could sow her wicked seeds.

That swastika, though! Hidden from Mother's eyes, because Mother hated it, as we all knew. I do believe that in the past Tante Gundhilde had deliberately flashed it for me to see. But that day, that January day, she wore it openly, and she seemed to be in a sort of euphoria.

I was glad when you left, Leah, as I could tell that Tante Gundhilde was bursting with news and I was eager to hear what she had to say. It was as if I knew it was nothing for your ears. And oh, how my heart lifted, once I was alone with her and she felt free to speak!

'Remember this day, Magdalena,' she gloated once you had gone. 'Today, our great leader Adolf Hitler has been appointed chancellor of Germany! Today is the dawn of a great new era. At last we Germans have something to be proud of. At last we can rise up out of the defeat of the war. Wash away the humiliation and stand upright in pride!'

And I was proud! Oh, how I was proud! As Tante Gundhilde spoke on she swept me up into her own excitement: the Day of the Seizure of Power, 30 January 1933! What a day, what an event! Here was the thing, the thing greater than myself, that I had so yearned for!

Mama, predictably, disapproved. But that censure only poured oil on the flames of my enthusiasm.

Over the past years I had turned more and more away from my strict Catholic upbringing, much to Mama's pain. I'd been baptised and taken first communion as a child, of course. I'd had no say in the matter, and that annoyed me terribly. Forced to go to church on Sundays, to confess my sins, to pray morning and evening and at every meal – over the years my initial boredom with the whole gobbledygook of Catholic teaching had morphed into open rebellion. Now, at almost sixteen, I had not been to church for at least a year. And I knew that Tante Gundhilde was also not a churchgoer. Mama complained about this now and then.

'I'd never have allowed her to be godmother if I'd known,' she grumbled; and she put my estrangement from the church down to Tante Gundhilde's 'subtle and malignant influence' (as she later called it). But now, starting on that thirtieth of January, that influence was to take me over body and soul, and how grateful I was for it!

For me it was my parents' bourgeois self-righteousness, the narrow-mindedness of their Catholicism, that I could not stand. And Mama's goody-goody selflessness and boring soft-ness also drove me more and more into Tante Gundhilde's ideological arms. Tante Gundhilde had hair on her teeth, as the saying goes. So fierce, so brave! I wanted hair on my teeth too! She was my model! For the first time, I had something grand and noble to live for: Germany! Something above my little puny self. Isn't that what we all long for, Leah? If it is not Germany, is it not some other noble cause, some ideal, some wonderful future of our imagination, towards which we can live and work and have our being?

You were so very different from me, Leah. You did not have a vision of a greater life; you were quite modest in your aspirations. If I'd asked you, then, what was your highest ideal and what you lived for, I think I know your reply. You would have said quite simply: Family. Those close to you, those you loved. God: yes, of course. But not in some exalted, I-will-die-for-you way.

For you, God was simply a part of it all; you and your family worshipped as all Jews do. You kept the Sabbath, more or less. You celebrated Hanukkah and all the Jewish festivals, but it was all integrated into your everyday living, the day-to-day mundanity of duty and community, and, rather than some grand euphoric ideal, it was all included in your simple daily life, in your thoughts and your prayers and in all your relationships. And you shared that perspective with me. We often argued about religion, and family. Your interpretation seemed to me too simple, too obvious. The definition of God handed down by my parents was too narrow, too stultifying. I wanted more, much more. And for me, family was just not enough.

And that's why for me, on 30 January 1933, everything seemed to naturally fall into place. A watershed moment, yes; but it had been ripening within me for a long time. That was just the day something in me burst open. I fell away from all the old concepts. This was IT. This was my new world. And you could never be a part of it.

4

MAGDA

That evening our parents took Markus and me to watch the parade on the Kurfürstendamm. I cannot describe to you my elation as we stood on the roadside watching the torchlight procession. The National Socialists were celebrating their victory, and they did it in style, marching for hours. Even now, I can hear the rhythmic thud of soldiers' boots as they marched past. I can see the forest of red and black flags displaying that proud emblem of might, the swastika. In the flickering flames of the torchbearers, I could see the faces all around me – laughing, smiling faces of spectators who, like me, felt the intoxication of the moment. Groups of youths marched past, boys and girls of my own age. I watched and envied them; their faces, too, were alight with the magic of the moment. They carried banners on which the names of their dead were written, and they sang, they sang with gusto and conviction.

'For the flag we are ready to die!' they sang, and those words only fanned the flame that Tante Gundhilde had ignited that very morning. I felt passion. I felt a gigantic resounding YES in my heart. Yes, this was it! This was the cause I could throw myself into, body, mind and spirit. A burning desire to

be a part of this swelling tide of dedication and selfless courage.

My parents did not share my enthusiasm. They stood beside us, silent, cold, distant, watching with disapproval. I did not care. I cheered with the crowd, waved wildly at the marching soldiers, thrust out my arm in the Hitler salute as the great man himself passed by in a black car surrounded by escorts on motorcycles.

A glance to my right told me that Markus also did not cheer. His face was blank, emotionless. He did not fling out his arm. I realised then and there that this, my greatest hour to date, had created an invisible wall between my brother and my parents on the one side, and me on the other. I realised that I was alone in my fervour, and that it would sweep me away from my family.

LEAH – BERLIN

The following day, Magda went to visit Tante Gundhilde again, and so, once again, I was on my own. Markus came to visit my brothers, Aaron and Mosche – the latter, though now at university, still lived at home. Those childhood days of easy camaraderie and fun were long gone, now; Markus was practically an adult, whereas I had become a shy, gawky girl who'd blush when he passed by, never knowing what to say. If we happened to see each other he'd always throw me a smile and a short greeting before retreating into the bedroom my brothers shared. Today, though, he stopped, and did more than smile and throw a greeting. He spoke to me.

'How are you, Leah?' he asked as he walked past me. I was sitting at the dining table working on my homework, and I looked up.

'I'm... I'm all right,' I replied hesitantly. I thought I should say more but was suddenly struck with a debilitating sense of wordlessness. I simply didn't know what to say. A smile was stuck on my lips which must have looked ridiculous, but I had no idea how else to respond to his friendliness. I thought he'd walk on and leave me to my studies, but he didn't.

'I was wondering, Leah,' he said now. 'If maybe... well, there's something I want to say to your Mosche and Aaron, and it might be good if you joined us too. Would you like to?'

'Oh! Well... yes, of course... but...' I was absolutely tongue-tied. This was completely bizarre. Why would Markus want me to join them in whatever they talked about or did in that room? Above all, what would my brothers say? I mean, I got on well with all three of my brothers, especially Aaron. But really, we lived in different worlds, now, and we now had few mutual interests.

'But...' I continued. 'Would they mind?'

'No. They won't mind. I told them yesterday that we need to include you in this, and they agree. Come along.'

He gestured to the door of my brothers' room. I hurriedly closed my textbook over a pencil and scraped back my chair. This was unprecedented. I hastily followed Markus into the room, aware of a sense of new privilege. As the only girl, I had my own bedroom, while the three of them shared a room. Now, I found Mosche and Aaron sitting on the edges of their beds. My younger brother Samuel was not there. He spent most of his free time in football training. And anyway, he was too young for discussions of the kind I was being invited into. It was just Aaron and Mosche and me in their room with Markus.

It was a small room, too small to hold three beds, but one of the beds had a bunk above it, and that was Samuel's. After greeting my brothers, Markus pulled two chairs away from the desks and gestured to me to take a seat. He smiled again at me in a most encouraging way, and I smiled back. I was still hopelessly tongue-tied.

Markus began.

'Well,' he said. 'So... It's happened. Did you hear the speeches last night, on the radio?' He looked from one of us to the other. My brothers nodded. Mother and Father had let the radio blare on well into the night. They'd left the television switched off. All those men, giving speeches. I had not listened but instead retreated into my room to escape the horribly grating sound of angry men ranting over the wireless. I've never been able to put up with ugliness, and the very sound of their strident voices had put me off.

'So you didn't listen, Leah?' Markus was no longer smiling, and his voice sounded concerned. His eyes, too, rested on me with a look of disquiet. 'Has Magda spoken to you today? About... what happened?'

I shook my head.

It had been a perfectly normal day. Magda and I had gone to school together as usual and returned home together, arms linked. I did notice a certain excitement at school, a certain unusual buzz. I thought that one of the teachers had looked at me in a funny way, but I hadn't given it further thought. I'd seen small groups of girls, huddled together and whispering, and I'd seen Magda in one of those huddles. Were they glancing my way? No, of course not. That was my imagination... Some schoolgirl drama, I thought. I cloaked myself in oblivion. Maybe it was some sort of intuition, whereby I refused to open my senses to what was going on. An innate need for self-protection. Certainly, Magda told me nothing.

After school we went as usual to her flat, where her mother, Tante Helga, served us coffee and biscuits; and then Magda rushed off to visit Tante Gundhilde – again! She said that Tante Gundhilde was sewing a dress for her, for her birthday. 'It's just another boring fitting, Leah,' she said. 'Why don't you catch up on that speech?' And off she rushed.

'That speech' was from Shakespeare's *Julius Caesar*: 'Friends, Romans, countrymen, lend me your ears.' I had to learn it by heart, and I was still struggling. Learning anything by heart was not my strong point, especially if it was in English. Magda could learn these things with a click of her fingers.

'No,' I said now to Markus. 'What happened?'

How gauche and ill-informed I must have sounded to him. I was apolitical for a reason; I knew instinctively that politics ran contra to my safe, happy little world and vision of the future. That politics would blow that world apart. He sighed. 'Leah, this is important. Very important. You really need to be aware of what's going on, especially in regards to Magda.'

'I don't understand,' I said. 'What's going on? What's Magda got to do with anything?'

And then he told me, told us. He told us about the previous night's parade. The jubilant cheering of the crowds, the speeches, the marching soldiers. The swastika, and what it signified. I was flabbergasted. My awakening was soul-destroying.

'The problem is, Leah,' Markus said, now looking at me directly, 'Magda is a hundred per cent with them. She agrees with everything they're saying and doing. She finally admitted it last night, when we came home from the parade. She and my parents argued deep into the night. She thinks this Hitler creep is going to lead Germany to greatness.'

Aaron and Mosche gasped at those words. 'She doesn't!' cried Aaron.

Markus nodded.

'She does. And, Leah, you have to be careful from now on.'

'Careful? Why?'

'You haven't been following the news, have you? You don't know what the National Socialists are saying about Jews?'

'No,' I replied. I barely glanced at newspaper headlines these days. I found politics too messy, too aggressively mascu-line. I was aware that there was something worrying going on but I was the typical head-in-the-sand ostrich. If I ignored it, it would go away.

'It's bad,' said Markus now. 'It's very bad, Leah, and if Magda becomes involved...' He shook his head before continuing. 'You can't trust Magda, Leah. Look, I don't think she'd really betray you directly. She genuinely cares for you. But she's... I don't know. She seems to have this bee in her bonnet now about a movement that will change the world and make Germany great again, and who knows where that will take her? Now, my parents and I recognise what's going on. We will always stand by you. You know that. But, Magda...' He shook his head sadly. 'She's my sister, and I love her, but in this matter she's become a stranger and she's not to be trusted.'

Not trust Magda? I couldn't believe it. 'She's my best friend!' I cried. 'We'd do anything for each other!'

'She's my sister, and I thought the same. But after hearing her last night...'

Sadness was written all over his face as he shook his head again, slowly.

MAGDA

What happened on that night of 3 January 1933 was to destroy all that was good and pure and healthy in my family. All that remains now is deep remorse, and sorry is much too shallow a word to express and contain it. Instead, I will describe in detail what it was that corrupted me and changed me into the warped creature I was to become.

I can lay the blame as much as I want at Tante Gund-hilde's feet, but of course she is just a scapegoat. I was a willing victim of the poison she fed me. I drank it all in. Mama must have wondered where I was always rushing off to in the afternoons, but she said nothing. Only you did, and perhaps Markus.

But then again, Mama was busy with her part-time job as a nurse and did not really monitor my comings and goings. Had she known of Tante Gundhilde's influence she would surely have objected. Now, after that January thirtieth, I went to visit Tante Gundhilde every day, and every day stayed at least an hour. I was a hungry listener. Her physical form might be ungainly, crude, shabby and – well, I'll say the word, primitive. But her words were not. Her words were beacons of light. They were, to me, poetic.

I grimace in hindsight. How could I, a lover of fine literature who drank in the words of Schiller, Goethe, Rilke, as well as Shakespeare and the great French and English poets, have been impressed with Tante Gundhilde's overwrought mawkishness when it came to what she called 'the glorious new dawn'?

'This, Magdalena, is the first day of a new era. The sun is rising over a new land, and you can be proud to have witnessed it. Germany's future is golden, and we are blessed to be a part of this transformation. Can you not feel God's grace streaming down upon us, through us, as He lifts our great nation to the heights, imbues it with His own divine and immaculate power?'

Oh yes, I felt it. Those words were like injections of supreme power that was almost divine in its influence. A power that surged through me, sweeping away all that was weak and impotent. It was history coming to fruition. God was on our side. I felt it in every cell of my body. It was a revelation. A new birth.

Which German did not feel inferior, our country having been so utterly defeated in the war? I speak, of course, of the first war. The 1914 to 1917 one. We had been crushed under the boots of the Allies and never recovered, politically, economically, personally. Not even geographically. The victors of the war had grabbed some of our most precious regions: Alsace-

Lorraine fell to France, Eupen and Malmedy to Belgium, Northern Schleswig to Denmark and, in the east, parts of West Prussia and Silesia to Poland. The list of our territorial and military losses goes on and on in; in all, 13 per cent of our European territories. Outside Europe, we lost all our colonies.

Economically, Germany was struggling to recover from our losses. Cities had been bombed, millions of our men killed. Psychologically, we were in a slump, a black hole of despair. And then this hero, this Adolf Hitler, came along, promising world dominion and glory beyond imagination. Can you, at least theoretically, understand why we were swept away by all the hubris?

I now understand fully that humiliation is not in itself a bad thing. It is an opportunity. An opportunity to bend low and humbly partake in the basic humanity that is beyond hubris, beyond an artificial sense of greatness. We can learn to be better people through humiliation; and the deeper the fall, the more there is to learn.

But how could I know that back then? I was just fifteen. All I knew was that I and all Germans were in this black cloud of defeat, and here was someone who promised to raise us up and lead us to glory. Hitler possessed the power of eloquence. His words seemed imbued with positive energy, which allowed our minds to soar. We believed every word. This was power: not physical power, but emotional power. It was heady. Ecstatic, even.

My parents, though, were immune to Hitler's potency. They were of that class of Germans known as Bildungsbürger: *cultured citizens. They were victims of a different kind of hubris. They'd never admit it, cloaked as they were in their Catholic self-righteousness. They thought of themselves as good Samaritans, helping the poor even as they looked down on those of low status, at what they considered the crude and primitive ways of the lower classes. People like Frau Krämer, who came once a week to do the laundry, would never be allowed to eat at the same table as us. I saw their hypocrisy: they called themselves Christians, Catholics, and yet they made clear distinctions between Desirable and Undesirable company. They told us not to mix with certain people. Low-life, they called them. Bad influences. I was determined not to make such distinctions. I believed in equality. (How ironic that sounds now!) I detested their Catholic hypocrisy. I believed in justice for all and a raising up of the lower classes so that they could, indeed, eat at the same table. And in this state of affairs, along came Tante Gundhilde, so conveniently.*

'You must join the Hitler Youth!' she whispered in my ear. 'In the League of German Girls, you will find everything you are looking for.'

And so, in 1933, I became a member of the Bund Deutscher Mädchen, the BDM. I did it secretly, for my parents would have been horrified. If joining in the jubilation on the day of Hitler's takeover of power was my first emotional step on my journey of downfall, then joining the BDM was my first physical step. It all went downwards from there. But in my delusion, I thought down was up. And this was just the beginning.

5

LEAH – BERLIN

From that day on, the day when Markus took me aside and warned me against his own sister, everything began to change. Of course, I was pleased that he had taken me into his confidence and that he considered me worthy of knowing what he knew about Magda, mature enough to understand. He knew she had embarked on a bad road, and he wasted no time in trying to convince me of the same.

Markus became a frequent visitor to our flat, and I found myself being drawn more and more into what was emerging as a secret society consisting of him, me and my brothers. Later, another girl who lived two houses down joined us. Her name was Elke and she was a gentile. I didn't like her at all and wished Markus had not invited her. She didn't like me either, I thought, but maybe I was imagining that.

We all thought that Markus's fears for the Jewish community were exaggerated. Yes, some Germans held prejudices against us; we'd always known that and lived with it. But we were Germans too, full citizens with all the rights that nationhood implies. We could not see the cloud looming on the horizon.

Markus did.

About a week after Hitler came into power, at one of our meetings, Markus made a prediction so preposterous, we all laughed at him.

'Hitler wants to remove all Jews,' he told us. 'Mark my words, this is just the beginning. Be careful.'

Aaron scoffed. 'Get rid of the Jews? Don't be ridiculous! It's impossible. It would be like removing' – he held up the multi-coloured blanket that was always folded at the foot of his bed – 'like removing all the red threads woven into the fabric. Just not possible.'

But Markus, unknown to us at the time, had contacts beyond our private little group. He was only eighteen, but his exploring mind took him to places and people who knew which way the wind was blowing. We continued to scoff. It was too ridiculous for words. This was all fearmongering! A wild notion of a scheme to get rid of us. A conspiracy theory. It just was not possible.

'We Jews are too strong, too much a foundation stone of German society,' said Aaron.

'But that's the whole point,' Markus said. 'According to the National Socialists, Jews hold too much power. Hitler is afraid that they might undermine his plans for Grossdeutschland, great Germany.' He paused there. 'I also think,' he said, 'he knows that Jews are more likely to see through him and his megalomania.'

Aaron and Mosche looked at each other and nodded. 'That's true,' Aaron said. 'I don't know a single Jewish person who likes him and believes in his dream of a greater Germany.'

'Exactly!' said Markus. He looked earnestly from one of us to the other. 'Anyway, did you hear what happened in the Prinz-Eugen-Strasse? A group of teenagers, our age, Aaron! Went into the apartment houses and vandalised the postboxes. Every box that had a Jewish-sounding name, they painted JUDE on it in big red letters. Or a swastika. They painted swastikas on the doors of Jewish homes. Jewish shops. They roam the streets at night, the vandals. Drunk and wild. Sometimes they belt out raucous patriotic songs.'

'How do you know all this, Markus?' Mosche asked. 'How do you know, and we don't?'

'I saw them myself,' he replied. 'Anyway, I'd advise you – your parents – to take precautions. Remove your name from the postboxes downstairs, and from your flat door. Gottlieb... Clearly Jewish. Now, all the Kaiserkorso neighbours know who you are, and we don't know if they'll betray you if anyone comes knocking at the door. But those thugs? If they decide to come and see who lives here, you never know. What if they decide to take it further: come up the stairs and look at the names on our doors? So it's a good idea to put a more neutral name on that box. Mayer, or something.'

'You want us to cower in fear?' That was Aaron.

'No, not cower, but take precautions. What's the point in inviting trouble?'

'Mother's maiden name was Heller,' said Aaron. 'It's less obvious than Gottlieb.'

Markus nodded. 'Heller's good. Try to use it whenever possible. I won't be able to legally change the name but at least you can use it informally. Change the name plate on the door.'

I stared at him, perfectly dumbfounded. He sounded so serious. He sounded as if there was danger afoot. Danger? To us? With Magda involved? It simply could not be.

I still refused to take Hitler's rise to power seriously. And I was completely unaware of how deeply affected Magda was by the change in government. I took our friendship for granted, and clung to the notion that Markus was mistaken. He had to be mistaken. Magda was my friend. I would not pull away from her. I refused to mistrust her.

But I did notice one thing: on our walks to school, our conversations became more and more political. We both had the best of intentions, and the highest ideals. We wanted to remove all ills from society. We wanted to do away with poverty, unemployment, homelessness, alcoholism, prostitution. We wanted to educate the masses and see them rise up. There was a difference, though: I wanted this for the world, but Magda seemed to think this betterment was only for Germany. And that Germany was the greatest nation, and had to lead the world. I didn't realise, at the time, that by 'leading the world' she meant 'absorbing the world'. And finally, 'conquering the world'. I didn't know of her vision for Greater Germany. But the politics of the day were slowly seeping into our friendship, spreading their slow poison, as I was soon to discover.

6

MAGDA

Reading back what I just wrote, dear Leah, I realise what a shock it must be to you to realise how captured I was from the very beginning. I still considered us close friends at this time, you my best friend.

You and I were in that stratum of society that was decidedly well-off in those difficult post-war years. We were what my parents called 'highborn daughters', destined to marry upwards and make a solid middle-class life for ourselves. To better ourselves. We were by now both in secondary school, along with our brothers – boys in the Gymnasium, girls in the Lyceum – most German girls did not attend the Lyceum, so we were already privileged.

My parents read the newspapers avidly and kept Markus and me well informed of what was going on in Germany. But their sense of complacency and superiority at not being like 'those down there' irritated me.

Berlin's population was 4 million. In the wake of our defeat in the war, unemployment throughout Germany had reached staggering heights – or should I say depths? Those people were truly in the Scheisse – pardon my language but there's no other word for it but shit. I worried about where we were going as a country; it seemed the only way was down. My parents complained constantly about the Weimar Republic and the way things were going: about the political murders and squabbles among the various factions and poverty and beggars. But what were they doing about it? Nothing.

I wanted action. Back then, most young people in Germany belonged to some youth group or club or other. My parents, worried about my blooming atheism, were eager for me to join a Christian, Catholic group, but naturally I refused. I was looking for something with more intellectual substance. I didn't want lectures or to be told what to do, which is ironic, considering what came later. I remember trying to convince you to join a group with me, but you refused – you were always more of an individualist, weren't you? You did not like to move in a pack. I did. That's the fundamental difference between us. As for Markus, he was more like you, always thinking and moving against the grain – but even he joined a club: Bismarck Youth or Bismarckjugend.

I must have been about fourteen when I found the KLUM.

Precocious as I was, I had made a new friend in the class above me, a girl who shared my enthusiasm for German culture. Her name was Ursula. And Ursula had already founded a club called Berlin Youth for Art, Literature and Music: die Berlinjugend für Kunst, Literatur und Musik. KLUM for short. What a name! How snobbish can you get! But I loved the name, and everything to do with it, and, young as I was, I soon became the most outspoken leader during our meetings.

My parents approved of the KLUM. They thought it was elevating. It was an informal group, not illegal, but unofficial, and as such we could not meet in an official clubroom at a youth centre; we held our meetings at the homes of our members, and because of the members' profiles my parents *accepted some meetings at our own home. That went on for a year or so.*

Naively, I wanted you to join the KLUM. You were quite a talented artist yourself, Leah. I remember you had a small sketchbook you took everywhere, and that you enjoyed drawing some of the flowers in the park. And you definitely had a gift for the human face. Remember that portrait you made of me? It's still hanging on my bedroom wall. And so I invited you to join us.

At the time, the group was reading a book called Foundations of the Nineteenth Century, *by Houston Stewart Chamberlain; yes, we read English authors, and French ones too, Flaubert and Racine. I had always enjoyed French classes and was already quite fluent, but KLUM went beyond what we learned at the Lyceum. We aimed to refine our minds. Cultural evolvement was one of our goals. I tried to explain this to you but you were having none of it. The meetings were intellectually invigorating, attended by like-minded girls – girls who like me strove to improve our minds with cultural nourishment.*

You were sceptical, mocking, even. 'It just sounds like a gathering of highborn daughters spouting on about how superior they are.' And you were correct. Most of the girls attended the Lyceum, which of course was already a sign of privilege, and a bit concerning.

But I placated my quibbles on this point with the thought of the club's aim: to integrate members of the working class who wanted to raise themselves up culturally.

LEAH

Magda has been urging me for some time to join some snobby girls' club called KLUM. We were about fourteen at the time.

'No,' I said when she tried to persuade me to join with her. 'It's not for me.'

'Oh, come on, Leah! You'll love it! All the girls are well educated, like you and me, and we all have cultural interests. We can meet regularly and discuss art and music and such things. I know you love art!'

'Yes, I love art,' I replied. 'But I love to *practise* art, not talk about it! And if I do want to talk about it, like after a visit to a gallery, I don't need some group to discuss it in!'

'But why not? We could have such fun! And it's educational, and mutually beneficial. I don't know much about art, but you don't know much about literature, do you? These are all like-minded girls, and we'd all benefit from each other. Educate each other. And literature. They read the classics! Come on, Leah, let's join together.'

'That sounds boring,' I said. 'Why would I want to sit in a group of girls and have them educate me about music and literature?'

'They don't just talk about it, Leah,' Magda said. 'They do events, Ursula told me. They put on plays, and have poetry readings. Some of them are in a choir; I'd love that! They have painting sessions and you could help me. And in the book group, I could share the books I love with you. And we could discuss the political problems of the day, like unemployment and homelessness. We could think up ways to solve these problems.'

I said nothing to that, but I shook my head rigorously; and there was that one word rattling around in my brain that I wouldn't say aloud, in deference to her: *abscheulich*. Ghastly. The very thought of such activities, a group of snobby girls discussing art and literature and culture – it made my skin crawl. Magda couldn't understand it. Meeting in groups sounded heavenly to her, and the KLUM brought out this inherently unresolvable difference between us.

'I just don't like the idea of groups and leaders and everyone marching in step and thinking in unison, and the leader telling everyone which way to go and what's the proper way to think and then everyone thinking the same.'

'But that's not what they do in KLUM!' Magda said triumphantly. 'That's the whole point of the group! They have no leader. It's a community of equals, from all walks of life.'

'I thought you said the girls were "culturally evolved"?'

Those were the very words Magda had used. Magda loved the idea of 'cultural evolvement'. Evolvement from the more primitive urges to eat and sleep, to make and nourish babies, to work for a living. She felt we needed to rise up to the noble ideals of any highly developed culture such as Germany.

But I would have none of it. 'It just sounds like a collection of snobby girls stroking each other's sense of cultural superiority,' was my final verdict, and I point-blank refused to join the KLUM. It was perhaps the first time I'd ever resisted one of Magda's brilliant ideas. A foretaste of things to come. So Magda joined alone, and went to the meetings alone.

And then I made a mistake. I laughed at her and her new group. I called them the KLUMPS. P for pedantic. Pompous. Pretentious.

'Just boring clumps of boring people talking about boring things,' I said. 'Art and literature and music speak for themselves. They don't need a bunch of pompous schoolgirls trying to make clever conversation. KLUMP!'

I shouldn't have teased her. I knew she hated to be teased, and much more so of late. She flew into a rage.

'You're just an ignorant, mundane clod!' she yelled. 'You'll never rise above the banality of everyday life. You'll end up married to some idiot just as boring as yourself, pushing out one baby after another and hanging up laundry in the courtyard, waiting for him to come home! A boring old *Hausfrau* with saggy boobs and stringy hair!'

We didn't speak for at least a week after that. But we made up. We always did.

MAGDA

Yes, Leah, you were obstinate. You would not join us. Already the split had begun. I think that you already felt, if not intellectually then somehow in your bones that there'd be a culture of exclusion in our club. It was a microcosm of society as a whole. You sensed that sooner or later you would be one of the ones excluded. And you were right. Your instinct was quite on target, as the future would show.

After Hitler came to power everything changed. KLUM became useful in a new way: it distracted my parents from the fact that I was, secretly, also in the BDM. Of course, they would never have allowed me to join the BDM, so KLUM provided a convenient cover. I didn't even have to lie. I'd just gaily announce to Mama that I was off to a 'meeting'; she'd smile and nod, assuming I was off to KLUM. And so for a while I was a member of both.

But in spring 1933 it became compulsory to join the BDM, and at last I could be openly a member. How I gloated! After that I could flaunt my membership, wear my uniform freely, my badge proudly displayed on my chest, and hold my head high as I strode out the door to attend the meetings, while Mama and Papa looked on worriedly.

But as time went on, I became sorely disappointed in the activities of the BDM. I found their discussions boring, of a low intellectual level. Primitive. And the disparaging way they spoke of Jews – it made me cringe.

You know, I hadn't even considered the fact that you were Jewish. I mean, I knew you were, of course, but since your family didn't make a big deal of it the fact held no significance for me. I was so naive! Yes, I knew the Party was against the

Jews, but at first only half of KLUM members belonged to Hitler Youth, and I was sure you would be accepted with open arms. I was such a fool. Of course, eventually we'd have had to unceremoniously throw you out.

Oh, Leah! Writing this has opened the floodgates. I am literally sobbing as I reflect on the fool I once was. An utter, absolute, dangerous idiot.

7

LEAH

Magda could be forgiven for not realising that my Jewishness was an issue. We were ethnic Jews rather than religious ones. Yes, we kept the Sabbath – if rather loosely – and Papa occasionally went to the synagogue, but that wasn't a regular event; and we certainly didn't place our Jewishness at the centre of our family life, as I knew the Orthodox members of our community did. Our Jewishness was simply another fact of life, like Papa's job as a doctor with his own practice, and Mama's part-time job as a librarian, as well as her role in the house taking care of us all. Good, solid middle-class citizens, not much different, outwardly, to the Bosch family, their Catholic middle-classness, their very typical German bourgeois-ness. We just happened, along with all that, to be Jewish.

Magda and I began to drift apart that year. She was drifting apart from Markus, too, even while he was spending more and more time in our flat, with my elder brothers, but also with me, and without her knowledge.

I did not need to be educated by the KLUM, because I was already being educated by Markus. If Magda's membership of the BDM was her secret, well, I had my secrets too. Markus told us everything. There was an open enmity now between him and Magda, and he kept us informed which way the wind was blowing. I still didn't want to believe everything he said about Magda; it seemed so disloyal. But the cleft was already becoming too wide to ignore.

One day, a furious Markus burst into the flat. 'The *Bismarckjugend*'s been disbanded!' he raged. 'Bloody Hitler! Bloody fascists! Didn't I tell you? I knew it!'

Markus had long been a member of the Bismarck Youth, and Magda teased him relentlessly about it. She'd call them the *Schlappschwänze*, the Floppy Tails – a name suggestive of impotence, sexual and otherwise – and liked to joke around that they were wimps.

'You can't even get a girlfriend!' she'd taunt him, in my embarrassed presence. 'You spineless monarchists! You should see the Hitler Youths! Strong, sturdy, full of vigour. That's the kind of man girls look up to, not you flippy-floppy fish, weak, wet and watery.'

Poor Markus! He couldn't even defend himself by letting her know that he *had* had a girlfriend: Elke, whom he had invited to join our private little dissident group. I had been insanely jealous of Elke, and nobody was happier than me when she stopped coming to our meetings. Had they broken up? Perhaps I was wrong and they had never been a couple? I couldn't ask him, of course, but I was happy that Elke never came again.

But Elke too had been a secret. Like most things in Markus's life these days.

Markus was by nature a rebel, a dissident, but his rebellion led in the opposite direction to Magda's and was forbidden by our government. So while she hid her BDM membership from her parents, he too was playing a game of espionage. In fact, the

Bismarckjugend provided a wonderful cover for him to discover secrets.

But that day, it seemed, she had crossed a line. He was furious.

My brother Aaron managed to calm him down, and he eventually told us everything. It wasn't just the Bismarck Youth; as of today, all youth groups were to be dissolved apart from the Hitler Youth, which was the only one now legitimate. 'This is how it starts!' Markus could hardly contain his anger. Again and again, it boiled over. 'It's going to be a dictatorship with Hitler at the helm. It's already started.'

I already knew some of this, as Magda had told me just that day, in confidence, that KLUM had been disbanded. 'It's not appropriate, in our new era,' she'd said with a sigh. 'I mean, I understand. It *is* a bit elitist, isn't it?'

'Well, it's in the name!' I said to her. 'How pretentious! Kunst, Literatur, und Musik, for the ignorant masses.' I put on a snobbish voice and lifted my nose in mockery of the highborn daughters she looked down upon even as she emulated them.

Again, she flew into a rage. That seemed to be happening more and more often these days. She could not abide dissent, especially not from me. It was as if she expected complete compliance with all her opinions and would not allow me a single thought of my own. And it's true that in the past I'd been a willing listener to her, and often compliant in her ideas. But no longer; and she resented that.

'You don't get it! You just don't get it, Leah!' she yelled at me and stormed off.

Get what? I thought. I understood very well that the Nazis – as the National Socialists were by now known – would not allow any opposing parties, not even a club of highborn daughters discussing art, music and literature. It seemed to me that the move to shut down that fairly innocent club spoke volumes. There was nothing to 'get'; I understood very well, I thought, particularly as I was now getting regular commentary and critical reactions from Magda's own brother.

A few days after the *Bismarckjugend* were shut down, Markus burst into our flat again. 'Magda is insane!' he cried. 'Completely and utterly insane! I can't believe she's my sister!'

After he had calmed down, the story came out.

'Two stormtroopers came to our door today, demanding I hand back my *Bismarckjugend* uniform. I stood up to them. I flat out refused. But they barged into the flat and began to search the place. They turned everything upside down, in all the rooms! But you know what? That lovely sister of mine – she knew very well that I kept my uniform in the ottoman, beneath some old curtains. She dug it out, handed them everything. You should have seen the malicious grin on her face! She's insane!'

We let him rage for a while over this mortification, and his sister's collaboration with evil. Yes, evil. That might have been the first time he used that word.

I was shocked, hearing that strong word, used against my best friend, his own sister. Surely it couldn't be that bad? Surely she didn't deserve such an appalling label? But Markus insisted that this was just the start. The thin edge of the wedge, he called it. Little acts of terrorism. One day, we would all feel the full weight of that wedge. The mallet, wielded at full strength, slamming down upon us in full force.

'At least they didn't take my breeches, or my boots,' he said. 'The stormtroopers handed them back. "You'll need them for the Hitler Youth," they told me. Magda stood by, smirking. She was delighted. She'd always been badgering me to join the Hitler Youth, and now here were two stormtroopers making it clear that I'd have to.'

He flashed a triumphant grin. 'I suppose I look young for

my age,' he said. 'They didn't realise that I was eighteen. Too old for the Hitler Youth. So I got the last laugh.'

MAGDA

I mentioned earlier that I had initially been disappointed with the BDM, after secretly joining in 1933. I could hardly admit it even to myself, but the girls who were my co-members were – I search for the right word and come up only with 'substandard'.

I was the only one in my local BDM group who attended the Lyceum; all the others were working girls of the labourer class or the lower middle class. They worked in shops and offices and factories, or they were learning to be dressmakers and hairdressers. Some were even servants. Cooks, cleaners. Their speech was crude, their ambitions and aspirations lowly. Their conversation was limited, centring on fashion, hairstyles, film stars. When I tried to turn our talk to political texts like Mein Kampf, *I found no response beyond silence. They hadn't read it. Our musical meetings consisted of learning the words to rousing patriotic songs, which we'd all then belt out together. I had nothing against patriotic songs per se, but a bit of Schubert's* Lieder *would not have harmed them in the least and would have brought them more in touch with Germany's great cultural heritage.*

I am describing this to you in keeping with my reactions at the time. Yes, I was a terrible snob, and arrogant to boot. I couldn't even admit it to myself. I was basically a hybrid creature: on the one side, I longed to escape my middle-class status and be part of the working class, which I thought noble of myself. But the reality was different, because there was absolutely no companionship between me and them. They had no political consciousness inasmuch as they regarded me as a highborn daughter myself, yet made no attempt to lift them-

selves up culturally. They had no interest in the workers' poetry I tried to push on them, no sense of the romance of cultural improvement. Their highest ambition was to marry and have babies. That, at least, was in keeping with Hitler's view of aspirational womanhood.

I wasn't fully aware of that particular aspect of National Socialism at the time, but it was most contrary to my own aspirations. Though I loved babies, maternity was the very last on my list of possible futures. Veterinary surgeon was in first place, but I also longed to be a writer. One of those ambitions had to be realised, but only one required an academic qualification.

But the BDM meetings weren't all boring. Sometimes we went on more pleasurable weekend outings: hikes, camping, youth hostelling, sports; and sometimes we met for field exercises and amicable competitions with neighbouring groups. I was shocked to see the way innocent rivalries could descend into outright brawls. The only word I had for such outbursts of violence was 'primitive'. I was often ashamed of my group members.

And I'm afraid I went too far. I've always been outspoken, as you know, and a little bossy. And one day I simply lost my temper and gave my teammates a proper dressing-down.

Some argument had broken out – I don't even remember what it was about. Probably hairstyles or film stars or boys or something just as shallow – the usual. I couldn't help it: I had to give them a good piece of my mind.

'You should be ashamed of yourselves!' I screamed. 'Just look at you! You call yourselves members of the BDM and you don't have the slightest notion of the greatness of your culture! Which one of you has read Goethe? Which one of you knows the difference between the Pastoral Symphony and the Emperor? I bet the only song lyrics you know are some stupid hit you've heard on the radio! You are Germans, but you behave like pigs in the trough!'

Just as I was yelling those last words Frau Schmidt, our dragon of a group leader, walked into the room. She had heard it all and was incandescent with rage. To my complete mortification I was the one now to be yelled at, in front of everyone else.

'What an appalling display of snobbery, Fräulein Bosch!' she cried. 'You're a disgrace to your group!'

She reached out and grabbed the badge I so proudly wore on my brown uniform. 'Do you know what this badge says? It says National Socialist Working Youth. That's who we are. This is not a refined space for cultural discussions, or a space to display our superiority of others! Do you understand that, Fräulein Bosch?'

Of course I understood. I always had! My behaviour was appalling, I now saw as clear as day, and I hung my head in shame. I'd been divisive and pretentious. It all came home to me as Frau Schmitz berated me. I felt as small as a pea and, almost in tears, I offered her my deepest apology.

'I'm sorry, Frau Schmitz, I'm so sorry. I was wrong. I behaved atrociously. Please, please forgive me!'

And I turned to the girls I'd yelled at and apologised to them as well.

But forgiveness didn't come at once and it wasn't going to come easily. I do believe that Frau Schmitz was making me aware of the assertiveness and no-nonsense attitude necessary for leadership, and the difference between assertiveness and pugnaciousness. That she was imprinting on my still-developing mind what would be needed. How I needed to become myself, eventually: uncompromising and unyielding, but with class. That was the kind of personality needed in our great venture. I was tall, but she was taller and towered above me.

By now I was quivering in my boots, and ready to crawl on the floor to lick hers.

That's when she finally relented.

'Very well, Fräulein Bosch. I think your repentance is sincere. And I also see that you might need an outlet for your so-called cultural strengths. As you obviously are too educated for the rest of your group' – I blushed again at her debilitating sarcasm – 'and you obviously enjoy reading and writing, I would like you to be responsible for the press section of our regional group.'

And so, Leah, that's how the BDM led to what was to become my career.

8

LEAH – BERLIN

One day Magda announced that they'd been forced to disband the KLUM and she wasn't even upset. She was almost contrite, aware of her mistake.

'You were right from the start, Leah,' she told me. 'It's quite snobbish, isn't it? And I admit that I was very judgemental about the other girls and their lack of culture. It's funny, isn't it: though you're a Jew, you're so much more tuned in to German culture than those girls. But I had no right to look down on them. The working class is Germany's future.'

I immediately picked up on her use of the word 'Jew'. There was a derogatory undertone to the way she spoke it, something I'd never noticed before. She was picking up on all the signals being taught in the BDM. That Jews were not the sort of Germans an upright person would mix with. That they were, perhaps, not really Germans at all...

Markus was far more attuned to Magda's change of attitude than I was – after all, he lived with her, and knew her inside out. He tried to warn me. He now spent most afternoons in our flat. I thought at first that it was solely because of my brothers, but I gradually caught on to the little signals that told me that he was as interested in me as I was in him. I couldn't help noticing how his eyes lingered on mine, and how he listened to what I had to say with far more interest than did my brothers.

Once, he came over when my brothers were not at home. I later discovered that they – all three of them – had gone with Father to a meeting at the synagogue, where Joachim Prinz, a young and charismatic rabbi, had started giving sermons that both encouraged and warned. Rabbi Prinz's talks at the Friedenstempel were drawing Jews from all over Berlin. Father had not invited me; as a girl, he thought, I should not become involved in politics. My parents were only trying to protect me from their own growing fears. Because slowly, the poison was spreading. Not only in Magda's heart but throughout society. We could no longer ignore it.

The thin edge of the wedge, Markus had called it.

That afternoon he suggested, seeing as how I was alone at home, that we go out together. 'When did you last go to the cinema, Leah?' he asked.

I shrugged. I hardly ever went to the cinema, but I knew that Markus loved film. He was an amateur actor himself.

'Come on, let's go!' he said. '*Laughing Heirs* is on at the Gloria. With Heinz Rühmann. It's supposed to be really good.'

I smiled up at him. 'I'd love to!'

'Let's go and have a coffee first,' he said.

I nodded and put away the book I was reading.

We went to a café not far from the Gloria cinema. Markus chose a corner table for us and pulled out a chair for me. I sat down while he went to the counter to place our order.

We waited what seemed like an age. Finally, a waitress with very stiff curls in her hair came to our table with a tray. She placed a cup of coffee and another plate with apple cake in front of Markus, ignoring me completely.

Markus said sharply, 'I ordered two cups, one for the Fräulein here as well.'

'Oh, really?' said the waitress. She didn't even look at me.

'Yes, really.'

We waited a further five minutes but a second cup of coffee and piece of cake did not arrive. I noticed that people at the other tables were throwing us surreptitious glances. I felt very uncomfortable. Markus had not touched his coffee or his cake. A glance behind me showed me the waitress standing in the doorway to the kitchen, chatting casually with another waitress. I felt really bad by now.

'Come on, Markus. Drink your coffee quickly and let's go.'

'I'm not drinking a drop!' he said and scraped back his chair. 'Let's go. This place is dirty.'

He said the last word so loudly everyone in the café looked up and stared at us. I wanted to sink into the floor. 'Markus!' I whispered. 'Not so loud!' But secretly I was proud of him. As we strode out of the café the waitress called after us: 'Not as dirty as your Jew-girlfriend, though!'

Markus stopped in his tracks and swung round, and I believe he would have stormed back in and challenged that girl right to her face if I had not pulled at his sleeve and begged him to go.

The film was a romantic comedy about a young salesman, played by Heinz Rühmann, who inherits a wine estate on the condition that he can't drink a drop of alcohol for at least a month. I followed the story only very superficially, and I thought Markus did too. We laughed in the right places, but I, at least, found myself more concerned with my own churning thoughts about what had just happened in the café.

In the middle of the film Markus reached over and grabbed my hand, and held it for the rest of the screening. And on the way home, he still held it. We did not speak much, but as he delivered me to my door he said, 'Don't be upset by what happened, Leah. But be careful. That kind of thing is just the start. We'll have to watch our step from now on.'

It was a warning, but I was distracted from it due to the fact that he had used the word 'we'. That one little word told me so much, and filled me with such elation. And I couldn't deny it: my upset at the café incident was more than balanced out by what I called the cinema incident. That precious moment when Markus took my hand in his.

MAGDA

I was elated, at first, by having been promoted to BDM staff despite being only sixteen years old. Voluntary staff, that is; I'm not sure how many, if any, of the BDM leaders were paid, and I most certainly was not. Anyway, I would have considered any offer of payment an insult. This work was in itself payment enough. It was service. Service to a higher, noble cause. The highest, noblest cause of all. It was an honour, and payment would have cheapened it.

But again, I was to be disappointed. I was now able to move and work among the established leaders of the BDM, the Old Guard. Even before meeting them I felt elated at the honour; it was almost like meeting God. Everything in me strained to respect them.

But the reality proved, once again, a let-down. It was plain that, rather than welcoming me into the fold as a young enthusiastic recruit, they looked down on me; they called me a March Violet because I had joined so late – I had not dared to join in the early days, when being a member called for risk-taking. I had joined only after the National Socialists came to power, when membership of the Hitler Youth was finally mandatory.

They made it clear that I was not one of them for another reason: I attended the exclusive Lyceum. I was a highborn daughter. And they, I noted, were from the very proletariat my parents despised, and behaved accordingly. They were uncouth, uncultured, gross. They spoke in such a base way my skin crawled. My term for them was 'primitive', my favourite word to describe such gross behaviour and language. I did not even like them – how could I respect them?

It was around this time that I first became aware of the growing antipathy towards Jews. As you know, I had no problem at all interacting with individual Jews and even making friends with them. You were my closest friend, after all. And almost a third of the girls in my class were Jewish, other Jewish families lived in our building, and we daily interacted with Jewish tradesmen. To be quite honest, I have to admit even to admiration of my Jewish classmates. So many of them were much more mature than I was that I felt like a child in their presence. They were physically and intellectually, and even socially, my superiors, a fact I could not help but acknowledge. Not one of them came from a poor home; one or two of them even came to school in chauffeur-driven cars. They represented old money. Those girls were well-bred and well-behaved, never forming the kind of cliques in which mean girls ganged up on certain victims.

I once did just that, to my shame. Joined such a clique, I mean. And I now have to confess to one awful act I committed. I was twelve at the time; a few girls had decided to play a prank on a certain Jewish girl who was, we thought, teacher's pet because she was so bright. Her name was Anna. Hearing or thinking of that name causes me embarrassment to this day. Anyway, on that day I was chosen as the perpetrator. It was on a summer outing to the Müggelsee lake. We had all brought a picnic lunch from home, and our teacher said we would swim first to work up an appetite, and then have lunch on the lawns a little way away from the water. I was friends with a mean girl named Gudrun, and it was she who thought up the prank.

'Come on, Gudrun and Magda!' the mistress called. We were whispering and giggling together. Gudrun pointed out Anna's lunch and handed me a little parcel wrapped in greaseproof paper she'd brought from home. Yes, she had it all planned out.

'I'm not swimming today, Fräulein Weber!' I called. 'I've got my... you know. My days.'

'All right then, so you stay here and watch over our things.'

'I will,' I replied, and sat down demurely on a picnic blanket.

As soon as they were in the lake, splashing about and enjoying themselves, I got to work. I quickly opened Anna's picnic bag and removed the packet of sandwiches wrapped in greaseproof paper her mother had prepared. I unwrapped it and the smaller packet Gudrun had given me. In it were several thin slices of pork sausage. I lifted the top slice of one of Anna's sandwiches and placed the sausage slivers on top of the egg slices she had, making sure that they were nowhere near the edges, and so invisible once I replaced the top slice of bread.

I giggled to myself as I worked. What a jolly prank! I thought it basically harmless, to be truthful; yes, I knew that Jews didn't eat pork, but the rest of us all did, so it wasn't harmful, I reasoned. Everyone loved sausage; perhaps she'd even like it. I was actually doing her a favour, I thought, introducing her to a delicacy she'd denied herself.

Then I sat back to wait for the others to return. But I was a bit envious: I wasn't at all indisposed, as I'd claimed, and I did love swimming. I loved the cold water and the exercise and simply having fun with the others. Why hadn't Gudrun played the prank herself? Why had she chosen me to carry it out?

So I changed into my bathing suit and joined the others. I told Fräulein Weber that I'd changed my mind; I'd come in for just a few minutes and wouldn't actually swim. I spent half an hour in the shallow waters near the beach, splashing the others and getting splashed myself, and completely forgot about Anna's sandwich.

Afterwards, we all ran laughing up the lawn to the picnic spot, flung ourselves on to the grass, and unpacked our lunches. We began to tuck in. Suddenly, Anna let out a loud scream, spitting out the contents of her mouth and throwing the sandwich far away. There was the evidence of my misbehaviour: pieces of red pork sprinkled among egg and cucumber slices and pickles and slices of buttered bread.

'It's pork!' Anna cried. 'Somebody put pork in my sandwich!'

Many of the girls broke into raucous laughter. Everybody looked at me. I turned red as a beetroot.

But Fräulein Weber wasn't laughing. I got into serious trouble. Mama was horrified; what I'd done was 'un-Christian' and malicious. I still didn't understand what was so wrong. That's how obtuse I was. However, later on Fräulein Weber had a long talk with me.

'Imagine if somebody played a prank on you by replacing the beef in your stew with dog meat and only told you after you started to eat it. Or rat meat. Or they made you eat cockroaches. That's how disgusting pork is to Jews,' she said, and finally I understood.

I went to Anna's mother to apologise, to her and her daughter. My apology was sincere, and they accepted it graciously. And my friendship with Gudrun was over.

Looking back, I see that as my first act of hostility towards a Jewish person, even if committed unwittingly – that is, not understanding the magnitude of my wrongdoing.

That had been years ago. Now, as a member of the BDM, I was regularly schooled in hostility and hatred towards Jews.

I remember marching down the Kurfürstendamm with my group. 'Stamp your feet as loudly as possible!' our leader told us. 'This is where all the rich Jews live! Let's wake them from their afternoon naps!'

9

LEAH – BERLIN

'Leah, you really need to step away from Magda,' Markus told me one day, soon after that cinema visit, but I couldn't do it. I didn't want to believe it. But then, that day came when the scales did finally fall from my eyes.

The cinema visit with its disastrous prelude – that was the beginning of me and Markus as a couple. We both knew we needed to keep it a secret, not only from Magda – that went without saying – but from both our families. It was something so precious, so intimate. A glance here, a touch there, a secret smile, that only he and I recognised. A little note pressed into my pocket: 'Zum Zoo, 4 p.m.'

We'd take separate busses from Tempelhof and meet at Zum Zoo, a small café close to the Bahnhof Zoo. Zum Zoo was now developing into the place for Berlin's 'homeless' youth to meet – homeless, not in the literal sense, but in an emotional and political sense. Young people who were lost, rudderless and oarless in a stormy ocean where the waves were lashing higher and the winds relentlessly blowing in only one direction.

I too was suffering under my sense of homelessness, in particular over the loss of Magda as my closest friend.

'I don't have to step away from her,' I said to Markus now. 'She's already stepped away from me. I mean, she's still friendly enough but it's as if we're going separate ways. I know she's a BDM member but it's compulsory so I didn't think much of it.'

'She's more than just a member,' Markus said. 'She works for them.'

'No!' I gasped. I hadn't had a clue! Of course I knew by now exactly what poison was being spread by the Hitler Youth. I knew that Magda had stars in her eyes regarding Hitler and his Grossdeutschland nonsense. And I knew that all German girls had to be members. But to actually *work* for them?

So naive I'd been! My friendship with Magda, my closeness to her, had placed a sort of protective cloak around her. And even when I'd felt her slow pulling away from me, I'd taken it to be solely because of her KLUM activities; I'd blamed the KLUM for the estrangement. But the truth was, she was being sucked into a vortex of poison – a poison that declared me and my community her enemy.

'How do you know?' I asked Markus.

I still didn't quite believe it; I wanted evidence. Magda had never spoken a single disparaging word to me. If we met in the hallway or stairs of Kaiserkorso Eins, her smile was just as warm, her words of greeting just as friendly. 'Just rushing off to my meeting,' she'd say, in the early days, and I would assume she was off to discuss the poems of Rilke or which Brandenburg Concerto was the best. She couldn't possibly be harbouring hatred! Not after everything we'd been through together. Not after those wonderful Bavarian summers, when we'd basked on lakeshores and soaked in the sunshine in almost unbearably green meadows.

'Oh, Leah,' Markus replied, 'you're so good, it shines in your hair. I'm not so virtuous. I've been snooping in her room and I found the proof. She's a full-blown Nazi, toxic to her eyeballs. See: she has this secret hiding place at the back of her wardrobe, behind a loose board. She's always hidden her secrets from Mama there; I've known about it since we were kids. Well, I went snooping and guess what I found? A shoe box full of her stuff. A bundle of pamphlets. And a tract, Leah, a tract, with the Blood Oath on it.'

'The Blood Oath? What's that?' The very name of this thing sent shivers down my spine.

'It's an oath the Hitler Youth members have to take. It's called the Blood Oath because they take it before the Blood Banner – it's supposedly soaked in the blood of martyrs who died at the failed putsch of 1923. And the oath itself... well, you don't want to know.'

'Tell me. I do want to know.'

'"In the presence of this Blood Banner, which represents our Führer,' he recited, '"I swear to devote all my energies and my strength to the saviour of our country, Adolf Hitler. I am willing and ready to give up my life for him. So help me God." That's what it says, Leah. Members of the BDM have to take that oath. Magda has taken it.

'Oh, Markus!'

'Well, all BDM members have to take the oath, so we can't really blame her for that. But there's worse in that box. She's writing articles for them, Leah. When she's typing away in her room, she's not writing harmless short stories anymore. She's writing articles for the Hitler Youth magazine, and she hides the carbon copies in that box. Letters from an editor, discussing the content. She writes Nazi propaganda, Leah.'

It was quite a warm day, but the skin on my arms broke out in goosebumps and it seemed that something was stuck in my throat, a lump so bitter it seemed to radiate all through my body and I wanted to run to the toilet and throw up. But I was stuck to my seat, to Markus.

Often we sat at tiny tables on tiny wobbly chairs but, luckily, that day we'd nabbed the cushioned bench in the bay window, where we could not only hold hands but cuddle together, and now Markus simply reached out and pulled me into his arms and let me heave against his chest with sorrow. That's when I knew it was over, completely over, between me and Magda.

Zum Zoo became our place of refuge. Markus, always one to make useful connections in useful places, had discovered it through some friend or other. It wasn't visible from the street, and that was its main secret. Either you knew it was there or you didn't, hidden as it was down a narrow alleyway, too narrow for vehicles, cobbled, picturesque, sunless because of the tall stone buildings walling it in. There wasn't even a sign above the café door designating it as a café. Zum Zoo was like a watering hole somewhere in Africa where the thirsty animals gathered; but Markus and I were thirsty not for drink, but for each other. For the chance to gaze into each other's eyes openly, to smile and laugh with each other, to speak in whispered tones about the unspeakable – but also to escape the unspeakable.

We continued to meet there several times a week, after school; Markus had just completed his final year of Gymnasium and was waiting for his university acceptance. Here, nobody would refuse to serve me: the waitress was a buxom, friendly girl who knew I was Jewish, who'd laugh and joke with us and with all the other customers.

The young people who came here – nobody over twenty, Markus told me, but that was an exaggeration – were all misfits. You could tell at a glance that they didn't fit in anywhere: artists, writers, dissidents, Jews, eccentrics of all kinds. If anything, we were the most conventional-looking couple in the whole establishment. Everyone seemed to know Markus. He was one of those rare people who everyone is somehow attracted to and wants to know. But since I was with him, they all quickly came to respect my place in his life and we had all the privacy we wanted.

Zum Zoo only served black tea and some excuse for coffee, served in mismatched cracked cups. Everything was free. There was an old biscuit tin near the entrance where you could donate money, and it went without saying that some donations were large enough to cover many cups. I was never sure who actually ran Zum Zoo. Markus may have known, but discretion was always paramount. Soon, the name was condensed to only its letters: ZZ. Or you could make the double-Z sign with your forefinger, and people would know.

But it wasn't just Zum Zoo that welded us together. Markus showed me Berlin in a way I'd never known it before. Berlin wasn't just the gloomy remains of the war that Magda so loved to complain about: a city of the homeless and the jobless, of prostitutes and pickpockets and down-and-outers. Berlin had just emerged from the Golden Twenties. It was a vibrant, exciting metropolis, a city of cabaret and cinema, buzzing with creativity and progress. If you had a certain antenna for that buzz, you felt it, even after Hitler's master strike. It would take more than a declaration of ultimate power to destroy Berlin's soul. Markus wanted me to find that soul, still bubbling away beneath the red, black and white swastikas that now festooned all the main throughfares of the city. Beneath the swastikas, beneath the pompous surface, Berlin's spirit lived on. Zum Zoo was one little example of how the underground kept that spirit alive; we kept it alive in our hearts.

Markus loved architecture and its history. I had never paid much attention to the city before but now he showed me all the iconic buildings and monuments that made Berlin one of the greatest cities in the world. I gazed up at the Brandenburg Gate in awe – of course I'd seen it before, but never holding the hand of the man I loved. That hand! An anchor, a point of safety when we'd lose ourselves in the faceless crowds.

. . .

From that day on, I kept my distance from Magda. I watched her carefully and critically. She didn't seem to notice this withdrawal. She also clearly didn't notice the mental wall I'd drawn between us, didn't miss the spirited political and philosophical discussions of the past. We still kept up the illusion of friendship. Still occasionally walked home from school together, or even went to the cinema. But we no longer visited each other. It was her outgoing personality, her chatterbox nature that kept the illusion of friendship alive.

The pretence she managed to put up! She'd somehow managed to create an artificial *heile Welt*, 'healed world', in which everything was *Friede, Freude, Eierkuchen* – Peace, Joy, and Pancakes – as we called it in local parlance.

Of course, for us Jews it was anything BUT peace, joy and pancakes. And so I had to be the one to draw the final line. A line that became thicker by the day, until the moment it became a wall falling between us with a resounding thud.

It happened later in 1933, before she went off to boarding school. A summer day. Magda and I were on our way home, walking down Bergmannstrasse, when we stopped in our tracks. All the other pedestrians were doing the same. A motorcade was on its way, led by an open Jeep in which stood a man with a loudspeaker, announcing the coming of 'our great Führer', clearing the street of traffic, driving all the vehicles away like cattle.

A veritable horde of motorcycles followed, all the bikes and their uniformed riders conspicuously emblazoned with swastikas. We stopped and stared. Then came a few cars. And then the Führer himself, standing in his open-topped car, right arm stretched out stiff before him in the required salute. All around us, pedestrians did the same. Arms shot out, voices raised in unison: *Heil Hitler!*

To my utter shock, Magda joined in. Her right arm snapped out, hand flat, palm down. There she stood, next to me but in a world of her own, straight and proud. And she, too, cried out: *Heil Hitler!* I could only see her profile, but pride and devotion and an uncanny fervour were written all over the side of her face.

There it was. Markus's warning words rang in my ears as I saw for myself what they really meant, and I froze in horror.

The motorcade passed by: it turned right down the Tempelhofer Damm and disappeared. Magda's arm dropped to her side; in fact, with that same arm she hooked mine and made as if to amble off on our way home, as if nothing had happened. And I knew it was time for me to confront her. I'd been putting off that confrontation for ages, but it had to happen. We could not pretend to go on as before. I had to make the declaration that would end it all forever.

'Magda! How *could* you!'

'But it was never a secret!' she replied. 'Hitler will bring long-needed renewal to Germany. He will end unemployment and get the economy up to speed. He's a breath of fresh air! We've spoken about this, many times.'

'Yes, but...' In fact, *we* had not spoken about this. *She* had spoken to me about this. I had deliberately held back my own opinion, still hoping to preserve our precious friendship.

'But he hates Jews!' I yelled it out to her. This was a new me, a me no longer struggling to hold together the tatters of our friendship. A me no longer trying to be kind even as I battled with sentimental memories. It was a loud, outraged, assertive me, a me Magda had never seen before. I was no longer the sweet friend who forgave and understood and made the first move of reconciliation when we argued. This was serious. I had never once before raised the subject of Hitler's rabid anti-semitism. That was the taboo subject we had somehow managed to leave untouched in all our philosophical conversations.

Loyalty had always been the foundation of our relationship.

That was why neither of us had touched upon the subject of Jews in Germany until now. And nothing, to date, had forced the issue. Yes, I'd seen much less of Magda since she'd joined the KLUM, and even more since she'd joined the BDM, but, I thought, it meant nothing much. I had wanted above all to preserve our friendship. I had been too naive to see how impossible that was, even after Markus opened my eyes.

Magda had been my other half! It had seemed like the ultimate betrayal, to drop her like a rotten egg just because our politics did not mesh. Who did that?

But now, I knew, it was well and truly over.

'Oh, Leah!' she said in that sing-song, half-mocking voice I'd always found so irritating. She always used it when she felt I was being ridiculous. 'Yes, Hitler does see there's a Jewish problem. But that doesn't mean *you,* for goodness' sake! Not *your* family! You're of a different calibre altogether! But you have to admit, there's a section of the Jewry that is really dangerous, and those are the ones we have to combat.'

I was so stunned I had no words. I said nothing but pulled my arm out from her tight hook.

'Oh, Leah!' she sighed. 'Don't be like that! You don't need to take offence. You're not at all like *those* Jews!'

Again, I did not reply. We walked side by side the rest of the way home in silence. We never used the lift in Kaiserkorso Eins, unless it was already at the ground floor; it was quicker to walk. I didn't walk, though, that day. I bounded up the stairs, along the corridor, and was in our flat before Magda had reached the top. That was virtually our last conversation.

10

MAGDA

The atmosphere at home was growing more and more tense. Constant arguments between me on the one side and my parents on the other, with Markus always siding with them, though not as a Catholic but as a rigorous Nazi opponent. Mama and Papa decided that I had been indoctrinated by Tante Gundhilde. They banned her from the house and forbade me from visiting her; but they soon realised they couldn't control a sixteen-year-old loud-mouthed zealot. Neither could they lock me in my room.

They came up with the brilliant idea of sending me away: to a Catholic boarding school in Bavaria. That September, 1933, Mama personally delivered me, kicking and screaming, into the hands of Mother Illuminata, the Abbess of the Heilig-Geist-Lyceum for Higher Daughters, not far from where she'd grown up in the Chiemgau area. Actually, I couldn't reject the school out of hand immediately. I almost gasped when I saw the beautiful building tucked into a verdant valley: it was like a castle, with turrets and towers, gables and steep roofs, strong brick walls, and I fell in love with the building at first sight. I had always loved medieval architecture, and this building sang with history and culture. It was simply German architecture at its very best. Who wouldn't want to make this place their home? And so, despite my basic resistance to being exiled to a Catholic prison – as I saw it – I resolved to at least give it a try. After all, the school had an impeccable reputation as far as the academic performance of the girls – the inmates, I called them – was concerned. And academically, I thrived. Not so much in my behaviour. Before long, it was one reprimand after the other. My behaviour was atrocious. I was forever spouting my view that the Third Reich was Germany's chance to at last rise up from the ruins of the war. I waxed lyrical in my praise for Hitler and what he would do for Germany. I argued with teachers and girls. I rolled my eyes during mandatory mass, and refused to pray kneeling in chapel. In fact, I would not kneel at all. I refused to make the sign of the cross.

I could not last long. After only one month, I was expelled.

Mama and Papa chose a different boarding school for me. This time, they were wise enough not to choose a Catholic school and instead picked a secular one, again in Bavaria, but this time in the city of Munich. Being a city girl myself, I found myself in my element – in more ways than one.

My parents, so eager to see me in an establishment far away from Berlin, would have been appalled had they known what went on in that school. After my first year there, a new headmistress took over and the entire style of teaching changed. From my point of view, for the better. Every member of the teaching staff was vetted for ideological purity. Those deemed contentious were dismissed as bourgeois and replaced by progressive hardliners in National Socialism. In this case, contentious meant those who did not toe the party line.

Needless to say, I thrived in that school. I did not miss Berlin and my BDM group one iota. We had our own BDM groups within the school – in fact, it was a hotbed for BDM activity. Oh, how wonderful it was to live, move and have my being with people of like mind, with whom I could have endless, deeply satisfying conversations about Germany's future role in world politics!

We'd join other BDM groups within the city and nothing was more joyous to me than to march through the city streets, proud in our brown uniforms, waving the red-black-and-white swastika flags, singing our rousing songs of victory and triumph, our throats raw from the effort of outshouting each other! I guarantee, Mama would have dropped dead, had she known.

I did not even come home for the holidays; I met girls at school from families who were compatible with my own world-view, and I never ran short of invitations to their homes during the holidays. We all egged each other on, as young people tend to do. I was in seventh heaven.

Of course, I did not keep in touch with you. I did not write you a single letter, nor did I hear from you. I hardly corresponded with my parents, and when they came to visit I was rude and dismissive, and naturally secretive. They certainly noticed that I was drifting further and further away, and that, far from being a solution, boarding school had actually cemented my allegiance to Hitler.

I think though that by this time they didn't care. They had admitted defeat, given up. In Berlin the old ways of thinking had now been completely obliterated by the new. It became a crime, almost, to not join the wave of Nazism sweeping through the city. Even if you disapproved of the new direction, you kept silent because it was dangerous to speak out. The Thought Police came after you. Not a real term; a term I coined in retrospect, after it was all over, once I could see with clear vision what had happened to me.

This was a new era. There was no room for sentimentality. No room for you. But you had already declared enmity, hadn't you, the day you'd confronted me on Bergmannstrasse? You'd

actually yelled at me for giving the Hitler salute! And much as
I hate to admit, I was shocked out of my mind that you'd dared
to confront me. That was a new you, Leah, a you I'd never seen
before.

LEAH – BERLIN

I was so relieved when Magda went off to boarding school. Even though we were no longer friends, no longer did anything together, and I no longer came to her flat or she to mine, we did occasionally see each other on the stairs or in the hallway or, in the earlier months, at the Lyceum, and it was awkward. Once she'd gone, the atmosphere in the building improved at once; immediately, peace descended on Kaiserkorso Eins.

But not on Berlin. Markus had been right. Hostility towards Jews was increasing day by day, and incidents like the one in the café with the hostile waitress were now a daily occurrence. Neighbours from down my street who had in the past always greeted me with a smile and a 'Guten Tag, Magda!', who had known me since I was a tot, now crossed the road if they saw me coming, or scowled into my face.

There was one neighbour, a nasty old man called Herr Wagner, who had always been a busybody. Over the years he had gained a reputation as the street's Order-Keeper. He seemed to have a broom permanently attached to his hand; he was always sweeping the road, clearing the gutters of every last leaf. Kaiserkorso Eins stood at a kind of open fork, with a small green island of trees and grass, and Herr Wagner always made sure that not a single leaf was left to lie on the street or even on the grass. He picked them all up, sweeping them into a large can and bending over to pick up stray ones individually. I'd always ignored him, even in the days when Magda and I would walk together, arms hooked. I could tell by the beady way he watched us that he'd disapproved of our friendship. It was the very same look as the one I'd got from Tante Gundhilde: disapproving, contemptuous.

Now he had been officially made block warden, *Blockwart* – or 'block snoop', the literal meaning of the term – by the Nazi authorities, and he wore a swastika proudly stitched to his shirts or jackets. The block warden's overarching duty was to form the primary link between the Nazi authorities and the general population; in other words, it was his job to supervise the comings and goings of Jews. On becoming the official warden – as he informed all the house's tenants by shoving a leaflet in every postbox – he was now the supervisor for our whole block and the official sneak, who would run to the authorities at the least suspicion of anti-Nazi behaviour (of which friendships between Jews and gentiles were considered the worst example!).

Markus and I agreed that we would not give Herr Wagner any reason to report us. This was not cowardice; it was simply good sense. Markus was becoming more and more involved in more intricate dissident activities, and it was better for him to keep his head down.

'The more undercover I am, the better work I can do,' he said, apologetically. 'It means I can play the game on the outside but dismantle it from the inside.' He sighed. 'At least, *try* to dismantle it.' He refused to give me any more details. The less I knew, the safer for me, he said. Jews were in danger, and he, as an activist, had to stay undercover. It was all part of the job.

But Markus stayed true. He was a stalwart. In my last year at school though, we never left the house together, and never gave Herr Wagner reason to suspect we were friends, much less sweethearts. That meant we had to avoid meeting anywhere in the Tempelhof-Kreuzberg area. We could never again leave the house together, never jump on a tram or visit the local cinema or ice rink together. We'd arrange instead to meet on the other side of Berlin, in crowded areas where we could merge into the hordes of people, be virtually invisible. Our relationship was *verboten*. I was *verboten*.

In our walks about the city he never left my side; I was not obviously Jewish to look at, and so though always inwardly on edge, I could somewhat relax in crowded central areas. Markus gave me confidence. By this time he had passed his Abitur with flying colours and had applied to the Technical University of Munich to study structural engineering.

'Why Munich?' I complained. 'Why not Berlin?'

'I need to get away from Berlin,' he said. 'I need to see more of Germany, learn how they think in other cities. And you know I'm half Bavarian!'

I did know that, of course, due to the wonderful childhood holidays we'd spent at his family farm. Markus, I knew, had a special affinity and love for Bavaria. I did worry a little – what if he found another girl there, a gentile, someone less problematic, politically, than me? I voiced my worries.

'You might find someone else there.'

He only wrapped his arms round me. 'No, Leah. I won't find someone else.'

'But how can you know that? What if you meet a nice blonde Aryan girl?'

'Why would I want a nice blonde Aryan girl when I have a beautiful, brunette Jewish girl?'

I nuzzled my cheek against his shoulder. 'I only cause you headaches. And trouble. It'd be much easier for you. Why get involved with us Jews? Why even care about me?'

Of course, I was fishing; not for compliments, but for a statement of commitment. I'd always loved him – I knew this now – but I nursed a permanent fear that he would find a better girlfriend, someone easier to be seen with, someone who came with less political baggage. *Why me?* I'd ask myself. *Why not another Elke, or a beautiful Renate or a bubbly Ulrike, solidly German, firmly risk-free?*

He pushed me away, then held me at arm's length, looked into my eyes, and said, 'Leah! Don't talk nonsense. Do you think I'm with you out of pity? Out of duty? That I'm fighting against the Nazis because – because of some grand idea of chivalry?'

I looked away. 'Maybe,' I whispered.

'Well, you're wrong. Even if I weren't with you. Even if I didn't love you. Even if I didn't want to make you, only you, my wife, I'd still be fighting against the scourge that has taken over my country. I'd still be a dissident, still be a rebel. Still be going up against the Nazis with every breath of my body.'

I smiled into his coat. 'What did you just say?'

'You heard what I said. I'd be fighting Hitler no matter what.'

'No. I mean the earlier bit. The bit about making me your wife.'

He chuckled then, and pulled me close. 'Of course, Leah. That goes without saying. It's what I want, one day, when Germany is free again.'

He pulled me closer.

'And anyway, why would I want some blonde Aryan girl when I'm lucky enough to have the most beautiful girl in the world in my arms?'

He tilted my chin up and looked into my eyes. 'Beautiful, inside and out.'

'Oh, Markus,' I sighed. I had no other words.

'We might have to wait a while, but we're young. We have all the time in the world.'

My brother Aaron had also hoped to apply to university, to study mechanical engineering at the Berlin Technical University. However, in April of 1933 the Law Against Overcrowding in German Schools and Universities, which drastically limited the percentage of Jewish students allowed in any one university, had come into effect, and he was not allowed to enrol. Mosche, my eldest brother, on the other hand, who had just managed to finish his medical studies before the law came into effect, now worked alongside Father in his private clinic in Steglitz. My youngest brother, Samuel, was not allowed to enrol in the Gymnasium due to same law forbidding or restricting the higher education of Jews.

I, meanwhile, had decided that an academic career was anyway not for me, and it was becoming clearer than ever that even if I'd wanted to study English and philosophy – both of which I loved – as a Jew and a woman, it would not be possible for me. It was against the law. I consoled myself that, anyway, one day I would marry and have children. Working with children seemed a sensible and practical choice, and so I decided to become a kindergarten teacher, and left school at sixteen with that goal in mind. I did need training, and so I found a post as an apprentice at a small Kindergarten in Kreuzberg, where the mothers of the young children were all working women of the class Magda would have admired as 'the proletariat'.

I loved my apprenticeship. I found much satisfaction in the company of little children – how innocent they were, how willing to learn; and little children did not discriminate. All they cared about was being loved and it was wonderful to interact with them. What a tremendous task it was, to help these children on their way to unfold whatever it was that was hidden in their depths! They were like tight little rosebuds, and we adults were the gardeners, helping them to blossom into their full beauty and happiness. Their full potential.

If only the times had been different.

By 1937 it was no longer a secret in Berlin that Jews were the scum of the Earth. We heard horrific stories of Jews being evicted from their homes by their landlords. But even ownership of a home did not mean safety. There was more and more talk, in the streets, in the newspapers, on the radio, that Jews were the worst threat and that Germany had to find a solution. More and more we heard about 'the Jewish Question', as if that was the one thing that stood in the way of German progress. In Zum Zoo, the talk became more dangerous, the faces grew longer and the disquiet so thick, you could cut it with a knife.

The new Nuremberg Laws were introduced in September 1935 and declared that Jewish people were no longer German citizens. And all Jews by law had to carry identity cards that showed a 'J' stamp.

Marriage and relationships between Jewish people and 'real' Germans became illegal; Markus and I were effectively breaking the law by even speaking of marriage, even by holding hands.

Jewish people were banned from becoming doctors and those Jews already practising medicine were banned from treating Aryan patients. Laws and decrees came into effect: public health insurance funds no longer reimbursed Jews for their medical expenses. Patients had to pay for all their own costs. Jewish physicians could not even call themselves doctors; they had to change their practices' signs to declare themselves 'health workers' or some such nonsense. And in some cities Jewish patients were no longer admitted to municipal hospitals.

Mother lost her librarian job and began to take on sewing jobs. Instead of applying to university, Aaron found work as an apprentice to a Jewish electrician; the pay was paltry, but at least he would learn a skill. I hid my new identity card in my handbag and hoped I'd never have to show it.

We struggled on. Markus and I grew even closer, though now he was studying in Munich I obviously saw much less of him. When he did come home, we would go for walks in parks far away from Kaiserkorso and hold hands and, yes, dream of a future together. I was sceptical, though. Our relationship was, after all, forbidden.

'Then we will leave Germany,' Markus said. We looked at

each other and he bent over and gently kissed my lips. 'I will never let such laws determine my future and my private life. We will go to England. Or America. Don't worry, my love, we will not let them win.'

But I did not believe his optimism. I knew he was only trying to calm me, to relieve my own fears, which were growing by the day. I could not forget that he had been the one to prophesy all of this long before the rest of the world had taken it seriously.

I had visions of armed Nazis storming into our flat and driving us out at gunpoint. Nightmares haunted me, of my family lined against the wall and a uniformed shooting squad pointing their rifles at us. The bang-bang-bang as they shot us one by one, and each of us falling to the ground in pools of blood. And Markus, who had sown the first seeds of fear in my heart, was now doing his best to uproot the weeds that had developed from them, and plant instead seeds of hope.

I saw behind his façade of nonchalance. He was as terrified as I was. Not just for our individual lives, but for Germany, and what was becoming of our homeland.

11

MAGDA

Ach, Leah! If only it were possible to turn back the clock. The clock of history cannot be reversed, but if we could go back in time and reassess our younger selves with the knowledge and wisdom we have gained as older people, how much better our lives would be! But then, perhaps it is better to learn the truth through bitter experience, no matter how painful that might be. Because truth learned this way digs deeper.

On the other hand: I always had a choice. The truth that I could have chosen a different path when I was young is hammered home by the fact that Markus did exactly that. I feel so ashamed, now, of the way I treated my own brother. The only mitigation that counts in my favour is that I did not denounce Markus. I was supposed to. As a good Nazi, it was my sacred duty to report any family member who expressed anti-Nazi sentiment, and Markus was doing this all the time, in the most appalling words. He must have known I could report him; but I didn't. Neither did I report Mama, who was much more cautious in her dislike of the Nazis. I suppose it is grasping at straws to add loyalty to Markus as a notch in my favour, when it comes to the final reckoning. But, to be quite honest, it wasn't that at all. I believed with all my heart that, one day, I could win Markus for what I thought was the right side. That's why I never denounced him.

Before I knew it, it was 1936 and I had graduated from the Lyceum. I was working in the Labour Service now and, having reconciled with my parents to a degree, was living at home to save money on rent.

Your brothers Aaron and Mosche, in the meantime, were associating with communists, and this came to the notice of the Gestapo. What better way to spy on what was going on, the Gestapo thought, than to recruit me to do the dirty work! I was to become a secret agent. My instructions were to renew my friendship with you, pretend that I had changed my affiliations, and that my sympathies now lay with the Jews and the communists. Can you even imagine a more ridiculous scenario? Who would ever believe that I, a hard-boiled BDM girl, could suddenly change my colours? It seemed, though, that they had intimate details of our once-close friendship. No doubt they had their own spies, first and foremost the despicable Blockwart, Herr Wagner, who had always watched the two of us walking off, arms round each other's shoulders, with beady, disapproving eyes; even before Hitler came to power. When he was just the street busybody picking up stray leaves from the ground. How could I possibly ingratiate myself with you, win back your favour, so as to spy on your brothers' suspected communist activities? I was told that the meetings were held in your flat and I was to find out more. I was called to the Gestapo headquarters, where one ghoulish-looking officer after another worked on me. It was quite frightening. You'd have thought I was the guilty party.

At first I refused outright. Such a ludicrous idea – how could they ever believe it would work? Did they think you were stupid? Brainless? I suppose they did. You were a Jew, after all. Not really human, in their eyes.

I pleaded with them, begged them to give up that plan. I could never act the part they wanted me to play, I patiently explained. I'd never convince you I'd changed colours. With stony-faced mien, one of the officers replied: 'Fräulein Bosch, it is your solemn duty to report on any wrongdoing you might be aware of. Should you refuse to do so, your loyalty to the Party will be called into question.'

On and on they lectured me. My former friends were a corrupting influence on young people. They were evil Jews who would lead Berlin's youth away from National Socialism. They were insurgents, a danger to the Party and to the nation. Should I refuse, there might be serious career implications for me. For weeks the Gestapo pestered me to do as I was told.

Finally, I relented. Half-heartedly, I tried to rekindle our friendship and to convince you I was now a Nazi-hater. Do you remember those ill-fated conversations, Leah? You saw through me as if I were as transparent as glass. The fact was, I couldn't do it. I couldn't spy on you; and, in fact, as I stumbled over my words, I hoped beyond hope that you'd see what was going on. I still cared for you, and I knew they'd come for you and your brothers one day. Not only that, I suspected that you were in cahoots with Markus, that he was involved too. I tried to warn you. I did.

I made a mess of it. Out of the blue, I turned up on your doorstep. Believe me, I was quaking in my boots! I had some pretext or other in my mind. I forget what I told the maid who opened the door to me. My falsehood must have been written all over my face – I am not a good liar. But even the maid saw through me. She shut the door in my face and that was that. I did not have the gumption or the acting ability to try again to convince her to let me in. I walked downstairs, my tail between my legs, to where I knew a Gestapo officer was waiting for me.

When I told him of my failure he abused me in the most

crude terms. I won't repeat his language here but, believe me, I turned red as a beetroot! Yet somehow I had managed to retain some measure of personal integrity.

And so, the next day, I went back. And this time, it was you who opened the door. And this time, I was able to stutter out the words.

'Oh, Leah!' I said. 'I miss you so much!'

'Really?' you said. 'I wouldn't have thought it. You seem quite happy with your new BDM friends.'

'They're not enough,' I pleaded. 'You were always my best friend. Why does it have to be this way? Why do we have to be strangers? Can't we meet somewhere and have a long talk, just like old times?'

I suppose that mention of 'old times' must have moved you. Old times can never be erased, can they? They are always there, calling. Because the old times are the true times, and these new times, they were steeped in hatred and falsehood and suspicion. I appealed to the best in you, your inherent good-will, and so you agreed. We met in a café, and I managed to warn you, clandestinely. I told you to warn your brothers, to get rid of any incriminating evidence in your flat. It was the least I could do.

I reported back to the Gestapo. I told them that you knew nothing, but that you had accepted my friendship and that I would sustain it for as long as proved necessary. Inside, I was burning up with shame and guilt. I was betraying both sides: you, and my beloved Party.

The very next day, the Gestapo came to your flat and searched it. They vandalised the place. They took everything they deemed suspicious, and arrested Aaron and Mosche. They also took your journal, in which you had originally recorded everything I'd told you, in which you'd noted that I had warned you of the coming search and told you to get rid of evidence.

And do you remember what you did, Leah? I do. And remembering what you did, the guilt in my soul is almost more than I can bear. You contacted me through my mother, and told me that they had your journal, and that I should be very careful what I said so as not to tie myself up in knots with lies.

I couldn't believe it. Somehow, a last remnant of our friendship remained. Yes, I had reluctantly agreed to spy on your family, but in the end I had warned you. And you had warned me back.

That night I wept myself to sleep. If there was at any time a point where I had the chance to wake up, to free myself from the indoctrination that had flooded my soul, the poison that was devouring me, it was then. Do you remember, Leah?

I did get into trouble with the Gestapo; they read your journal and knew I had warned you, which was why apart from that journal they found nothing incriminating against Aaron and Mosche in their search. They hauled me before my supervisor and gave me the dressing-down of my life. They called into question my very loyalty to the Party and considered dismissing me from the Hitler Youth due not only to my failure as a spy, but also to my collaboration with the enemy (you). In the end they kept me because I had become invaluable to them through my other work.

It seems to me that my fate hung in the balance. Perhaps, had I been expelled from the BDM, from the Nazi Party, perhaps that would have been my big chance. Perhaps I would have woken up. Perhaps I would have become a normal-thinking young woman again. How many forks there are in the road of life, and how even a slight change of heart, change of direction, can change the very course of our lives! But it was not to be. I was too valuable to them by that point. I was a good Nazi, and they knew it.

LEAH – BERLIN

In normal schools, boys were trained to become 'swift as a greyhound, as tough as leather, and as hard as Krupp steel', while girls were trained in domestic sciences and taught how to become good wives and mothers. In sending Magda to that school, it seems, her parents had set her on track to follow the male curriculum. Magda too, was destined to become 'swift as a greyhound, as tough as leather, and as hard as Krupp steel'. Unusual for a girl, but there we have it. That's what happened. And yet: there was that day when she almost turned soft.

One day, there she was on my doorstep. I happened to be at home.

'Leah!' she cried, as if delighted to see me. She opened her arms and didn't really give me the choice to enter them or not, because they closed around me and she dragged me into a bear-hug. I was so confused. What on earth was going on? Why was she hugging me, after all that had taken place between us? Was there some little spark of heart left in her? I met her eyes. I searched them. What did I see there? In the past, I'd been able to read her like a book, and even now I could see guilt, lies, falseness, more guilt, more lies, shame. *What is she up to?*, I thought. *What does she want with me, why has she come here?*

Markus's warning not to trust her rang deep within me; I knew from him that she was well on her way into the very heart of Nazism. I was still in contact with her parents, who were as anti-Nazi as ever but who now kept quiet and complied out of self-preservation, as many good Germans were forced to. As such, they had taken her back into their fold for the time being. I knew she was staying with them but had hoped to avoid her. No such luck. There she was, holding me in this bear-hug, and I didn't know what to think.

But I had manners, so I greeted her back. And somewhere

within me, I wanted to give her the benefit of the doubt. I
wanted my old friend back.

'Guten Tag, Magda,' I replied to her overly hearty greeting.
My words were flat and free of emotion.

'How lovely to see you again!' she said. 'I've been thinking
of you so much, the whole time. I miss you!'

'Really?' I replied. Did she notice the longing in that one
word, 'really?' I meant it. I would have loved, at that moment, to
overturn the last few years. Something inside me pined to
rekindle our friendship, and to trust her again. In my naivety, I
longed to erase all the bad things she'd done with one stroke and
forgive her and start again. But as well as longing in that question, there was irony. *You, Magda?* I wanted to say. *You miss
me? You, who were the one to cast aside our friendship for a
wicked ideology that wants to destroy me?*

She didn't detect that. Her reply was a very non-ironic: 'Yes,
really! Oh, Leah! I have so much to tell you! Can we go off and
have a long chat somewhere? In a café, or something? What
about that nice little café in Kreuzberg, the one we used to go to
on Saturday afternoons?'

Was she joking? She must know that Jews by now would
not be welcome in any old-school Berlin café. She must have
known! She must have seen the signs, *JUDEN VERBOTEN!* She
was not wearing her BDM uniform. She was dressed in normal
clothes: a simple pleated woollen skirt and one of her old hand-
knitted sweaters. I believe it was one her Tante Gundhilde had
once given her for Christmas. She had not grown much since
then and it was still a good fit and in good condition. She looked
like an ordinary German girl, not like a Nazi. I longed to
trust her.

But I also longed for her to see the reality I now lived in, so I
shrugged and said, 'All right.' Let her find out the hard way, I
thought. When we were thrown out of the café, or refused
service the way Markus and I had been, she'd feel how it was.

She'd know how impossible it was to be friends again, however much we might want it.

She went back to her flat to fetch her coat, and I put mine on. It was a fairly mild December day, I remember, in the run-up to Christmas, though there was nothing Christmassy about life in Berlin. No lights and trees and carols. No *Alle Jahre wieder, kommt das Christuskind!* No: the Christ child would not be coming this year, or any year after 1933.

Suitably attired, we marched down the pavement, elbows hooked. She was the one to do that. I would have preferred to keep my distance, uncertain as I was; but by now I was curious. What did she want? Had she really changed her colours? Or was this a ruse? Suspicion nipped at my yearning for a new beginning, for a turnaround on Magda's part.

I was so surprised when they let us into the café. The same waitress as before was there and I saw the dirty look she gave me. She would have been well within her rights to refuse us entry, but she didn't. Perhaps she recognised Magda as a BDM member, I thought, and that's why she let me in, despite the sign on the door. But why had Magda ignored the sign? And would the waitress serve me? And the other patrons: many were locals, who knew who I was, and I saw the foul looks they threw me. Magda must have too. But she ignored them. I actually thought that was a good sign. That she was standing up for me in the face of stark prejudice. That's how much I longed for reconciliation.

Magda ordered coffee and *Lebkuchen* for both of us. *Lebkuchen* was a luxury, and fairly expensive. I had not had any for years. I was sure that waitress would refuse me a serving. But she didn't. This could only be a result of Magda's presence.

We were sitting at a table in a far corner, where it was unlikely that we'd be overheard. Magda started with a few polite questions about my family, and about what I was doing now, and so on. But very soon, she leaned in towards me and in a conspiratorial whisper said: 'Leah, I've so much to tell you! I've changed so much since 1933, and I need to apologise. You see, I was swept away by the whole Nazi message, like most people. I couldn't help it. But I've changed since then. I've had a change of heart.'

'You have? In what sense?' She couldn't know it, but guilt leaked from her eyes. Magda had never been a good liar. She was the kind of person who threw herself 200 per cent into whatever it was she was passionate about, and now, pretending to be something else – well, she was as transparent as glass. Something was wrong, and I couldn't put my finger on it.

'In the sense that – well, my friends come first. And you are my friend. I can see now I was wrong to go along with Hitler's message to cast out the Jews. You, all your family, are my friends! You are not Jews to me, you are good people. And I hate the Nazis for trying to turn me against you.'

Again, the guilt was right there in her eyes, written there in plain sight. Magda had no idea what a bad actress she was. Much as I longed for her words to be sincere and true, I knew instinctively that they weren't. Much as I longed to forgive and forget, for her to be truly contrite and as keen as I was to be friends again, every sense in my body was trembling with warning. Red lights flashed: it's all a lie! Be careful!

She continued to talk, more garrulous than she'd ever been as she tried to resurrect the past.

'So what are you up to these days?' she asked. I told her about my job as a nursery teacher. 'And how do you spend your time after work?'

Was she prying? Had she noticed that Markus and I were often out at the same time?

'Oh, I have a few friends and we like to play music together sometimes,' I said. 'Nothing formal, of course.'

'Jewish friends?'

'Of course.' I'm sure that I lied more convincingly than she did.

She said she regretted the fact that she saw so little of Markus even now he was home for the holidays. 'Markus seems to be almost invisible!' she said with a too-casual chuckle. 'He's always gone, gallivanting around town. Have you any idea where he goes off to?'

Was she spying on her own brother? Was she planning on betraying him to the Gestapo? I would put nothing past her.

I was quick with my reply. 'Well, what do you think? He's a good-looking young man. He probably has a girlfriend.'

'Haha! You're right, I should have thought of that. I hope you're not jealous, Leah!'

I wonder what she'd have said if I'd told her then that I was that girlfriend!

'Markus was right all along,' she went on with a sigh. 'I was wrong. I shouldn't have gone along with the new regime. I should have opposed it, as Markus did, and my parents. I'm so sorry, Leah, because I lost my friendship with you. It was so precious!'

I could almost believe that the sigh she let out was genuine. But I didn't. I let her talk and she went on for a while in that vein, trying to convince me that she was now suddenly anti-Nazi. But by now I was truly on red alert, and it didn't work. I went along with the farce, interjecting with things like 'Really?' and 'Oh, I'm glad of that.'

What game was she playing? I was bursting with curiosity. The only way I could think of to find out was to play along. To pretend I believed this act.

I noticed a couple at the table next to ours. Their conversation had been lively at the beginning, but I had noticed that they had gone curiously silent once Magda had started on her anti-Nazi rhetoric. I was convinced they were listening. Intently so.

Eventually, after this long sob story about how she really, truly regretted having joined the BDM and how she was trying to gradually extricate herself, she finally came to the point.

'Mosche and Aaron,' she said, 'what are they up to these days? Aren't they worried about the Nazis?'

'Of course,' I replied. 'We all are. Didn't you see the sign on the door? I don't even know why they let me in. That waitress knows I'm Jewish.'

Magda ignored that dig. She was determined to talk about Mosche and Aaron.

'They must be worried about the whole anti-Jewish direction of the Nazi Party,' she said. 'I wonder if they're doing anything against it. I know that the communists are fighting it. I would love to be able to discuss such matters with some real Jews, people I trust. And I do trust them.' She started to ramble, obviously trying to put me at ease by recalling the past. 'Remember how I had a crush on Aaron, years ago? Remember how you and I used to have these crazy dreams, of marrying each other's brother? Crazy, right? I was so infatuated. And you know, I never really got over Aaron. And I was wondering if the dream really was crazy. I knew you and Markus were close. I wonder if Aaron could ever forgive me? I do believe he liked me, back then. I know I went astray, for a while. Dear Leah, I would love to visit you at home! Do you think your parents would forgive me? And Aaron and Mosche? Imagine if we could all get together again! Since my conversion I've been thinking up all the ways I could maybe help the Jews and...'

I didn't believe a word of it but I played along. I was curious. I was sure that the couple at the next table were listening to every word; Magda was speaking loudly enough. Was she so stupid as to think she'd convinced me? Were the couple so stupid as to think this strategy was working?

Soon, Magda stood up and excused herself. She needed to

go to the lavatory. When she came back, she was as falsely gay as before. Like I said: Magda couldn't lie to save her life.

'Shall we go now?' she said then. I nodded. Magda signalled for the waitress to return, paid our bill, and we left the café. But just as we were walking out the door, and before the other couple could follow us and observe, Magda pressed a note into my hand.

'*Careful*,' it said, when I read it later, at home. She had obviously written it in the lavatory. '*Tell Aaron and Mosche the Gestapo is watching them. Your home might be searched soon.*'

LEAH – BERLIN

I always associated Tante Helga with Christmas. As Jews, we did not of course celebrate, but back in the old days, in the run-up it was impossible to escape. Tante Helga would throw herself into a frenzy of baking; the entire stairwell would be filled with the mouth-watering smell of *Weihnachtsplätzchen*, Christmas biscuits. *Zimtsterne, Pfeffernüsse, Kipferl, Linzeraugen, Engelsaugen, Nussecken, Spitzbuben...* oh, the list goes on and on.

I was always welcome in Tante Helga's kitchen. 'Would you like to help lick the bowl, Leah?' She never had to ask twice. Magda and I would sit at the table and lick the remains off the spoons and bowls, laughing and joking together. We each had our favourite *Plätzchen*. Mine was *Zimtsterne*, Magda's was *Kipferl*. 'Leave some for the others, girls!' Tante Helga would cry as we tucked in. I can still smell the sweet aroma of cinnamon, nutmeg, cloves, allspice, the warm comforting feeling that baked goods implanted in the hungry heart of a growing girl; the special magic of flour, butter, sugar and eggs, so basic each on its own but, expertly combined, cut or moulded into special, distinct shapes and rounds on a baking tray, and placed in a hot oven by Tante Helga's loving hands, and then cooled on her kitchen table, sprinkled with white icing sugar or almond slices or desiccated nuts – oh, it was heaven on Earth. If anything could have converted me to Christianity, it was Tante Helga's biscuits.

Tante Helga was determined that the Christmas season should be filled with the aroma of baking. With Berlin still suffering the economic consequences of losing the war, it was very difficult to obtain all the necessary ingredients, but she had a good supply of the main necessities, sent from her parents' Bavarian farm. Sugar was in short supply, but a Bavarian neighbour kept honey bees, and so Tante Helga was able to sweeten her baked goods.

In earlier years she'd prepare little paper bags of biscuits and give them to Magda and me to distribute to neighbours. We'd tramp from door to door, handing them out with a big smile. She would put a few of those bags in her voluminous handbag and take the two of us for long walks through the poorest streets of Berlin, and, whenever she passed a beggar on the street, he or she would receive a little bag, dropped on their lap or pressed into their hand. Tante Helga would take Magda and me to the Christmas Market and there again, the smells would envelop me and swirl me away into a magical world. Mulled wine and roasted chestnuts and baked caramel apples – oh, the very memory makes my mouth water!

Sadly, though, by the time Magda took off after graduation – I assume on some BDM mission – it was all over. No one was celebrating Christmas by then, at least not in the way they used to. And anyway: Jews were not welcome.

We weren't welcome anywhere, and what was left of the Christmas markets – well, I'd never know as I would never now venture into one.

To make matters worse, I saw little of Markus at this time. He was still mostly in Munich and, even when he returned home, our contact consisted mostly of little notes sent to me clandestinely, in which he reminded me that he was still with me and warned me never to get involved in anything. Zum Zoo was no longer our refuge: it had been raided. I suppose it was inevitable: some *Blockwart* or other must have noticed all these undesirable characters turning into that narrow back alley, and reported them. Two of Markus's friends had been arrested and had disappeared. 'Be careful, Leah,' he warned me again and again, and I was. I didn't dare venture that far from home without Markus.

This was because he was by this time so deeply involved in 'other matters'. He told me nothing, but it was easy to guess. There were communist resistance groups in every German city, but especially in the university towns. I knew of the local group through my brothers, consisting almost entirely of Jews.

As Magda had warned, our flat was raided, but thanks to her warning my brothers had been prepared and the Gestapo found nothing incriminating. They arrested Mosche and Aaron anyway, but released them after a week.

I was worried sick for all three of them, Markus, Mosche and Aaron. I desperately wanted to join the resistance, play some part in it, however small. But it was not to be. They were all three so protective of me. 'This is just the beginning, Leah,' Markus told me. 'The best you can do is to stay safe and keep your head down.' It's what Father kept telling us all as well.

It was at my job in the kindergarten that I met Trude, and we became firm friends. Trude, on noting that my surname was Jewish, immediately let me know that her mother, too, was Jewish as she had three Jewish grandparents. That was the criteria for being classified as a full Jew. Trude, however, having only one Jewish grandparent, escaped the damning designation. She was worried sick for her mother, who lived in Frankfurt.

It was Trude who told me about Sonnenhof.

'It's closed for the winter,' she told me, 'But next summer,

I'll take you there. We can always do with an extra pair of hands!'

She wouldn't tell me anything more about it. 'Let it be a surprise!' she'd say with a smile when I pestered her for more information.

So I just had to wait.

The net was tightening around us. Jews were fleeing Berlin: to England, to America, to Canada. We would have fled too, but a sponsor was needed in the country one hoped to emigrate to, and that's what we didn't have. All we had was each other. Family, friends and, in my case, my boyfriend. And Tante Helga.

Tante Helga, too, was worried on our behalf, and I became particularly close to her during this time. She was battling demons of her own. She was deeply ashamed of the path her daughter had taken, and, now that I was working in childcare, she seemed to regard me as something of an expert.

'Where did I go wrong, Leah?' she once wept. 'I loved her so much. I gave her all I had. I was a good mother, I always thought! I raised her in good Christian values: love one another. Love your neighbour as yourself. Be kind, be generous; follow in the footsteps of Christ. But what I have now is the very opposite of that.'

'I'm sure Magda still has those values,' I reassured her. I still believed it myself. I could not quite imagine that she had completely turned into the hate-machine that we were seeing more and more of. And there was the note she'd passed me, warning me of the Gestapo search. That showed she still had goodness in her, surely? I told Tante Helga of this. Her eyes opened wide in surprise.

'Really? Magda warned you? She did? Oh, Leah! That surely means she's not all wicked!'

'I'm sure she isn't,' I said again.

'You know, Magda was always against the Church. She

hasn't been to mass for many years. And yet, deep inside, I always thought she was in fact a real, true Christian. She was so – so passionate. So kind. To animals, especially, and anything helpless. She loved babies!'

I chuckled. I remembered that quirk. Magda could never walk past a pram without stopping to peek inside, throwing the mother a smile that meant 'may I?' Inevitably, the mother would stop and allow her to admire the baby. What mother doesn't want her baby to be adored? And that's what Magda did.

'She's adorable!' she'd tell the mother, who would bask in the compliment. And yet, Magda never wanted children of her own. I certainly did. I could even put a face on my future husband: Markus's face. But Magda always said she would never marry and have children. So it was strange that she joined a movement that held up marriage and motherhood and child-raising as the only valid role for a women. But then, Magda was full of contradictions.

To Helga, I said: 'Yes – there was always something soft-hearted about her, in spite of her brash exterior.'

'Magda was a Christian through music,' Tante Helga said. 'She would be swept away by religious music. Remember the "Ode to Joy"?'

Oh yes! I certainly did! It was her favourite; she loved the lyrics. Called them inspiring, uplifting. And, although she didn't have much of a singing voice, she had a habit of bursting into song at odd times, and this was her song of choice. She loved the grandiloquence, the magnificence of great music, the pompousness of 'Ode to Joy'. 'Freude!' she'd cry out. 'Freude! Freude! Freude!' A loud, exuberant cry for Joy.

> *Joy, fair spark of the gods,*
> *Daughter of Elysium,*
> *Drunk with fiery rapture, Goddess,*
> *We approach thy shrine!*

Thy magic reunites those
Whom stern custom has parted;
All men will become brothers
Under thy gentle wing.

And at the other end of the spectrum: death. She had often declared Mozart's *Requiem* to be the most magnificent work of music ever written. That Mozart was an instrument of God, through whom God's voice could be heard. Nothing else, said Magda, could explain the sacred grandeur of the *Requiem*.

How could someone who appreciated such music, who could understand the miracle of divine grandeur shining through humans in art, in music, in architecture, in literature – how could such a person fall prey to the Nazis? Tante Helga and I often pondered this mystery, and my explanation was lame.

'I think she was just swept away in a wave of Nazi propaganda. I hope and pray she'll wake up one day.'

'If it's not too late!' said Tante Helga. 'If there's a war, Leah! If Hitler wins! What then?'

We had to leave it at that. We found no explanation.

'All I can do,' Tante Helga said in despair, 'is pray for her. Whatever else she is, she is still my daughter.'

Meanwhile, the word 'war' was being bandied around more than ever in these days, 1936. We couldn't believe it. Not so soon after the last war! Hitler couldn't be that mad!

But what if he was?

12

LEAH – BERLIN

One morning in the spring of 1937, Markus dropped by just before breakfast, a very unusual time for him. He was now a fourth-year student at Munich's Technical University and lived in student digs in Freising, where that faculty was located.

Markus always came home during longer university breaks. That Easter holiday I was nineteen, and working at the nursery, and he was twenty-two.

I still lived at home with Mother and Father, though we were all beginning to worry, by now, that we'd be evicted. Scores of Jews were facing evictions. With all his patients now being Jewish, Father heard day after day dismal and sometimes terrifying stories of whole families being put out on the street. Jewish-owned homes being repossessed by the authorities. Jewish tenants being evicted from their homes by their land-lords. People sent away with only a suitcase, forced to leave their lives behind.

Most frightening of all, we heard about people being taken away by the Gestapo, to camps throughout the country. These camps were all rumours, of course; nobody knew anything for sure. But we all heard the stories.

It was coming close to home. The old Levy couple on the top floor came down to say goodbye. 'We're moving,' said Frau Levy with a sigh. 'Our daughter in Freiburg – she's persuaded us to move in with her.'

'That's in Baden, isn't it?' said Mother. 'About as far away from Berlin as you can get.'

Herr Levy nodded. 'She says it's not as bad down there. But you never know. It's spreading. The whole family is hoping to leave Germany. We've all applied for visas.'

A week later, we all helped them load their suitcases into the van that would take them to Freiburg. We all wept: the Jewish community in Kaiserkorso Eins was breaking apart.

But worse was to come. Just a week after the Levys' departure, I came home to find the Bienstocks from upstairs being escorted, hands clasped behind their necks, down the stairs by several Gestapo officers. Frau Bienstock threw me a look that haunted me for days afterwards, her face distorted by a melange of terror and outrage and sheer desperation.

I rushed into my own flat.

'Mother! Mother!' I cried. 'What's going on? Where are they taking the Bienstocks? Are they under arrest?'

Mother was weeping. 'They've been evicted,' she said. 'Their flat is only rented and the goyish pig of a landlord has thrown them out. They've lived here all their lives; they were here before we were!'

'Will we be evicted too?'

'We can't be, technically,' Mother said. 'We're leaseholders; the lease has many years left on it and it's supposed to be secure. But in these times, nothing is secure.'

I ran outside, down the stairs and out the front door. I was just in time to see Herr and Frau Bienstock being pushed into the back of a sinister-looking van. It had no windows in the back, but through the open rear door I glimpsed other people within. The van drove off; where to, we did not know.

I saw another such van a while later, just down the road, outside a Jewish haberdasher's shop. The owner, an old man, was being beaten on the street by two Gestapo officers, screaming for mercy, and then he too was pushed into the van. And he too disappeared into nowhere.

Markus told me of trains leaving stations pulling cattle carts filled with Jews.

'The camps are real,' he said. 'And nobody ever returns.'

Not only Jews were in these camps, the rumours said. They were also filling up with dissidents, people like Markus, or like my brother Aaron, who was both a Jew and a rebel. Sent off to labour camps, where young men especially were to provide labour for the factories and the pompous buildings and whatever other projects Hitler was planning. Markus hinted at a weapons factory near Munich.

We all knew that according to the terms of the Versailles Treaty, Germany was not allowed to rearm.

'But of course they will!' Markus told me.

'He can't be planning another war!' I said in shock. How ingenuous I was! Of course that was exactly what the Führer was planning.

In the middle of all this, Aaron was arrested. Again. The first time, back in 1936, when he had been arrested along with Mosche, they had both been released fairly soon. This time, Aaron was not so lucky. Or rather, it wasn't luck. He had deliberately placed himself in harm's way, just as he had been doing from the very start, from that first clandestine meeting back in 1933. Now a fully trained electrician, he worked so hard that we saw little of him at home. I knew he was up to something, but I didn't want to know and didn't ask.

We all knew by now that both Markus and Aaron were in some kind of underground movement, but we weren't allowed to discuss it, or ask questions. The less we knew, the better; but I feared for their sake. I feared they might be getting into something over their heads.

'I can't tell you more,' Markus always said when I asked. 'Please. It's dangerous for you to have too much information. I want you to be safe.'

'But I want *you* to be safe!' I'd reply.

I was in a constant state of tension on his and Aaron's behalf. The fact that they were endangering themselves added another degree of tension to the noose that was already tightening round our necks.

And now Aaron had been caught. In January 1938 the Gestapo once more burst into our home and dragged him into the hallway. I was at home at the time. Mother and I ran into the hall with them all, screaming uselessly at the Gestapo to let him go.

'He's not done anything!' Mother yelled. 'You brutes!'

Of course they ignored her. I had no idea what he had been up to; like Markus, he had been shielding me from too much knowledge. But there it was. The first time Aaron had been arrested, they had had to release him due to lack of evidence. This time, the charge stuck. Aaron's arrest came as a huge shock to my parents, who had been oblivious to his underground behaviour; they deemed all such resistance foolish and advocated a 'keep your head down' policy. A policy I, too, had been adhering to. But things were just about to get serious, and we were all waking up to the fact that the Nazis meant business. It was time to take our heads out of the sand, and Aaron's arrest and imprisonment was the wake-up call.

We waited and waited for him to be released: in vain. Rumour had it that he'd been sent to Sachsenhausen concentration camp for 'asocial' behaviour, under an order that was not subject to judicial review, and that he'd be there indefinitely. But nobody knew for sure. It was all just guesswork.

Rumour also had it that these prisoners would be put to

work in factories around Berlin, but no one told us anything and no one knew for sure. Of course, we could not visit him. Not his Jewish family, nor his Jewish friends. Germans could visit him, and Markus longed to; but visiting would arouse suspicion; a good, Nazi-loyal citizen would never visit a Jew. Markus, too, had to keep his head down. At least in public.

'Now I'm the one who feels like a coward,' he said. 'Choosing between my friendship and secrecy.'

'I think Aaron would want you to preserve your secrecy,' I told him.

In the end, my desperation to know of my beloved brother's whereabouts forced me to abandon my pride and do the one thing I'd sworn never to do: ask Magda for help. I wrote her a letter asking her to meet with me, and gave it to Tante Helga to pass on to her.

Much time had passed since our last disastrous meeting, and we both knew that that whole 'I'm no longer a Nazi' line of hers had been a complete farce from the beginning. I wondered if she'd have the gall to meet with me again, knowing full well that she'd lied to my face.

But then, a knock on the door. I opened it and there stood Magda, pink-cheeked and bright-eyed, and not a trace of shame or embarrassment.

'You look well, Leah!' she said after a short greeting. 'Shall I come in, or should we go out?'

'Come in,' I snapped. I could not put on an air of friendship. Not after what had happened the last time. Yes, we had both had the decency to warn each other, but we could never be friends again – and her 'you're looking well' was a lie: I looked terrible. Who wouldn't, under the circumstances?

I happened to be alone at home and so led her to the sitting area. I didn't bother offering her tea, I got straight to the point. 'Aaron has been arrested,' I said.

'I know. Mama told me.'

'We don't know where he is. You have friends in high places, I've heard. I'd like you to make enquiries for me. For *us*.'

She stuttered. 'I-I, oh, Leah. I don't know if I can do that. It's a bit awkward. I mean, it's awkward for me to—'

'To ask your higher-ups about the whereabouts of a Jew. I know that. I can imagine. You're not supposed to care. But you can do it and I want you to. Aaron used to be your friend, too. If you have a last decent bone in your body, Magda, you'll do it. I don't care how. Just do it.'

At the words *a last decent bone in your body* Magda turned beetroot red. I took that as a good sign. It meant she had a tiny vestige of conscience left.

'I'll see what I can do,' she murmured, and got up to leave. She knew by now that this wasn't a social call. She knew that this time, there'd be no small talk or pretend friendship. I showed her out the door, not sure if she'd simply conveniently forget my request or just refuse to do it.

But hardly a week later a letter arrived for me.

'Aaron was in the Sachsenhausen camp,' she'd written, 'but he's now working in the Siemens labour camp. They recruited him as a trained electrician. I'm sorry, I don't know more than that.'

We all had to be satisfied with that. Of course we knew about the Siemens factory just outside Berlin, a huge complex with thousands of employees. It was a very desirable place of employment for engineering graduates; in fact, Aaron's original aim had been to get a job there once he had qualified as an engineer. A dream that had come to a full stop in 1933. But with the growth of Germany's economy, the demand for labour was higher than ever.

'I'm not surprised,' Markus said when I told him what Magda had written. 'I've heard that armament contracts are being negotiated between Siemens and the government.'

I thought about the Versailles Treaty. 'Germany isn't

allowed to manufacture armaments!' I'd protested. 'It's forbidden!'

'Do you really think Hitler cares what's forbidden or not? Don't you remember what I told you? They're planning a new war, and they need workers, and a trained electrician like Aaron? Free labour? Of course he's there. It makes perfect sense.'

Knowing that Aaron was at the Siemens factory – so close, and yet so far – brought no small amount of comfort to us. It sounded as though he'd be safe there. They needed his manpower, we thought; we clung fervently to the hope that he would be exempt from the executions rumoured to be taking place in some of these camps. It was slave labour, but he was valuable to them and so they'd keep him alive. That was the best we could hope for. We had to be satisfied with that.

Now, unexpectedly back from Munich, Markus explained that he'd arrived home late last night, spent the night in his own bed, greeted his parents, and immediately come over to see me. My heart soared, especially at his first words: 'I miss you so much, Leah!' He held out his arms and I rushed in. They closed around me.

'I miss you too,' I murmured into his shoulder.

He nuzzled the top of my head and we stood there for a few minutes. Mother walked by and greeted him, a half-smile on her face. She of course knew of our relationship by now, and though she didn't exactly approve of it – she and Father would have preferred a Jewish man for me – she tolerated it because she knew what a fine, brave fellow Markus was. And he was not only my sweetheart – he was one of Aaron's best friends, and he was as outspokenly anti-Nazi as could be. A good German.

Now, we couldn't even trust devoted Christians as good Germans. Last year, the Catholic Church had started to collaborate with the Nazis by informing them of who had been baptised and who not. I'd discussed this with Tante Helga and she had been shocked: she regarded it as a betrayal of the Church of the central teaching of Christ.

'Jesus was a Jew!' she'd said. 'How can this be condoned? How can His people be treated as outcasts?'

'Well, at least now Magda might approve of *something* the Church has done!' I'd said wryly.

Since then, everything had worsened; the Aryanisation of the economy continued at a brisk pace. In January, Jewish business owners had been forced to sell their companies, almost always considerably below the value of their goods. Jews were prohibited from working in any office in Germany. Everywhere, outside shops and cafés and restaurants, signs were being posted: *JEWS NOT WANTED*.

Now, Markus managed in just a few words to increase our worry. When Mother passed through the dining room again, he called to her and asked her to listen.

'I don't want to scare you,' he said, looking from one of us to the other, 'but I think you should all leave Germany. Things are going to get much worse for Jews and there's no telling where it will end.'

'We'll never leave!' cried Mother. 'It's what we told Aaron before he was arrested. We are a strong people – we will stand up to whatever comes, hold our heads up high. My husband is not a coward. He told Aaron: we'll never run.'

Markus nodded. 'But think of your children,' he said. 'Think of Leah and Samuel.'

Mother turned ghostly white at those words. She said nothing more, just ran back to the kitchen.

'You scare me, Markus!' I said when she'd left. 'What more can they do to us? How much worse can it get for us?'

'You don't want to know,' he said grimly.

'Anyway, I'll never leave you!' I told him.

'Knowing you're here makes it all so much harder for me!' he sighed. 'Just be careful, Leah. Please. Don't do anything rash.'

'Well, I could say the same to you, Markus. Please, please be careful!'

'Don't worry about me. Everything I do is undercover. On the surface I'm a good law-abiding Aryan. But you...'

I knew what he was saying. Nobody, looking at Markus, would suspect him of being a dissident. He had those tall, strong, blond, blue-eyed good looks that according to Hitler epitomised Aryan superiority. Whereas I – I didn't look particularly Jewish, but my hair was dark and my eyes brown. Hardly an example of perfect German womanhood, the counterpart to Markus.

And quite apart from his looks, everyone liked Markus. He was one of those thoroughly disarming people whom even strangers like without understanding exactly why, whom people trust on sight. That was probably one of the reasons why, in spite of his passionate opposition to Hitler's seizure of power, he hardly ever attracted suspicion.

'I feel so useless. I wish you'd let me join your group.'

'No. You stay out of it.'

'Because I'm a girl? You don't think I'm capable?'

He reached for my hands. 'Oh, Leah! I know just how capable you are. And women can fight this just as well as men. There are several young women in our movement. I can't say more. I just believe, I know, that you need to keep out of the madness. Most of all, I wish you'd get out of Germany.'

I repeated what I'd said before: 'I'll never leave you.'

He sighed. 'So be it. We'll find a way. But we have to be more careful, Leah. We can't be seen together any more. Not by people who know us.'

13

MAGDA

After my refusal to spy on you and your family – which I think was a signal that I had not yet been 100 per cent won over; that a tiny part of me rebelled – I was in the BDM's bad books for a while. But they forgave me as I was essential for their press work. They had discovered that I had quite a talent for writing inspiring articles. They began to publish my words in their youth brochures, pamphlets and newsletters. Becoming a writer had always been one of my ambitions, and the BDM – and Hitler Youth in general – gave me that opportunity.

As a dedicated soldier of the cause, I threw myself into my first full-time job with the press and propaganda department of BDM in the Berlin head office. My salary was small. In truth, I would have been happy to work for free, as I regarded my work as service for Germany. But the pay was so paltry it hardly covered my living expenses. It was really just pocket money. I was de facto a volunteer.

My new position was perfect, in terms of my long-term ambitions and the role I saw myself playing in what would one day be Grossdeutschland: Great Germany. At the core of everything, we have youth. Germany's youth, I knew – or

thought then – had to be moulded and carefully curated so as
to make them fit for their roles as tomorrow's citizens and leaders. From my perspective today, I would say they had to be
made compliant. Children absorb what their elders teach them,
usually without question. If society is to run like clockwork,
there is no room for autonomous thinking. We had to get them
when they were young, feed them the grand idea of Grossdeutschland ruling the waves – no longer Britannia! I had
long admired the power and glory of that patriotic British song,
'Rule, Britannia!', and was actually working on a German
translation, which we could add to our collection of stirring
patriotic anthems. I never got beyond: 'Herrsche, Deutschland! Deutschland herrsch die Welt!' I'm really not much of a
poet. I couldn't find a suitable rhyme for 'Welt', and anyway,
ruling the world somehow doesn't have the same poetic impact
as ruling the waves.

Propaganda! That was the watchword. Joseph Goebbels,
chief propagandist for the Nazi Party, and from 1933 the
Reich Minister of Propaganda, had long been the Gauleiter,
the district leader, of Berlin. I had listened to many of his
speeches over the radio and was already an acolyte, just as he
was an acolyte of Hitler. I listened with particular ardour to
his speech on New Year's Eve of that year. Imagine, now,
hordes of young, bright-eyed Aryans, vast arenas filled with
rows of blond, young people in brown uniforms, the Führer
himself crying out these words to us till they were emblazoned
in every heart. Can you see, Leah, what such an oath, sworn in
the company of all your peers and your appointed leaders,
would do to the spirit of a young person? Can you understand
how completely our hearts and minds, our very souls,
were won?

That, Leah, is what we call brainwashing. It really is a
literal removal of any kind and loving thought towards others,
any trace of Jesus' teaching about the Good Samaritan and

loving your neighbour, and impregnating that mind with this sole replacement thought: Love of Germany.

Did I not once experience some pinch of conscience, a stab of cognitive resistance? How, you may well ask, could I reconcile those words with my passion for the works of Bach and Beethoven, steeped with the love of God above all?

The truth is, Leah, I suppressed it all. Any doubt that arose in my mind – why, I simply pushed it away. The very act of pushing it away was making me hard as Krupp steel. As for God: I firmly believed that God, if there was such an entity, was firmly on our side. It never once occurred to me that He might be on the side of the Jews, or those who opposed the notion of Greater Germany. That's how green I was, we all were. How brainwashed.

I feel now as if I am telling you those words personally as you sit here beside me; my eyes are locked on to yours as I beg you to believe me. Beg you to believe that deep inside, you were always there. There is no indoctrination that can completely wipe clean the goodness once implanted in a child's soul, because – and I believe this with all my heart – goodness is innate to the human psyche. Our parents are there to manifest that goodness, to bring it to the fore, and there is no doubt Mama did that for me. Goodness is innate – but it must be nourished.

That is why all religions are rooted in goodness, no matter how they are later corrupted by men to serve their own evil ends. That is what history tells us. Since the war I have studied many religions (I will get to that later) and this is the ultimate truth I have gleaned. A single spark of goodness at the core of our being. It can never be completely erased. But in a young person, yes, it can be obliterated to the point of complete invisibility. That is what happened to me.

As an official employee – well, volunteer – of Hitler Youth, I knew that I had to leave my parents' home for good. I rented a cheap room in a poor district of Kreuzberg, and towards the end of each month I always went hungry. I knew I could move back in at Kaiserkorso Eins at any time, but pride prevented me. Also, poverty helped expunge my guilt at being a highborn daughter.

One day, I found a stray dog on the street that had been in a fight, with half his ear missing. You know I'd always wanted to be a vet – and I knew also that Mama, a nurse, had all sorts of healing lotions and bandages at home. That was the one occasion I returned home during this time. I came secretly, took what I needed, healed that dog and made him my own. I named him Flocki. I even shared my food with him. I had always been thin, but by now I was all skin and bones. I basked in my poverty. It was a self-imposed penance for being born into the wrong family, a family that did not support Hitler or my dedication to him, and I positively glowed with self-righteousness.

I had always had a somewhat combative nature, and at work I often argued with my colleagues and superiors and found fault with them. Perversely, instead of it putting me in their bad books they kept their eye on me for promotion and education. I had the makings of the perfect Nazi leader. Needless to say, I went that route willingly.

Where were you at this time, Leah? I had no idea. As I write I can almost feel your physical presence right by my side, though in reality you were completely absent back then. Purged from my life. I was forging ahead, oblivious to all that had been good and pure and uplifting in my life, and that was the way I wanted it. But now I do wonder – where were you? What were you doing?

14

LEAH

One day, walking together near Alexanderplatz, Markus and I heard the distant thrum of drums, and then a Jeep festooned with swastikas drove slowly past. We stood aside to watch it pass; we knew a parade was on its way. The Jeep was followed by a marching band: young women in brown uniforms, some beating on those drums, others holding swastika banners aloft, waving them. They marched to a strict and perfect rhythm, every movement synchronised.

After the band, another group of brown-uniformed girls marched past, singing. Something about Jewish blood; I couldn't catch all the words. Some of these girls, too, held banners on long flagpoles, which they swung firmly from side to side. Their heavy boots thumped down on the cobbles like a single gigantic boot, causing an eerie thudding pulse. They sang with full lungs, almost shouting. There was nothing musical about that song. It was bellowed out in a belligerent chant that was only faintly related to melody of any kind. The faces of the girls were stony, their eyes staring straight ahead, their mouths opening and closing in absolute unison as they belted out the words. The columns of marchers seemed to go on forever. This must be the entire membership of Berlin's BDM.

Suddenly, Markus gripped my arm tightly. 'There's Magda!' he cried.

'Where? Where?'

He indicated, pointing into the crowd. The girls were organised in straight lines, both lengthwise down the street and rows of six across it. It was easy to see her, though she marched at the far end of her row, progressing slowly towards where we stood together on the pavement. She carried one of the flag-poles, and swung it back and forth boldly as she marched. She didn't see us. How could she? Her fiery gaze was fixed straight ahead. Her torso, neck and head were stiff and upright, anchoring those swinging arms and those marching legs. Her mouth opened and closed, wide and fierce; her jaw moved up and down as she, in one accord with all the others, belted out the militant words of the Horst-Wessel song, the anthem of the Nazis:

Clear the streets for the brown battalions,
Clear the streets for the storm-division man!
Millions are looking upon the hooked cross full of hope,
The day of freedom and of bread dawns!

My own jaw dropped at the sight. There she was. My one-time best friend, the closest female friend I'd ever had, unambiguously declaring before all the world her allegiance to the dictatorship that would see me and my people banished from society. Banished not only from workplaces and restaurants and schools and our homes, but from the streets too? From Germany?

I'd seen one or two parades before, marching bands, men in brown uniforms tramping past with metrical precision, their boots stomping in collective unity. The sight of such militarised shows of power had always driven fear into my heart. But this: to see Magda among them, to witness her unwavering allegiance to this menace – it was terrifying. For the first time, I understood how deeply she had been sucked into the movement. Now, I knew that Magda was my enemy.

When she had marched past, I stared up at Markus. The horror I saw in his eyes was a perfect reflection of the dismay I felt myself. We both knew then, at the same time, that the Nazi threat was not just political, not just societal: it was personal. In Markus's case, it was familial.

He grabbed my hand then and squeezed it tightly. No words were needed. He pulled me through the milling throng. Many were cheering. Many were waving small swastika flags of their own. Many around us had given the Nazi salute as the march stomped past. We edged our way through them all. Eventually we came to a quiet street and from there found our way to the bus stop. Markus waited with me for a bus that would take me home.

'I'll come later,' he whispered as he kissed my cheek. 'I've got to see some people.'

I only nodded, unable to speak. My stomach was twisting and turning, knotting and unknotting as the nausea rose up my gorge. I pushed it down. By the time I arrived home my cheeks were wet with the tears I'd been unable to hold back. I opened the front door, rushed to the bathroom, and dry-retched over the sink again and again, until there was nothing more to vomit, because disgust had scraped me empty.

15

MAGDA

Do you remember that Hitler Youth slogan, Leah; the one that had been seared into our very psyche: 'swift as a greyhound, as tough as leather, and hard as Krupp steel'? *I understood that last section not as being hard towards others, but hard towards oneself: unrelenting. In fact, never giving in, working to the bone for the good of Germany.*

There's another slogan that was seared into our being. It was a vow we had all taken, we Hitler Youths. It's most embarrassing to me to repeat it to you in these pages, but I must. Here it is. These are the words I clung to with all my being whenever some latent prick of conscience caused doubts to rise within me. Forgive me, Leah. We swore on the Blood Banner.

We swore oath upon oath. We pledged obedience unto death to him and those he appointed to lead. We swore to believe in Germany as firmly, clearly and truly as we believe in the sun, the moon and the stars. We swore to believe in Germany as if Germany were our very selves, and as certainly as we believed our souls strive towards eternity. We swore to believe in Germany, or our lives are but death. And that we must fight for Germany until death.

I don't suppose you know much about how the Hitler Youth had developed and was organised, so I'll give you a short run-down. By this time, the movement was entirely responsible for the physical, mental, and moral education of Germany's young people. All other youth groups, whether their scope was political, religious, or for leisure activities, had been disbanded. You'll remember what happened to KLUM! So when children turned ten, they had to join either the Deutsche Jungfolk for boys, or the Deutsche Jungmädels, for girls, both flowing into the Hitler Youth. There was no choice, Leah. It was compulsory. Even if their parents, like mine, disagreed, children had to comply, lambs offered on the altar of Nazism.

I was a victim of this implacable law. I was just fifteen when the Nazis swept me off my feet and pulled me into arms of Krupp steel; when they replaced my beating, feeling heart with a machine.

The BDM absorbed me. It became my entire life. It sucked my blood.

16

LEAH

To my dismay, I soon had to part with Trude, at least as my colleague. Our little kindergarten was a state-run institution, and Jews had been banned from any kind of state employment. My employer, a wonderful older woman called Dagmar, had kept me on as long as she could, but one day the Gestapo came by and asked us all for papers. Yes: we were now required to carry papers on us confirming our Aryan descent. Of course I failed that test. I had that ominous 'J' in my identity document, and I had to go. Trude, not being a full Jew, passed the test and so could stay on. But we remained friends, and saw each other often in our spare time. I had lost Magda, but I was building a new circle of female friends, of whom Trude was the first.

By now there was an active information-sharing network among Berlin Jews. I found another job with a private Jewish nursery school, financed by the children's families. I learned that these were families where both parents were forced to work through economic need. My pay was negligible, but I was nevertheless grateful that I still had any work at all. Not everyone did. Jews were being dismissed from their jobs right, left and centre. They were expelled from schools and universities. Many now worked practically as slaves at the Siemens factory, including Aaron, as we had discovered. Electricians, plumbers, builders will always be needed, and his training had at least meant he was not put on a cattle car. Because that's where many of us ended up. Cattle cars, disappearing into the East.

My mother was fortunate. She had had to give up her librarian job, but at least my father was a doctor and still had a reasonable income, so we as a family were comparatively well provided for. Still, it was a struggle and we all played our little part in making ends meet. Eventually, Mother took in private work as a seamstress, which her mother had been before her.

'What are you doing this weekend?' Trude asked me one day in early 1937.

'Nothing much,' I said. 'I'll just be at home with Mother and Father. We don't go anywhere any more.'

All the joy had been sucked out of Berlin life. The vibrancy, the laughter, the sheer gusto that Berliners had been known for in the Golden Twenties had been obliterated. We Jews cowered at home behind closed doors. We emerged only to go to our jobs and to secure food, to queue up for ages at the few shops where we were allowed to purchase what we needed to survive. Indeed, it was now only about survival.

'Why don't you come out to Sonnenhof with me?' she said.

There it was again: this mysterious Sonnenhof.

'I'd love to!' I replied. 'If I only knew what it was, and where.'

'Just come,' she replied. 'You look so pale and disheartened, you need a break.'

I did. The very name intrigued me. Der Sonnenhof. It sounded like some sunny oasis, far from the bleak stone walls and streets of Berlin. *Hof*, farm: it reminded me of Tante

Helga's country refuge in Bavaria, of the childhood summers we'd spent. An idyll, far away from the hellhole Berlin was becoming. A place to escape. To breathe again. I know my idealised image could not possibly be true, yet I allowed my imagination to run away with me. I dreamed of a place in the sun, far away from everything to do with the Nazis and their reign of terror.

'Of course I'll come!' I said. 'If I may.'

And so, that sunny afternoon in early May 1937, Trude and I took streetcar 46 to the end of the line – an hour outside of Berlin – and then we walked a further half-hour through a forest. And there it was, spread out before us, shining in the sunshine.

'Silbersee,' said Trude. *Silver Lake*. And, indeed, the expanse of water shimmered silver in the afternoon light; and there, not far from the shore, was what looked like a green jewel, sparkling in the sunshine. An island. The living reality of my imagined vision of paradise.

'So that's your Sonnenhof,' I said. 'An island in the sun.'

'It is.'

I took a deep breath and simply stood there, gazing. After the brick and tarmac and pavements and crowds of the city, I already felt that I stood on the shores of paradise. I drank it all in, breathed it all in. The cloudless spring sky, reflected blue in the lake. The lush green of the island. The twittering of birds in the trees above us. Trude must have felt my emotion, for she said nothing and simply stood beside me, breathing deeply as I did.

Peaceful and idyllic, that green island beckoned to me, and already from the shore I felt my heart widening, reaching out in longing for a place of serenity where I could once again be myself without fear of the future. A vague memory of that glorious day on the Zugspitze, so very long ago, rose up in me.

Markus, sighing the words *This is IT.* That sense of inner perfection I had glimpsed.

Here it was again. Just looking out from the shore, I knew that was again, this was IT.

I could simply *be,* without fear of the Gestapo knocking at my door. Without those ugly signs, JEWS NOT WANTED. The far shore beckoned to me. I looked at Trude and smiled. She smiled back. It felt like an eternity since I had truly smiled from the bottom of my heart.

Awakening out of my reverie, I realised that. But I didn't see a boat. There was a boathouse to our left, but its doors were open and it was clearly empty. No boat.

'How do we get out there?'

She laughed. 'Like this!' she said and called out loudly: '*Hallooooo!* We're here! Come and get us!'

Shading my eyes with a hand and looking out across the glittering lake, I glimpsed movement on the island, and then a human figure walking down to its shore. Presently, a boat edged away from the island and made its way towards us. As it drew closer, I saw that it was rowed by a handsome young man, who grinned broadly at both of us.

Arriving at the lakeshore where we stood, he got out and stood before us.

'Leah, this is Dieter von Berg,' said Trude, and to him, she said, 'Dieter, this is Leah, my good friend.'

'Welcome, Leah!' said Dieter. 'Trude's always talking about you.' He stretched out a hand to help me into the boat. Once we were both settled, he pushed it away from the shore and rowed us over to the island.

From the shore, a small path led to the interior of the island. I looked around in awe. What greeted me was not some version of a luxurious holiday island. Instead, I found myself on a farm. Rows and rows of earthen beds stretched before us, with several people, mostly young women, bent down or kneeling with their hands in the soil, or digging, or pushing wheelbarrows. I looked around in amazement, a hundred questions burning on my tongue, but, as we were walking single file, they would have to wait. Dieter led the way, followed by me, with Trude bringing up the rear. Dieter led us to a sort of open-walled shack, in front of which a middle-aged woman was laying a table with cups and saucers.

'Mutter, this is Trude's friend, Leah,' said Dieter. 'Leah, my mother, Lisa von Berg.'

We shook hands. 'Pleased to meet you, Frau von Berg,' I said.

'Call me Lisa,' she replied as she shook my hand. 'Trude told us all about you. Welcome to Sonnenhof!'

I took another deep breath, so deep it was as if I was drinking in the entirety of the sun-drenched air, the slight breeze wafting in from the lake, the sky itself.

'This is... this is paradise!' I said.

And it was. But not for long.

We'd arrived on a Friday evening, too late to work but just in time for supper, taken at a long wooden table outside the kitchen, prepared by Lisa herself. It was delicious.

'All vegetables from the garden!' said Trude.

I found out that these girls were all friends or relatives of Lisa von Berg, come to help for the summer. Some went home at night, others, like us, slept on the island in tents. That first night I retreated to my allocated tent, which I shared with Trude, in a state of euphoria, a happiness I had not known since the carefree days of childhood. I fell asleep right away, in spite of the hardness of the earth beneath me.

The next thing I knew, someone was shaking my shoulder. It was still dark, and yet, apparently, it was morning.

'Wakey wakey, rise and shine!' Trude said in a sing-song

voice. 'It's off to work we go! Potatoes are calling, wanting to be planted!'

Trude led me over to a large field of newly turned earth, arranged in long beds, that was to be the potato field. Lisa was there to greet me.

'Have you ever planted potatoes before?' she asked.

I shook my head.

'Well, now's a good time to learn,' she said with a laugh, 'I'm sure you've eaten them all your life.' Next to her was a wheelbarrow filled with seed potatoes, and a bucket of dark, crumbly compost. 'These are all ready for planting,' she went on. 'We prepared them in the greenhouse. The last frost was two weeks ago, so they should be fine planted out.'

She demonstrated what was to be done: how to push a piece of tuber into the earth, the eyes upwards. How far apart to plant the next one. Explaining all the time in soft, soothing words, as if I were a child. And then she left me to it: to the field, and the potatoes, and the cold raw earth. I worked all day, not only planting but digging, weeding, pushing wheelbarrows.

It was a revelation. Paradise, I realised, is not a reprieve from work, a permanent Sabbath where work is sin. Work is part of paradise. I threw myself into it and, to my astonishment, as I got used to it, as I pushed my hand into the cool moist earth and deposited my seed potatoes there, happiness, pure and sweet, welled up in me. Happy just doing what had to be done with a small hoe, earth and potatoes, and my own two hands.

Trude and all the others – Lisa had six adult children, who in turn had partners and friends – had all become part of the small community that kept the island running. I was the only one, beside Trude, from a Jewish background. But for once, I was able to ignore the danger that posed.

Lisa, though, was quite aware. 'Be careful, Leah,' she warned me urgently when we had a moment together. 'Things are only going to get worse. Germany seems completely brainwashed.'

But I was already in a state of denial. I laughed her off. This place was too perfect and I basked in a sense of having already escaped it all. Here, being Jewish didn't matter. Here, we were safe.

After dinner we all went to bed early, in preparation for an early start the next day. I fell asleep the moment my head touched the makeshift pillow, consisting of a roll of clothes. I had not fallen asleep so easily in months. Perhaps years.

17

MAGDA

Hardly had I started my work writing for the press office in Berlin when I was called up for Land Service, a duty every young German had to perform. Land Service had the aim of removing urban youth from their unhealthy home environment and returning them to the delights of the countryside and working on the land. This meant working on farms all over Germany, from springtime to harvest.

I was sent for my Land Service to a farm belonging to the Rittergut Schwanditz in Thüringen, a stately home still occupied by the eponymous aristocratic family, descendants of the fourteenth-century knights and princes who once reigned here supreme. I was accompanied by a ragtag group of other BDM girls. We came from all walks of life: factory girls, students, civil servants' daughters, waitresses, typists. It was service to Germany. No one was better than the other. No one was privileged. And let me tell you, Leah, that work was hard! It never once occurred to me that we were providing free manual labour to a wealthy family, landowners of high status. No: to me it was work given from the heart. It was service; almost religious in nature.

I was a city girl, like you, Leah. Imagine me, then, on my very first day on a peasant farm, planting potatoes on a cold and rainy morning, in a dreary field where the last snow still lay in the furrows! The earth was sodden and lumpy and above all cold, and I had to plant the seed potatoes one by one, my hands numb with cold, my back aching from the wire basket I carried and from the endless bending over.

Oh, it was dreadful. I have never been so close to tears before or after. Dreary, backbreaking work – but I instilled in myself the firm decision not to break; to carry on, to do my best, that this was service for the greater good and I could not be lax. Laziness would be the greatest crime, and, whether it was planting potatoes or washing loads of filthy laundry or harvesting corn or mucking out the cowsheds or driving horse-drawn wagons to and from the fields, I had to do the work in the spirit of service and lift my mind out of the attitude of complaint. You know: that whingeing sense of self-pity we both used to get when our mothers roped us in to do some harmless chore.

During the harvest, the farm work went on for up to fifteen hours a day, sandwiched between sessions of physical training at dawn and dusk and political instruction from the camp leader, as well as dancing and singing to keep our spirits up. You can imagine just how exhausting it was for a city girl! But ever I strove to lift my mind above complaint, and, often, if I were alone in the fields, I did this by singing.

Do you remember how I used to burst into Beethoven's 'Ode to Joy' at random times? Well, picture me now in a potato field, beneath a grimy grey sky, belting out Freude! Freude! Freude! *at the top of my voice! If there were any witnesses, they would have thought me quite mad, yet it helped to get me through the days.*

You might not believe this, but in retrospect that was the happiest period of my life. There is indeed a certain joy that comes from pushing oneself to one's very limit, while refusing to give in to that whiny voice that comes from deep within. Pushing oneself through the mire of grumpy self-pity to a state where there is, indeed, joy; joy without cause, simply bubbling up from within. I reached that joy several times in that period.

It was an innocent time. I did nothing evil. I helped the farmers, as we all did, even if we were not compensated. It was service, beyond individual gain. It was, in a way, seventh heaven.

18

LEAH – SONNENHOF

Oh yes, she worked us to the bone, did Lisa; but we did it joyfully, laughing and chattering as we worked, our hands deep in the rich moist earth. I spent that weekend on the island, and every other weekend of that whole summer. I wished I could stay forever, but apparently the island was unliveable during the winter. *What a pity*, I thought. I simply wanted to escape to this perfect little refuge and live here always. No Nazis, no Gestapo, no *JEWS NOT WANTED* signs. The only thing missing was Markus.

On my second day on the island, Trude placed in my hand a book by one Leberecht Migge. 'Read it!' she said. 'It'll tell you what we're doing here.'

I took the book and read the title: *Jedermann Selbstversorger! – Eine Lösung der Siedlungsfrage durch Gartenbau – Everyone Self-Sustaining! A Solution to the Settlement Question through Horticulture.*

I looked up at her. 'What's it about?'

She spread her arms wide, indicating the garden, the small buildings on its other side, and all the activity going on between.

'It's about all this. I couldn't possibly explain before you

came – I think you'd have run a mile!' She smiled, rather hesitantly. 'You're a city girl, Leah. I know – I did deceive you. I
made you think you were coming for a holiday, but you're not.
It's going to be work, today and tomorrow. I just wanted you to
see it first before you ran. I wanted you to meet – *her*. Lisa.'

As I was to discover later over that weekend as I read the book,
and over the many weekends and holidays and summer days
that followed, this Herr Migge – or simply Migge, or the more
familar Der Migge– was the hero of the day, not only to this
little group of enthusiasts but to all of Germany's foremost
architects and landscape gardeners and city planners of the day,
for his innovative work in modern environmental design. Migge
had been a close friend of Lisa's, and I could see how she had
taken on his vision: a vision of everyone owning a piece of land
and developing it enough to completely maintain ourselves, our
families, our communities. And as I worked, I understood how
being close to the earth, and the wealth it produces, made me
feel wealthy too: rich in an internal, spiritual way. United with
all of nature. Migge had died in 1935, but his ideas lived on,
here on this island, carried forward and put into practice by
Lisa.

This island, this little oasis of peace just outside Berlin,
floating in the shining sunlit Silbersee, was the result. Lisa had
taken over the lease and decided to turn it into a living experi-
ment of Migge's futuristic dream. A workspace and farm and
vegetable garden and homestead and community, all rolled into
one. And I was privileged enough to be an active participant.

It was she who inspired and encouraged and, yes, drove us.
She was a hard driver. I had never even touched a proper
vegetable bed before, just the little pots of herbs that Mother
kept on the kitchen windowsill, and which I watered regularly.
That first weekend on the island, by the end of the day – my

back aching from bending over, my thighs and calves sore from squatting, my upper arms in pain from stretching and carrying, my bare skin scratched from thorns, my hands raw and blistered from pulling, cutting, scraping at the earth – I was an exhausted wreck of a city girl.

But happy. So happy. Happy with a joy that welled up from within; breathing clean, green air into my lungs, rejoicing at the sun's gentle May caress, delighting in the many chats, casual and not so casual with my workmates; I joined the others at the long wooden table and the soup and bread I filled my stomach with seemed the best meal I'd had in my life.

It was that day on the Zugspitze all over again. I longed to share all this with Markus. I longed to tell him about Sonnen-hof, for it to be his refuge as well as mine. Here, we could be safe. Safe from whatever ugly winds were blowing through Berlin and all of Germany. It could be our own little oasis.

MAGDA

We are getting close to the crux of my story. Dread invades my heart, because I know what is to come and you don't, and I will have to write it down, and you – if you are reading at all – will read and know the worst. But it must be done. There is no escape from truth. For years, I held my own truth, the truth I had created for myself, to be THE truth. The one and only. But that was tunnel vision. There is no my truth and your truth. There is only what actually happened, what I actually did, uncoloured by my own biased interpretation. THE truth, without personal distortion. I must see it myself in order to be freed of it. Freed of myself and my own distortions, coloured by my personal bias and feelings. That is true freedom, Leah. Freedom from the self-deception that modifies all events to flatter and primp oneself and so to distort what actually happened. That is what I must do now, however much it hurts my sense of self.

I won't bore you with more details of my work in the Land Service. I'll just say it taxed me to the limit, but I accepted it all at the time as character-building. And I stand by that assessment. I do believe that no matter what, hard physical labour develops a strong inner core that will stand us well no matter what route we eventually take in life, and no matter in what capacity it is done. No matter what our ideology.

At the time of my service I was a full-blown BDM girl, but the actual work was not politically driven. It was simply work, done to put food on the table or to maintain life. And that is always good. You know the saying: Fleiß bringt Brot, Faulheit Not – Diligence brings bread, laziness brings woe. It's true. There's nothing like hard physical work for building strength of character, and I was to experience this first-hand in this period of my life.

You and I, we were brought up as privileged highborn daughters who were excused from the need to contribute to the work that keeps a household running; our mothers did all the domestic work, now and then aided by paid help. I remember your mother had a maid who came once a week to clean your home from top to bottom, even though, at least when the children were younger, she was a Hausfrau herself.

And my mother, even though she worked part-time, took it upon herself to keep our home spotless, and only occasionally roped me in to help. Do you remember my beating the carpets in the courtyard? That was one job I loved. Maybe it wore away some of the latent aggression that lurked in me when I was a girl. I remember how I loved smashing the carpet-beater into those rugs hanging on the line! Smash, smash, smash. I loved it! But it wasn't work. This, in the fields and on the homesteads, this was actual knuckle-breaking work. And it *was good for me. I wonder if you were ever called to physical labour. I have no idea where life took you after we parted.*

Anyway, after two seasons of Land Service, it was back to journalism, writing articles, mostly propaganda, for the BDM. I was good at it, very good, and my work was recognised, not in any monetary way but in promotions and praise. Believe me, praise from a higher-up in the Nazi hierarchy was as wonderful a reward as any financial gain.

Do you remember how fierce was my ambition as a young girl? To be a vet, or else a philosopher. A writer. I remember once trying my hand at poetry and short stories; but even I could tell that the results were not up to scratch. You, of course, did not hold back in your critique. This is dreadful! you'd say, when I showed you my work. Fiction and poetry were simply not my forte. But there it was, in embryo. I wanted to be a writer. Propaganda, it turned out, was exactly up my street.

One thing I can promise you, Leah, I never wrote for Der Stürmer. I'm not sure if you know this, but that nasty rag was not an official publication of the Nazi Party. That's why it did not display the swastika on its front page. It was published privately and made millions for its owner. I abhorred that paper. I remember once a vacancy came up on its staff and word got through to me. Somebody, I forget now who it was, encouraged me to apply. I did not.

Those Stürmer journalists were paid a good salary, whereas I was working for peanuts, and I could have done with the extra money. I could have found myself better living quarters, for a start, and bought better food and kept a dog (remember Flocki, the stray dog I told you about earlier? When I went off to Land Service I'd had to find a new owner for him, and luckily, I did find a well-positioned BDM leader who gave him a loving new home).

But what I want you to know is that the Stürmer was beyond the pale in its antisemitic diatribes. Gross, despicable, primitive. I could never have worked in that set-up, though what I was doing for the BDM was bad enough. My articles at first focused on building confidence in young people, confidence in their heritage, their culture, in the idea of Great Germany. Grossdeutschland. *That was our clarion call.*

We were called to a higher duty. To the service of something greater than ourselves, in which we could lose ourselves and thus become great ourselves. I saw myself as a leader from behind, leading not by standing at the front lecturing and giving speeches, but from the ground up, with words of encouragement, words of inspiration. Written words, not spoken. Words that could change hearts and minds.

Perhaps, one day, I would write a book. A book that young people would read at night before they went to bed, a book that would lift their spirits and give them the power to be living parts of this great enterprise: Grossdeutschland. *And:* the pen is mightier than the sword! *– that I believed with all my being. I did not believe in war. I did not want war. I thought we could create* Grossdeutschland *with words alone. Words that would move hearts and build a new society, a society founded on higher ideals that would, eventually, encompass the entire world.*

I knew that Hitler's book, Mein Kampf, *was not that book, not a book that would inspire the young generation. I had to admit that I found it boring, exaggerated, pure polemic, and his antisemitic focus gave me heart palpitations. This was not what I wanted for* Grossdeutschland. *I believed that this new society could not be built on disparagement of a certain section of the community but should focus on the positive.*

My imagined book would be different. It would grip young people just as I had been gripped. And not just the young. Back then, we had not yet incorporated the word 'bestseller' into the German language, but that was what my book would be. I was certain of it. That was my task in life, my God-given calling.

But there was no time left for writing books at this point. I had to put my dream on hold. It would have to wait, as other duties called. And that's where my sorry tale takes me now. Brace yourself, Leah. It's not pretty.

19

LEAH – SONNENHOF

After that first weekend I was smitten. Smitten with Silbersee, smitten with Lisa, smitten with the very idea of a self-sustaining lifestyle outside the mainstream, outside of city life. Perhaps I'd always been a farm girl at heart; I certainly took to this life of burying my hands in the earth, to looking up to the blue spring sky above, to the lake. No streets lined with buildings, no traffic. Above all, no swastika signs everywhere you looked. No Nazis. No fear. I breathed in the fresh air and the freedom, the sheer contentment that this lifestyle brought. I came as often as I could, and, one day in late June 1938, I brought Markus.

I was not yet capable of rowing the boat across to pick him up as he yelled from the lakeshore, but I went across with Dieter in the boat and threw myself into his arms.

'At last!' I said. 'I've missed you so much!'

'And I missed you!'

We climbed into the boat and settled on one of the seats. He immediately turned to me and kissed me, strongly, on the lips.

'Hey, you two!' Dieter chuckled. 'Time for all that later! Pleased to meet you, Markus!'

They shook hands, Markus laughed, and in the twinkling of

an eye they were friends. That's how things worked on Sonnenhof. No formalities, just instant friendships, instant communication, instant connections. Something that was so desperately
lacking in the world outside, that dismal world of suspicion and
fear and dark shadows round every corner. Here, there was only
sunshine.

Markus was immediately as enamoured of this new life as I
was; him being a newly graduated structural engineer, our work
on the island was right up his street. When he found out that
Leberecht Migge's ideas were the foundation of the island's
work, that Lisa had personally known Migge and, with his
support in the early days established the homestead using those
very ideas, he was delighted. He held up Migge's book: 'I refer-
enced this in my dissertation!' he said. 'All of this, landscape
architecture, his notion of resettlement outside the city as a
means of connecting back to the land, organising space, the
concept of urban regional planning, incorporating gardens into
city development – that was the basis of my own theories! This
is the future, Leah. This is how I see society moving forward.'

He and Lisa became the closest of friends as soon as they
met. Markus thought it was all brilliant and innovative and the
future of cities; that instead of concrete jungles, they could
become places where buildings and earth could be harmonised,
where humans never lost sight of the power of nature. Where
brickwork and green life – *grünes Leben*, he called it – went
hand in hand.

That night, Trude, who had shared my tent up to now,
moved out.

'You'll want to share with Markus,' she said, with a twinkle
in her eye, which slightly shocked me. At home Mother would
never have allowed me to share a room, much less a bed, with
Markus, and neither would Tante Helga. Here, it was different,

I found out. Trude had only been sharing my tent to keep me company; she had known I wasn't ready to sleep there alone. Now that I had Markus... well. Back she went – to her Dieter.

But that night as Markus and I snuggled together, each cocooned in a sleeping bag, I was shy and he was considerate. He enfolded me in his arms, stroked my hair, and that's how we fell asleep. We were in no hurry to take things further. *We have all the time in the world*, Markus had said; it seemed like so long ago. That's how one thinks when one is young and innocent. *All the time in the world. We will never grow old. We'll always be young.* Foolish notions!

But Markus was actually far from foolish. He had been invited to an interview for a job on Hitler's pet project, the new airport at Tempelhof. The interviewees had been hand-picked; only the best new engineering graduates would be invited to work on the project. One didn't apply for the job; one was selected for it. The enormous building site was practically opposite our families' homes at Kaiserkorso, and so it would be perfect for him logistically – he could live at home. But more to the point, it was a huge professional challenge and came with enormous prestige.

'Think of it!' he told me in excitement. 'This would mean working on one of the most progressive and innovative building projects in all of Germany, in all of Europe! In the world!'

I couldn't help being sceptical. 'But it's Hitler's project.'

'Engineering isn't political,' he said. 'It's neutral. Like all the sciences. It's mathematics, calculation, logic. The opposite of politics and ideology.'

'Didn't you say that the entire university was flooded with Nazi propaganda? Even the science faculties. How can you escape it, anywhere in public life?'

'I admit it – there's always pressure to fall into line. But the scientists I've worked with don't give a hoot about Nazism. They just want to do their best work. To progress, to research, to develop new ideas. And that's all I want to do. Work with the best engineers at the highest level of my ability. It's such a challenge, such a chance!'

'How come they invited you, out of all the students?'

'Well, I don't want to boast, but I was the top student of my year. I graduated summa cum laude and my dissertation was published in a leading industry magazine. It's a great move for me. And the pay isn't bad, either. I suppose somebody noticed and recommended me to the Tempelhof functionaries.'

But career progression was not the driving force in Markus's life. Career progress, of course, was important to him, but though he longed to realise his ideas, there were bigger matters at stake right now. His heart and soul were focused on the need to rid our country of the scourge of Nazism. In Munich, as in Berlin, he had made contact with other young people who were equally appalled, banding together to secretly work against the Nazis. Though he told me no details of what they were doing, he did tell me the names of his closest friends: Christoph Probst and Hans Scholl. Hans had a young sister, Sophie, who, Markus said, reminded him of me.

'In what way?' I asked, suspicious.

'I can't really put it into words. She's just so – genuine. Like you. Committed. Sincere. Passionate.'

The word 'passionate' worried me.

'Is she pretty?'

He laughed. 'Pretty? I suppose so. But don't tell me you're jealous!'

'I am, a bit! I miss you so much, and you're down there with all these friends, all these gentile girls who aren't a problem. Girls who're revolutionaries, like you. Not cowards, like me, hiding from the Nazis. I feel so – useless.'

'You're not a problem, little mouse. You're an inspiration. You're not a coward at all, and you're anything but useless. And Sophie is a mile away from being a revolutionary. She's only fifteen, and she's even in the BDM.' He squeezed me tight, kissed me on the nose. 'So, don't worry. There's only you. I promise.' He pulled me close and whispered in my ear: 'And I love you. I will always love you.'

I pulled away and looked him in the eyes. What I saw there told me what I longed to hear: Markus was true to the bone. In those eyes I saw strength, and loyalty, and courage, and, yes, love.

'I love you too, Markus.'

He pulled me close again. 'We'll come through this. Together.' But his voice wavered at that last word, and I knew that even the strongest love was no guarantee of a safe future. That future, *our* future, remained a huge question mark. Neither of us knew what tomorrow would bring, or next month, or next year. Our future was not in our own hands. It was in the hands of a criminal organisation called the National Socialists, and my one-time best friend, Magda, was a part of that reign of terror. That hurt terribly.

Markus came many times during that summer. He made a point of studying Migge's ideas in practical detail; he was thinking ahead, he said, of what he wanted from life. When 'all this' was over. He seemed to have no doubt that 'all this' would one day be in the past and we could build a life together.

Though he'd grown up in Berlin, Markus was at heart a land boy. He loved the countryside, he loved the earth, he loved nature. He loved the idea of humans living in perfect compatibility with nature. He loved farming, and hoped one day to live, not in an urban centre like Berlin or Munich, but on the land. Growing food, raising chickens, founding a family in a place where his children could run barefoot through the fields. Apple pie and roast chicken on the table. An idyll, nestled in the hills and valleys of Bavaria, hopefully on his grandparents' farm; and he hoped to one day build a house there for his own family and live the perfect life. *When all this is over.* That was the promise he made, over and over. We had to cultivate faith, he said. Faith plants a sense of certainty in the heart, and that certainty brings the strength to carry on, even when the storm is upon us. That strength will pull us through.

Now that I had had my first taste of living on and from the land, I was completely on board with Markus's dream. It became my dream too. One day, it would be all over. Jews would no longer be vilified. Jews and gentiles would be loving neighbours and friends again. They could marry. *We* could marry. We *would* marry. When all this was over.

Sometimes, we had doubts. In fact, often we had doubts. Over the previous years, the rules and regulations that made pariahs of Jews had became stricter and more outlandish. The noose was tightening. But at Sonnenhof, we felt that here, this little haven capsuled away from the chaos outside: *this* was reality. We clung to that notion, that vessel of all our hope. This is how it should be. This is how it *would* be. *When all this is over.*

'Hope is all we have,' said Markus. 'We cannot give up, Leah. One day we will be free. I will spend my last drop of blood fighting for that freedom.'

'That's what I'm afraid of,' I said. 'That you'll go too far. You're too brave, Markus, too outraged, too rebellious. And here I am, cowering in fear on this island.'

'Don't call it that,' he replied. 'You have reason to fear, but you're not cowering. You're doing the best you can, building up something and keeping your faith alive. If you had no faith you would not be here, working on the land. You'd be hiding in a dark cellar somewhere. We must have faith, mouse. We must lift our hearts to faith, because that's where our strength lies.'

I cuddled closer into him. I loved those words, but sometimes I thought they came too easily, too pat. That Markus was fooling himself, or at least trying to fool me.

And so 1938 crept by in this strange world in which I commuted precariously back and forth between day job and the Sonnenhof idyl, between the gloomy shadow spreading through Berlin, and the sunshine and free air of Silbersee. A world in which the darkness could all be put aside. Here, we lived each moment just as it came, and fear stayed on the far shore.

20

MAGDA

Oh, Leah. How I dread what must come next. I dread looking my delusion and my blindness in the face. But it has to be.

All through 1938, I worked on at my job as a staff writer and propagandist for the BDM. I would have loved to go to university and study philosophy or the classics, but it was just not possible. My parents could only afford to send one of us to university, and that was Markus – who not only was older and male, but was studying something that, my parents claimed, had 'hand and foot', a substantial basis, unlike my useless subjects of choice. As for veterinary medicine, even if it had been financially feasible, it would have been another dead end in that day and age; nobody had money for vets. But with the Grossdeutschland Hitler had planned for us all there would be building projects galore, and Markus's choice of structural engineering was the right one. Germany, we all believed, would lead the world. Our cities would be futuristic, innovative, progressive. We needed men like Markus.

Markus was my big brother. I was happy to give him a leg-up.

One day, just after Markus had graduated, I made an impromptu visit home to pick up my old typewriter and some clothes. He happened to be there. Though he still claimed to despise the National Socialists and refused to join the Party – much to my chagrin –he was talking to Mama about possible jobs, and waxed lyrical when he described Tempelhof Airport, which was practically across the road; we could virtually see and hear what was going on just by crossing the street. It would be the chance of a lifetime to work there, he said.

I pricked up my ears. 'Why don't you apply?' I said.

He made a sceptical face. 'You need vitamin B to get in there.'

Vitamin B: Beziehung. Connections. A helping hand. I had a sudden idea but said no more.

Mama had listened with interest while Markus was talking, though I doubt she understood what he was going on about, especially when he went into technical details. But everyone knew about Tempelhof. Everyone was talking about it. It was to be the pride of Berlin.

The physical structure, Markus had said, was made up of an elliptical airfield and an enormous building complex. The massive steel structure of the hangars, the monumental terminal buildings: everything was designed to demonstrate power and superiority. There was no grander building in all of Europe. I was so proud of Germany's technological dominance. I could see that, despite his wrong political opinions, Markus, too was proud – not necessarily of the powerful symbolism, but because it was such a professional challenge for engineers. He would be even prouder if he landed a job there, I thought to myself, and maybe I could help. Maybe I could be his vitamin B. The very fact that he was so impressed by the prestigious venture was proof that he was slowly waking up, I thought.

How could he not! Hearing him wax lyrical about Tempel-

*hof, my brilliant idea would not let me go. I was delighted that
Markus was obviously beginning to see the light. He needed
only a nudge, and I knew I could help. I could kill two birds
with one stone: help Markus get this job, and give him that last
little prod he needed to open his eyes to the right way of
thinking.*

*When Mama told me, very proudly, that he had graduated
as one of the best students of his year, I determined to take it
upon myself to ensure he also got the best job available.
Markus was my big brother; I had so adored him as a child,
and it broke my heart every step he took along the wrong political path. It was as if he were living in darkness, quite literally
in the Dark Ages of Germany. I felt that if only he was given
the chance – if only he could really see where we were heading. If only he could be among the right people, the leaders of
the new era who would take us forward into Germany's
New Age.*

*And so I spoke with one of my superiors, a very influential
army man (whose name won't mean anything to you), and told
him about my talented brother. I told him he was young and
gifted and that the new Germany needed forward-thinking
men like him, and that I wanted to give him a hand up. This
man told me to write a letter about Markus, give it to him, and
he would pass it on to the right person, with a recommendation
as well as a mention of me as being a devoted and hard-
working Party woman. Markus having a connection to me
would give him a hand up, make him more visible than all the
other graduating students of his year.*

'Is he in the Party?' this man then asked.

*I shook my head sadly. 'But,' I said, 'one thing leads to
another. Once he is absorbed in this prestigious and monumental project, I'm quite certain he'll join. After all, Party
members are the ones who get promoted, and he's definitely
interested in progressing his career. I heard him say so.*

Anyway, who wouldn't want to work on the greatest airport in Europe? My brother is a perfect Aryan. He just needs that final push.'

I showed him a photo of Markus. Yes, I carried a few photos around with me, of Markus and also Mama and Father. I believe in family as the foundation stone of society; and I desperately wanted the best for my brother. I wanted him to understand. I wanted us to be friends again. I hated the discord between us.

'Write that letter,' my supervisor advised. And I did, and as promised, he added a note of his own, assuring whoever was to read it that I was a highest-calibre BDM member and my brother was the perfect Aryan of the kind we needed to establish the Third Reich.

And so, I was not in the least surprised when Markus was called in for an interview. Apart from being pleased for him professionally, I was completely convinced that he would soon open up to what, in my eyes, was so very obvious politically. I was doing him a big favour, I thought, and one day he'd thank me for it. One day, we would be friends again.

Of course I could not possibly tell him, yet, that he owed this interview to me. One day, though, once he was converted to The Truth, I would tell him, and he would be proud of me, and grateful. That was the plan.

At this time, I was living in Berlin, but generally avoided going home. There was still so much tension between my parents and me. On the one hand, they had to accept, now, that I was playing a leading role in Germany's renewal. Eventually, history would prove me right, I believed, and I needed to exercise patience with them and not argue so much. They were resisting, I thought, the way a petulant child resists its parents' wisdom. I felt infinitely superior to them, and they had no option than to concede to me, since the entire government *apparatus, including the Gestapo, was on my side. I even had the right to turn them, and Markus, in for their criticism of the Party.*

Yet for me, it was hard to deal with. Nobody likes an opinionated child, and that's how I saw them: stubbornly clinging to their wrong opinions. I told myself to be patient, but it was hard and, whenever we met, there were arguments. In spite of my better knowledge, I tended to lose my temper and shout at them, which was not good and pushed them even more into resistance of the truth.

You realise, I hope, dear Leah, that I write those words in great irony, my tongue firmly in my cheek!

And so I avoided home, and confined my contact with my parents mostly to letter-writing. I couldn't even phone them, since they still used the phone in your family's home and I couldn't encourage them to go there. But I loved my parents and kept in touch, despite the arguments.

I admit there was another reason for me avoiding home. There were too many Jews in the house. Not only your family, but the Levy couple, and the Bienstock couple in the attic. It would have been too embarrassing for words to run into any of that lot, as I referred to them.

I found myself wishing the building could be 'purified'. Yes, that was the term I used now. I had been well brainwashed. I had made Nazi terminology my own, not even questioning it. Not even inspecting the glaring discrepancy and contradiction between what I knew from experience – that these were all decent, perfectly ordinary human beings who ate, slept and had their beings in no different way than we did – and the poison I had been inoculated with. And then the building was purified, Mother told me on one of my rare visits home. Almost. The Levys had moved out voluntarily, and the Bienstocks had been removed. I didn't ask where to. I didn't

want to know. But there was still one Jewish family there:
yours.

And you, I wanted to avoid above all.

Eventually, I heard from Mama that Markus had been
approved for the job and was due to begin in September. And
so I wrote him a gushing letter of congratulation. He still
didn't know that I had had a hand in the whole process, and I
could hardly tell him now.

But I felt such pride! My brother would be working on this
magnificent project with which Hitler could display the power
and grandeur of the new Germany. It would reflect positively
on me, too. We were the vanguard – and he was to be a part
of it!

I congratulated him not only on landing the job, but on
finally acknowledging that Germany was the leading world
power in every way, as evidenced by this monumental
construction. Well done! *I wrote.* Now you are with us!

To my astonishment, Markus replied in great fury. How
dare you! *he wrote.* How dare you assume that just because
I've been given this job, I'm now a Nazi! Yes, Tempelhof is
indeed at the cutting edge of construction work, not only in
Berlin but in all of Germany and even Europe and perhaps
the world. But I won't be working there as a Party func-
tionary, and you can be sure that my motive is not to promote
Grossdeutschland and Nazi political power! This is purely a
professional move. And all this hoopla about it being a
demonstration of Hitler's power: what balderdash! What
arrogance!

Oh dear. He was a long way from what I had hoped, which
was conversion. And such opinions could land him in trouble.
I immediately destroyed that letter – I burned it in the fire-
place. I could not let it fall into the hands of any of my supe-

riors – it would be regarded as almost treason, and who knew what the repercussions could be, for Markus and for me.

I remembered how he'd in the past dismissed Hitler himself as a pompous ass. I'd been horrified at the time. But at the end of the day, I thought, I was right and he was wrong. In accepting this job, he had aligned himself with Hitler's vision. How could it be otherwise, I thought. Markus had been a little bit slow in coming to his senses, but now, like it or not, he was with us, and would be swept along with the tide, as all Germans were. After all, by not going with the tide one put oneself and one's family in grave danger.

Just writing and reading those words – the thoughts I had at the time – I am once again astounded at my own complete blindness. How lacking in perception! And I thought myself so superior at the time! So easy it is for an otherwise intelligent human being to become so completely distorted in thinking that she does not realise her own madness. That was me.

Markus insisted that Tempelhof was nothing but an empty spectacle and he had taken on the job purely for the professional challenge. That was an incendiary concept to me. I replied, of course, and tried to prove him wrong. A few letters flew back and forth as we argued about that airport. Such a useless, empty argument, Leah, looking at it with the wisdom of hindsight.

In the end, I had the last word. I wrote him a three-page letter letting him know that he and his ilk were going to lose because the National Socialists were Germany's future and the little people holding out – people like him – would eventually be silenced. He never replied. How smug I felt, knowing that he had no arguments left to counter mine! But what a waste of time and energy, I thought. Why didn't he just concede defeat? Even our parents had done so – well, more or less, in that they simply ignored the topic. That to me was proof that they knew there was no point in resisting the inevitable.

Because serious matters were just round the corner. My account of this will shock you now as it must have shocked you back then.

We have arrived at early November 1938. You know what that means.

21

LEAH – BERLIN

When I saw Markus the night after his interview, I could tell by his drawn face, the tension in his jaw, the frown across his forehead, that something was wrong.

'The interview didn't go well?'

'It was an absolute disaster!'

'Why? What happened? I thought you were perfect for the job?'

'I am, and the job is perfect for me. I want it so much, Leah! But...' He slowly shook his head.

'Well? What happened?'

'The moment I walked in to face the interviewing team, I knew it would all be a flop. There they all were, in their brown suits, all with their swastika badges prominently displayed. And the swastika on the wall behind them, and the oversized portrait of Hitler. You were right, mouse.'

'Oh no!'

'Yes. And all those right hands flying out in the Hitler greeting! *Heil Hitler,* they all yelled. Yes, yelled. Every one of them. At me.'

'So what did you do?'

'Oh, Leah! I feel so ashamed. I can hardly admit it. But... I wanted this job so badly. I need it. It's well paid, and Mama and Papa need the money, and... well. I did it, Leah. I gave the greeting. I said the words.'

'You didn't!'

I was shocked. I couldn't believe that Markus had complied. It seemed a betrayal of enormous consequences. If there was one thing I truly believed in about him, it was his absolute integrity. He was simply not capable of lying or pretending to be what he wasn't. What he had done today was a complete repudiation of everything I knew him to be. Tears gathered in my eyes.

'Oh, Markus! You didn't! How could you!'

My sense of disappointment in him almost broke me in two. I stood up and paced the floor. I began to cry, properly cry. He stood up, walked towards me and took me in his arms. I resisted at first, then I let it happen. This was still Markus. The love of my life. Straight as an arrow, as true as gold. I could not reject him, no matter what he had done, no matter how deep my pain at his apparent cowardice. I tried to understand. To listen to him. How could he?

'I'm sorry, Leah. So sorry. Yes, I did it. And it was the worst thing I've ever done in my life. I felt like a traitor. I just wanted to be interviewed for the job. I knew that that was the first test, and it seemed a small price to pay.'

'A small price? Markus, it's a huge price! How can your personal integrity be a small price? How can you stand there and tell me it was right, to do that thing?'

'On the surface, no, it wasn't right. But, Leah, something went through my head at that moment, and I knew I had to. I had to get this job. I had to get this interview. I couldn't fall at the first hurdle. It was important to play along. It wasn't real. It was as if I was playing a role in a play.'

'No, Markus! You were letting them know you're on their side! You should have just turned and walked out.'

'No, Leah. You need to understand. I couldn't do that either. To refuse the Hitler salute, to walk out... You don't play with the Nazis. See, it's not just the salute, little mouse. There's more to it, and I'll explain – just trust me, and let me finish, all right?'

I nodded. I had to give him the benefit of the doubt. My Markus. Maybe he could give a plausible explanation to what seemed like betrayal of his own ethics. I took a deep breath. 'Go on,' I said.

'See, Leah. It's now becoming dangerous for any German *not* to give the Hitler salute. Giving it is the sign: *we are together. I agree with all that is happening.* Not giving it exposes a person as a villain of Germany. It can lead to arrest. We're already at that stage. I could not expose myself. Do you see? Do you see the risk of showing my true colours?'

'Still!' I said, not quite convinced.

He continued.

'In the split second it took for me to decide, to give the salute or not, I realised that not complying would put my work at risk. They'd want to keep an eye on me, now; because why had I put my career in jeopardy? they'd ask. And...'

'But your integrity, Markus. Your integrity!'

'Just hear me out, Leah. Just listen. So: they interviewed me, and it all went very well, from a professional perspective. It really is a wonderful opportunity. But, at the end of the interview, I was told that a prerequisite of getting the job was joining the Party. They had noticed that I did not wear a swastika. They told me I had to join, if I wanted the job. They asked me if I would do that. Join the Party.'

A long pause ensued. I held my breath.

'And I said yes.'

I gasped.

'You agreed to become a Nazi?'

He nodded. 'Yes. But don't judge me, Leah, let me explain.'

'What more is there to say? You're going to become a Nazi?
You?'

He shook his head slowly. 'Yes – and no. Yes, I will in
theory become a Nazi, if offered the job. I will make the
salute when necessary. I will pay lip service to the *Heil
Hitler!* and *Sieg Heil!* Greetings. I will play the game. But,
Leah, I will never be a Nazi in my heart. You know that. It is
all a ruse. A cover. Because, in the background... in my
heart...'

He stopped speaking again. I knew he was searching for the
right words. I waited.

'In my heart, I will be true to myself. I will be playing their
game, yes, but as a spy. Spies are actors. They have to be. They
play the game, but with purpose. And I've always been a good
actor.'

Yes. I remembered how when Magda and my brothers and I
were younger we'd gone to all his plays, how we'd applauded
and cheered. Markus could act. I shut up then and let him
continue.

'As they explained the project to me, what my work will be
– it will involve working with some of the most brilliant and
prominent engineers in all of Germany – I had the glimmer of
an idea. And even as they showed me a plan of the airport, the
public terminal, the hangars, the control towers – even as I
listened, my mind was working at top speed. Could there be a
secondary reason for this project? I thought. Could there be a
military reason? We all know that there are secret rearmament
plans. Could Tempelhof be part of those plans? I began to
suspect there's more to Tempelhof than meets the eye. That it's
a cover for something more. And if so, what a great opportunity
for me to investigate.'

His explanation was beginning to make sense. I nodded,

and seeing that I'd relaxed a little, he took my hand and squeezed it.

'But anyway, Leah, I don't really have a choice. If I were to walk away now, there'd be a target on my back. Because why would any young, gifted, ambitious graduate turn down a job like that? They'd investigate me. And me being investigated would put my friends and co-conspirators in danger! I'd have to stop altogether. A thought leapt up in my mind during the interview: a wolf in sheep's clothing.'

He lowered his voice, now, as if the walls had ears.

'Leah, in my group we are so very careful. We are wary of spies, of people pretending to be on our side but really being the eyes and ears of the Gestapo. You know what it's like: they're everywhere, pretending to be so innocent, one of us. And I had this thought: I'd do the reverse. Pretend to be one of them. Wear the trappings of Nazism, because that's how to get close to them. And I thought this: play the game, Markus. Just play the game.'

'In other words, pretend to be a Nazi, to spy on them.'

'Exactly!'

I leaned forward then, and he met me with open arms and clasped me close. I nuzzled my face into his chest and a wave of murky emotion swept through me. It was fear, mingled with pride, mingled with the terrible uncertainty that haunted our lives. I pulled away.

'But, Markus, that's so dangerous!'

'Not really. At least, not right now. But don't you see: if I can win their trust, if I can play the part well, who knows? Who knows where it will lead? We have to use all the weapons we can, Leah, and the most important thing is to get behind the scenes to know what these devils are up to. The only way to do that—'

'—is to break all your personal rules. To be someone you're not, so as to investigate.'

He held me at arm's length, then, and we gazed earnestly into each other's eyes.

'But can you do that, Markus? Can you maintain the façade of being complicit, over time?'

'I don't know, Leah. That's why... well, anyway, let me tell you what happened. Once I'd passed the test, given the salute, spoken the desired words, all went wonderfully well, from both sides. They told me about the plans for the airport and gave me a tour of the site. I have to say, it's magnificent. If they get it done, it's going to be the most technologically advanced airport in the world. But they also tested my knowledge, and I passed with flying colours. They'd read my final dissertation and called it brilliant. They loved me, as an engineer. One of them praised my very Aryan looks: he said I looked like the quintessential hero Hitler's looking for. The kind of hero they'd put on posters encouraging young people to sign up! Tall, blond, handsome.'

I pulled away. 'I never thought of you as vain!'

He only laughed. 'Don't you see, that's a good thing! It's my best disguise!'

'So they offered you the job?'

'Not quite, but from what they said it seems certain they will.'

'And you? You're certain?'

He hesitated then. 'I'll have to, Leah,' he said eventually. 'I told you: rejecting it would put a target on my back. But it'll mean a totally different kind of work and I won't be able to do my undercover work any more. I'll have to be so very careful. It means keeping up the pretence maybe over years, just waiting for a chance to do some good. This is just an airport, after all, and I'm just an engineer. I'll hardly be working in Hitler's head-quarters. But on the other hand...'

A strange light burned in his eyes, a light that hadn't been there before.

'Go on!'

'At the same time, it's Hitler's pet project. He takes a personal interest in it. It's his personal vanity venture, a thing he wants to showcase to the world. And you know what? He comes regularly to inspect it. To be shown its progress, to revel in the sheer grandeur of the project. He's involved in every step, every little innovation. He inspects the blueprints and the 3D models. And, Leah, my mind has been working non-stop since the interview. I can't help it...'

He paused, and then continued: 'Leah, what I'm about to tell you is absolutely, one hundred per cent, confidential. You cannot let even a whisper of it leave your lips. You cannot tell your best friends nor your parents nor anybody. Do you understand?'

I nodded. There was a lump in my throat and I swallowed it down. 'Go on.'

'Yes. Hitler comes to Tempelhof regularly. But what if... what if...?'

I frowned, and tried to read his face, his quizzical smile, the elated glow in his eyes. What if... what?

His eyes gleamed now with a passion I'd never seen before. A zeal was there: alive in them, a fire, a fervency. And a strange thing happened. It was as if his eyes could speak, and my eyes could listen. In silence he told me. He did not need words. I knew. I knew with all my being, with every cell of my body, exactly why Markus was going to become a Nazi. Clarity struck like lightning.

I had never understood the saying *My blood ran cold* before. It seemed such a cliché. But now I did. It was as if every vein in my body had turned to ice. I struggled to find words, but my tongue seemed sewn to the floor of my mouth. Eventually everything in me erupted and I flung myself at him.

'Markus! No!'

He wrapped his arms round me and there we sat, folded together, both weeping.

'No! No, Markus, you can't do that, you can't—'

He quickly placed a finger on my lips. 'Shhh, Leah, don't say it out loud. Never say it out loud. It's not for you to know. You never heard it from me. But... yes!'

'No, no, no, Markus! Don't even think it! You can't! And-and... it's so dangerous! How could you? They'd find out! They-they'd be ruthless! They'd...' I whispered the last forbidden words: '...kill you.'

'But, Leah, just imagine. Wouldn't it be magnificent?'

I threw myself against him then. 'Please, please, Markus. Don't take the job. Please don't take it. Please don't even think of that... that terrible thing.'

'Well, they haven't even offered me the job yet.'

I fervently hoped they would turn him down. Choose another candidate, a loyal Nazi. Not my Markus.

He stroked my head, so gently, so lovingly. 'Don't worry, mouse. Please don't worry. Or if you have to worry, worry about yourself, about keeping safe from those monsters. Don't worry about me. Please don't. Maybe I won't even get the job.'

But he *was* offered the job, and he accepted it. He told me the very next week.

I wept.

I wept openly. He took both my hands in his and held them tight and looked straight into my eyes. What I read in his own eyes – well. What I read there confirmed everything I believed about Markus. I knew he would go to any lengths to stop this thing.

And yet, and yet. The price he had to pay... pretending to be a Nazi, day after day, maybe year after year. The constant propaganda, the constant brainwashing. Magda had succumbed to it from the start. Being bombarded with it day in, day out would require an unimaginable mental armour. Was

Markus up to it? Could he be corrupted, the way Magda had been?

The next time I saw Markus I finally found the words that had stuck in my gorge at our last meeting. The direness of both our situations finally forced me to stop hiding my head in the sand and to face the facts. We were both in terrible danger: he with this ridiculous plan he had concocted, this dangerous job he had accepted; and I, for the simple fact of being a Jew. We met, as usual, at Sonnenhof, where I now spent almost every weekend. Markus came out whenever he could. He slept with me in my tent; inevitably, as the weeks went by, we had also become closer physically and we were now an established couple, and recognised as such by everyone who came to the island. And so, three weeks after the conversation that had caused me such devastation, I once again tried to change his mind as we sat together in the little tent, only a flickering candle flame as light.

'Please, Markus. Don't do it. Don't do this terrible thing. Play the game, if necessary, keep the job and play the game, but let that be all there is to it. Just be a good engineer, not a spy. You cannot possibly keep up the façade. You cannot do this thing. They will find out. They will kill you! They are not fools – these are Nazis.'

'You have so little faith in me?'

'It's not that I don't have faith in you. It's that I fear *them*. I fear for you. No career is worth this risk. Promise you won't.'

He sighed then, put an arm round me, drew me closer.

'I can't promise, Leah. I know myself well enough to know that, given the opportunity, if there's even the slightest possibility... I wouldn't be true to myself otherwise.'

I knew he had to do it. He wouldn't be Markus if he didn't.

He'd already agreed to take the job. And now his mind had

a new and perilous focus: to get close to Hitler. To assassinate Hitler.

Much as I wanted it done, I didn't want Markus to be the one to do it.

Markus's father, whom I had always known as Onkel Reinhold, took the rift in his family particularly hard. He was, of course, Tante Gundhilde's brother, and knew of her leanings. But he was also Tante Helga's husband, and a kinder, more Christian woman has never walked the Earth. Obviously, what with Magda being who she was, Aaron in prison, and Markus a secret dissident, things had grown most awkward between the two sets of parents. Our mothers rarely knocked on each other's door to borrow some ingredient, and our fathers no longer exchanged newspapers. It was a sad state of affairs.

Then, one night in the summer of 1938, there came a furious rapping at our door. I opened it, and there stood Tante Helga, obviously in a panic.

'Leah! Quick, quick!' she cried, pushing past me into the flat. 'Eli! Eli!' Her voice was hysterical, terrified. Without waiting to be invited – she had not been in our home for years – she burst into the living room, where Father and Mother were both reading. I followed her, and saw Father jump to his feet. 'What's the matter, Helga?' he asked.

'It's Reinhold! Oh, Eli! I think he's having a heart attack!'

Tante Helga was a nurse, but this was beyond her expertise. She babbled on as Father pulled on his shoes: 'He had an angina attack earlier on and I gave him two aspirin, but then he passed out and I tried CPR but it didn't work, and...'

We didn't hear the rest. Father, medical bag in hand, rushed out the door with Tante Helga, down the hall to their flat. I wanted to follow, but Mother held me back. 'You'll only be in the way,' she told me sternly.

And so we both waited in anxiety until Father returned. 'He's going to be all right, I think,' he said. 'I gave him nitroglycerin. That helped. But I advised that he be taken to hospital for observation.'

We had the only telephone on the floor, and so Father picked up the receiver and made the call. About half an hour later we all watched as the emergency crew carried Onkel Reinhold away on a stretcher.

Tante Helga later came weeping to us and explained that Onkel had been admitted for a few days so that he could be stabilised.

'Thank you, thank you so much, Eli!' she said, still bawling her heart out. 'We don't deserve it, I know. I promise to be a better neighbour in future.'

And she was. Hardly a day passed when Tante Helga did not bring some treat over to us; it might be a cake, or a cut of beef from her mother's cattle, or a bag of apples, or a bowl of butter, also fresh from the farm. And though we could never be seen outside the building having even a casual conversation, Tante Helga once more became part of my life.

22

MAGDA

I swear, and you must believe me, Leah, that I knew nothing of what was to happen in advance, on the day of 9 November 1938. Oh, I had picked up a hint or two. I had been to a meeting in one of Berlin's town halls, and as it came to a close the SS leader asked us if we'd like to participate in a 'special action' that night.

I was not even vaguely interested. The meeting had been extremely boring, and I longed for home, which at the time was that small room in a Kreuzberg converted mansion. There I had a table and my trusty old typewriter, and I had started that book I had promised myself I'd write. That inspiring book that would one day be read, I hoped, by every young German. I would write it in an engaging, populist style so as to inspire young people. It would light up their hearts just as my own had once been lit up. So I, and many of the other attendees of the meeting, declined to take part in that 'action', whatever it was.

I am so glad I didn't go, Leah. You know why.

The following morning on my way to work, I walked through one of the cobbled side roads that would take me to my

*office, and I was surprised to see all the shop windows that
lined the street had been smashed. The pavements were filled
with broken glass. The shop windows were empty holes, and it
was plain to see that some had been raided of whatever
contents they'd once held. Everywhere I walked, broken glass
crunched beneath my shoes. Large jagged-edged pieces of pane
lay on pavements blanketed with shards and tiny slivers.
Everywhere, shattered glass, sharp and ugly and threatening.*

And everywhere, painted in big, ugly, black letters: JUDEN
RAUS! *Jews Out!*

*When I arrived at work, I asked the office manager what
had happened. He snickered.*

*'Oh, you know. All of those shops were owned by Jews. It's
long past time to give them a clear message.'*

'A clear message? You don't mean...'

*'Of course I mean that. It's time to stop pussyfooting
around the matter. Out with them all! We want a Germany
free of that scum!'*

*I swear to you, Leah, that was the first time it was spelled
out to me in such unambiguous words. You probably don't
believe me. I can hardly believe it myself; after all, I had read*
Mein Kampf *and I knew what Hitler thought about Jews.*

*But eliminate them all? I truly had not known that that
was the final aim. Or maybe I had known, but had suppressed
the knowledge, pushed it so deeply into the dark regions of my
mind that it never surfaced, not even as a hint.*

*Just as I had suppressed any discomfort when it came to
discrimination against Jews, just as I looked away whenever I
saw a sign saying* Jews Not Wanted, *just as I refused to read*
Der Stürmer *with its disgusting attacks on the Jewry, just as I
walked away from any conversation that maligned Jews, or at
least shut my ears and never joined in: so, too, had I disre-
garded any hint that Germany should, one day, be free of Jews.*
Judenfrei. *I had heard the term, but I had never, once, taken it*

*seriously. I swear it, Leah. I swear to God. I know you don't
think much of my faith in God, but more of that later. For now,
I simply beg you to believe me.*

LEAH – BERLIN

That night, that 9 November 1938: that was the breaking point.
Kristallnacht. The Night of Broken Glass. The night they
showed their face and let us know, finally know without a
doubt, that they meant serious business.

Father had been working late that evening; he often did,
these days. He was more dedicated than ever to his patients,
and long after nightfall he'd still be seeing some of the poorer
Jews who could not afford to pay the full fees now that their
health insurance no longer paid. In some of these cases he made
house visits, sometimes only coming home at midnight.

That night, Father did not come home.

He came home in the early hours of the tenth, a broken
wreck of a man.

Mother had been up all night waiting for him. She had tried
to ring his practice, again and again, but there had been no
reply. I had tried to stay awake to keep her company, but had
eventually given in and gone to bed, but only to a restless half-
sleep; I'd woken up every half an hour, got up to check if Papa
was home yet, and gone back to bed for another restless session.

Mother, exhausted, had fallen asleep on the living room
couch when finally, my father's key turned in the lock. I'd left
my bedroom door open and, on high alert as I was, I heard it,
sprang up and ran to the living room.

Mother was holding Father in her arms. He was bleeding
from a head wound. He could hardly speak; he seemed dazed,
stammering out words we could not understand.

'Leah, run quickly and fetch Helga,' Mother said, and I was
out the door in a flash. It was an unearthly hour before dawn,

and she'd still be asleep, so I pressed the doorbell and kept my right thumb on it, and at the same time hammered on the door with my left hand, and called out: 'Tante Helga! Tante Helga! Open up!'

Eventually she came to the door, a shawl wrapped round her shoulders, in her long nightgown, her hair bundled into a nightcap.

'Father's been hurt!' I cried. 'Please, please come over!'

She was wide awake in a flash. 'Of course!' she said. 'Just let me get my dressing gown.'

'Is... is Markus at home?' I asked.

She shook her head. 'He didn't even come home from work yesterday,' she said. 'Now let's see to Eli.'

And oh, what a morning it turned out to be.

Father by now had fallen unconscious; together, Mother and I had helped him to the bedroom and when Tante Helga and I got back to the flat he was lying on the bed, Mother dabbing at his head wound with a folded towel.

Tante Helga, in the doorway, said 'Jesus Christ!' and turned right round again.

'There's a medical cupboard in the bathroom,' Mother called after her.

'I know!' she called back, and soon returned with her arms full of bandages, lotions, medical implements. She set to work immediately, cleaning and bandaging the gash on Father's head. He had concussion, she said; it was a miracle he'd been able to find his way home, to even walk. But that wasn't all. When Mother removed his shirt, she found his upper body bruised and battered; in fact, the bruises were just forming and would turn violently purple and black over the next few days.

Tante Helga gently touched his hand, which hung limp, and he flinched. 'I think it's broken,' she said.

'What can we do?' wept Mother. We all knew that Jews were banned from almost all Berlin hospitals.

'We'll take him to the Jewish hospital,' said Tante Helga. She was the picture of calm efficiency. 'But not now. Tomorrow, when things have calmed down. I'll put a temporary splint on it.'

'What things? What's going on?' I asked.

'I don't know, but something definitely is,' said Tante Helga grimly. 'You should have heard the noise outside, all last night. Red Baron Street seemed to be having a street party. Shouting and cheering, rowdy bands creating havoc.'

Father was slowly coming to, shaking his head from side to side and groaning. Mother, on Tante Helga's instructions, had fetched a wooden spoon from the kitchen and Tante Helga had made a splint for his wrist.

Father was beginning to talk, but he didn't make sense, not yet. He only murmured names, and asked how a Herr Gold-schmidt was, and if his office was locked. We reassured him that everything was in order, though of course none of us really had any idea.

At about 6 a.m. there was a knock in the door. I opened it, and there stood Markus. No words were spoken. We exchanged a look that said everything. He came in and sat with us, and it was from him that we heard what had happened on Kristall-nacht. Markus, defying his own decision to refrain from further underground activity, had been active all night, it seemed, working in a Kreuzberg cellar that had been a sort of temporary refuge for threatened Jews, some of whom had managed to flee in the early hours of the destruction.

Markus had till now labelled all the little acts of anti-Jewish aggression as the thin edge of the wedge. 'The axe has fallen,' he said now. 'It's open warfare.'

But for my family, the axe had fallen long before Kristall-nacht. It had fallen at Aaron's arrest. We could put his arrest down as a consequence of his own actions. But this was different.

These Jewish shop owners whose businesses were attacked that 9 November: they had done nothing. They were just innocent businesspeople trying to make a living. How could a simple Jewish cobbler, or clockmaker, or haberdasher, be in any way responsible for Germany's economic woes? Yet that was the excuse the Nazis gave for the wanton destruction of their lives. Broken glass. That was the symbol for all that was to come. That night, that day, we had no inkling where it would end, but we felt, deep inside, that a nightmare worse than anything we had imagined was just about to begin.

We knew now without a doubt that this was not just a temporary insanity from which Germany would one day soon wake up, shake its sleepy head, ask, 'What just happened?' and return to normal. There was no longer a *normal* to return to. Or rather, *this* was now normal. Anyone could now be attacked at any time for any reason. Being Jewish was in itself a crime. And it was about to get worse.

My parents had been taking it seriously enough since Aaron's arrest, but on that night a new sense of urgency overcame us all. There was no more hiding one's head in the sand. This, we all knew now, was just the beginning.

23

LEAH – BERLIN

Unknown to us at the time, it was not only us, and not only Jews; the entire world woke up on that night. The entire world had been watching and worrying on behalf of Germany's Jews and now the world – or at least, the United Kingdom – finally decided it was time to take action.

Soon after Kristallnacht, an appeal went out on the BBC Home Service asking for British families to come forward if they were willing to foster a Jewish child from the endangered area. In no time, hundreds of offers came in, and volunteers began to visit possible foster homes to assess their eligibility. The foster families did not have to be Jewish; all that was required was that they seemed respectable and capable of caring for children, and that the homes were clean.

As soon as they heard of this action – which was called the Kindertransport – my parents applied for my youngest brother Samuel to be sent to England. A volunteer came to our home to assess his eligibility. Samuel, three years younger than me, was fast approaching his eighteenth birthday; that meant he was only just still eligible under the age criteria. There were other criteria too. Priority was given to the children who were most in peril: teenagers who were in danger of arrest, Polish children or youths threatened with deportation or residing in Jewish orphanages. Young people with impoverished parents, or with a parent in a concentration camp.

None of these criteria applied to us. We were too well off, my parents upright and well-adjusted citizens. But during the interview – at which I was present – my mother broke down.

'I already have one son in a concentration camp! Already our family is being watched! Please, please take my little boy!'

Somehow, Mother's heartbreaking appeal won the interviewer over. Two weeks later we received news that Samuel had been accepted for the Kindertransport. He was given a January date when his train would take him away.

My eldest brother Mosche was also in luck. Now married to his sweetheart Rachel, to whom he had been engaged for a while, he too was about to leave. His father-in-law, a prominent cardiac surgeon from Hamburg, had a brother in the US who had agreed to sponsor the entire family. They had been issued visas; their departure, too, was planned for late 1938. Now there was just me, Mother and Father living at Kaiserkorso Eins.

There was no hiding from the facts. We might cling to our home, but 'home' by now was little more than a sentimental idea. Germany was no longer our home, as Markus reminded me day after day. And now, Mother and Father conceded that it was over. One evening soon after Kristallnacht, they too were forced to confront the problem, and to force me into confronting it.

'We will have to leave,' Father said.

Those were the words I'd been dreading, and to hear them spoken out loud was heartbreaking. It meant we'd reached the end of hope, when hope had been all we'd had to cling to. Hope had been a raft that had carried us across such choppy waters. That raft was about to capsize.

'But where will we go?' The words came from my lips, broken and desperate. There was nowhere for us to flee to. We had discussed leaving the country years ago, but you really had to have a sponsor in another country, like Mosche's in-laws, and we didn't. The only relative we had abroad was a distant cousin of Father's in Warsaw, whom we'd never met, and of course Warsaw was as bad as or worse than Berlin. Perhaps Mosche, once he was settled in the US, could send for us; but that would take years. And even those who had relatives abroad were often denied visas, despite spending hours in long queues at all the foreign embassies. Our faith that Germany would wake up from the nightmare had been broken, and it was too late: there was nowhere to go. We were trapped, in the country that was supposed to be our home.

'Leah,' said Father now, gently. 'Germany is now engaged in civil war, and nobody knows the outcome. We should have left as a family years ago, but we refused to accept the signs and now it is too late. No Jew is safe in Berlin, and, much as it goes against everything I believe in, we will all have to hide. And...'

They looked at each other and I saw an expression of immense sadness pass between them.

'We will have to separate,' said Father. 'We will be dependent on Germans willing to hide us in their homes – a risk for them. We, your mother and I, have found a family who will take us in. A colleague, a doctor, will take us into his home... but there is room for only two, for us two; your mother and myself. I said he should take you instead, but he thinks it will be easier for you to find a refuge on your own, than we would. So...'

'So, I will be on my own? In hiding?'

Father nodded.

'We will find a place for you, too!' Mother said. 'We will not go until we know that you are safe. We will never leave you, but, just as we have sent Samuel away, so we must prepare to lose our last remaining child.'

She wept then and wrapped me in her arms. 'Oh, Leah, Leah! We must get through this. We must survive, all of us!'

I wept with her. A young person relies on his or her parents to provide that safe haven called home, and it is probably ingrained in all of us that wherever they are is our home.

I knew that survival for any one of us would be in God's hands. We all prayed together, then. It was the only thing we could do. Father recited the Hashkiveinu, the Jewish prayer of seeking comfort through the night. In this case, the night was not just the end of the day; night would be the long, terrifying darkness that lay ahead. Night would be the unknown future, as we prepared ourselves to retreat from the daylight of living openly in our own country. It was to be the night of hiding, of separation from our most dearly loved ones. Father prayed slowly and solemnly. All our cheeks were wet as he invoked protection.

'Grant, O God, that we lie down in peace, and raise us up, our Guardian, to life renewed. Spread over us the shelter of Your peace. Guide us with Your good counsel; for Your Name's sake, be our help. Shield and shelter us beneath the shadow of Your wings. Defend us against enemies, illness, war, famine and sorrow. Distance us from wrongdoing. For You, God, watch over us and deliver us. For You, God, are gracious and merciful. Guard our going and coming, to life and to peace evermore.'

MAGDA

Oh, Leah! As I sit here writing on this old typewriter I can almost feel you here, sitting beside me. I feel your presence. I want to put my arm round you, hug you. To say sorry, from the

*bottom of my heart. Sorry I was not the one to protect you.
That I was on the side of those who wanted to destroy you.*

*Slowly but surely, we were administered the poison. We
absorbed the poison. And slowly but surely, I, your best friend,
I too absorbed it. I was so young, Leah, when they first administered it. How could a fifteen-year-old girl know that it was
the wrong choice? How could I refuse the poison, when it was
whispered into my ear, shouted from the rooftops, at every turn
I made?*

*As a young girl I truly didn't realise what was happening.
How could I?*

*I did not at all make the connection between my liking for,
and friendship with, individual Jews and the frightening
image of the repulsive Jews we were being fed. We took no note
of the contradiction. We were friendly with our Jewish neighbours and we had Jewish friends; this had technically nothing
to do with 'the Jews'. 'The Jews' were a nebulous collective of
the secular and the Orthodox: intellectuals, university graduates, professors of literature, doctors, lawyers; skullcap-wearing
rabbis, but also carpenters and plumbers and shopkeepers,
greengrocers with carts at the local markets; Yiddish-speaking
housewives, jewellers, haberdashers, communist agents, Zion-
ists, medal-wearing ex-officers, tradesmen. They were everywhere. And slowly, gradually, we were being weaponised
against them. They were not real Germans. They were the
enemy.*

*They were not our friends and neighbours. They were a
menacing anonymous horde. They were wicked, the bogeyman. They were a progression from the wicked witches and
wizards of our childhood fairy tales, and they were out to
destroy us well-behaved Germans and take away our prosper-
ity, our jobs, our way of life.*

*I never put you in the same category as 'the Jews'. You and
your family were different. Your father was much-respected in*

the entire neighbourhood. He was a doctor who had been awarded the Iron Cross in the war, a kindly man who would treat the poor even if they could not afford his fees. I liked your brothers, and for a while I even had a crush on Aaron. How could things go so dreadfully wrong?

PART TWO: WAR

24

LEAH – BEXHILL-ON-SEA

Since opening the letter I'd been reading almost non-stop, getting up only for lavatory breaks and to make myself a cup of tea or grab an apple. I had not cooked, not slept. That letter held me spellbound. With every word, Magda had been drawing me more and more into her depraved life.

It was now midnight. And time to take stock. Now and then while reading, I'd felt floods of nostalgia, understanding, even sympathy overtaking the basic longstanding sense of betrayal that had separated me from Magda all these years. But now, reading those last words, the decision Markus had made came back to me with full force and a wave of unmitigated, uncensored rage came over me.

Markus had made a choice: but so too had Magda.

I had to stop reading. I needed to scream out loud. I needed to see her before me, shout at her, maybe even slap that smug trying-to-be-kindly pseudo-tolerant grin off her face. And I did. I jumped to my feet, right there in my cosy safe Bexhill-on-Sea living room, and yelled at her.

'NO!' I screamed. 'A thousand times no!'

I am not sitting next to you at your desk listening and

nodding attentively in understanding, while you spout off about how much you loved me and my family and how broad-minded you were, and how you admired my father, and how I was the best friend you shared everything with! You cannot force me to read your filthy justifications – and according to you, we haven't even reached the really bad part yet! All this is just a build-up to ease me into a coma of empathy, so that, once you have spouted all the vile actions you want to confess, I will forgive you! You seek redemption with me but I cannot give it – only God can give that, or one of your Catholic priests in the confession box!

I don't care how much perception you have gained over the post-war years. This so-called perception is a result of Germany losing the bloody war! Had you won there would have been no hand-wringing *mea culpa*, no tears of contrition, no begging for forgiveness!

I want to vomit. I want to throw this damn letter in the fire! I want to dig out your eyes! I will never forgive you, not ever! The only reason I have read to this point is to learn the depth of your depravity, and no amount of sweetening it up with all your saccharine tales of how good you really were deep inside, no amount of sugar-coating can erase that. I'm not sure I can bear to read further. I don't want to know. What good will knowing do? It won't bring back the dead.

The thing is, Magda, and I wish you were sitting – no, standing – with me now so that I could tell you to your face in no uncertain words: YOU HAD A CHOICE.

Letting me know that you are basically a decent person who knew good from evil changes nothing. Letting me know you were brainwashed as a very young person changes nothing. YOU HAD A CHOICE. You could have listened to your mother, your brother, your father, but you chose not to. You *chose* to listen to Tante Gundhilde and all the Nazi monsters and that choice remains with you. No excuse!

In a way you are even worse than a Nazi who was not raised

in goodness, in the true Christian spirit, because that person did not have the choice to turn from evil. You had the choice and you chose evil, so you must carry that guilt: forever.

I cannot read on. There's only so much of your so-called confession I can take in one day. I need to sleep. I will go to bed. It is past midnight. Tomorrow, there is laundry to be done and I need to go shopping. I will go to bed and try to sleep. Tomorrow I will make the decision to either read on, or destroy this creepy, sneaky way to get into my good books and my heart. But I can tell you right here and now: NEVER!

25

MAGDA

*If you don't mind, I'll jump forward a bit. A year later, almost.
September 1939. Germany marched into Poland, against the
warnings of the British and French leaders, who immediately
declared war on us.*

*And so we were at war once again. Who could believe
such a thing? Up to now, 1939 had been a brilliant year for me
and my BDM friends. It had been a summer of pure sunshine
and joy. Yes, there were rumours and rumblings of an outbreak
of war: but what young person takes such warnings seriously?
We went for lazy trips on lakes, we swam and splashed in cool
waters, we frolicked in gardens and held midnight campfires
and admired the night sky. It was an idyllic year.*

*Not for Jews, of course; but we BDM girls resolutely closed
our ears and eyes to anything that would mar our blue-eyed
vision of where Germany was heading. We did not acknowledge the suffering of others, those close to us, people we had
once been friends with. Mama told me in her letters that there
was no longer health insurance for Jewish patients. Jewish
doctors were only allowed to treat Jewish patients, and they
had to pay for treatment themselves, treatment hardly anyone*

could afford as they were losing their jobs, their businesses, left, right and centre.

Mama wrote:

Poor Dr Gottlieb! He is really struggling to keep afloat, and since that attack on Kristallnacht he is a shadow of himself. You know him – he always treated the poorest of the poor without charge. And I told you how he saved Papa's life after that heart attack. We are so indebted to him. But now, even those who had once been rich have no money.

Magda: you must be honest with me. You must tell me the truth. Is it true that Jews are being sent away to camps in Poland, never to be seen again? It surely cannot be true; but the rumours are everywhere. Please tell me, Magda, and tell me you are not a part of such an atrocity!

I destroyed Mama's letters of complaint. They were dangerous. Anyone complaining about the new rules and laws could land in trouble. Anyone showing any support for the Jews could be arrested. Mama was taking a great risk, putting her fears into words in a letter – and to me! What if one of my colleagues was to read those letters?

I wore my blindfold with ease and enjoyed that final pre-war year with as much gusto as possible. It was as if in refusing to accept the ugliness of reality, the very revulsion we all felt deep inside propelled us into a gratification of all the senses. To indulge in any and all sources of entertainment, of false pleasure, false laughter, false gaiety.

Oh yes, that was a good year, 1939. Before it all fell to pieces. We refused to see the cracks. We rejected reality. We were the offspring of parents who had lived through the previous war, and we had grown up with stories of suffering and deprivation. With the megalomania of youth, we refused to accept that this was our fate too. That the shadow of war hung, a dark cloud, on the horizon; that even as we enjoyed the last sunny summer days that black cloud hovered there, menacing, not promising more sunshine and laughter, but threatening the end of days. That it was over. That it was the last summer we'd ever know sunshine and gladness.

So yes, we were stunned as the news of war hit us. That dream of Grossdeutschland had turned into the awful nightmare of war. But, Leah, you know me. There's not much that can keep me down for long, and I quickly rallied my strength and my optimism. Poland, I reasoned, was now ours. The Führer knew best. This was the start of Grossdeutschland, and I had a part to play in it all. I was ready. We all were. We were stalwarts, after all, and Hitler was our living example. He had lived through the Great War as a soldier, as a hero, and he knew first-hand the misery of war. He had obviously done all he could to prevent a new one; if there had been even the slightest hope for peace he would have grasped it. It wasn't our Führer's fault that he had failed.

And now, all we could do was be brave and follow his instructions. This was the way we could, one day, all live in peace and freedom – which, after all, is what every German wanted. So, Leah, with such hollow arguments I excused Hitler and validated the war. The end justified the means. There was going to be one Reich, one Vaterland, and we would all put our shoulders to the plough to make it happen. Or, as may be, march forward into battle. In England you have that hymn, 'Onward, Christian Soldiers'. The analogy of war as a Christian aim seemed perfectly fitting: we were soldiers in a great battle that would finally fulfil our dream. We were ready for combat, loins girded. Oh, the clichés! They pushed us into lunacy.

I'm not going to waste your time discussing how I felt then about the displacement of Jews in the Sudetenland, or about who I thought the land belonged to, and who had a right to be where. You will probably be sick and tired of all the discus-

sions and orders that were going on at the time. I will cut to the
chase. I will tell you what I did, personally, because that's
what this whole letter is about. It's not a geography or a history
lesson. It's a mea culpa. *And I need to get it off my chest.*

Quite literally: there's a burning sensation right here in my
heart region, like a swelling, and in it is a silent voice insisting
on being heard, and it needs to be heard. By you. So here goes.
Before you start to read I am asking you with all my heart,
when you realise what is about to unfold, not to ball up the
letter in a fit of rage and throw it in the fire. Please. Listen.
Read.

LEAH – SONNENHOF

Markus began his work at Tempelhof in early 1939. So much
had changed since then. Aaron, as far as we knew, was still
working at Siemens as a political prisoner. Samuel had been
sent to England and goodness knew when or if we'd ever see
him again. Mother and Father were planning to go into hiding,
and were only waiting for me, too, to be settled. We all relied on
Markus to help.

Markus, in the meantime, was playing a dangerous game.
He had called himself a wolf in sheep's clothing, but it was actually the other way round. He was the sheep – the innocent,
good, one – entering the wolf's lair. How could he possibly
maintain that role, pretend to be a Nazi, a Jew-hater?

'How can you do it, Markus? How can you?' I asked him
again and again when he came to Sonnenhof in early May.
After the winter, Lisa von Berg and her loyal troupe were back
and the new season of planting had begun. This year, there
were far fewer of us. The threat of war had changed everything.

'I can do it, because I know it's for a good cause,' he said.
'It's true I have to be more careful than ever now, but really it's

no worse than an acting job. The only difference is that now I have to play a role in real life.'

That much was true. 'But this isn't just a game, Markus. It's civil war. And your real life is filled with peril. It could get you killed!'

'I know. You just have to trust me in this, mouse. Remember I am doing it for you, for Germany, for all of us.'

He shook his head and the expression of sadness on his face, a play of light and shadow in the flickering candlelight of our tent, was almost too much to bear.

'Tell me, Markus. Tell me about your work. I know you've kept it secret to protect me but now there can be no more secrets between us. Because I know your biggest secret.'

He nodded. 'You're right. It's time for you to know.'

He drew me closer yet, and then began to speak. Slowly, each word leaving his lips filled with so much weight I could actually feel the burden of his admission accumulating within me, heavy, powerful, formidable.

'It started with Aaron,' he said. 'He got himself involved with a Jewish organisation, a young married couple, Herbert and Marianne. I won't tell you their last name so as not to compromise you, and maybe them, but they are quite a force in the Jewish underground of Berlin. Anyway: Herbert and Marianne had met as very young members of the Young Communist League – you remember, Aaron was a member too. They've managed to organise a network of nearly a hundred young Germans, most of them Jewish, who oppose the Nazis. You know how Aaron was arrested? It's because of his membership of this group. I was one of the few non-Jewish members and managed to stay undetected. The group became a kind of refuge for young Jewish members who had not managed to escape.'

'People like me,' I said. 'Why did you not tell me, Markus?

Why didn't Aaron tell me? I'd have loved to be a member of such a group.'

'We wanted to protect you, Leah. We both did. Being a group member was dangerous. You saw what happened to Aaron. When they arrested him that second time, God only knows what they did with him. I couldn't let that happen to you. Aaron made me promise to keep you safe.'

'You should have let me decide that,' I said, but squeezed his hand to let him know I was not angry, just disappointed.

'Anyway, it soon became clear that our work could not just be confined to Jews. We needed Germans as well, anti-Nazi Germans who were willing to work underground so as to protect Jews. The parents, for example, of our young members as well as they themselves. As the years passed, we became aware that everything would only get worse. That Hitler was building towards an all-out war against Jews. That they'd have to escape to survive that war and those who couldn't escape – they'd have to hide somewhere in Berlin. And only Germans could hide them. So a group split off from the original group.

'I was at the spearhead of the new group. It consisted of young people who would try to make contact with ordinary Germans prepared to help Jews, hide them in their homes if need be. So that's what we've been doing over the years. Slowly finding out who can help. Which families, which households, would be willing to not only hide a couple of Jews but maintain them, protect them from discovery.'

'And you've found people who'll do that?'

He nodded. 'Yes! There are good Germans, Leah. Brave Germans, who'll take the risk. It's not easy finding them because obviously we can't ask directly. But some members of the group had accommodating and helpful family members. Parents, aunts, uncles, grandparents, who pledged to help. And now, for me it's personal. I've been looking for a place for you, in Berlin, but it's hard. We have so many fugitives on the list. Mothers, with small children. Old women, people who're ill and need care. They get priority, mouse, before strong and healthy young people like you.'

'Of course you have to give them priority.'

'I'm doing my best. Of course I am. But nothing's come up, and I can't show favouritism by pushing you to the front of the queue.'

'Of course not. But I feel terrible, knowing that my parents have somewhere to go but they're waiting for me to go first.'

He hugged me. 'I'll keep on looking, privately. If push comes to shove, there's always my grandparents' place in Bavaria. They hate Hitler. I think I can persuade them to hide you, but it would mean getting you down and across-country into Bavaria. That's tricky, and dangerous.'

'Oh, Markus! I'd hate to put your grandparents in danger! I'd hate to put any German in danger. I hate that I put you in danger, just by loving you, and you loving me.'

'That's what it means to love someone, Leah. Don't even think about it.'

That was my Markus. My beloved Markus.

Later, he told me more about his work, and the problems involved, and how it came into being. I was so impressed, so touched, I flung my arms round him and pulled him close and kissed him all over his face

'Oh, Markus. I love you so much. So much. If only...'

He kissed me back. Stroked my hair, my face, with gentle fingers. 'I know, my little mouse. I love you too. If only this was all over, and we could build a life.'

'Do you believe we ever can?'

In the candlelight I half saw, half felt, that he nodded. 'We will win,' he whispered. 'There is a great power, a power of righteousness and justice. That power will win. There will be peace, there will be freedom again. For all of us.'

'But not for all, Markus. Some of the righteous people have already lost.'

'Not for all,' he agreed. 'We can only pray that we'll be among the lucky ones.'

'But if we aren't?'

'Don't even think it, my love.'

He blew out the candle, and we nestled down beneath the blankets, warm in the comfort of our love and our desperation and our longing for peace on Earth.

And then it came, the day we were all dreading. It was just Lisa, me, Trude, Dieter, and Lisa's eldest daughter, Hiltrud. Markus was not with me on the island that weekend; he couldn't always get away to make the long journey. But on Friday, 1 September, Lisa gathered us all together. We all knew what was coming as we took our seats around the long oak table. Trude gently patted my shoulder. Lisa squeezed my hand. And then that hated voice, that voice that drove daggers of terror through my being, boomed over the transistor radio. After much prevarication, Hitler finally came to the point:

> *This night for the first time Polish regular soldiers fired on our territory. Since 5:45 a.m. we have been returning the fire, and from now on bombs will be met by bombs.*

And though we had all been prepared, a horrified gasp went around the table. I burst into tears, and so did Trude. She and Dieter clung to each other. Lisa edged close to me and, stony-faced herself, allowed me to cry into her shoulder. Hiltrud stood up. 'I think we need a drop of brandy,' she said, and walked off to fetch it.

On the following Sunday came the response from Neville Chamberlain in Downing Street, London. Lisa of course received the BBC's German service and we all listened, this time without tears, as an unemotional voice gave us the German translation of the words that would usher in the next chapter of the nightmare:

> *This morning the British ambassador in Berlin handed the German government a final note stating that unless we heard from them by 11 o'clock that they were prepared at once to withdraw their troops from Poland, a state of war would exist between us. I have to tell you now that no such undertaking has been received, and that consequently this country is at war with Germany.*

So that was it. This was war. There was nothing left for it but to find out how we could protect ourselves.

26

MAGDA

Leah, I am prevaricating. Everything in me is telling me to skip this part. We have arrived at the crux of the matter, and I don't want to continue this letter. In fact, I put it away for three months to avoid finishing it. I don't want you to know. And yet I must confess. This whole letter is worthless if I do not. At least on paper. Will I ever send it to you? Right now, I do not know.

I am right now sitting at my kitchen table – you know the one. The one where we once all sat together sharing one of Mama's beef stews, laughing and joking together without a care in the world. Now I sit here all alone, my old typewriter before me. Yes, I am back, but so much has changed. West Berlin is an island, contained by a wall. Fortunately, Kaiserkorso Eins is on the right side of that wall, and so I am free to travel back and forth; but right now, here I am, at the table.

The kitchen is basically bare. There are a few potatoes in the pantry and two green apples in the fruit basket on the table. Some old bread in the breadbasket. In the fridge, there is butter and cheese – bread and cheese being my staple at the moment. I am thin; I do not eat much. I say this not for sympathy but just so you can make a picture of my present state. And again, I am prevaricating. I do not want to tell you this. But I must.

My job was clear. I was to be the bearer of good news. I had been working as a journalist for years now, of course, practically since my teens when I had started writing BDM propaganda. Now, I was given a camera and some training in how to use it. I was to go eastwards. The campaign for Grossdeutschland had started, and I was to bring the joyous news back to the eager German public. I was not working for a regular news outlet – no, they were as yet forbidden access. I was working for the Nazi Party. I was given a specific job: I was to write positive articles about the process, which would be curated and distributed among the print media.

The land we once called Poland was to be enfolded into the German Reich. The double meaning of 'Reich' did not escape me: a noun, meaning realm, empire, kingdom; but also an adjective, meaning rich. Poland was ours. Our realm. Our Lebensraum, living space. Our realm was our wealth.

In conference with some of my leaders, I made a suggestion that was accepted with open arms. I wanted to make my first articles exciting, relatable, and so, I said, why didn't I simply join one of the teams of BDM girls moving into what was once Polish territory, now a part of Greater Germany, to prepare the way for new German settlers? This was exciting pioneer work. I would live and move among the girls, photograph them at home and work, and tell the people back at home how wonderful it all was. At the back of my mind, of course, I had bigger plans. History was in the making, and I was going to be a major player in the recording of it. I would be right there as Poland melted into Germany. I would be telling the stories of victory, taking photographs that would be unique. Sometimes,

I would be filming the process – though I wasn't so confident at this part of the task. The film camera was bulky and heavy; really, I needed a strong man at my side to do this part of the work. But I would have the words and the photos, and I would be the first to report back. I was euphoric!

As part of my training, I had a year previously taken on the role of leader of a BDM group. I had grown close to those girls, and now that very group was about to embark on this great adventure. The group now had a new leader, a blonde, very Aryan-looking, very tall and smart-looking woman called Adelheid: an old Germanic name that, containing as it does the word 'Adel' – 'nobility' – suited her perfectly, because she was the very image of a woman of aristocratic birth and upbringing. The kind of woman I would once have aspired to emulate, though by now I was confident in my own skin, sure of my skills and my future. Adelheid epitomised the Nazi motto: tough as leather, swift as greyhounds, hard as Krupp steel. She was all those things, and a great example to me, a model of what I wanted to be.

Adelheid and I became unlikely friends. Off we went with 'our girls' to prepare this new dawn, this new Grossdeutschland. We were pioneers! We would march into this new dawn waving the flag of victory, and all the propaganda brochures depicted this.

Did you ever see that pamphlet, showing on the cover a tall blonde woman with pigtails over her shoulders, striding boldly forward against a rising sun, her swastika flag held aloft as she swung it back and forth? That particular brochure was all over Berlin in 1940. Well, that woman was Adelheid, and I was the proud photographer, and it was I who wrote the text.

The specific job of our girls, led by Adelheid, was to prepare abandoned homes for the new settlers so that they would feel comfortable, welcome. The BDM girls were to do the groundwork for the German pioneers, who would then arrive to much fanfare. My job was to document it all. To create historical evidence, without which the actual creation of Grossdeutschland would sink into the sand without trace. To me, my job seemed monumental. I was creating the history books of the future.

We all – I, Adelheid and the girls – felt honoured. Of course, we all, and the history books that would come after us, would always omit one little detail.

In our euphoria we completely ignored the fact that resettlement began with evacuation. For these new pioneers to move into this shining new world of Grossdeutschland, those who had been there before, who had lived in the homes and the farms, the cottages and the mansions we were preparing for the new settlers, had first to be removed.

But that was not our business. That was dirty business. Someone else would do it.

You surely know by now, Leah, just how dirty this work was in reality. Everyone now knows of the suffering caused by the Germanisation of Poland. That nefarious project was founded on the mass expulsion of Poles living in the region. Those homes, the cottages and farms and mansions that we so joyously prepared and handed over to ethnic Germans: their former owners had been simply driven out. Deported, sent to the ghettoes or to forced labour, their houses and property handed over to Germany.

These expulsions came, of course, with economic exploitation, looting, and confiscation of Polish enterprises and farms covering millions of hectares. But that was not our business. We did not care. We turned our faces away from that reality, because the end justified the means. We had our specific task, which we did to the best of our abilities, and proudly so.

We, young people who had almost all been raised by the tenets of Christian ethics, turned a blind eye to anything unpleasant that had gone before, and simply did the job we

*were supposed to do. We were creating Grossdeutschland –
literally, we were creating this wonderful new world. We
could ignore anything that left a bad taste. The end justified
the means, so we did not care about the means. We were there
to make the end glorious.*

*You ask why. Why didn't we see that what we were doing
was profoundly wicked? You ask: how could someone who had
supposedly been raised to Love Your Neighbour as Yourself
(you remember Mama!) be a party to this? Someone who had
had Christian values inculcated into her since she was a
toddler, in whom Christ's teaching of loving kindness had been
instilled from the time she had ears to hear –* how could you,
Magda? *I hear you cry.*

*I will try to explain. And yes, I know this is yet another
attempt to delay describing what I have to describe. And you
will reject what I have to explain as an attempt to excuse
myself and vindicate our actions. But no. I really want you to
understand what was going through our minds. I have thought
about this intensely in the intervening years, and have developed a theory of my own. Please hear me out.*

*We were young. Young people have a need to build their
confidence and their sense of identity, which is implanted in
them by a collection of attributes, all of which either enhance
our self-worth or detract from it. These are the attributes our
society has imbued with positive or negative values. Let's
name some of them. Our family's reputation, for example, its
standing in society. Our father's profession. Is he a doctor, or is
he a dustman? If the former, we feel pride. If the latter, we feel
shame. A notch up or down on the scale of self-worth. Our sex:
we are raised to believe the male sex to be the more important,
the leading, the stronger, the superior sex. So males feel superior, females inferior. Our race. According to Nazi ideology, we
Germans are superior, above all others, while Jews, Negroes,
Indians and the like are inferior. More notches up or down.*

Our educational level: university, high school, or none? More notches. Our homes: mansion or hovel? Our looks: beautiful or ugly? Our wealth: rich or poor?

In each case one of these attributes is better, one worse, and every one of them makes a notch on our internal self-worth scale, either up or down. Our dignity, our self-esteem, our pride, are all based on the attributes we have collected, the notches up or down. We collect and cling to the positive attributes to enhance our self-worth, and do our best to eliminate or at least improve the negative ones: we go to university, or get a better job, or buy a bigger house, or wear cosmetics to improve our looks. All in the name of enhancing our sense of value.

We young Germans came of age in the post-war era (of course, I mean the first war, the 1914 to 1917 one), an era in which Germany was the bogeyman, the loser, the failure. We had failed as a nation. We had lost a great war. We were at the bottom of the heap of nations. And because our nation had failed, so too did we youths feel that we were failures. Our self-esteem was at rock bottom. The once-great nation of Germany, the nation of thinkers and poets and composers, of innovative science, engineering, and great architecture, had been ground into the dust and was struggling to get back on its feet. And so we come to perhaps the most important attribute of all: nationality. We want to feel pride in our nation, to triumph in its successes in order to feel triumphant about ourselves. It all comes back to the personal – do you see? Do you understand?

Now, add to this present post-war sense of failure, world history as we had been taught at school. We had learned that the great heroes of the past were Napoleon, Caesar, Alexander, Nelson, Hannibal. All of these had waged war to get where they did, to go down in history. Their names and their deeds survive the ages. All of them had earned their greatness through conquering other nations. Britain had practically conquered the world, and acquired colony after colony, with

France hot on her heels. Even little Holland had a few colonies.

These nations had all fought and won, and in winning, they had increased their Lebensraum. In the animal kingdom the strongest wins, the weakest loses. Survival of the fittest is the rule of law. Strong animals demonstrate their might in order to maintain their status. Historically, it's been the same with nations.

Do you see where I'm going, Leah? We young Germans had grown up with a debilitating sense of inferiority because of our nation's failure. Remember, in 1933 we didn't know the lengths Hitler would go to in order to achieve superiority and Lebensraum. Psychologically, we were ready for the brainwashing that followed. And so, when it came to preparing Polish homes for Germans, we excused the atrocities committed as being no different to those committed by other great nations in the course of history; it was simply our turn to earn our spurs as one of the great conquering nations.

But I think, beyond all the philosophising and the explaining, it all boils down to one thing: We did as we were told. We had taken the Blood Oath. We were sworn to obedience. And we had a new bogeyman: Jews. It was all their fault.

And yes, of course I am now horrified, and all the explanations in the world cannot bring me peace of mind. I was guilty. I am guilty.

And so, having said that, I must at last get down to answering your burning question: what did you do in the war, Magda?

To put it into a few simple and direct words, down to brass tacks, as you say in English: Poles were driven from their homes. Those same homes were subsequently occupied by ethnic Germans, or Reichsdeutsche, as we called them then. Germans of the Reich. The better people, as we thought. I was a part of that action. I was there. I watched and wrote and took *pictures and said nothing. Not a word. I was there as a silent observer, and now my silence condemns me.*

My typewriter is waiting. I will now make myself a cup of tea in order to find the strength to continue. Or pour myself a shot of brandy. Keep reading, Leah.

27

MAGDA

Around this time I received a telegram from Mama, one that crushed me completely. Papa was dead! He had died of a heart attack. It was not his first one; he'd had an attack a few months previously and Mama had called Uncle Eli. I think even that you were there at the time. That was a huge scare and from then on, Mama kept not only aspirin but nitroglycerin in her medical cabinet. But this time it didn't work, and Papa died at home. There was no Uncle Eli to save him, for you had all gone into hiding, according to Mama.

I was devastated. Yes, communication between me and my parents had been reduced to almost nothing, but, exactly for that reason, the news of his death crushed me completely. I had always thought that one day there would be a great reconciliation. That they would come to not only accept my political affiliation but even appreciate it, and understand my excitement about Germany's future. They would apologise for not accepting the truth earlier, and for not listening to me. I'd been so sure that Papa would come to see my side of the situation, and now, to know that this was never to be – well, along with my grief I could not help but feel annoyance. Why were he and Mama so stubborn, so blind?

The funeral would be the following weekend, and there was not a chance that I could make it home in time. Mama indicated this in her telegram, and hinted that I wasn't wanted anyway. And so I had to grieve alone, without the comfort of family: Mama, and Markus, and Papa's sister, Tante Gundhilde, the only person in the family who understood me. I cannot properly express my inner devastation. I had to suffer it on my own. It was the first time someone close to me had died.

Of course, over time I would experience more than my fill of that phenomenon. But this first personal bereavement, and the challenge of facing it alone, did in some way help to steel me against an over-sentimental approach to that final life passage. Death exists. We all have to face it, through our families, our loved ones, and, eventually, our own death. It helps to be stoic about it. Finally, it is just a life passage, like birth. I girded my loins, to put it poetically, and grew strong.

LEAH – SONNENHOF

As soon as possible after the declaration of war, Markus returned to Sonnenhof.

He came late. Night had already fallen when he popped his head into my tent. My little gas lamp was burning, and I was reading, as I usually did before falling asleep.

'Squeak squeak, my little mouse! Need some company?' Cheery as ever, my Markus, trying to keep my spirits up, to get a smile out of me. And yes, I smiled and held out my arms for him.

But even in the flickering half-light, I could see the worry etched on his features. And it wasn't long before we began to speak in earnest.

'Leah, listen. it's time to get serious about a place for you to hide. Your parents are worried sick, and of course they won't go themselves until you're safe. And... I think you should stay here. At Sonnenhof.'

'Here? But that's not possible, Markus. Nobody is here over the winter. The house is unliveable. I would be snowed in. And it's freezing cold. There's no heating. And what about food?'

'All problems that could be solved, with a little creativity.'

'But... How?'

'Leave it to me, Leah. That's my job. Structural engineer. That's what I am, what I do. As I see it, the only problem would be getting Lisa's permission. Do you think she'd be open to the suggestion? We'd have to make changes, serious changes. Store food, make the house winterproof. All kinds of things.'

'I don't know, Markus. I really don't know. I hate to ask. She's so nice, so kind. It would be imposing on her generosity. It's such a terrible risk for her! How can I possibly ask? There's already the fact that she lets me come, putting herself in danger. How can I ask for more?'

MAGDA

I'd like to backtrack a little. Before going to Poland, I'd been on a career ladder in journalism. My final aim was to be editor-in-chief of a newspaper or magazine, or even, one day, to work at a publishing company as an editor, discovering new great books.

And write my own. Yes, as I've told you, I wanted to write a book myself, a groundbreaking book for girls in the Hitler Youth as well as young women facing the challenges of adult-hood. A book that would fire them with that same spirit which had brought me to this point, and catapulted me forward into the trusted position I now held. I knew the internal struggles involved in being a good Nazi. The effort involved in dealing with conflicts of conscience. I had been through it myself and was in a position to guide and help other women. That was a book I longed to write, but at the same time I wanted and needed a steady, responsible job, not only one that would pay the bills but one that would put me at the top of my field.

This new job, documenting how the first pioneers came into Poland, and how the BDM prepared the groundwork, was a perfect start to this new future. I already saw the book I'd one day write for publication, complete with photos I had taken. I could see such a book as an important work, documenting as it did the first steps towards the founding of Grossdeutschland.

And so I came to the city of Poznan in Poland, and the area called the Warthegau, which corresponded to the pre-Versailles province of Posen (Poznan). As you might know, the Militärbezirk – military district – of Poznan had been created in September 1939, and later annexed by Germany. I don't suppose you know all the details, so I'll make it brief; in short, so you understand. The new Gauleiter immediately embarked on a programme of complete removal of the formerly Polish citizenry. They had to be chased out. And after they were gone, their homes were to be resettled by ethnic Germans from the Baltic and other regions. Basically, these settlers were to be welcomed into farms and homes formerly owned by Poles and Jews.

That's where I came in, as a member of the German occupying power.

Oh, Leah! In retrospect I can only feel shame. I have lived through this period again and again in the decades since my Awakening.

'Awakening' is the word I give to the final opening of my eyes to what I have done, the basic criminality of my actions in this time. There are no words to convey my sorrow and my guilt. But it is not my place to wallow here in such guilt. I'm very aware that my genuine remorse, and this entire confes-

sion, could very well be interpreted as an attempt to mitigate the horror of the role I played, the lives I helped destroy.

And now I need to take a break from writing. The memories overrun me in wave after wave of supreme guilt and sorrow and regret. The images crowd my mind. I cannot bear it! It is now night and I have been writing all day, for hours on end. I am emotionally exhausted, and hungry. I must eat something. And then I must sleep. But I know I won't sleep. Or if I do, that sleep will be haunted.

Good night, Leah. I will continue my story tomorrow.

What did you do in the war, Mummy? *Thousands of young Germans, born in the war years or soon after, are now asking that very question of their parents. Many of those parents refuse to answer.*

If I'd had a child, I would have one day faced that question. But I have no children. I only have you. You are the one I must confess to.

LEAH – SONNENHOF

I had never before lived away from home, but last summer, in 1938, something new had happened. I had fallen in love with a little island, a place in the sun that had settled in my heart as a refuge. Now, in 1939, I was an integral part of the small island community and was already thinking of Sonnenhof as my second home, the people who inhabited it as my second family.

Lisa von Berg in her motherly way had made me welcome from the start – yes, she worked us all hard, but her straight-talking, unsentimental way of speaking appealed to me and more and more I was drawn to her, not only as my gardening teacher but as my mentor and a living example of independent living. Lisa was the exact opposite of the cowardly rule-followers who made up the majority of German citizens, who drank in Hitler's words as if they were nectar. Unafraid of society's censure, she embodied those attributes known as *Berliner Schnauze, Berlin Snout*: outspoken and articulate, rude, if necessary, she did not suffer fools gladly. She said what she thought, smoked what she wanted, and did it all with a heart of gold. She was much loved by everyone – especially, I found out later, by the late Leberecht Migge, with whom she'd had a very close friendship.

My friend Trude, I knew, loved her like a mother. I, too, leaned into her, and found myself again and again opening up to her, pouring out my burden of fear into her open heart. Fear for myself, my parents, for Markus, my brothers – all of this she listened to in silence, nodding along in sympathy and offering, occasionally, solutions.

Now, in late 1939, it had become serious. But I could not bring myself to ask her if I could possibly stay at Sonnenhof over the coming winter. It would require a complete repurposing of the living quarters. That was far too huge a request. But worse yet: how could I ask her to put herself, and her family, at such risk?

Markus had told me that he and his network of dissidents had been unsuccessful in their search for a family who could take me in. Demand was high, as was the danger, and it was becoming harder and harder to find host families.

'There's only one solution, now,' said Markus. 'The farm. All the more reason now that Mama moved back in with Oma and Opa. So she'll be there as well.'

Onkel Reinhold had recently died of a heart attack. Markus had told me this when he first came back to Sonnenhof. Tante Helga had moved back in with her parents to help them run the farm.

'But that's putting them all at risk! Tante Helga too!'

'And they know it. I've asked them, Leah, and they've agreed. It's the long trip down I'm worried about. With your papers, and that big J identifying you as Jewish – it's just too risky.'

I could tell we were both still thinking about the possibility of me staying on Sonnenhof. But surely it was just too much of a risk for Lisa? After all her kindness to me, I could not impose further. But, as it turned out, Lisa approached me soon after my latest conversation with Markus, and brought up the subject herself.

'You and your parents have to leave Germany,' she said. 'Germany is not safe for any Jew. Don't you have relatives abroad you could go to?'

I shook my head. 'No,' I said. 'It's too late. They wanted to go to England to be with my youngest brother but it was always difficult to get a visa, and now...' I spread my hands in a gesture of hopelessness. 'Now England has stopped issuing visas. It's the same with the US. We should have tried to leave long ago, but we always thought... we always hoped... Berlin is our home. We didn't want to leave! Where would we go? But now...'

Lisa placed her hand over mine.

'You must stay here, of course,' she replied. 'Let this be your home. No one will find you here. You love it here, don't you? On the island.'

'Here? Yes! Of course I love it. But...'

She smiled. 'No buts, Leah. Don't worry, I've already discussed it with Markus. We will make the house winterproof. I had anyway planned to do so one day, but never got around to it. But the time has come. Sonnenhof will be your home, Leah. For as long as it is safe.'

28

MAGDA

Poland was to be repopulated with ethnic Germans, right up to the Urals. Adelheid's job was quite straightforward and very practical: her team of BDM girls had to turn up at the homes and farms of the Polish people who had formerly occupied them and make them fit for the Germans who would now be occupying them. And I was to accompany them, to record this significant moment in Grossdeutschland's history for posterity. My pen and my camera were the tools of my trade, but what motivated me, what carried me forward, was my immense pride at being a part of this historical moment.

Adelheid's team's job was rather basic: cleaning. The houses' former occupants had known what was coming in advance and had, in many cases, deliberately left a mess. Some of the floors we found were thick with dirt. Some had left a path of destruction behind, no doubt an attempt to show their contempt for the German occupiers who had chased them out.

Adelheid did her best to keep the spirits of her girls uplifted. 'Onwards, girls!' she'd shout as they all spread out through the rooms, armed with brooms and buckets.

As for me: I was there as a neutral, but immensely proud,

reporter. I took photo after photo, and even as I watched through the lens of my camera I was writing my articles mentally, describing what I saw: Adelheid's brisk efficiency as a leader, the willingness of the girls to do even the dirtiest work. (Not the REAL dirty work, of course. I speak here of literal dirt, not the horrors that would later be revealed to the world.)

I did my bit, too. I encouraged them to sing as they worked, songs of inspiration and triumph. 'You are doing vital work for Germany!' I told them, and led them in the rousing patriotic choruses I had learned myself as a BDM girl. I might only be there as an observer and a reporter, but I took joy in giving them great words of inspiration and courage.

I pushed away the fact that for the new settlers to move in, others had been expelled from these homes. We all ignored that reality. We had a job to do. No time for softness or senti-mentality.

Adelheid herself intrigued me. I hoped we could become friends, and at the end of every day, when the two of us and our BDM girls sat around campfires and roasted sausages and sang invigorating songs, I felt great companionship with her.

In fact, though, she was certainly my superior in many ways, and I looked up to her. Two years older than me, she had that certain je ne sais quoi that some people simply radiate. That certain gravitas and self-possession I wished for myself. Yes, I had a loud voice with which I could always win the attention of others, but with her it was a certain aplomb, a bearing, which came not only from her impressive outer appearance but from deep within.

She was not only tall, but strong and sturdy, with the muscular physique of a sportswoman. It did not surprise me to learn that she had been a candidate for our last Olympic Games, as a swimmer. I, on the other hand, had never been interested in sport and was not particularly good at any such endeavours. I was tall and slim, thin almost. An academic.

Adelheid had presence. She was a born leader. I often managed to hold her back once the girls had gone off to bed, so that we could have private conversations. I wanted to know all about her. I learned that she had grown up as the daughter of a prominent administrator in a smallish town in Württemberg – something ending in '-ingen', as so many Swabian towns do. As our conversations became more intense and more intimate, her Swabian roots came to the fore in a pronounced dialect, which encouraged me to revert to my own beloved Berliner brogue.

We laughed and joked about keeping up the standards for the girls, above all by always speaking in High German and encouraging them to do the same. Once I managed to get hold of a bottle of beer, which we shared, and as the night wore on we became ever more relaxed. We exchanged Swabian jokes with Berliner jokes and laughed ourselves silly. But then, as we began talking about our respective childhoods, things got serious. Adelheid mentioned that there had been Jews living on her street. I was just about to play the one-upmanship game by saying there had been Jews living in my building, when she added, '...of course, the Gestapo quickly swept the vermin out, and good riddance.' The words I was about to say stuck in my throat.

And that was the moment I realised just how much of a fish out of water I was. I could not erase the past, nor did I want to. You would have to remain my little secret as long as I lived, as long as I was a Nazi. There could be no compromise. I could never, ever reveal that truth: that I had never succeeded in tearing you from my memory and my heart. That I would never, ever, betray you, personally. I had the living proof: that day when I warned you of the Gestapo search. And you warned me back.

I knew then that much as I admired her, Adelheid could never be a friend. She was a colleague, and my role was to document the great work she was doing. But that work, too, required that I monitor my reactions closely and not get too sentimental, because there was another side to our job, one we did not often see. One that required qualities that I most definitely lacked. There was a soft side to me, and battling it was my constant challenge. In one of the booklets that were required reading we had been given clear instructions:

You are now the master race. Nothing was yet built up through softness and weakness… That's why our Führer Adolf Hitler expects from you that you are disciplined, but stand together hard as Krupp steel. Don't be soft, be merciless, and clear out everything that is not German and could hinder us in the work of construction.

My job as reporter for the Hitler Youth was to cycle between the farms and villages and towns and take photos of all that was going on, make notes both mentally and in my notebook, and write them up as articles. These articles, along with the best photos, would be published in the Hitler Youth Monthly *magazine.*

The new German settlers who would be escorted over later that day or even in the night, by an SS officer from the Resettlement Office. Adelheid and her team did an excellent job, and by documenting their work, I made sure she would go down in history as the face of the resettlement programme – not just a figure on a brochure, but a hero in her own right.

But as time went by, I found it harder and harder to ignore the other side to the resettlement task. The families to be expelled could only take with them, on the one hand, possessions that fitted on their handcart, and on the other hand, nothing of potential value. Adelheid had to inspect the houses and the carts before they left, and she had to be very strict on that account. On a few occasions, she made the family unload every single item from their cart as she suspected they had smuggled in a few 'forbidden' items that they were supposed to leave behind. It's not surprising that all of them were furious; and poor Adelheid would bear the brunt of that fury.

In particular, they took advantage of our ignorance of Polish by unleashing diatribes in that language, and though none of us understood a word we nevertheless knew exactly what they were saying from the sheer explosive nature of the verbal abuse they hurled at us.

Adelheid didn't care. 'Pigs!' she would snort, and shake it off. For me, it was not so easy. It was easy to guess the content of their expletives, and I hated being on the receiving end of what were obviously curses. It threatened the heroic image I had of myself. But again and again, I pulled myself together. Tough as leather, swift as greyhounds, hard as Krupp steel. That was how I aimed to be, and Adelheid was my living model.

In retrospect, I can say it's true that we deserved all the contempt that came our way. And I want you to know, Leah, that I did not take the verbal abuse like some soulless robot entirely without feelings. It did hurt, deep inside. I had to make the conscious effort to create a sort of mental shield, so as not to let the vituperation penetrate my armour and get to me. I had to be hard as steel and just do the job. I had to learn to let the Polish diatribes run off me like water off a duck's back. Thank goodness, I did not understand the words.

The English have an apt saying, 'Sticks and stones may break my bones, but words will never hurt me'; but it's only half true because words do hurt – just not in a physical sense. And on those occasions when I was vociferously cursed in Polish, in words I could not understand but which I knew *expressed uttermost hatred and revulsion towards me, I had to consciously push that hurt away.*

Like everyone, I prefer to be loved rather than hated, and such powerful animosity was a lesson for me in making myself tough as leather and hard as steel. That, after all, was the goal. I considered myself at the time to be something of a martyr. Of course, I was really the abuser... but we'll get to that later.

As it was, I straightened my shoulders, hardened my features and strove to emulate Adelheid. I was just doing my job, I reminded myself again and again. This has nothing to do with me personally. I am serving my country. Preserving history for future generations. It is for the greater good. I wore my badge proudly and held my head high, and knew it was all in the service of Grossdeutschland.

And I have to say that some of the people we evicted did not rage and rant and curse me. Many left in floods of tears, weeping their hearts out. Especially the women. And those tears hurt more, far more, than the curses. And that hurt, too, I had to shove behind my mental shield. I could not allow the agony of these people to affect me. I could not break. I would not allow it. And that was the greatest challenge of all. I had to constantly remind myself of the good we were doing: Creating Lebensraum*! Lebensraum, for the magnificent project that was* Grossdeutschland. *I did my best to banish from my conscious mind all thought of the people who had been removed so that the German settlers could take over. Mostly, I only succeeded in subduing my conscience, because all I did was push my natural reactions underground, by concocting justifications for what I was doing.*

After all, I told myself, the people who had been removed: they were just strangers. We did not know them. We were ships passing in the night to each other. And even when we met them as they were about to leave, when we faced their anger and received their abuse, it was not our job to care. We were tough as leather, hard as steel. No sentimentality permitted.

But it was all a lie. In my case, a deliberate attempt to ease my guilt. And it didn't always work. Because I did care.

I didn't want to care, but somewhere, deep inside, I did.

There were times, Leah, when I struggled to stand firm.

Those times when the evacuees weren't just faceless strangers. Those times when we arrived in a village in the grey of early dawn; when we invaded Polish homes with half-eaten meals on tables, and unmade beds where small children had obviously been sleeping; beds that were still warm, in a small patch, from the little bodies that had been snatched from them. Sometimes in freezing weather we found Poles huddled together in cattle carts, along with the cattle, to keep warm. We knew full well that many, especially children, died in those carts, the bodies unceremoniously removed by the local police force.

Occasionally we would see a cart laden with a family's paltry possessions. Its owner would invariably keep their face averted, as if they could not bear to look at us. I taught myself to steel my heart; it wasn't my concern. That is, I tried to teach myself. I was there only to take photos, to document the exodus, I told myself. This was, after all, history in the making. The photos were half of the job, the articles I'd write the other half.

Just doing my job. I could not afford to be sentimental; I was documenting history. Tough as leather, swift as greyhounds, hard as Krupp steel. How often I recited those words to myself! This was the living challenge, I told myself. My job was to rise to it. Wasting thoughts on the dispossessed did not come into it, much less feeling sympathy or pity. Where did they go? What would become of them? Not my concern. I had to be strong, to actively cultivate strength.

But once, I was caught out. It was in the home of a family

who presumably had been well off, judging by the size of their house and the high quality of the furniture in that home. They had four children, including a baby.

I walked through the house taking photos, accompanied by the mother with her baby in her arms, and we went through the rooms together, me clicking away, creating my vital historical document in photos. But I could not help but notice the love with which she walked from item to item. She opened drawers and cupboards, showing me their precious contents: Silver cutlery. Delicate crockery. Antique art objects. Paintings. And everyday, mundane things: tablecloths and napkins. Laundry for the beds. Carpets. Every piece, I knew, was valuable; but it had to be left behind for strangers, because my government had said so.

When all was documented, we stepped outside together.

Their cart, outside the front door, was already packed full. They had a small homestead, with cows, pigs and chickens, all of which they had to leave behind. Unusually, they had a dray cart, and a horse to go with it; the father had just harnessed that horse to the wagon and then gone into the barn to fetch fodder. I do not know how much food the family had for the journey, and how long it would last them. I tried not to care, but despite myself I did. I took some wonderful photos. They would all one day be published in my book, I thought.

This was a family of the same class as me. The girls, had they been allowed to grow up here in peace, would have been highborn daughters, like me and you. They were not peasants, whom I could easily dismiss as 'not my business'. They had a bookcase packed with books. The woman was clearly cultured; as we passed it, she stopped and removed two books. One book was a Bible. As the title of the other one —and of all the books on the shelves – was in Polish, I could not read it, as I would have liked to do, but I recognised the names of some famous authors and a whole row of leather-backed books: The

Complete Works of Shakespeare. *I made an internal note to advise Adelheid to ensure that a cultured German family moved in here, one who would appreciate all the valuables left behind, and care for them. Adelheid would understand.*

That mother and I did not speak a word of the same language, but she spoke anyway. All through that last tour of supervision, she spoke. And I knew exactly what she was telling me. I could tell, from her tone, that she was furious, that she held nothing back. She would have known that there was nothing I could do, not only because I did not understand, but because she and her family were leaving, and I was just a woman, like her, and unarmed. I doubt she would have behaved like this with the SS officer in control; but in doing so to me, she was showing me up. She was addressing my own lost humanity, putting the woman in me to shame. Yes – in spite of myself, I felt shame.

But worse was to come. As we went back outside, one of the small children sitting on the loaded cart fell off it, landing in the dirt. The father was still in the barn. Without a second thought, the mother turned to me and placed the baby in my arms, then bent down to pick up the fallen child, to hug and comfort it and dry its tears. There I was, holding a Polish baby!

Well, Leah, you know about me and babies. I could not help but look into that baby's face. Big blue eyes stared back at me. Those eyes, Leah! So candid, pure. Wise, all-seeing eyes. Eyes that did not judge, but simply saw. Eyes that saw right through me, that saw it all, that saw me as I was, right down to my depths, digging away at all the filth buried down there and throwing it all into the light of consciousness. An immense wave of guilt swept through me, impossible to suppress and push back down, as I had in the past. Those eyes were not Polish and not German. They were the eyes of purity. Eyes of light. They exposed my filth completely.

It lasted only a few seconds; then the woman lifted up the fallen child and placed it on her hip, and with her other arm recovered the baby from me. She did not acknowledge me with even a glance. She certainly did not thank me for holding her child. She simply turned away from me without a word, and stepped away. The baby looked at me over her shoulder, still as serious as ever, those huge eyes seeing right through me. The woman, striding away, spat on the ground beside her. I knew that spit was meant for me.

There are few times in my life, Leah, when I have been left speechless. That was one of them.

If the ground could have swallowed me up, I would have willingly sunk into it. That baby was the straw that broke the camel's back of my conscience.

29

LEAH – SONNENHOF

The next time Markus came to Sonnenhof, he brought someone with him, a rather unkempt fellow in his late-twenties, introduced simply as Waldi.

'Waldi's a trusted friend,' said Markus, 'he's a carpenter, and he's going to stay here for a while to help us get your home fixed up for the winter.'

When I was alone again with Markus, I laughed. 'What kind of a name is Waldi?' It was typically a dog's name.

'A code name,' said Markus. 'We all have them.'

'What's yours?'

It was his turn to laugh. 'I'm Fido,' he said, 'but don't you dare call me that to my face!'

What Waldi had been doing up to now turned out to be living underground, in shadows and in dread of being captured. He had been called up to join the Wehrmacht, but instead of fighting for Germany had disappeared and become an active member of Markus's group. Waldi, it turned out, was also a quarter Jewish: his mother was half-Jewish, which meant that he did not have the 'three Jewish grandparents' necessary to make of him a pariah. As a deserter, he would be shot if discovered.

It was now October, and hardly any of the other helpers were on the island. The community was anyway much diminished, for several members of Lisa's family had been called up to serve the war effort in one capacity or other. Now it was just me, Trude and Lisa herself. Lisa and Trude lived in the log cabin that was to become my winter refuge, while Waldi and I slept in tents, warm in our down sleeping bags.

Waldi and Markus inspected the cabin to determine what needed to be done.

'The main thing is to maintain heat within the cabin,' Markus said. 'You'll have the little cannon stove and we'll chop wood to keep you going all winter, and the walls themselves are fine. And it's great that it's made of whole logs; that means there's natural insulation. Your problem will be the windows, the floor and the ceiling. And the front door is very flimsy– we'll probably have to replace it. And the windows.'

'How are you going to do all that?' I asked anxiously.

Markus and Waldi exchanged a glance. 'There are ways,' said Markus. 'We can get the materials. The main problem will be getting them here unseen by the authorities. We'll need glass for the windows, and fibreglass for the insulation of the roof and the floor.'

'What's fibreglass?'

'It's a very modern material,' said Markus. 'It's made using glass fibre; they make flattened sheets, like mats. These have to be nailed on to the area to be insulated. I researched it for my final dissertation. That's how I know about it. Not many companies manufacture it. It's mainly produced by an American company, DuPont. But there's also a German company that produces fibreglass, in convenient mats. The company is called Rex-Isolierungen, and the factory is close to Schwäbisch Hall, in Swabia.'

'So you can get some for us? Can you get enough?'

'Yes. Luckily you won't need it for the walls. The solid logs are good enough. And it's only a small cabin.' He glanced around and up at the roof. 'This cabin is only three by four metres. So in all, for the floor and the ceiling, we need about twenty-four square metres—'

'We can cut that amount in half,' Waldi interrupted. 'We'd need to pull up the floorboards anyway. But instead of this fibreglass underneath the boards, we can use woodchip. It's not perfect, but easy to get hold of it. Any sawmill will supply it, almost for free.'

'What about transport?' I asked. 'How will you transport the materials over here?'

Lisa, who had been listening in, interjected: 'Don't worry about that. I've been bringing supplies over here since time began. I'll do it. No one will question me.'

I could believe that. Lisa radiated authority and, as far as her credentials for Nazi approval was concerned, hers could hardly be better. That 'von' in her name hinted at noble, pure-blooded German ancestry.

'But what about this fibreglass stuff?' I asked. 'How can we get hold of it? Surely we can't just turn up at the factory and buy it off them?'

Markus nodded. 'Actually, we can. I'm authorised to put in orders for necessary building materials, and we do need fibre-glass for some of the Tempelhof buildings. I'll just order some surplus to what we need for the airport and siphon it off for us. Nobody will check. That'll do for the roof. All you have to do then, Waldi, is nail the mats to the ceiling.'

Waldi nodded. 'I can do that,' he said.

'And the windows?'

Markus smiled. 'Thermopane!' he said. 'Two panes of glass, with gas between them. A really good method of insulation – a lot of heat escapes through windows. I predict that one day it's going to be standard.'

He turned to Waldi. 'You can do that, can't you?'

'Of course! There are only two windows anyway.'

'And then the door,' Markus said.

'If you give me the measurements, I'll get a new one,' said Lisa.

There was a small trapdoor set into the floor and, lifting it, we found a ladder leading down into darkness. Lisa explained: 'We've never used that – it's an underground storeroom; when we built the cabin we dug it out, for storing all the preserves we hoped to make in future. We'll stock it full. Try it out, Leah; go down and have a look.'

I cautiously climbed down into the darkness. Markus handed me a box of matches and a candle, and once I reached solid ground I struck one and lit the candle. In its flickering flame I looked around. It was, indeed, a primitive cellar, with an earthen floor and rough brick walls, lined with empty wooden shelves.

'It's good!' I called up. I blew out the candle, pocketed it and climbed back up. 'Perfect!' I said. 'It's as if the cabin and the storeroom down there's been waiting for me all these years.'

'Well, they do say I have second sight!' said Lisa with a chuckle.

Markus turned to me. 'See? All arranged. We'll have you as snug as anything this winter.'

The next time Waldi came, it was at night, and he brought several sacks of woodchip. Over the next few weeks, more and more supplies came over, brought by mysterious boats both day and night. Lisa, as she'd promised, took charge of the transport of supplies. Everything was stored in the lean-to behind the cabin. I, meanwhile, took care of another matter: the preparation of enough firewood to last me through the winter.

While Lisa and Trude took care of the harvesting, I chopped wood. Over the past years Sonnenhofers had already felled (and replanted) a good number of trees for this purpose, so I wasn't short of material; and before long, I was swinging my axe with better precision. The heap of chopped wood grew by the day.

At the end of every day I felt a sense of complete fulfilment; I was looking after myself, making a home, providing myself with a safe future – as far as it was possible to judge safety; no one knew how long that safety would last or, indeed, how safe it really was. But my sense of achievement was real, and by the end of October, when Waldi came over to stay for two weeks to do the building work, it felt to me personally as if there were no war raging at all.

That was a good time. I was busy; we were all busy, filled with a sense of purpose, a sense of retreating back into ourselves and into a natural world that would always protect us. At night, we would light a bonfire and sit before it, huddled in blankets, revelling in the fire's warm comforting glow. There is something so fascinating, so healing, about a live fire. But the best part was that Waldi had a guitar and proved to also have a good strong voice. He would sing for hours, late into the night, into the fire: traditional German folk songs, Schumann's *Lieder,* ballads and humorous songs in Bavarian and Flemish dialect.

'The one thing I'm going to miss is music,' I sighed on one of the last nights before I was left to myself. 'I wish...'

Immediately, Waldi handed me his guitar. 'Here. Keep this,' he said.

'But I don't play the guitar! I haven't a clue!'

'Then I'll teach you,' he said. 'All you need are a few chords. You sing along and provide the melody. It's not like the violin.'

By the time he left, I could sing several of my favourite songs and accompany myself on the guitar: 'Die Forelle', and 'Wie Schön Blüht uns der Meien', and 'Muss I Denn': The Trout, The Month of May is Blooming, Must I, Then.

One song in particular, 'Five Wild Swans', filled me with such melancholy, such a welling up of sentiment, that I could sometimes hardly sing. But sing I did. No other song so poignantly told the story of the hollowness and cruelty of war.

It told the story of five beautiful wild white swans, flying off, never to return. Five birch trees next to the brook: never to bloom. Five soldiers, marching off proudly to war, never to return home. Five pretty girls on the beach, never to weave their bridal wreath.

Oh, it was heartbreaking, that song. The soldiers, and the girls. Was I one of those five girls? Yet still I sang it and I played it, night after night.

I might be relatively safe, now, but I worried. I worried for Markus, who I felt had played a dangerous game in stealing twelve square metres of fibreglass matting from the Tempelhof delivery. He never told me how he'd done it – as ever, he brushed off all enquiries with a wave of the hand and a simple, 'Don't worry, little mouse. The less you know, the better.'

And I worried for my parents. I knew they were holed up in the cellar of one of Father's wealthy colleagues. How safe were they? We'd had no contact now for weeks.

I worried about Aaron, too. Was he still working at the Siemens factory? How safe would he be in the long term? One heard such horrible stories. We had all heard of those trains, packed with Jews in cattle cars, chugging off to the east in the darkness of night. No one knew where they were headed. Allowed to take one suitcase, and all their money and jewellery. I wondered if Mother and Father would have been safer on one of those trains. But every time I had that thought, I repelled it. No. Those Nazis could not be trusted. We were all better off where we were, in hiding.

No need to worry about Mosche, who had made the escape to the US along with his new wife and his in-laws. No need to worry about Samuel, who we knew was safe with his foster family in England.

And no need to worry about Magda. She was safe with her new Nazi family and friends.

30

MAGDA

After that encounter with the baby, I broke down. I made some excuse or the other to Adelheid and my supervisor and returned to Posen, found a cheap room in a guesthouse, and buried myself for a few days in self-pity, self-condemnation, and an overwhelming sense of worthlessness.

I was too soft for this job. I could not do it. I could not align it with my conscience; but then, I wasn't even supposed to have a conscience! I had made my oath; I was supposed to be as tough as Krupp steel, but I wasn't, I couldn't, I had failed. What was I to do? By now, Germany had invaded France and there was little doubt that soon all Europe would be ours. Denmark, Norway, Belgium and the Netherlands had fallen and the British had been driven into the sea. Germany had taken more than 1 million Allied prisoners. And then Paris itself fell – the jewel in our crown. Parisians, having decided not to fight for their capital, fled the city in droves. Pétain signed the armistice. First Poland in the east, now France in the west: Grossdeutschland was forming right before my eyes. Berliners filled the streets in their thousands, cheering and waving flags, when Hitler returned after signing the new treaty with Pétain. As a good Nazi, I had every reason to rejoice with them.

I alone did not.

I alone was a failure. A bad German. I couldn't do my job. Such an easy job, too – just take photos and scribble a few lines about what I saw. But even at that I had failed. I hovered on the edge of a black hole of depression. I holed myself up in Posen for weeks. I was at the lowest point in my life.

By now, it was mid-1941. Up to now all the work I had done for Hitler Youth, and the BDM in particular, had been on a voluntary basis. Working as a volunteer had been my personal proud contribution to the great mission that was Grossdeutschland. It was intended to prove that I was doing my work not for personal or professional advancement, but as my sacrifice to the noble cause. Instead of a salary I had been provided for: I had received room and board – albeit always in cheap and basic accommodation, always at a low level, to prove my dedication – and a certain amount of petty cash as pocket money. But basically, I was free to resign at any time. And so I did. I returned to Berlin, handed in my resignation as a volunteer, and went about searching for a proper job.

I scoured the employment ads in the papers and very soon found what I was looking for. The Berliner Volkszeitung, one of the leading newspapers of the city, had placed an ad looking for a trainee editor. That was exactly what I was looking for. No longer out in the field, facing the horrific reality of what National Socialism looked like in the real world. No more investigative journalism. No more photographs as eternal evidence of the horrors I had seen. No more reporting live from the field, full of enthusiasm and passion. The sigh of relief I breathed out on reading that ad told me everything. I knew the job was made for me.

I sent in my application and in the meantime tied up the loose ends of my work for the Hitler Youth. I wrote up my final reports in as neutral a way as possible. I felt as if I were treading water. Not sure what to do next. I had lost my passion for my work. And without passion, who can do a good job?

As expected, I was called for an interview at the paper, which went well – I did an excellent job of self-presentation, putting on a show of competence. But I'd always been good at that; I had always pretended to be more than I was, always convinced others of my superiority. I got the job. With my experience in the field, they felt that I was perfect for it; and it was perfect for me.

I was near the end of my training when another piece of Nazi propaganda fell into my hands and I had the lightbulb moment that would propel me into action, give me back the passion that I so missed. France was now the focus of the war, and there, in that leaflet, someone had written an article about 'winning back the Alsace'. That's when the light went on.

Alsace! Alsace in eastern France, tucked between the Rhine river and the Vosges mountains, a land of rolling vine-covered hills, historic castles, and pretty villages, called to my heart. Alsace, one of the regions stolen from Germany at the end of the First World War, had a long history of being some-times French, sometimes German, and in 1918 the Versailles Treaty had awarded it most unfairly to France. Now, Hitler had taken back what was inherently ours. Alsace was still full of Germans, the article said; proud Germans who were happy to be back in the Reich and speaking their own language. Happy, and proud. Moreover, Alsace was a beautiful place, a land flowing with – well, not milk and honey, but wine. I cheered up instantly.

That's when I had my brilliant idea. I wrote and suggested it to my former supervisor, the editor of Hitler Youth Monthly. I was ready to go back into action. I would once again report on the Germanification of Europe, but *now, instead of the east, I would go west. I would go to Alsace and report on the wonderful work being done there. The Alsatians rejoiced in being once more 'home'; we needed to document this. I would visit the homes of these grateful Germans, speak to them in German, laugh at Alsatian jokes, go rambling in the beautiful Alsatian hills, sit around in picturesque Alsatian villages sipping wine with the German locals at pavement bistros. I spoke French fluently; that was another asset. And I would take photos of happy Alsatian Germans who had never felt French, and who were delighted to be once again officially German. What more fulfilling task!*

As I knew it would be, my suggestion was approved and the next thing I knew I was taking that long train ride all across Germany, east to west, Berlin to Strasbourg. My supervisor had already made arrangements for me to stay, at least at first, at the home of a certain Major von Obermeyer, who was the Kreisleiter *for the entire district. This, of course, was a huge honour for me, but I was to find out that Major von Obermeyer and his wife regarded it as an honour to have me as a guest, to introduce me to the region, and to be able to promote their work to the world. I was to be their spokesperson.*

Strasbourg had its own history, and Major von Obermeyer soon filled me in on the details. That very first evening we all went out to a restaurant in the quaint cobbled Old Town. It was called Zum Ochsen. How happy I was to see the German sign in bold letters, and to remind myself that hardly a year ago this had been officially France! How wonderful to see such a smooth transition!

We sat at a pavement table and sipped at our glasses of Riesling and I was happier than I had been in years. This was it. This was how Grossdeutschland *was supposed to be. France, converting seamlessly back to being Germany. While my plan was to research the annexation of Alsace by talking to* the people themselves, Major von Obermeyer was keen to fill me in on how smoothly the process had been up to now.

'After the declaration of war in 1939, all Strasbourg citizens were evacuated,' he told me. 'Every last one of them. They were relocated to southern France for strategic reasons. The same happened in other border towns west of the Rhine. We had to plan this all very carefully, of course, because France had been working to turn the citizens French for the past two decades. So for ten months the city was completely empty except for garrisoned soldiers. That was such a strange feeling, Fräulein Bosch! An entirely empty city. Meanwhile, I and the other administrative staff were busy at work reorganising everything. Eventually, we created a city of proud Germans. We are happy to have you here, Fräulein Bosch, to document this historical transition.'

And I was delighted to be here. My heart swelled at his words. This was how it was supposed to be. People proud and happy to be German, even if they had once called themselves another nationality. After Poland, this was going to be like an extended holiday. No bad conscience, no witnessing of things I'd rather not witness. No burden on my moral principles.

Yet the more Kreisleiter von Obermeyer boasted about the New Strasbourg, as he called it, the more a sense of disquiet began to creep through me. I couldn't really identify it logically. I was usually good at analysing my own mind and its vagaries and contradictions, but here – I was confused. It was a vague sense of dissonance, like a wrong note in an otherwise perfectly harmonious symphony.

'Everything here is now German,' Major von Obermeyer proclaimed. 'All the books in the library are German. All the shop signs are German. The citizens now all have German names and speak only German. With Strasbourg as the central hub, all of Alsace will soon follow suit.'

'What did you do with the French books?' I asked hesi-

tantly. Perhaps they were preserved in the archives of the libraries. Those wonderful works of literature I had studied for my Abitur, those great French authors. Racine, Molière. And the French language; a language I loved. The rhythm, the lyricism of it. The sound of it. I had prided myself on my ability to watch a classic French film in its entirety and understand every word. It had to be preserved!

And what would happen when we conquered England, I wondered. Would we burn every single copy of Shakespeare? The horror! I'm ashamed to say that this idea was as appalling to me as the brutality towards humans I had witnessed in Poland. I was forced to face up to certain facts I had, up to now, ignored in my euphoric dreams of Grossdeutschland. I had somehow imagined that, as German culture spread across the world, it would absorb, amalgamate, ancient cultures like the Greek, the Persian, the Japanese and the Indian, but that these cultures would somehow continue to exist along with the new; subordinate, of course, to German culture, but still alive, and appreciated. The languages would continue to be spoken, in addition to German. Italy would always be Italy. The great Russian writers and composers would live on, Tchaikovsky and Tolstoy alongside Beethoven and Goethe. I had never worked out the details of how that would happen. I just never imagined that the Grossdeutschland dream meant the entire uprooting and erasure of other, non-Germanic, cultures.

In my enthusiasm for all things German I had neglected to complete the equation. Even now, I could not think this through. I swallowed my confusion and accepted the offered hospitality gladly.

Frau von Obermeyer was extremely proud of what Strasbourg, and eventually the whole of Alsace, was becoming, and I as a polite guest put aside my disquiet for the moment and went along with her as she played the tourist guide over the next few days. I marvelled at the magnificent cathedral and delighted at the picturesque architecture alongside the canals and bordering the cobbled streets. Strasbourg was picture-post-card perfect, cultured and uplifting, the complete opposite to what I had seen of Poland. I took many photographs.

The Kreisleiter's wife's main focus, however, was shop-ping, and mine was not. I was never interested in accumu-lating things, especially not the things other women seem to treasure. She was particularly proud of the fact that Paris couture was easily available here; it seemed that, along with French perfumes and wines, couture was the only thing French she appreciated. She introduced me to her friends. They were all German, having moved here from various towns and villages all over Germany. But this was not what I had come to the Alsace for. It seemed rude, as a guest, to ask for more, but eventually I did.

'I'd really love to meet people who have lived in Alsace since before the annexation,' I told her. 'People who had considered themselves French and are now German. Do you know anyone like that?'

At first she frowned, as she tried to think, and then her face relaxed into a broad, radiant smile.

'Yes! Of course! You must meet Margarethe Kurtz.'

31

LEAH – SONNENHOF

And then it was November. Markus came to visit me for the last time that year. He came seldom anyway, as it was risky, but knowing that this time would be the last for several months – well, it was poignant.

In the meantime, all had been prepared. I was beyond grateful for everything my friends had done for me. Trude had knitted me a thick pullover and several pairs of socks, mittens and caps. Waldi had made my home snug against the winter's cold. Everyone in the Sonnenhof community had contributed something to make sure I'd have as comfortable a winter as possible, given the circumstances.

The harvest had been good, and now the underground storeroom was packed full of winter vegetables –potatoes, carrots, turnips, beetroots – enough to last me three months, as well as jars of preserves: beans, peas, cucumbers, what have you. I had apples and pears. The chickens did not lay in winter, and so Lisa had removed them to a mainland farm. She had offered to leave a few, for me to slaughter and eat, as well as the rabbits, three of them, in cages in the menagerie section behind the cabin.

'Do you know how to slaughter and prepare chickens and rabbits for eating?' she asked.

I shook my head no.

'Hmm. Too bad. And no time to teach you, now. But you'll find instructions in Migge's book.'

I knew for certain that I'd never read those instructions, never slaughter or skin a rabbit or a chicken. Not if I wasn't starving. We were in war; innocent lives, even those of chickens and rabbits, I felt, had to be preserved. I sent them back to the mainland. At most, I was prepared to go fishing, if necessary. Yet the idea of sitting for what could be hours on a grey winter day, waiting for a fish to bite, was not appealing. Again: only if I were starving.

I had instruments – shovels, spades, a heavy broom – ready for clearing snow, and vessels for collecting and storing water, and a shed full of chopped and stacked firewood. The outdoor toilet was ready and waiting. The cannon stove – a small, cylindrical, wood-burning stove made of cast-iron – as well as a small kerosene cooker had been prepped for me to boil water and prepare basic meals on. There was a cosy carpet on the wooden floor, friendly curtains at the windows, several blankets stacked in a cupboard for the really cold nights.

Lisa handed me a small transistor radio. 'Just so you can know what's happening in the world.'

'I was wondering,' I said hesitantly. They had all been so helpful, so confident that I could do this. I hated to ask, but I had to.

'What would I do in an emergency? I mean, there's no phone. No way to contact you. If something were to happen...'

'You're right,' said Markus. 'If you were to fall on ice and break a limb. Or an accident with the axe. Or if you get ill. You do need a way of getting in touch. Lisa?'

We both looked at Lisa, and she smiled reassuringly.

'The lake will be frozen over for most of the winter,' she

said. 'And usually, it's possible to walk across. If it's not frozen, there's the canoe, hidden in the rushes. But if it's a serious emergency, like an accident, or the cabin caught fire, or you need to contact me immediately...'

'I was thinking of a walkie-talkie or even a proper radio set, but that'd be almost impossible to get hold of,' said Markus.

'And the range would not be enough. My house is a kilometre away. No, you need a more workable method – and we do have one. I was going to tell you.'

She paused, and Markus and I both looked at her expectantly.

'Pigeons!' she said triumphantly. 'Homing pigeons.'

She explained: her late husband, back in the day, had kept the birds and trained them as homing pigeons for exactly this: an emergency; someone being stuck on the island and needing help.

'It was in the early days, when the children were small and rambunctious. He worried that I'd be out here and one of them would fall out of a tree and their head would be bleeding, or someone would cut off a finger by accident, or something, and I'd be out here with six children and unable to call a doctor. So he got a few pigeons, trained them, and eventually breeding and training pigeons became his hobby. He kept them in our loft, and we've had pigeons up there ever since.

'We've never actually needed them up to now – in summer people come and go regularly. But I still keep pigeons. I've still got the batch he trained in his last year. Their cooing reminds me of him. So comforting. They're at my house, up in the loft, ready to be used. And the cage my husband built for them, here on the island – well, it might need a bit of repair, but it's still standing. I'll show you later, and Waldi can do any repairs needed. All you need to do is feed them. I'll tell you what to do, just in case.'

She paused. 'Any other worries, Leah?' She patted me

gently on the back. 'I know it's a bit terrifying, if you've never lived on your own before. Loneliness will be the biggest problem, I think, more so than an accident. That's why I brought these.'

She pointed to several crates, still unpacked, sitting at the back of all the supplies. 'Books,' she said. 'They'll be your company. You'll be fine.' She bent over one of the boxes and brought it into the cabin, where she bent over again, opened it, removed the books one by one and placed them on the empty bookshelf, 'Books will be your only friends for a while.'

She chuckled. 'I'd have brought you a crate of wine as well, but I don't think it's a good idea for you to have that much if you're going to be drinking on your own. But here's one bottle from our vineyard.'

She handed me a green bottle. The label read *WEINGUT VON BERG, TALHEIM-FLEIN. 1928* TROLLINGER.

'You've thought of everything! Thank you so much, Lisa!'

I hugged her then, grateful for her generosity. She really had thought of everything, for my comfort as well as my safety. A bottle of wine, but not a crate. Books. A wireless. Warm flannel pyjamas, and a sheepskin coat. What a wonderful woman.

Over time I'd learned so much more about Lisa. What a dark horse she was! I knew by now that she had grown up on a vineyard south-east of the Württemberg city of Heilbronn. She had been an only child, and when her father died in 1929, he had left her everything. Since then, the vineyard had been managed by competent supervisors who kept Lisa's cellar well supplied with excellent Trollinger and Riesling wines.

Of course, Lisa had always impressed me with her confident and assertive attitude towards life, but what I hadn't known until now was even more extraordinary.

'You'd never have known it,' Markus said, 'but Lisa actually runs the main dissident group around these parts, and she manages a delicate balance between them and the Nazis. I've been able to link up with that group; the members are older, and more experienced than us amateurs. There's someone who was an actual undercover spy in the last war, and someone else who's sort of taken me under his wing. And they have resources we don't have. Like homing pigeons, for communication. And a forger. I'm going to get you new ID documents, mouse, and then maybe you can come out of hiding. All through Lisa.'

'She's incredible!' I said. 'She seems to know everyone who's anyone.'

Markus nodded in agreement.

'She's got the Gauleiter for this area eating out of her hand – she bribes him with wine. Crates of it. Same with any too-curious Nazi officer. They leave her alone. And the locals all look up to her.'

I learned that Lisa's late husband had been mayor of their village for many years and had died just before Hitler became chancellor.

'Probably better that way,' Markus said. 'He was a loyal Social Democratic Party man and would have faced strong opposition even in the early Nazi years. Probably ended up in prison, like most of the SPD leaders. Lisa is more diplomatic. She keeps the local Nazis in check; there's something about her. A kind of charisma that somehow gets through even to savages.'

I nodded. I knew what he was talking about. Lisa had not only won my heart by now; in taking me under her wing, I looked up to her for everyday guidance, not only in practical matters but in making vital life decisions. Knowing her made me see how important it is for a young person to have a wise and competent older figure they can respect unequivocally – a mentor, to be a guiding influence through those formative years. Good parents can fulfil that role, but to find someone outside the family – well, that's gold for a young person. If such a person is lacking in a young person's life there's the extreme danger that they might fall victim to exploiters, to passing trends, to manipulators.

That was what had happened to Magda, I felt. She'd rejected her parents' guidance and values, listened to her Tante Gundhilde's rhetoric, and ended up with Hitler. It's as if there's a pliable void in the young mind, an openness coupled with a yearning for absolute truth, and if the wrong person comes along with the wrong message – well, it's trouble.

Because without wise guidance, who can really distinguish between right and wrong? Hitler's message had filled a void, convinced swathes of young people of the 'truth' of his message, harnessed their righteous passion. That was how Magda had fallen. My best friend was now this ugly, distorted version of herself.

She, like hordes of young Germans, had been unable to recognise the basic wrongness of it all. The inhumanity of it. Because only when coupled with humanity – humanity towards all humans, not just a select few – can a message be deemed right.

Lisa's humanity shone from every hair on her head, from the warmth in her eyes and the sincerity of her voice. I had no doubt that had Magda, as a young person, had a Lisa in her life, she would have grown in the very opposite direction to the course she'd actually taken. Who could not love Lisa? Who would not want to follow in her footsteps, learn from her, become like her?

On this last visit, Markus had brought a camera and, as well as taking photos of us all working on the cabin, he asked me to pose for a close-up of my face. 'For your new papers,' he said. 'We're organising a new identity for you. You'll be Lena Gebhardt when all's ready.'

I spoke it out loud. *Lena Gebhardt.* A new name, a new identity, a new me. A new level of safety.

A strange memory emerged: Magda, suddenly deciding, at about twelve, that she wanted to be called Lena, the other short version of Magdalena. Tante Helga shrugged and went along with it, as we all did, but in the end she found a change of name too complicated and became Magda again. Now I was to be Lena. It would be my safe identity.

But now it was time to say goodbye to everyone; not just Lisa and Markus and Waldi, but also my dear friend Trude, who had brought me here in the first place. Trude by now was engaged to Lisa's son Dieter. But now Trude, too, was leaving, along with all the others.

Markus was the last to go.

'Keep strong, mouse,' he said on that last morning. 'And I'll see you in March.'

Before he left he placed one last item on the table. I looked at it in trepidation: it was a gun.

'Just in case,' he said. 'You never know.'

'In case of what?'

He shrugged. 'Probably you won't need it. But it's good to have some protection.'

'I don't even know how to use it,' I said. I picked it up with the tip of my forefinger and thumb, as if it were dirty, and handed it back to him. 'Take it. If Nazis come rushing up from the pier, well, a little handgun won't do me any good. They'd shoot me as soon as I fired my first shot. Which would probably land in a tree somewhere.'

He sighed, and took back the gun, slipped it into the canvas bag he wore over his shoulder.

'You're right. I just hate to leave you here all alone, without protection. I feel like a deserter. As if I should be with you.'

He reached for me and drew me close. We hugged. 'You are with me,' I whispered. 'I will think of you every minute of every

day. Pray for you to be safe. Take care, Markus, take care. I hate
to think of you in that nest of vipers.'

We walked together down to the pier. A final kiss, and he
climbed into the waiting boat.

I blew him one more kiss as he pulled away from the pier.
He blew it back, and then he was off, rowing towards the shore
across the lake. I watched until I saw him reach the far bank,
climb out, and pull the boat up the beach and into the little
boathouse, where it would spend the winter months. Lisa's own
house, I knew, was hidden behind the forest trees beyond the
boathouse; near enough for me to think of her as my closest
neighbour, but still too far to feel her neighbourly presence. The
winter season had begun. The boat, moored either on the island
or the mainland, symbolised active life on the island, Now,
locked away for the winter, it symbolised my isolation.

Markus waved once more from the shore and I waved back.
Then I turned to walk slowly back to my cabin. I was alone.
Surrounded by water that would soon be freezing and turning
to ice. The weather forecast had already predicted the first
snowfall.

My exile had begun.

32

MAGDA

Margarethe Kurtz lived in an apartment building in a fashion-able part of Strasbourg. A concierge opened the front door to me (I had convinced Frau von Obermeyer to let me go on my own) and escorted me into the lift, a clanking metal pen similar to the one at Kaiserkorso Eins, pulled up and down by a complicated set of pulleys, axles, chains, shafts, cogs and cables, a groaning mechanism fully visible through the grid of the iron cage. This cage stood in the centre of the hall, a dark vertical tunnel next to the stairwell.

The concierge, a dour, hunched woman whose beady, suspicious eyes seemed to accuse me of some unknown despi-cable crime, ushered me into the pen and pushed a button. The lift groaned and clattered into action, before finally grinding to a creaking halt on the fourth floor. The concierge pulled apart the jangling concertina doors, and there stood Margarethe Kurtz, a very beautiful woman of a similar age to me. A woman whose eyes were dead.

I had seen dead eyes before. There are many kinds of dead eyes. I had seen them in Nazi top brass, who could look at you with eyes that seemed made of steel. Eyes flat and soulless, with no indication that someone lived behind them. I had myself tried to cultivate such eyes: hard as Krupp steel, hard, dead eyes, deliberately flat. But I saw arrogance behind the deadness.

I had seen dead eyes in the faces of Polish refugees chased from their homes, forced to be refugees, who looked into an empty future. But I saw hope beyond that deadness.

I had seen dead eyes in beggar children on the streets of Posen, children who had given up on life because nobody loved them, nobody cared. I'd seen 'please love me!' in that deadness.

The eyes that stared at me as I greeted Margarete Kurtz were a different kind of dead. They were the eyes of a woman who had become a ghost. There was nothing there. Not soulless steel, not arrogance. No hope. No appeal for love.

She did not smile.

The concierge grunted as if reluctant to leave us alone, but Frau Kurtz dismissed her with a cursory wave of the hand, greeted me politely, and showed me in through the open door of her flat.

I was surprised to see that the flat was in the modern art deco style. Frau Kurtz led me through an immaculate, rather sterile living room to an oblong, glass-topped, sharp-edged dining table with no tablecloth, already laid out with delicate pastries of a sort I hadn't seen for years.

'From my favourite patisserie,' she said, and her voice too was dead. We sat down on matching chairs, severe with tall, perpendicular backs, and Frau Kurtz served me a variety of delicacies on what I supposed to be art deco plates, and real coffee. I tucked in hungrily while she spoke.

'Frau von Obermeyer told me on the phone that you wanted to interview me,' she said, 'about life in Alsace for the original inhabitants.' Her voice was dead. Lifeless.

'Yes, indeed,' I said, swallowing hastily. It had been ages since I'd tasted anything as delicious; even Mama's baking couldn't match the light fluffiness of a fresh Millefeuille. 'I'm very interested in how the local Alsatians welcomed the incoming Germans and how they feel about their province once again being returned to Germany. How they feel about becoming German once again.'

She looked me straight in the eye. 'Are you a member of the Nazi Party?' she asked.

'Well, yes. Of course. We all are. National Socialism is—'

'So I suppose you want the usual lies, and not the truth.'

I was shocked. How dare she speak to me in such insulting terms? It went without saying that she should play the game, the way we all did. The way I had played the game with Kreisleiter von Obermeyer, never once letting on that I'd been shocked that the Germanification of Alsace meant the erasure of French culture. This was how one behaved; even if one's innermost feelings were of hatred for the current reality, even if one wanted to resist some new insight or the other – insight, of course, referring to those nagging doubts that nipped at one's established certainties like an angry lapdog at its owner's heel. One resisted. One repeated the words and the slogans and the prevalent ordained concepts. That was how this game worked.

I hemmed and hawed for a few seconds and then I said, 'Just – just tell me where you grew up and how – how you came to be here.'

'I will tell you the truth,' she said then, 'because I have nothing more to lose. I grew up in a lovely mansion in the heart of the wine-growing region to the west of Colmar. My family owned acres of vineyards and we produced some of the best wine in the province. My mother now runs the vineyards. She is French. We are all French. We love France. I had a beautiful childhood and we all lived in paradise until the Germans came and told us we had to be German. I married a monster. I married him because he raped me and left me no choice. He raped me again last night. I am trapped here in this *ugly sterile apartment that he has placed me in and all I want is to go home.'*

So saying, she burst into tears. Her face distorted into an ugly mask as the violent sobs racked her body. Hands raised to cover her face, she let out the most guttural sounds I'd ever heard from a human being, almost animal. She pushed away her art deco plate with its uneaten slice of Tarte Tatin and fell forward on to the table, head buried in her arms, and actually howled. I looked on helplessly, uncertain as to what I could do.

'Shall I – shall I get you a glass of water?' I said eventually, as she raised her head and began to dab at her cheeks with a napkin.

'No – yes please. I'm so sorry. I'm very sorry. I didn't mean that. Please, please don't publish that. I just broke down and I – I couldn't help it. There's no one here. No one understands. And you – I'm sorry. You're a Nazi too so I suppose you're going to turn me in now. I deserve it. I deserve to die. But – no. I'm sorry. Please, don't tell anyone this happened. If my husband finds out... I'm at my wits' end; I just don't know what to do...'

That last 'do' came out as a long, drawn-out wail. I was flummoxed. In the end I brought her a glass of water and patted her on the back and murmured what I hoped were comforting words. I had never had to do anything like this in my life before. I had never seen anyone break down like this before.

But now this stranger poured out her heart and her entire history to me. Her eyes were no longer dead. Her eyes bled agony. Her name, she told me, was not even Margarethe Kurtz. It was Marie-Claire Gauthier, and her real home was the Chateau Gauthier-Laroche outside the village of Ribeauvillé and she was homesick but could never, ever go back.

'Why not?'

'I told you. Because I am married to a Nazi monster.'

She gave me no more details about the monster, but she talked on about her family; her mother and her dear sister Victoire and her brothers Lucien and Leon, her friends Jacques and Juliette and an Uncle Max and many more names I later forgot. It all came pouring out and all I could do was nod along. I knew my duty. I needed to report Margarethe and her terrible act of betrayal to the Kreisleiter, at once. As a good German, a good Nazi, that was what was required of me. But as I rubbed her back, as I held the glass of water to her lips, I knew I wouldn't. Instead, I did something just as dastardly.

'Can you give me the address of your family?' I asked. 'I'd like to visit them.'

33

LEAH – SONNENHOF

The first week on my own was the worst. The first morning, I woke up to a world of white. As the forecast had predicted, the first snowfall came, early in December, and did not relent for two whole weeks. Snow on snow on snow. I had no time to ease into living on my own, providing for myself with the rations left for me and learning the idiosyncrasies of the wood-burning stove as well as the kerosene cooker; I had to deal with snow and ice from the first day of my exile.

At first, the snow was just a light feathering on the grass outside my cabin, and the skeletons of trees etched in white frost against a brilliant blue sky. The sun, rising over the far eastern shore, cast a golden glow on my little world. I gasped in delight – how glorious the sight!

But the snow returned by midday and kept up all that day and into the night. I swept away the first dusting from the path to the toilet, but by the end of the day I was shovelling it away in thick wads.

It snowed all through the night. By morning, there were twenty more centimetres. I shovelled and shovelled all day, and by dusk – which came, of course, early – I was already in a state of panic. What if this continued throughout December? Into January and February? What if we were looking at a terrible winter in which the cabin would be buried under two metres of snow? Too much for me to shovel?

Only one little thought comforted me: my friends knew I was here. In an emergency, I knew, Markus and Lisa would somehow look out for me, rescue me. Besides, Lisa had said that when the lake froze over it was possible to walk across the ice between the island and the shore; I would not be entirely isolated.

But it was a week of anxiety before, at last, at the end of the second week, warmer weather came and the snow melted away. I had never been so relieved to see the dull greys and browns of a dead winter landscape. But I had had a glimpse and a fore-warning of just how hard it could get out here. Last winter had been mild, and that's what I'd been hoping for. That first week taught me that nature has its own timetable, one which seldom aligns with our own desires and plans. But at least now I could prepare for the worst.

But the snow never returned; now, the long evenings were the worst. By then, though, I had made friends with the stove, and I found delight in the saturating warmth it gave off. It had a small window at the front, and I could sit for hours before it, on a thick cushion, swaddled in one of Lisa's wool blankets. I'd read books in a lantern's glow, now and then looking up to gaze into the glowing orange of dancing flames above shining red embers. I played Waldi's guitar, and grew better and better at it, singing along to the songs he'd taught me, and more besides.

Comforted and warmed through by the stove's radiance, I knew a peace that was at complete odds to the dire stories of war and devastation transmitted by the radio. At first I had sought human company through that radio; just hearing human voices conveyed the sense that I was not alone. But the news was terrible. England, London, was being bombed. What about my little brother Samuel? Was he safe? Would the Allies retaliate? Would Berlin be bombed one day? Terrifying thoughts. After a while I stopped listening. I kept the radio permanently switched off. I didn't want to know.

More and more I found my refuge in books; I slowly journeyed through the shelves Lisa had packed full for me. In books I could escape into safe and pleasant worlds and mentally shut myself off from the real one, just as I was physically shut away.

The days and the weeks and the months ebbed away, indicated by the crosses I drew on each day of the wall calendar. I developed a rhythm of my own: chopping wood, carting it back to the cabin in the wheelbarrow. Taking care of my cabin, my little home: heating up water for washing myself and my clothes, for making tea. Cooking: vegetarian meals, bland but in their own way delicious, because I learned to savour and value every mouthful. Apples and pears were my dessert, and they, too, tasted like nectar. Yes, I missed Markus, Lisa, Trude and the others; and yet I gave thanks that I was safe from the ravages of war, and knew that I was in a much better position than others of my people.

I worried, though. I worried about my parents, my brothers, Markus. About those I loved, and strangers; those not as fortunate as I was. The people being shunted off to the east. What would become of them? As I nestled into my own sense of safety, concern for those I cared for grew stronger.

I did not worry about Magda. She had made her bed and was now lying in it. I did not care whether that bed was comfortable or not.

February drew to a close with one last heavy snowfall, one strong storm in which the cabin rattled and heaved as if it would be blown away. I spent that night wrapped warm in my eiderdown, unable to sleep, for once more it felt as if the end of the world was nigh. This too shall pass, I said to myself, and, indeed, it did.

But then, the German officers came, and my safe little world fell apart.

34

MAGDA

'Margaux Gauthier,' said the woman waiting for me as I stepped down from the bus in the Ribeauvillé village square. 'Or Frau Gauss, which is the name my new government has bestowed upon me.'

She held out a hand; its skin was dry and cracked, the hand of a farmer. A hand that knew physical work.

'Pleased to meet you, Frau... ah, Madame... Gauss. Gauthier.' I didn't know what to call her. She'd given me a choice, but I wanted to be polite, and correct at the same time, which was probably impossible. But at least I was here, with her, having taken the train down to the southern Alsatian town of Colmar, and from there boarded a bus to the village.

Major von Obermeyer and his wife had been very much opposed to my visit to this part of Alsace. 'It's not properly Germanised as yet,' the Kreisleiter had told me when I returned to their home after my visit to Margarethe. 'We still have work to do down there and you might meet with some resistance to the new administration.'

He offered to intervene by putting in a telephone call to his Colmar counterpart in the Colmar Mairie, the Town Hall. I could meet the staff and receive their hospitality. They would explain everything.

But the previous day, Margarethe had informed me that she had once worked in that very Mairie and said that if I truly wanted to meet the citizens of the district and know what the original inhabitants really thought of the annexation, then I had to do so independently. And so I politely declined the Kreisleiter's offer and ventured off on my own. An independent, freelance journalist. That wasn't exactly the job I'd been contracted to do; but it was the job I now chose to do.

Ribeauvillé turned out to be a village torn from a child's fairytale picture book: rows of tall, slightly wonky, half-timbered houses flanked narrow cobbled roads and higgledy-piggledy bridges and barns. Boxes filled with hanging geraniums graced many a windowsill, and tubs of many-coloured flowers clustered around doorways. It was hard to believe that this was in a country at war with all its neighbours. Swastika signs were pasted on a few doors, but there was nothing like the blanket coverage of swastikas I'd seen in Strasbourg, or, to a lesser extent, the station square of Colmar. And for that very reason I found myself breathing a bit deeper. My love for the swastika, it seemed, was somehow diminished, no longer the unquestioning adoration of my early years as a Party member.

I took note of this change with a sort of dispassion. Since my minor breakdown in Poland, and since Margarethe's breakdown, a subtle reassessment was taking place within me and I wasn't sure what to do about it. My only recourse was to stand back, apart from myself, so to speak, and go through this phase of my life as an uninvolved witness. The professional journalist, simply observing without personal commitment or bias. It turned out that Margarethe (or Marie-Claire, as she preferred to be called) was not on speaking terms with her mother, but she'd allowed me to use her phone to call her.

'Don't tell her you're with me now,' she whispered as I dialled. 'But you can say I gave you her number.' I did so, and arranged with the brisk-voiced woman at the other end that I would take the afternoon bus into Ribeauvillé the following day and she would pick me up in the village centre.

And here she was now, waiting for me as I descended from the bus, waiting for me, as promised, in the village square. Margarethe's mother, a middle-aged, sturdy woman with salt-and-pepper hair and wearing worn overalls and gumboots, standing beside her van. It was a somewhat battered white van with, on the side in bold lettering, the words DOMAINE GAUTHIER-LAROCHE and the image of a bunch of plump grapes, and beneath that, in smaller lettering, VINS EXTRAOR-DINAIRES.

'I've been ordered to change that,' she said, pointing to the French words. 'I'm supposed to replace the French words with "Besondere Weine". Ha! Over my dead body. And I'm supposed to rename the whole domaine. "Weingut Gauss-Laroche", it's supposed to be called. They can't change the Laroche part, at least, because that's still trademarked.'

Her voice bristled with resentment and outrage. I was astonished that she could even begin to voice such an anarchist viewpoint so openly, to a Nazi Party member wearing a swastika badge. Had she no fear, not even respect? Back across the border, in mainland Germany, I could denounce her for such open defiance of the rules. But maybe it was different here in Alsace.

'But it's the law,' I argued. 'Alsace is now German and everything has to reflect that.'

'Is that what Marie-Claire told you? And what's this about anyway? You said you're a journalist, investigating. But I can see your affiliation.'

She clapped her own breast pocket to indicate my swastika badge. Perhaps I should have removed it before coming here for the interview, and with any other interviewee, that might have made sense. But this Frau Gauss – or Madame Gauthier or whatever she was to be called – obviously didn't pull her punches, as her next words showed me.

'Alsace will always be French,' she informed me as she reversed the van into the square and drove off. 'That's who we are. You can bring in your soldiers and your swastikas. You can burn our books and pull down our flags. But you will never extract the Frenchness from our souls.'

I could not believe the frankness of her statement. Her open rebellion. In my entire time as a Party member, I had never encountered such barefaced defiance. Yes, there'd been the endless quarrels with Mama and Markus, but in the end I'd always had the upper hand because they knew they were on the losing side, and their arguments were those of losers. This woman was unlike anyone I'd ever encountered. She was fearless, and as she drove – with one hand on the steering wheel, the other holding a cigarette, an elbow on the open window ledge – she let me know this in no uncertain terms.

'You will not find a genuine Alsatian who will welcome you invaders,' she told me.

We drove through countryside all covered with parallel lines of vines, as if a giant comb had been pulled over the undulating hills, leaving them perfectly coiffed. After about twenty minutes she turned in to the courtyard of a lovely ivy-covered chateau.

'Here we are,' she said, 'Home sweet home.' She said the last in English.

A couple of dogs came racing out to greet us, prancing around and jumping up against us both. I patted them and asked their names and that seemed to earn me a few plus points. A young woman with long golden hair emerged from the house, and Madame Gauthier introduced her as her daughter Victoire.

Although: 'Probably Viktoria to you,' she said with a laugh. 'That's the name you Germans inflicted on her. To us, she remains Victoire.' Her voice was mocking.

Victoire smiled and led us into the kitchen, where Madame Gauthier invited me to take a seat and offered me a glass of wine.

'Wine?' I said, 'At this time of day?' It was only two thirty. She shrugged. 'Suit yourself. All I know is, I have the best wine in the entire province. Why deny yourself a special treat?'

She broke out in peals of laughter, and with those words I had cracked her code. Madame Gauthier kept her status as French alive, even in the face of opposing German Kreisleiters and Oberbefehlshabers and other impressively titled military men, simply by dint of her impressive wine cellar.

'Men are weak,' she said. 'Women and wine, that's the way to conquer them. Here, try this Gewürztraminer.'

I'd never been a drinker, as you know, Leah. Every Nazi knew that Hitler disapproved of alcohol, and was himself a teetotaller, so, strictly speaking, our loyalty demanded that we emulated him. Drinking was, however, a vice not seriously resisted by most Nazis I knew. They loved to gather in pubs and down bottle after bottle of beer and engage in rousing and rowdy singing. Hitler might disapprove of alcohol consumption but perhaps he knew his men well enough to know that enforcing abstinence was not a rule that could ever work. Personally, I simply didn't much care for alcohol.

Yes, I'd drunk Riesling with the von Obermeyers and shared a few beers with Adelheid back in Poland, but that was only to win approval and to demonstrate camaraderie. That afternoon, Madame Gauthier tried a similar tactic on me. Once she'd dropped her 'you nasty Germans' combative stance, her ploy of in vino veritas began.

I accepted her offer of a glass, and then another. It was indeed delicious...

'Let's move into the garden,' said Madame Gauthier after my second glass, and we did. The kitchen led into a stone-flagged terrace, which on one side was enclosed by a magnificent garden in full flower, and on the other open to a splendid view of the rolling vine-ribbed countryside. All around, magnificence. We sat at a solid wooden table and Madame Gauthier brought out a selection of her wines that I 'simply must taste'. She launched into a lecture about all the different wines produced by her chateau.

'The Germans are as fond of good wine as the French,' she said with a laugh. 'How else do you imagine I keep them all to heel?'

'Aren't you afraid?'

'Me? Afraid? Of what?

'You know. Of bribery or something like that.'

She laughed. 'Pas de tout. Not a bit.'

And I believed her.

She laughed again when she saw that I had finished my glass. 'Santé! There's plenty more where this came from.' She popped open another cork. 'This is my best Pinot Blanc.'

I felt a delicious lightness of head, a sort of giddy euphoria. The sun was warm but not scorching; perfect. Birds sang in the bushes. The dogs came out and lay at my feet and I stroked their heads. One laid his head on my lap. I remarked that Madame Gauthier herself was not drinking. 'Oh, I can drink any time,' she said. 'You are my guest. I like to spoil my guests.' I understood perfectly.

As the afternoon turned golden I became slightly garrulous.

I told her things I perhaps shouldn't have. I told her about you, Leah. I told her about Markus and about Mama. I can't remember what I said, but at one point I cried. When I spoke of Mama, she nodded and said she understood completely, from personal experience. I knew she was *thinking of Marie-Claire. I told her about Marie-Claire's breakdown, and about my own, in Poland. I told her about the terrible things I'd seen there, and I cried again. She handed me a handkerchief, went back into the kitchen, returned with a bottle of some new wine and poured me another glass. In return she told me things she also shouldn't have, things that a sober Nazi officer would have arrested her for.*

At one point she said something in French. Just a few words.

'Oh, I love the French language!' I said, slowly, in perfect French. 'We studied it at the Lyceum!' Of course, French had been dropped from the curriculum in the thirties but she needn't know that.

'Really! Then let's speak French from now on!' she said, also in French, and launched into a speech of which I only understood 'Bahnhof', as we joked in German, meaning not a single word.

'Slow down, slow down!' I laughed.

'See?' she said. 'You don't speak French at all. A language is not just words, it's a whole world and you cannot enter the French world. All you have are words. But we Alsatians can enter yours, and that's our advantage. It's why you'll never conquer us.'

We spoke German again after that.

It was, perhaps, the strangest afternoon for me of the entire war – of my entire life – and Madame Gauthier the most perplexing and inscrutable human being I'd ever met.

'I need to get the bus to go back to Colmar,' I said at last, my speech slurred.

'Certainly not,' she said firmly. 'You must spend the night. We have lots of empty beds here.'

'But... but... I must ring that bitch...'

'What bitch?'

'The one I'm staying with in Strasbourg. She expects me back tonight.'

'Oh. You mean the Kreisleiter's wife. Don't worry, I will do it for you. I do know the Kreisleiter, you know. I once offered him and one of his colleagues my hospitality.' She chuckled. 'An interesting evening.'

'Why are you so kind,' I slurred, 'to bad people?'

I remember saying that, even if I remember little else of our conversation afterwards. I do remember her reply: 'Magda, you are merely playing the role of a bad person. There is more to you than that, but you need to dig deeper to find that real you.' Somehow those words seared themselves into my consciousness and, even long after, I remembered them. As well as her knowing smile. I wondered what she meant by 'dig deeper'. But later, I understood.

Victoire brought out a large pot of soup she had made herself and a loaf of home-baked bread and we had supper. I learned that it was she who was responsible for the beauty of the garden; gardening was her hobby.

The evening grew long and yet more golden. As the sun sank behind the hills, a sense that I belonged here overcame me. A feeling of at-home-ness I had never experienced before. A longing to stay and settle and live here forever; to forget everything in the past and start again, fresh, with just the people I knew and loved. As if the Magda who had fallen in love with Hitler and the idea of Germany had never existed. As if she were a fiction conjured out of my own mind.

And then it was night and I could hardly walk and Madame Gauthier bundled me off to bed, supporting me as I stumbled up the stairs. She made me take a 'tisane' before bed. 'To prevent a hangover,' she said, and it did.

The next morning, she was quite taciturn. I was incapable of eating the breakfast she offered; my body, unused to wine, demanded a fast. And so she packed me into the van and drove me to Ribeauvillé for the early bus. She did not talk during the drive, but just before we arrived she said, 'Go back to Marie-Claire, and ask her to ask her husband to give you a tour of his workplace. And when he does, be a good upstanding Nazi.'

'Why?' I asked. 'What's his workplace?'

'Have you ever heard of Natzweiler-Struthof?'

'No.'

She nodded. 'No, I suppose you wouldn't have.'

Silence.

'What is it?'

'Just do as I said. Ask Marie-Claire to get you there. You'll find out.'

Another silence. Then 'And...' She paused. We had arrived. We climbed out of the van. The bus was waiting.

'And what?' I prompted.

'Give my love to Marie-Claire.' She turned away abruptly, not even saying goodbye, and climbed back into her van.

35

LEAH – SONNENHOF

The morning after the February storm I woke up to find a devastated world. The winds had played havoc with the garden, and many of the young trees had been torn up. Branches and twigs lay all around the forest's edge. I tidied up as best I could but, while I was working at filling the wheelbarrow with twigs for kindling, I noticed movement on the far shore. Shading my eyes, I peered across the water.

Yes: there on the landing beach I could see two figures, who seemed to be staring at the island. I slipped back into the cabin, which I knew was not visible from the shore, hidden as it was behind the boxwood hedge that separated the house from the vegetable beds. There was a pair of binoculars on a shelf; I grabbed them, stole back outside and, hiding behind a tree trunk, peered through them. That was when my heart stood still. Two uniformed officers were standing on the far shore, in conversation, showing great interest in my little island. One of them pointed up to the sky above the island. I looked behind me. It was unmistakable: a white tendril of smoke swirling upwards and dissolving into the blue of the sky. They had seen it, and were wondering who lived here. Why had we never thought of that? From their black uniforms I knew they were SS officers.

I had to hide! But where? The island was small, and if they were to search it I would be a sitting duck. The cellar? No: it seemed a perfect hiding place, but was actually useless, as I'd need someone to close the trapdoor after me. I was trapped, my heart pounding so hard I was sure they could hear it.

But I was lucky in one thing: the lake was no longer frozen, so they could not walk across. I saw them approach the little boathouse. Would they take the boat and come over? But they moved away, and through the binoculars I saw that the double doors were firmly secured with a huge padlocked bolt. And then they walked away, back down the path through the forest, back to the village. A respite only; I had no doubt they'd be back. Possibly with a boat, or a tool to cut through the padlock. They'd get here – somehow – and invade my sanctuary. It would be over. I had to think fast, despite the hammering of my heart and the fear nipping at my mind.

My first thought was the canoe, hidden among the reeds along the shoreline. I could escape in that. I went to look for it.

It had been completely demolished by the recent storm.

And then, one word, one name, rose in my mind: *Lisa!*

Lisa was in danger, just as I was. Yes, she'd managed till now to keep the Nazis in check, but this was serious. Harbouring a Jewish girl on her property? That could get her killed. A few bottles of wine as a bribe wouldn't buy her way out. Not this time. I had to warn her; not just for my sake, but for hers. But how?

And that's when I remembered the pigeons. How could I have forgotten? I had been feeding them and looking after them as my only living companions, but now I remembered their real purpose.

I recalled the instructions Lisa had given me: write a note, secure it to one of the pigeon's feet and set it free. It would fly straight home to Lisa. But would she see it arrive? Could she help? If so, how? Even if the pigeon served as a warning, when the SS officers returned, she'd be in as much trouble as I was. She owned the lease to the island. The boathouse was hers. She had obviously deliberately hidden a Jew. Sooner or later, they'd arrest her. I had to warn her. Give her time to flee. To protect herself. Somehow. Even if I couldn't protect myself.

I scribbled a note and secured it to the leg of one of the pigeons as she'd taught me, held it in my hands as I walked as close to the pier as I dared, raised my hands and let it go. It flapped its wings and flew away, straight towards the shore. Now there was nothing left for me but to wait. And to watch. And to hide.

An hour later, I again saw activity on the shore. The two SS officers were back. They had somehow managed to negotiate a blow-up rubber boat through the forest and were laying it on the water. Climbing in. Heading towards the island.

A new panic overtook me. I had to hide. They couldn't find me! Had Lisa received the pigeon, and my note? What would she do? Lisa's house was near to a road that led past the forest. She had time to flee – but where to? Now it was she who had to hide – but where? Who would take her in? We were both in big trouble. This was the end. After all our efforts, all our preparations: this.

They would find the cabin, enter it, and start looking for me. They would scour the island, and eventually find me. I would be arrested, thrown into jail, or put on one of those mysterious trains one heard of, chugging off eastwards into the night, carriages stuffed full of Jews. It was just a rumour, I knew. But what if it were true? I tried to keep my heart from hammering so loudly. *Think, Leah! Where can you hide?*

As I looked around in desperation, I saw it. The little outhouse. The aptly named 'plop-loo': the *Plumpsklo*.

The *Plumpsklo* took a pride of position in Leberecht Migge's vision for sustainable living from the land. In the cabin Lisa had hung up a framed document, the plan for how the *Plumpsklo* was constructed, how it worked, converting human excrement into compost to recycle into potent fertiliser. Our *Plumpsklo* was housed in a small wooden construction at a discreet distance from the cabin. There was a certain whiff around the building, which would, hopefully, keep the curious away.

I slipped into the *Plumpsklo*, closed the door, slid the bolt that locked it from the inside. It was my last, and only, resort. I sat down on the wooden bench, over the hole. I could hear voices outside, male voices calling, asking if someone was there.

'*Hallo! Hallo? Ist jemand da?*'

Then, all of a sudden, I heard a new voice. A female voice. A voice I recognised.

Lisa's voice. She was calling – but *what* was she calling?

'Halli-hallo! Lena!' she called again, loud and clear. 'Lena, where are you? Come on out! It's important!'

At first I didn't understand. And then, all of a sudden, I remembered. The new identity they had arranged for me: Lena Gebhardt.

I stood up, pulled back the bolt, opened the door. I called: 'Lisa? Here I am!'

'Oh, there you are!' Lisa came into view, along with the two officers. 'I was just telling these two gentlemen about you. Gentlemen, this is Lena Gebhardt, the writer. As I told you, she is here to do some historical research for her next book. She needed peace and quiet, and the island is perfect. Lena, this is Major Schmitz and Major Bachmann. They saw smoke coming from the chimney and came to investigate.'

'Why didn't you come when we called?' said one of the officers, frowning.

'I-I was in the toilet,' I mumbled.

'You could have called back when you heard us, to let us know where you were.'

I looked at my feet, feigning embarrassment. 'I'm sorry. I was just... it's a bit... a private matter. I didn't want—'

'Don't tell me you're going to interrogate a lady about what she does in the toilet!' said Lisa, in false outrage. 'That's not your business!'

'She was in there for ages!' replied the officer.

'I-I was hiding, because I didn't have my papers with me!' I managed to stutter. 'I knew that would get me into trouble. And I knew I had lost them, somewhere. I-I didn't...'

I looked at Lisa for help.

Lisa said, 'She sent me a carrier pigeon asking for help. I came right away. She'd left her papers with me for safe keeping. Why would she need papers out here, on the island, where she's all alone, she said. But I did try to tell her it was silly.'

'And where are those papers now?' It was the officer introduced as Major Bachmann. He frowned, and spoke sternly. 'You need to be able to show them. Everyone needs to have their papers with them at all times. It's the law.'

'Yes, indeed, and here they are!' said Lisa, and, miracle of miracles, she rummaged in the handbag slung over her shoulder and pulled out a wad of documents, which she waved in Bachmann's face.

Major Bachmann frowned, looked through the documents, handed them to Major Schmitz, who took them, looked through them, regarded the photo, looked up to compare it with my own face, nodded, and passed them back to his colleague.

'Seems to be in order,' said Major Bachmann. He handed them to me. 'You need to keep them with you at all times! Even out here on the island.'

'Yes, sir. I will. I'm sorry.' I gripped the papers with white knuckles. I couldn't believe that this was over. I'd been caught out, yet not caught out.

The officers both tipped their hats at the two of us. 'Sorry to have bothered you, Frau von Berg, Fräulein Gebhardt,' said one of them.

'Oh, no bother at all. Give my regards to Herr Gauleiter Schneider. Please tell him I've got some good Trollinger he might like. And you too, of course! Why not pop by some time. You know where I live. I'll have a bottle for you.' She winked then, and, to my complete astonishment, they both gave a half-bow, clicked their heels, muttered their thanks, turned and walked away.

I looked at Lisa. 'How did you... where... those papers! When did you get them?'

'They were ready about a week ago. From now on, Leah, you're Lena. Never forget it.'

'Oh, Lisa! I don't have words! What can I say?'

She dismissed my gratitude with a wave of her hand. 'Nothing at all! It's all in a day's work.'

36

MAGDA

It was ridiculously easy to arrange my visit to Natzweiler-Struthof. All it took was a call from Kreisleiter Obermeyer to Oberbefehlsleiter Kurtz. The very man who, Marie-Claire had confided to me just two days ago, kept her in check through rape. The monster.

Far be it from me to condone Kurtz's behaviour towards his wife. Of course I was on her side, but I was not here to judge or rebuke her husband. This was a game of tactics and strategies, and Madame Gauthier had made me more than curious. Why had she insisted I visit his workplace? Why was there such secrecy about that name, Natzweiler-Struthof? What was it? Where was it? Why had she placed a finger on her lips when she spoke that name, as if reminding me to be cautious, discreet? I had to play my cards well if I wanted to find out.

When Kurtz picked me up in his Mercedes-Benz the following Monday, it was the professional Magdalena Bosch, senior staff member of the Hitler Youth, who climbed into the passenger seat. Next to me sat the chauffeur. Kurtz himself sat in the generously upholstered back seat.

Kurtz picked up two more passengers on our way out of Strasbourg, two unprepossessing men in full Nazi uniform who sat in the back seat with him and spent the whole journey into the mountains speaking about some party they had all attended the previous Saturday night. I had never known that men could gossip to that extent. They completely ignored me, all three of them, and so, as the car wound its way up a mountainside in the Vosges mountain range that separates Alsace from Lorraine and the rest of France, I was thankfully not obliged to make polite small talk.

At first we drove through softly undulating hills striped with the typical ranks of grapevines. Up and up we climbed, up and down and around the hills, and then into the forested hills of the higher mountains. In the distance, snow-capped peaks rose up against the brilliant blue of the sky, providing a picturesque view that rivalled the Alpine peaks of my childhood Bavarian holidays. By this time, I wanted to interrupt their conversation, ask where we were going, what was so special about this place, why it was so high up. So isolated.

I soon found out.

The first sign that we were approaching our destination was, in the middle of nowhere, a security gate with a sentry box. It opened automatically as we approached; Kurtz's car had been recognised. The two sentries standing there clicked their heels and gave the Hitler salute as we passed. We all saluted back in return.

A few hundred metres later we came to a huge gate and high wire fences, completely isolated from the rest of the world, and I knew all at once, without explanation needed, what Natzweiler-Struthof was. It was a camp. A concentration camp.

I don't suppose you have heard much about Natzweiler-Struthof, Leah. It was never part of Germany's official concentration camp system. It had a unique history of its own, as I later found out.

The location of the camp had been chosen specifically for its proximity to a granite quarry. The goal was to extract and cut blocks of granite, out of which magnificent palaces and grand edifices would be built all over Germany, all for the glorification of Hitler and the Third Reich. A new Renaissance, a grandiose undertaking reflecting all the megalomania our Führer is known for.

But who was to extract that granite? Fit German men were needed for a more noble cause – fighting the war. Cheap labour was needed. And so, the labour camp Natzweiler-Struthof, near the village of Natzwiller, was created specifically to provide workers for the quarry. Work on the camp began in July 1940, two weeks after the fall of Strasbourg, and it went into operation in 1941. The only concentration camp established by the Germans in the annexed region of France, it sat 800 metres high, hidden away in the mountains, a perfect location.

We all emerged from the car and I saw that we were at the rounded top of a mountain, with wide terraces descending the slope. On the terraces stood long wooden barracks.

'That's where the residents are housed,' said Kurtz. 'Residents' rather than 'prisoners', as if they were hotel guests, tourists come for a holiday.

'As you can see, the view is magnificent,' he added, quite offhandedly spreading his arms out to embrace the panoramic vista of forested slopes and snow-capped peaks etched against a cloudless blue sky. Not a city, not a village, not a house in sight, only forested hills beyond the high wire fence that enclosed us. A chill settled on me at his words. Was he really so apathetic as to believe the view outside the fence could distract me from what was inside it? From those ominous rows *of single-storey barracks? Apparently, yes. His voice was casual, unconcerned, his face grey and soulless. I took out my notebook and pencil and began to take notes. Then I raised my camera and took the first photos.*

I noticed on the highest terrace what looked like a gallows, and turning to take a photo, I asked, in as casual a voice as I could muster. Kurtz confirmed it. 'Yes, now and again we have cause for an execution. You must remember that these prisoners are dangerous. Many of them were violent criminals before their incarceration. The vast majority were dissidents, men actively fighting with all means at their command against our Führer, which in itself is criminal. Many were Jews.' As he spoke the last word his face took on an expression of complete disgust.

I am good at reading people, and I could tell from the start that Kurtz personified through and through the Nazi ideal: tough as leather, and hard as Krupp steel. Being in his late forties, he probably was no longer swift as a greyhound, but I was sure he was swift in the execution of punishments. I could see that in his face. Some people do carry their entire personality in their features, and Kurtz was one of them.

I wondered if others could read my face as well as I read theirs. Was it beginning to show, the beginning of the wearing away of my initial zeal? Could people tell that something in me was no longer tough as leather and hard as steel? Since Poland, since my meeting with Marie-Claire and then with her mother, I could feel that erosion within me. Doubt had started to sprout, and doubt was toxic for the Nazi message. Did it show?

We walked down the terraces to the very bottom. Kurtz showed me the interior of what he called the prison quarters, where troublemakers were incarcerated as punishment. I saw certain gadgets that I could only surmise were instruments of torture. I did not ask, and he gave no details, but I took photos.

Neither did he give me a tour of the barrack to the extreme right of the prison cells. This had a chimney rising high above its roof. As he led me away, back towards the staircase between the terraces, I had to ask. I turned and pointed.

'What's that building?'

'It's the crematorium,' he said. 'It's where we dispose of dead bodies.' He left it at that, but, against my will (I was still trying to be the tough professional) my blood ran cold. 'Can we go inside?' I asked.

'Certainly,' he replied, and led me in through the door. The interior was quite simple. Two rooms. A simple one with what was obviously an enormous oven, its chimney extending up and through the roof. Next door, a bare room in the middle of which stood a large concrete slab, waist-high, man-sized in length. Question after question burned on my lips, but I held those questions back, for I'd be incapable of speaking in the neutral tone required, that tone of factual disinterest that Kurtz exemplified. The hands on my camera shook as I raised it to my eyes. I wondered if he'd noticed.

Just as we were walking back up the terrace stairs, a group of prisoners, all in striped uniform, began walking down from the top. Kurtz gestured me to step aside on to the terrace and allow them to pass. The first thing I noticed was how thin they all were. Their faces looked like transparent fabric drawn tightly over their skulls. Many had no hair. Many limped and had to be helped down the stairs by others. Something within me rebelled. I took a deep breath and pulled myself together, reminding myself that I was a professional, a journalist, a dispassionate observer.

All along, I had been taking photographs of the place; of the view, the fences, the barracks, the inside and the out. But as I raised my camera to photograph these walking skeletons, I hesitated. It seemed somehow... rude. Intrusive. I turned to Kurtz to ask wordlessly permission, bobbing the camera. He

*gestured at the prisoners as if to say, 'do as you please,' and so I
snapped away.*

*And then something happened. Oh, Leah. This will be so
tough for you.*

LEAH

February 1940 came to an end and merged into March. I had
survived the winter and my exile was just about over. Nobody
knew how long this terrible war would last. One more year?
Two, three, or more? Five, ten, even? The last war had lasted
four years. We were only into the second year of this one. How
much longer? And most terrifyingly, how many of us would
survive? And which of us?

Lisa came to the island in the first week of March, with
Trude. The new season was about to begin. Together, we set
about repairing the damage the winter and that last fierce storm
had wrought and, for me, it was a new beginning – I had
survived. I was an older, wiser, stronger version of myself, and
as the last snow melted and the days began to grow longer, I felt
a new confidence. I would survive this war, however long it
lasted. We all would. We would not let the Nazis win.

Of course, much later I would come to see that it was all
bravado. But I couldn't know that then.

Markus arrived on the second weekend of March and, for
the first time, stayed with me in the cabin, in the snug little bed
in the corner. I cannot describe the sense of uttermost relief and
comfort, being in his arms once again.

'I missed you so much,' I murmured into his shoulder.

'Not more than I missed you,' he said, and hugged me closer
yet. That, it turned out, was the weekend that determined our
destiny, that moulded us together forever. No matter what, we
belonged together. We were a family. I knew it right from the
first. It was a sense of deep, abiding unity; a sense of new life

pouring into me, literally. A new beginning, a bigger, rounder sense of what we were and what we always would be.

Several weeks later, I told him. 'I'm pregnant, Markus. We're going to have a baby.'

His delight was beyond description. 'And that's why we will fight on, Leah. It's not just us now. We must end this scourge for the sake of our child.'

'Oh, Markus.' That was all I could say. It sounded like such a cliché. How many other parents had said those exact words, and how many had still perished? But I knew exactly what he meant, because I felt it too: a renewal of my strength, my courage, my determination. My hope. My belief in a good future.

Right from the start, it was clear to both of us that I could not spend a second winter in the cabin. The baby was due in December or January, I calculated, the darkest days of the cold season. I could not give birth here, nor care for a newborn. In fact, I thought, I could not give birth anywhere in Germany; as a Jew, or as a fictitious Lena Gebhardt, I could not go to hospital, and my own father, a doctor, was in hiding.

But Markus did not hesitate for even a moment. 'I'll take you to Mama,' he said. 'It's what I always wanted – for you to move in with Oma and Opa on the farm. And now that Mama is there too, a nurse, who can help you with your pregnancy and the birth. It's perfect.'

'But – I don't want to impose. Put them at risk.'

'It's Mama's first grandchild,' said Markus. 'Of course she'll help you. She'd have helped you anyway, but now – all the more reason.'

'But...'

'No buts. You'll be safe there, as Lena Gebhardt. We'll make up a story for you. Trust me on this. Because where else can you have a baby? Berlin has been purged of Jewish doctors and probably of midwives too. It's the only solution, Leah. And I promise, they'll help. They'll all help.'

I couldn't help breathing a sigh of relief. And I still had a 'but'.

'But how will I get down there?'

'I'll take you, openly,' he replied. 'You're Lena Gebhardt with papers to prove it. We'll travel by train, openly, together.'

And so I settled into another summer at Sonnenhof, knowing it would be my last; the last, that is, until this damned war came to an end and I could return in freedom, with my child, and my husband. My family. How old would that child be, when the war ended? I could not begin to guess. I just knew that we'd return here one day, to thank Lisa, to see my island home again, to celebrate our survival. How could it possibly be otherwise?

Having a child, even knowing that a child is on the way, shifts one's perspective in inconceivable ways. There can no longer be even a sliver of doubt. Survival and safety become more than words conveying a dubious hope. Survival and safety become the first necessity. Hope becomes certainty. Entertaining even the slightest doubt for even a moment means betraying the new life, this infinitely precious being. Survival and safety become one's sole mission in life, one's sole focus; and a miracle occurs: with that focus comes the strength and vigour and passion to defend that being. And so it was with me and Markus.

I spent the summer working on the land with Lisa, Trude and the others, making sure that whoever came after me in the cabin the following winter – for Lisa had declared that for the duration of the war, that cabin would always be available to anyone who needed refuge – would be well provided for. But my mind was elsewhere. My mind was contained, centred around the life growing within me, and I had no fear, but only confidence and scintillating joy, a joy that met the terrible things going on outside me with defiance and certitude.

In September Markus and I took our leave from the island and from the friends we had grown so close to, who had helped me and kept me hidden and alive. I hugged them all, weeping, as I said goodbye.

Lisa took me in my arms and kissed me on both cheeks. '*Lebwohl!*' she said, 'Farewell. God willing, we will meet again when all this is over.'

'I will never forget what you have done for me,' I said through my tears. 'Thank you so much.'

There were similar hugs and final words of hope and gratitude for Trude. As she embraced me, she whispered in my ear: 'I'll be having a baby too. Dieter and I will be parents, early next year.'

My heart leapt and I squeezed her tight. 'One day, our children will play together,' I whispered back.

'I know.'

And then we were off, Markus and I. As Lena Gebhardt, his pregnant fiancée, I embarked on this new phase of my life. We did not take the train after all; he had managed to borrow the car of one of his higher-up Tempelhof colleagues; and, though we were stopped several times on the drive down to Bavaria, the showing of not only his own ID but also his impressive papers identifying him as Project Manager at Tempelhof Airport was all we needed. To me, it was quite shocking, seeing Markus in action.

The first time was the greatest shock. We were stopped at a security post a few kilometres outside Berlin. 'Don't worry about this, mouse,' Markus said, squeezing my hand, as we drew to a stop. I had to fight to stop my trembling, but luckily the sentry's eyes were on him, not me.

Markus rolled down the window; the sentry bent over to speak to him.

'Sieg Heil!' Markus announced. His arm shot out in the Nazi salute. The sentry stood to attention and did likewise. The car had various emblems stuck to the windscreen and a unique number plate that, it seemed, identified it and its occupants as VIPs. And that was really all it took. The sentry did not even ask for papers. Markus was plainly of rank.

'Where are you going?' was all he asked.

'To my parents' farm in Bavaria,' Markus replied truthfully. He turned to smile at me and, with a hand gesture, explained, again truthfully, 'I'm taking my fiancée to my parents, where she'll be safe from enemy bombs.'

'Gute Reise!' said the sentry, and waved us on.

'You're good at this,' I told Markus once I'd calmed my nerves.

'I am,' he said. 'I told you I was a good actor!'

'When this is over, you should try to get a part in a film!'

He laughed. 'Maybe I'll make it to Hollywood.'

Joking aside, I was petrified, and it was not until the car rolled safely up the drive to Tante Helga that I was able to relax. She welcomed me with open arms, and before long, I was settled in an attic room in the farmhouse.

At last, for the first time in years, I felt safe, normal. And I also felt tremendous guilt, knowing how many members of my community could not enjoy the same sense of safety. It was now no secret that Berlin, Germany as a whole, was being depleted of Jews. It was no secret that there were trains departing the city, bound for the distant east (although the exact locations were still secret, as was the fate of those on board). I felt guilt, because I had managed to save myself. But what about my parents? What about Aaron? Where were they?

Were they still safe? I had no way of knowing. Markus had done his best to procure information, but what he knew was unreliable at best, sketchy at worst. And some information was best kept secret.

'I don't know which family is protecting your parents,' he'd said, 'and it's best for me not to know. It's their secret, and needs to remain that way. As for Aaron...' He shook his head. 'I've been able to find out that he's been transferred from the Siemens factory. But where to, I don't know. He counts as a Jewish dissident: double trouble. Their fates are kept secret. We can only hope and pray.'

That worried me no end. We had all thought Aaron was safe at Siemens. Practically a slave, but at least valued for his labour and thus secure. Now? Would he be shunted off to some dark hole in the east, in one of those horrendous cattle cars? It was one more fear on top of the fear for my parents, myself, my baby, my people. I was safe, for the time being. But at what price?

I even felt guilty at being safe, when so many others of my people were far from safety. I had to live with this guilt; and it was tempered with the joy of the impending birth. A luminous, irrepressible joy. No matter how often I told myself that happiness of any kind was inappropriate considering the circumstances, that joy refused to be quenched. It rose like a gurgling mountain spring through the annals of my mind, through all the fears and the uncertainty and the sheer agony that comes with living through such dire times. A new life, growing within my body. Something so precious, not even the scourge of war could destroy it or the joy it brought me.

MAGDA

One of the prisoners stumbled, but not from weak knees. He stumbled because our eyes caught and just as I clicked the camera, I dropped it in shock. It fell to my waist and dangled there on its leather strap as I stared.

His jaw dropped and mine must have too, even as the whispered word Aaron! escaped my lips. It was him, Leah. Even beyond the skeletal mask that was his face, I knew him. I knew him in the eyes, in the look that flashed between us, imperceptible I'm sure to Kurtz but a seeming eternity to me because I can see it now before me: the eyes I had known all my life, from back when we'd all been kids together, teenagers together. From that very short-lived flirtation when I was fifteen, from the laughter and fun we'd had together, dancing, ice-skating, all four of us linked as we walked through a Berlin Christmas market with the aroma of mulled wine and roasted chestnuts wafting around us, and a brass band playing jazz in the background.

You know, of course, that we had once had the silly idea of marrying each other's brother. We were about twelve or thirteen at the time, an age when girls start to become women and to dream of the great love of her life, and there were these two handsome young men escorting us all over the place, to ice rinks and up Alpine mountains. What could be more obvious, that we would stay a foursome?

But while your crush on Markus was genuine, I knew even at the time that my flirtation with Aaron didn't have a future. The fact is, Leah, I could never have loved any man the way I loved you. I was aware that that love was hopeless. No wonder I was able to give myself to an even greater love: the love for Germania, and the man who cultivated it, pushed me into it.

But Aaron was a friend, my very closest male friend. And here he was, little more than a walking skeleton. And yet, looking at that skeleton, I knew that a fire still burned within him. It was his eyes. The very same eyes I had known since my childhood. Those eyes, once bright and filled with fun, now sunk deep into the skull that formed his face.

In them, now, a haunted, yawning emptiness, something dead. Yet something alive, as well. A tiny spark, the last remains of that fire. Not just the spark of recognition. The spark of defiance, a defiance that had still not been extinguished.

Leah, before I dropped the camera, I had managed to press the shutter. I later developed that photo. I did not want to enclose it in this envelope as it would have shocked you too much. If you reply to this, I will send it to you. One day. Or give it to you personally, if you allow me to.

I will close this account of Natzweiler-Struthof right here, as that was the crux and the climax of my visit to that place of horror.

Later that day the chauffeur drove me back to Strasbourg. Kurtz and most of his Strasbourg colleagues, it turned out, always spent the week, Monday to Friday, in a Nazi hotel close by.

I did not stay much longer in Alsace.

I had found there all that I needed. My job was done.

37

MAGDA

Alsace – the entire experience, Margarethe, and then Madame Gauthier, and finally Aaron – was the straw that broke the proverbial camel's back. I knew then for sure that I could no longer be a devoted member of the Nazi Party. Devoted is the pertinent word: I could be a Nazi in name alone, speak the required slogans, make the required gestures. But I could no longer pretend to myself that I was hard as steel, or aspire to that end. I was too soft for this job, and always would be.

Aaron. I couldn't stop thinking about him. Those eyes! That spark of life, a tiny ember buried in ashes, glowing bright! I was filled with the urge to tell you, your family. You must all be living in constant fear for him, I thought. I needed to let you know he was still alive. Only just, but alive! I needed to tell you his whereabouts. You would not be able to visit him, but at least you'd know.

You, Leah. Since I'd seen Aaron I was thinking more and more about you. If I had pushed you from my mind in the years gone by, the years of my full delusion, now, in the years of my gradual awakening, you kept pushing yourself back into my consciousness. You forced yourself into my mind, uninvited, in memories of our closeness, our love. My love for you. How deep it had been, Leah, and how much it had cost to root it out completely and replace it with love for an evil man and the monstrous philosophy he had created. I had erased you from my mind, but now you returned with a vengeance.

Where were you? Had you managed to flee Germany in time? Had you been in one of those dreaded cattle-cars, shunted off to the east and a dire future, a dire end? I grew frantic with worry. Were you even alive? I had to know. And if you were alive, you had to know that Aaron was too. And your parents had to know. What could I do? How could I find you?

I also had to let Markus know. Aaron was his best friend, after all. Markus, now firmly ensconced in his fabulous Tempelhof job, might have some idea where you were, and pass the news on to you, or your parents.

But then again: the whole point of my intervention, in getting him that job, was for him to become a full Nazi. Now I could only hope and pray that Markus had stayed true to his original convictions. If so, he might know where you were, and if it was possible to contact you. And so I wrote to Markus with the news, addressing the letter to him at Kaiserkorso Eins, where I knew he still lived. I had by now moved back to Berlin-Kreuzberg, into another cheap, dingy room rented by the week, and that was the return address I put on the envelope. Secretly, I hoped that with this letter Markus and I could rekindle some sort of a relationship. I would love to discuss what I had seen in Alsace with him. Let him know of my growing doubts. On the other hand, I had never been good at admitting my mistakes. Would my pride ever allow me to speak honestly to Markus? Time would tell.

By now I had developed the photo I had taken of Aaron. I did not send it with the letter. It was too shocking, the photo of a man half-dead who happened to be Markus's best friend and your brother. I could not do this to either of you. I wanted the *news of Aaron to give hope to both Markus and you, and your parents, of course. If you were still alive.*

I wasn't surprised at all when the letter plopped through my postbox unopened. 'Return to Sender' *in bold writing – Markus's writing – on the envelope.* 'Annahme Verweigert.' *Acceptance Denied. I remembered then that in his last letter Markus had told me never to write to him again. Disappointed, I put the same letter in a clean envelope, addressed it to Mama at the farm in Bavaria, and added a note asking her to forward it to Markus. There. Job done.*

And now I had to rethink my own status within the Party, and my next moves. A tricky undertaking. I knew my love affair with Nazism was over. But how to proceed?

One had to be careful. One could not simply leave the Party and expect to live a normal life. But I could take one step back. My first task was to fulfil the obligation I had undertaken in going to Alsace in the first place: my report. And so I dutifully did what I'd set out to do, but keeping my wits about me and picking my words carefully.

These were quite different reports from the ones I'd sent from Poland. I wrote about the most successful Germanification of Alsace. Of the happy Germans in Strasbourg, and the incredible completion of the Natzweiler-Struthof camp – emphasising the spectacular views from the camp, and the wonderful work being done there through the extraction of granite that would be utilised to build grand edifices all over Germany. Hoping that my cynicism did not show through the carefully chosen words.

I did not mention who did the work of extraction, and what condition those labourers were in.

I carefully sorted through my photographs, as I had always done. Even back in Poland, once the photos had been developed I had always carefully curated which ones would be sent to the Hitler Youth for publication and which ones I would keep for myself. The photographs had to show a positive front, and in that I complied.

The disturbing photos, those showing scenes that threatened to shatter the image of myself as 'hard as steel', stayed in my own private collection. And so, here too, I selected only one photo of the prisoners as they stumbled down the terraces, one that did not reveal their wrecked bodies. Those photos, I kept for myself.

In the meantime, I returned to the Berliner Volkszeitung. *I had not yet completed my training as an editor, and hoped they'd take me back, and they did; I completed my training, and was taken on as a full-time editor.*

An impartial desk job. Just what I craved. And a salary, so that I could afford to live in a somewhat nice dwelling and eat nice things. I found an affordable flat, again in Kreuzberg. How I wished, though, I could live again in Kaiserkorso, in our old home!

Not only had I found the perfect job: my life situation was now calm enough for me to devote more time to a private enterprise. I've already told you about my desire to write a youth-oriented equivalent to Mein Kampf. *Something more reader-friendly, something that would speak emotionally and powerfully to our eager young people and fill them with that same ardour that had catapulted me into the BDM, against my parents' wishes, so long ago. My new job was the perfect environment for such an ambition. Yet everything had changed. As a press and propaganda journalist, I had been anchored in the very heart of the youth movement and feeding them information that would help mould their impressionable minds in the 'right' direction. That had once been my aim.*

But since Alsace everything had changed. I was still writing my book. But the concept was now a different one, and I knew for certain that this reformed version would never be published. Not in Hitler's Grossdeutschland. But I neverthe-less had to write it, as a labour of love. A labour of truth.

I was by now well aware, as were we all, that conquering the entire world, starting with Poland and up to the Aral Sea far in the East, and perhaps beyond, was impossible, a megalo-maniacal fantasy. World domination, he had wanted. East-wards towards China and simultaneously, western Europe and North Africa. The pipe dream of a madman. Yet I could not even begin to entertain the notion that Germany could lose the war. Even the thought was, well, unthinkable. But my over-confident arrogance had taken a devastating hit. Nothing was going according to Hitler's plan. It was all falling apart.

Yes, we had taken France, but England was proving to be far too resistant. The fact that the United States of America had joined in the war effort since the attack on Pearl Harbor in December 1941 had thrown up some terrible obstacles. But, of course, we always had our great Führer's reassurance that eventually we would be the victors. Germans listened to his speeches for comfort and confidence, and never, not even for a moment, lost faith. We clung to the dream of eventual triumph.

Please, Leah, understand that I wrote that sentence decid-edly tongue in cheek! As I've already stated, I had lost faith. But there was nothing I could do. I was already a part of this huge juggernaut of oppressive power and my only option, now, was to play the game and not show my doubt.

And so 1942 crept slowly by. Slowly, slowly, we all began to realise: conquering the world was megalomania gone berserk.

And then, there we were, in the middle of 1943. The Blitz of Berlin.

I had never once expected that Berlin would be bombed. But here we were. A city under siege. On 30 January – exactly ten years after Hitler's rise to power, as if in mockery of it – our enemies launched a deliberate air attack, disrupting an important speech by Herr Goebbels to mark that anniversary. The attack came precisely at the hour of his speech, which was completely disrupted. The irony was not lost on any Berliner.

I thought at the time it was a terrible omen, but I tried to dispel such superstitious notions. Still, that particular attack was a severe embarrassment for the German leadership, and there couldn't have been a German alive who was not seriously alarmed.

Night after night of bombing raids. Civilians fleeing for bomb shelters most nights; civilian areas of the city completely destroyed. Streets full of rubble, entire buildings reduced to heaps of broken bricks. I loved my city. To witness its destruction was soul-destroying.

Then, three months later, on 20 April, came Hitler's fifty-fourth birthday, which the enemy decided to disrupt too, with another devastating bombing raid on the capital. All year so far there had been similar attacks, and Berliners were now accustomed to seeking refuge in bunkers when these attacks came at night. I, too, found myself running for underground safety when the warning sirens came. After the hubris of the early years, how humiliating!

And then in November of that year, just six months after I had started employment, came the attack that would later become known as the Battle of Berlin. Horrendous! Thousands of Berliners were killed, hundreds of thousands were rendered homeless – and in winter. I was so glad, now, that Mama had moved to Bavaria, and I wrote to her regularly to reassure her of my own survival. She must have been worried sick but, apart from a few words on a Christmas card, she did not reply. I knew that she was still devastated by the choice I had made to join the Nazi Party and had never forgiven me, but I loved her still and tried to keep in touch. The less she knew of my *actual work, the better. I knew she would not have approved of anything I'd done over the past three years. I myself did not approve, after all.*

But back to Herr Goebbels, and his New Year's Eve speech. You cannot imagine the confusion that speech let loose in me. On the one hand, my confidence was restored – that Germany would win this war. Despite the reversals we had endured over the past year, we would win; 1944 would see us on top again.

Herr Goebbels gave me much-needed peace of mind: 'What worked for the enemy in the First World War will fail him in the Second World War. There is no point in even speaking about it. Our people survived so brilliantly the test of enemy air terror during the year 1943 that the enemy can bury the hopes he had for it. The nights of bombing have indeed made us poorer, but also harder. The misery of air terror is to some degree the mortar that holds us together as a nation amid all dangers. Our people have not fallen apart during the nightly firestorms as our enemies hoped and wished, but rather has become a firm and unshakable community.'

On the other hand: what kind of a Germany would we end up with? The entire foundation of my confidence had been shaken. I was torn in two. If the Axis crumbled into dust, what then? Where would I go, what would I do? I was certain that all those who had participated in the project of world domination would be brought to trial and punished. All those involved in the resettlement of Poland. That meant me. The Allies would come after me. After all of us. I was terrified of the punishment that would be meted out for the part I had played. And for that reason alone, we had to win. We had to! Somehow!

It was clear that Hitler himself was not going to allow a single doubt to cross his mind. God was on our side! No matter how bleak the prospect of victory seemed, by a last-minute miracle we would win! Out of ruins, we'd stand triumphant! I clung to that hope.

For the present, all I could do was my job, as well as I could. As an editor, I was in the wonderful position of being able to maintain a neutral stance. I did not have to stand heart and soul behind the articles we published. I only had to make sure they were well written. It was not my job to judge. That remit belonged to those higher up.

And in that spirit I continued my work, which I loved, though my work conditions weren't exactly what I would have chosen. For a start, I was the only woman among the journalists and editors. But I was good, and pretty soon I was promoted, and then promoted again, above some of the men. Still, my male colleagues tried to establish a hierarchy that would have relegated me to the lowest level. I soon clarified my position, however. Even through all my conflicts of conscience, my doubts, my mental breakdowns, I had preserved my basic characteristics: my ability to assert myself and not suffer fools gladly.

Perhaps they'd never yet encountered a woman quite like me, one so perfectly gifted with that wonderful trait known as Berliner Schnauze. Yes, that was me: rude, outspoken, loud, and, when needed, coarse. A big mouth. I paid no attention to the rules of etiquette that dictated that women had to be sweet, gentle and subservient. Not me!

You know me, Leah. I haven't changed in that respect. Remember how I chased the bullies away from you on our way to school, just by barking my contempt at them? Well, so I barked at those men and, amusingly, they backed off.

Having established my position, I ignored them for everything that did not relate to the job. These men were coarse themselves. Primitive. I could not abide the way they spoke of and to the female secretaries, much less the way these poor women were treated. One of the areas with which I had disagreed with the Führer from the very start concerned the roles of women, and it pained me now to see that these men considered women the human equivalent of brood mares. Women had to produce the next generation of good Aryan stock, tomorrow's children. In all my previous propaganda work, I had downplayed this aspect and encouraged my female readers to develop themselves as well as they could: physically, culturally, educationally. I did not believe we were inferior to men, and, much as I loved babies myself, I knew I never wanted one of my own; and I would stick up for any woman who chose a single and childless life, as I had done.

But this was the first time I'd had to actually work with male colleagues in an office, and I was shocked at their behaviour. These men were extremely promiscuous, and so very coarse in their boasting of their proclivities. They did not understand me and my ascetic way of life at all; nevertheless, since I did not appoint myself their moral arbiter, we managed to carve out roles for ourselves in which they moved as a pack and I was the lone wolf.

I did, however, also carve out a role for myself among the women. Not just the secretaries; also, cleaners, canteen workers and so on. I tried to warn them about making casual liaisons with the men and was always a little astonished at how easily they fell into the trap of male seduction. I felt that women in general needed to be a little more circumspect in this area, and many a time I had to comfort a cruelly discarded cleaner or secretary.

I tried, and mostly failed, to foster in them a certain personal pride and bodily integrity. I never quite understood why they were so pliable. But maybe, as far as women and female behaviour are concerned, I'm just an anomaly, and I should just let it rest. It's simply not possible to change others, and I refused to judge my fellow females.

As for the men: there's a way of letting someone know you disdain him them without using words. Unless they were rude to me first, I was never rude to their faces, and in our day-to-day work it was simply live and let live. I did notice that they were a little surprised that I chose a celibate life. They seemed to think that men were God's gift to women and couldn't fathom the fact that I did not behave as such. The poor things. Frankly, there have been very few young men in my life who I could really respect. In fact, I can only think of three: your brothers Mosche and Aaron, and my brother Markus. And of course, I worried terribly about Markus.

38

LEAH

The next two years, 1941 and 1942, seemed to fly past. Once more I retreated into a bubble, a bubble occupied by just me, my daughter Naomi, Tante Helga and her mother, whom we all called Oma. Markus came as often as he could, but it was a long journey from Berlin to Munich and then from there out to the farm and his visits were rare. But when he did come, it was like a warm, cosy piece of heaven torn away from a ragged world outside, a world that was falling into tatters, not only in Europe but in Asia and North Africa. Now the Soviet Union, too, was our enemy. I hoped and prayed that Germany would lose. That was the only hope for my family's survival.

But I could not follow the news outside. Here on the farm, we lived in an oasis, we three women and our baby. Four generations. When Opa died two years ago most of the cattle were sold off, and now there were just enough for our little group to manage on our own, without outside help. The young farmhands had anyway all been recruited for the Wehrmacht and were fighting for their lives somewhere in France or on the Eastern Front, and so it was just us. Then in 1942 Oma's health deteriorated and Tante Helga became more involved in her care; I took over most of the farm work, milking the cows, feeding them, cleaning the stalls. Naomi lay in her pram nearby, kicking and gurgling. I would pick her up and feed her when she cried, sitting on the side of the stone trough in the farmyard, drinking her in with my eyes, talking to her, watching her grow.

And grow she did. When she began to crawl, I left her with Tante Helga in the house, as we could not have her on hands and knees in the stalls. Oma died in June of that year, after which Tante Helga and I shared the farm work and the child-care and the household chores. Markus came only twice that whole year.

'I can't believe you're still working at that terrible place, pretending to be a Nazi!' I said on one of his visits, when he was granted compassionate leave for Oma's funeral. I spoke half in jest, half in rebuke; I wished he would find another job, but I knew it was difficult. He had been promoted several times over the years, so I knew how valuable he was to the project, which was still not complete; resigning would probably result in punishment of some kind.

'It's not so bad any more,' he told me. 'The colleagues I work with – they're scientists, professionals, not politicians. We just don't discuss politics or ideology; that's for the men in adminis-tration. We just check in for work, do our job, go home.'

'What about your great plan? Does Hitler ever come to inspect?'

His face fell. 'I think I was letting my imagination run away with me with that idea,' he said. 'There's no way I could carry out something that enormous on my own. I was hoping I could find accomplices within the project, but the only one I've found is in a minor position, in reception. He'd be of no help at all.'

We had gone for a walk across the fields surrounding the farm; Markus had said he wanted to show me something. We came to a large gate; he opened it and we walked through. He closed it again, and took my hand.

'Hitler does come occasionally. It's still his pet project and he likes to see how much progress we've made. When he comes, he's in and out. He likes to tour the place, give us all pep talks. He shakes all our hands... it's so disgusting having to touch that man. I feel I need to wash my hands afterwards. But that's as far as it goes. I wouldn't know where to begin if I were to... you know. He doesn't eat any food when he comes, so that option isn't possible.'

'What option?'

'You know, poison. And anyway, it seems he has a few tasters who go everywhere with him. Young women who have to sample everything he eats beforehand, to check that it's not poisoned. Only when he sees they're OK does he actually eat.'

'But if you're not making any progress there, Markus, why don't you simply leave? Get another job? The Siemens factory would snap you up!'

'They're all Nazis there too!' said Markus. 'So what's the difference?'

He shook his head. 'And anyway, if I quit, they'll probably make sure I'm sent to the Eastern Front in disgrace. They don't like disloyalty, and that's what it would be.'

'Then what, Markus? Surely you're wasting your time there?'

I could feel his dissatisfaction. Markus was simply not made to fit into a job at the service of others. He was a fighter, a rebel, a maverick, and much as I knew that at least he was safe in his present job, I also knew he was made for more, that his true talents were being wasted and that he longed for more. But for the time being, he could only dream.

We walked on, hand in hand, in silence. Markus carried Naomi on his shoulders, holding her little feet to keep her steady while she clung to his head. She kept throwing off his hat, and I would pick it up and hand it back, only for her to throw it down again with a peal of laughter. I put it on my own head, and she found that even funnier. She was an easy child, happy and affectionate. She was my whole world: she and Markus. If only we could build that world, together. If only this terrible war would end.

We walked along a lane and then, following a path leading off it, I gasped in delight. We had reached a part of the farmland I had not yet seen, a beautiful valley, nestled between emerald-green hills. A small river ran through the valley, bouncing down from a spring hidden among a grove of trees further up the hillside. Pure bubbling water bounced among rocks and gathered in a small, shallow pool at our feet.

Markus lifted Naomi from his shoulders and set her down. It was a beautiful summer day, the sky as blue as sapphire and cloudless. The sun was warm, yet not too hot, and shone silver on the leaping water.

'Oh, Markus! This is wonderful!' I cried. I removed all of Naomi's clothes and set her in the pool, where she squatted down in delight and began to play with the water and the stones, laughing and looking up at her father. Markus laughed too and they played a little game of throwing stones. And then he spoke, solemnly and slowly.

'One day,' he said, 'one day when this is over, I'll build a house. A home, for all of us and the children who'll come later. It'll be like your Sonnenhof cabin, just much bigger, with room for us all. It'll be made of whole logs, Norwegian spruce instead of pine, and it'll be a warm, snug home, modern and yet charming, in the old Bavarian style. I'll build a home where we have everything we need. We'll grow our own food. We'll be safe there and we won't need anyone. Just us.'

I laughed. 'Dream on!' I said. 'What about electricity? What about school, for the children? What about a job for you, and money to maintain us?'

He laughed too. 'Yes, it's just a dream. But a house right here is possible, Leah. It's the perfect spot. We can sort out the details as they arise. I'd like to follow Migge's lead, and be as self-sustaining as possible. If this war has taught me one thing, it's that you can't trust a government to do the best for you and your family. Yes, we'll need to compromise. But it's good to have a dream, something to work towards, and that's mine.'

'Then it's mine too,' I said. 'There's nothing I want more.'

'When all this is over,' Markus promised, 'we'll work on the reality.'

But then his leave was over, and he was gone. He actually left a day early, so as to catch up with old friends in Munich: the brother and sister Hans and Sophie Scholl, and other friends.

He shared with me some of what was going on in Munich. 'They call themselves the White Rose,' he said, 'and they are working mostly to awaken young people, to grow the resistance in Munich. We all believe that if the different groups in all the cities work together, we can achieve something great.'

'Just be careful,' I warned him. 'Please be careful. Don't take any risks. That's all I ask of you.'

'I'll be careful,' he promised.

39

LEAH – THE FARM

Markus might have promised me that he would be careful and take no risks, but he couldn't speak for every dissident, and in 1943 disaster struck. On 22 February he turned up on the farm unexpectedly, distraught and almost hysterical with grief. I hadn't been listening to the radio and I hadn't read the newspapers – I was sticking to my method of maintaining my little bubble and keeping my world whole – and so I had no idea of what had taken place.

'Sophie and Hans!' he cried. 'They've been caught. Oh, Leah! They're dead!'

He opened his arms and I fell into them. His body heaved with wretchedness. His face distorted with agony. He blubbered like a baby. Naomi, on the floor beside us, pulling at his trousers, burst into tears as well, and for once we both ignored her.

I offered what comfort I could, but there was nothing I could do to turn back the past, and bit by bit, the story came out.

Sophie and Hans had one day decided to distribute anti-Nazi fliers at their university. They had left piles of them at strategic points around the corridors and halls, and Sophie had toppled a pile into the main auditorium. She and her brother were arrested, put on trial, found guilty of high treason by the People's Court.

On 21 February – yesterday – they had been executed. By guillotine.

I actually screamed when I heard that word. It could not be! But it was. Sophie was only twenty-one, younger than me. I did not know her, but I felt the agony in every cell of my body.

'That's it,' Markus said before he left us again. 'It's time to get serious.'

'But what will you do, Markus?' I wept. 'Where will you go?'

'Back to Berlin,' he replied, and his voice was grim and his eyes, as they held mine, were no longer soft, no longer warm. 'I'm going underground,' he said then. 'I'm sorry, Leah. I have to get serious. I do it for you and Naomi and every mother and every child. I have to fight this terror, with every last bone in my body.'

'You promised to be careful!' I wept. 'Not to put yourself in harm's way!'

'And I will keep that promise,' he replied. 'I promise to keep that promise. And I'll let you know.'

Cold dread filled every cell of my body. Up to now I'd felt secure, knowing that Markus worked at Tempelhof as a Nazi. I knew him to be safe there. But I also knew in my bones that that safety could not last forever. That one day it would end, and he'd enter the darkness that was the underground. When that happened, all contact would cease. All visits would cease. It would be the beginning of the end. Neither of us knew what that end would be, but I knew I would not see him again for a long, long time.

We wept together, then, and Naomi wept with us, not

knowing the reason but in sympathy with our grief and our fear. We huddled together, all three, and wept. And as we wept, I somehow knew. I had a premonition.

40

MAGDA

I realise now that over the last few pages I've omitted to speak of the one subject that must be foremost in your mind as you read – if you are reading at all. Not just omitted. Avoided. Yes, I have deliberately avoided this particular subject.

Jews.

Of course, by now it was common knowledge that all Jews had to be removed from Berlin. We all knew of the trains that day after day rolled out of Berlin's main station, heading eastwards. We all knew that Jews had been rounded up and stuffed into those primitive carriages like cattle. They were being sent to Poland, we were told, where they would be housed in appropriate camps. They would be allowed to take a suitcase with them, to start a new life in Poland. This reminded me somewhat of the resettlement in Poland that I had observed so closely.

It's true that in that work I had been more involved with the newcomers than with the evacuees, but I had constantly reassured myself that they all would find a new home somewhere. We heard, too, about the Warsaw Ghetto. We were the press; of course we knew.

But as humans, we were all inclined to gloss over the details we could not reconcile with whatever conscience we had. At least, that was how I dealt with the unpleasant knowledge. I did not go deeper into the matter. It is how I placated my conscience.

I refused to confront the vague questions that rose up in my mind. The reality I had faced myself was bad enough.

And yes, there were questions. With the wisdom of hindsight, I now know that my conscience, some sense of morality, of right and wrong, was sending constant messages into my conscious mind – messages that I pushed away with the relentlessness with which I had watched the banishment of the rightful owners of Polish homesteads, with the neutral stance of a reporter, denying all personal responsibility. I had pushed all awareness of their misery away from myself. I didn't want to know, and so I did not know. I had long ago mastered the art of pushing away from me every unwelcome thought the moment it tried to tickle my brain. Except when I couldn't. When I'd had my little personal moments of crisis. But were the rumours true? No. Just No. They couldn't be. See no evil, hear no evil, speak no evil. The Jews would be fine. They would be resettled, just like the Poles. We just didn't want them in Germany. Hitler didn't want them in Germany. They had to go.

Did I once think of you in that situation, Leah? Did I ask myself where you and your family had disappeared to? I knew you were no longer at Kaiserkorso Eins; the time was long past when Jews could live in normal housing and all Jews had left the building. If I had been inclined to care – well, I didn't. I didn't allow even a thought of caring. It was Orders, from above. The Jews had left the building and the city. So be it. Not my concern. Other departments were responsible for the Jewish problem. Not me.

Tough as leather, swift as greyhounds, hard as Krupp steel.

I had finally achieved that coveted goal. My mind was steel.
Not my job to question or to care.

41

LEAH

The silence that followed Markus's departure was, for me, the most terrifying thing of all, because it was so personal. I knew that the stakes were higher than they'd ever been: for him, for us, for our family. Knowing that he'd gone underground just when the Nazis were turning on themselves in the most vicious phase of the war catapulted me into a state of permanent panic, a panic that simmered beneath the surface because, still, I had to carry on. I had to feed and milk the cows and clean the stalls and care for my baby. I had, for her sake, to present a serene and comforting front, because she could read my eyes, read my smiles, feel every tendril of fear that escaped my body. I could not let her know that things were so very wrong. That her father, instead of being here with her, was out there as a shadow in a savage world, his life at risk.

And that, as contradictory as that seems, it was a good thing, a noble thing; that he was fighting not only for her future but for the future of all children born into this madness. I had to support him against every instinct, every need for him to be right here with us.

Before he left, I had told Markus how useless I felt, sitting at home and waiting for news, bad or good, instead of being out there, fighting alongside him. I began to wish that I, too, had chosen to go underground and fight. I knew there were women in Markus's group, in all the dissident groups. There was a Jewish group, called the Baum Group, with several girls as members, girls braver than I was myself. I felt cowardly for having chosen, instead, to hide.

But Markus was adamant that my form of resistance was as worthy as any other. My resistance lay in survival.

'What use would it have been if you'd joined the Baum Group?' he argued. While they were active, Markus had kept me up to date while at the same time dissuading me from joining. The Baum Group had done wonderful work, just like the Scholls: they circulated anti-Nazi leaflets, they organised demonstrations. They even did some bombing. I'd been so envious, at the time. But what was the result? Mass arrests, executions, and more reprisals against Jews.

'What's the point, when in the end there are no Jews left? No, Leah. You're now a mother, and that role is vital. Naomi is the future. She is our future. You must live for her. You did the right thing, mouse. Never call yourself a coward. You and Naomi represent the future, and it is for you that we fight.'

I had to be satisfied with that.

In fact, that year, the year the Scholls were executed, the year Markus went underground, was the year everything changed. Though German propaganda of course filled the news channels with stories of glorious victories, news of Germany's terrible defeat at Stalingrad, and other devastating defeats in the Soviet Union, trickled through, as well as news of the Warsaw Uprising, defeats in North Africa, the Mediterranean. Italy: the arrest of Mussolini, and news of the imminent surrender of Italy. The bombing of Hamburg. We knew. We heard. We allowed ourselves to hope. These positive reports came at unexpected times, from unexpected sources. Markus had said he would never try to contact me or his mother, and yet he managed to send reports of Allied victories through anonymous channels. I knew these reports were from him. And I knew that, whatever he was doing, it was good.

And yet I feared. In spite of all the hope I had gathered and stored in my mind, no matter how often I told myself that all would end well, a deep chill had settled in my heart that I could not shake off, no matter how hard I tried. It was the fear of all women everywhere whose country was at war, wives and mothers whose husbands and sons were out there, fighting in wars in which everyone was a loser. It was the cold hand of terror wrapped around my heart, on behalf of our loved ones; because whether they were out there in open battle or, as in Markus's case, fighting from below, from the shadows, the spectre of death lay over us all.

Tante Helga feared for her daughter. Where was Magda? What was she up to? Despite having cut off all contact with her Nazi daughter, she worried nevertheless.

And then, out of the blue, a letter plopped through the postbox. It came after lunch; the postman on his country rounds always delivered our mail at this time. Naomi was having her nap, and Tante Helga was upstairs. I picked up the small pile of post lying on the floor, three or four letters in all, and before placing them on the hall table glanced through them; by habit, because of course nobody was writing letters to Lena Gebhardt. Not even Lisa, or Trude; we had all decided it was better to have no contact at all for now. But I recognised the writing on the top envelope, and gasped aloud from shock. I knew that handwriting: Magda. What could she possibly be writing to her mother about?

'Tante! Tante!!' I shouted as I ran up the stairs, two at a time. Tante Helga was bringing in the fluffy eiderdowns from the open windows where they'd been airing and making the beds, mine and hers and Naomi's little one. My voice must have been wildly panicked, because she came running out of her bedroom and said urgently, 'What's the matter?'

'A letter! From Magda. For you!' I was out of breath; I gasped the words. Tante Helga tore the letter from my hands, glanced at the address, and ripped it open. Unfolded the single page of writing. Typewritten. Typical Magda. She frowned.

'It's actually for Markus,' she said. 'But she's scrawled a few lines at the top telling me to read it and forward it to him, and—' She stopped talking as she read on. And then: 'Oh!' Her left hand flew to her mouth, covering it in shock, and her eyes sought mine, caught mine, sent a silent but unmistakable warning.

'What is it?' I cried.

'Oh, Leah! Leah, it's about Aaron. Dear Aaron, news... Magda's seen him. He's alive...'

'Oh, thank God!' I cried. 'Thank God! I've been sick with worry... I thought they'd—'

'He's alive, Leah, but it's not good. He's in a camp in France. Well, Alsace. Germany now, I suppose. Natzweiler-Struthof. Magda says he's in a terrible condition and that it's a brutal camp and she fears for his life... Here, read it yourself.'

She handed me the letter. My knees were already giving way and I sank to the ground. Sitting on the top step of the stairwell, I read Magda's devastating words:

Markus, this is a death camp. They work the prisoners till they can no longer stand. I've seen those men. They are like walking skeletons. Living corpses. Some are executed, by gallows. There's a crematorium, where the bodies are disposed of. It's a terrible, terrible place, Markus. I was invited to view it due to my job but all I can say is, if this is how the Jewish problem is to be solved, then something's very wrong.

I crumpled the letter in my hands, and right there, sitting on the stairs, I buried my head in my arms and cried until my lungs ached from the effort. At some point I felt Tante Helga's arm round me as she, too, sank to the step next to me, and murmured comforting words.

'I have to let my parents know!' I wept. 'They're so worried!' But we both knew there was nothing to be done. At least we now knew he was still alive – or at least had been when Magda saw him. Goodness only knew if that had changed. Yet still, it was a small comfort compared with the dark hole of not-knowing we'd lived in before.

Right then Naomi, waking from her nap, began to howl, and so I stood up, drained of every last tear. On legs numb from being bent double on a low stair seat, I stumbled off to give comfort to my daughter.

The shock of Aaron's situation changed nothing. Though it was a relief to know that he was at least still alive, I now knew that he was, according to Magda, basically a living corpse, and there was no respite in my worry for him. Indeed, my fears only worsened.

And the news grew worse by the day. November of that year brought the beginning of the Battle of Berlin. We listened in petrified shock to the reports of our beloved city's destruction as the Allies reduced it to rubble. My fears for my parents emerged once more with a vengeance: it was all very well to hope for an Allied victory that would free us from Nazi terror, but at what price?

The bombs' targets were not military ones, and they seemed indiscriminate; they fell on poorer districts and on the homes of the rich too. Would my parents survive the bombs? And Markus: was he still in Berlin? Had Tempelhof been bombed? Surely it was a prime target. Was Kaiserkorso Eins still standing? What about Lisa von Berg, her family, my dear friend

Trude? Trude must have had her baby by now; were they safe? I imagined her giving birth during an air raid, in a bunker some-where, and prayed for her. Prayed for us all. I had always loved the Psalms of David, and Psalm 23 now became engraved into my being:

'Yea, though I walk through the valley of the shadow of death, I will fear no evil, for thou art with me, thy rod and thy staff to comfort me...'

The comfort was small, just a thin thread of hope, but I clung to it with all my strength. The knowledge that Nazi Germany was now clearly losing this terrible war, the spectre of Nazism fast diminishing. There WAS hope. Perhaps the Allies could save us all in time. Save Aaron. My parents. Me, and Markus, and Naomi, my precious little family. I clung to that thin thread, that psalm, as to a lifeline.

42

MAGDA

There is another subject I have avoided writing about until now, and you know exactly what it is. A chapter I've omitted. I wish I could keep this secret forever, but something deep inside forces me on. So here goes.

The news – it came to me through the grapevine; everyone knew I had a brother who worked at Tempelhof – was that Markus had walked off the job. Not given notice, not resigned in the proper manner, but simply walked out and never returned. It hit me like a bolt of lightning. The fool! How could he abandon such a privileged position! Where was he?

I had a dreadful suspicion that Markus had gone into the underground, that murky place of homeless rebels living in the shadows and hunted by the Gestapo. That he was a dissident, actively opposing the Nazis. That realisation was in itself confusing to me. How could he have lasted so long at Tempelhof, if he had retained his opposition to the regime? I had thought that being soaked from top to toe in the great purpose of creating the most advanced physical symbol of our power would have done the trick of convincing and converting him to Nazi ideology, or at the very least curbed his most passionate *impulses. Made of him a meek and obedient employee, keeping his head down and his lips sealed. I know, I know. That's the very opposite of Markus's nature. But still, I'd hoped. Tempelhof had been a safe place for him.*

If that was not the case, if he had run off to join some protest group, then his very life was in danger. The Party did not tolerate dissidents. Earlier in the year, a group of amateur troublemakers had been unearthed in Munich and eliminated, including a very young female student called Sophie Scholl. Surely her fate – execution by guillotine – would have been enough to show Markus that resistance is futile? Also, it did not reflect well on me if my brother, whom I had personally recommended for the job, proved to be an enemy of the state. Luckily, my own stance and reputation were, at least on the surface, impeccable, and I had no fears that I would be implicated and punished. I had managed to play the game well, never letting on that my faith in Hitler and the ideology as a whole had suffered a terrible blow.

I loved Markus. Back in the early 1930s I had truly believed he had been deluded; I had helped him nab that wonderful job at Tempelhof Airport in the hope that he would eventually see the light. I had done it as a favour, as a true believer. But now I was a true believer no longer. I myself entertained doubts, and I could very well imagine that so did Markus; and I could no longer blame him.

Now he had disappeared without a trace. As the months crept by, at the back of my mind was the urgent need to track him down, wherever he might be. I had to find him! I had the feeling Mama might know something about him and his whereabouts but, if so, she wasn't telling. I wondered if she had received my letter about Aaron and forwarded it to Markus. Perhaps that was the reason for him quitting the job? Perhaps he had developed some insane plan to find Aaron and rescue him from Natzweiler-Struthof?

His disappearance, however, brought an advantage for me. Now that Markus had vanished into thin air, our flat at Kaiserkorso Eins stood empty. I lost no time in moving back in. It was by far the cheapest option for me and was of much better quality than some of the dumps on offer. Now that you and your family were gone from the building, I no longer had to fear an unpleasant, guilt-ridden encounter either.

Moving back gave me a bit of nostalgia. Again and again, your face floated into my inner vision. Memories of us together, racing up and down the wooden staircase, playing in the courtyard... You might not have been physically present, Leah, but your spirit lived on in that house and, against my will, I thought of you constantly. Where were you?

It was so strange, being back at Kaiserkorso Eins. Everything had changed. All the people I had known and loved were no longer there. The fact that all the Jews had disappeared from the house caused me one crisis of conscience after the other. Mother had written to me some time ago that the Levys and the Bienstocks had left, but facing the reality was a different matter.

A family with three young children had moved into your old flat. I saw them now and then but refrained from making conversation or getting to know them. The name on their postbox and their doorbell was Fuchs. Whenever the siren went off, warning us of a raid, we all ran down to the cellar, everyone in the house, but even then, when we were all squashed together, I did not try to engage. By this time I did not care: I was merely surviving.

And then fate played into my hands; or rather, fate called me into action. I was invited – that meant ordered – to an interview at the Hitler Youth Berlin headquarters. To be honest, the call came not only as a surprise but as a shock. I was well aware of my own doubts and failures regarding Nazi ortho-

doxy, and I wondered if they had somehow got wind of the fact that I had, over the past couple of years, lost faith. That I was no longer the loyal Nazi willing to die for the cause, that, in fact, everything I was doing now was in the interest of my own self-preservation. Could they read minds? Was I in trouble?

But no. I was interviewed by a tall, thin officer called Major Bödigheimer, and his stance towards me was anything but threatening. In fact, he was most pleasant and understanding, praising me for the outstanding work I had done for Hitler Youth and for my unwavering loyalty and proven willingness to serve the Führer. In fact, he was quite sycophantic – which should have made me suspicious. But on the contrary, it made me grateful, so fearful I'd been that my faithlessness had been discovered and that I was about to be denounced.

Very soon he came round to the main subject: Markus.

'You must be aware, Fräulein Bosch, that your brother Markus suddenly left his job a few weeks ago. He did not resign in an orderly fashion, which we would of course have accepted. No: he left overnight, so to speak. In Nacht und Nebel, *night and fog. This puts him, and us, in an awkward position. The suspicion has arisen that he may have joined a dissident group. If this is the case, it would be extremely dangerous for him. Such renegades are invariably found by the Gestapo, and, unfortunately, his fate would be dire.'*

He regarded me quizzically, demanding a reply with only his steel-grey eyes. And so I gave him one.

'Y... yes, Major Bödigheimer, I'm aware that Markus left his job unexpectedly.'

'On the other hand,' he continued, 'his reasons for running off might be even more sinister. Your brother, you see, has in a short space of time proved to be something of a genius as far as engineering is concerned. He is our top man and we don't want to lose him. But the suspicion has been expressed that he has been recruited by the Americans. That they seek to build

an airport in their country even grander than ours, and have secretly recruited your brother to this end. A member of our organisation saw him once speaking to a man who had an American accent. We think this is the more likely explanation. That he is a spy, and has been from the start. We need to find him, if he is indeed still in the country, before he is whisked off to become a traitor to his Fatherland. Nothing could be worse.

'So; Fräulein Bosch: do you know of his whereabouts? We do know that you have moved back into your old building. We have been keeping an eye on it, but he has not been seen turning up there and we believe he is keeping his distance. Especially since you moved back in. It would after all have been stupid to return there, and he is anything but stupid. However, we were hoping that he has tried to contact you, and that you know where to find him, and can help us.'

'No, I'm afraid I don't. Markus and I have no contact at all. I have no idea where he is.'

I hoped he did not notice the trembling of my hands. I'd spoken the truth, but fear as well as a lie can cause trembling and mine was caused by fear. He nodded.

'Well, if you do find out, Fräulein Bosch, it would be in your brother's best interests if you let us know immediately. In fact, it would be in both your best interests, whatever the reason for his disappearance. Because if he does get involved in any subversive behaviour, or traitorous behaviour concerning Tempelhof, the consequences would be dire. For both of you.

'You love your brother, don't you? We know it was you who first recommended him to us. And should he indeed be found to be involved in subversive or traitorous actions, some of the responsibility would inevitably fall on you. You would be implicated, for having helped him get the job. Far better, now, for you to help us find him.'

He paused, then leaned forward and said slowly, as if trying to implant his next words into my brain, 'In fact,

*Fräulein Bosch, if you find him and return him to us volun-
tarily the outcome would be most advantageous, for both of
you. You see, he is extremely valuable to us. We want him
back. We want him to continue his work with us. If we find
him, he will return to his Tempelhof job. Obviously, he would
be kept within the building; we do have accommodation in one
of the wings. He would of course be watched for any further
attempts at escape. This is the best-case outcome, for both of
you. If you help us find him, you too will be rewarded. Do you
understand what I am saying, Fräulein Bosch?'*

Those eyes of steel bored straight into me. I knew exactly
what he was saying. And I knew then that I had to find
Markus, for his own safety. I had no doubt that, if I didn't get
there before them, the Gestapo would eventually find him.
Unless, of course he had been recruited by Americans and
already spirited out of the country. In which case he was safe.
But if he were still in Berlin, or anywhere in Germany, and
they did find him, it would be the end. For both of us.

And so I nodded. *'I understand.'*

*'If, on the other hand, we find him engaged in subversive
activity, or associating with subversives, there is no hope. He
will be killed on the spot or put to trial and found guilty. We
do not tolerate such behaviour. You have certainly heard of the
Scholl brother and sister. These people must be punished. Do
you understand?'*

I nodded again. *'I do.'*

*'So he has one chance. To return to us and continue his
work. And that's where you can help. Bring him back,
Fräulein Bosch. Deliver him to us, and he will be safe. He will
have his job again. His life will be spared.'*

I left that interview as a wreck. Desperate to help Markus,
and fearing for his life. Knowing I could help, but not knowing
how to do so. Where was he? What was he up to? Which was
it? Was he in the underground, a man they considered a dirty

traitor, who would be shot on sight? But who, if he handed himself in, still had a chance, because they wanted him to work for them? Or was he a spy, a brilliant scientist, who had escaped to safety long ago? I fervently hoped it was the latter.

If I found him – if I could somehow get there before them – I could help him avoid the worst. If I did find him then just maybe I could persuade him to return to Tempelhof. Surely he valued his own life? It was the only way to save him. They would keep him safe; in custody, perhaps, but unharmed, because they needed and valued him. He could not survive very long in the underground. I was sure of that. The Gestapo were everywhere. Their spies were everywhere. If they caught him, and he tried to escape or fight – which he would, knowing Markus – they'd kill him. Of that I was certain.

Of course, I secretly hoped that he was, indeed, a spy for the Americans. That they had spirited him away and that he was now safe. But I was realistic. I knew that the chances of me finding Markus were slim. If he didn't want to be found, he wouldn't be found: Markus was smart. All the same, whenever I walked the streets of Berlin after that, I kept my eyes open for Markus. Not only that, I actively searched for him.

43

LEAH – THE FARM

Tante Helga worried too. For her, though, the worry was more material: would Kaiserkorso Eins still be standing at the end of it all? The loss of property was, of course, incomparable to the loss of human life and loved ones; yet still, there was something elementally disturbing about the wanton destruction of homes, the places we'd lived in, the safety afforded by those buildings. Berlin, our beloved Berlin, was becoming a dystopian waste-land. A heap of rubble.

The year 1943 exploded into 1944 in new waves of destruction. Now it was Munich's turn to be bombed – so much closer to home. Our farm lay far to the south-east of Munich and so the bomber planes did not fly overhead – but we heard the distant explosions, and we saw the night sky turning red with the fires of devastation. The three of us – me, Naomi and Tante Helga – drew closer for comfort. We were relatively safe, out here in the idyllic folds of the Bavarian hills, but our loved ones were out there, somewhere, and we had no way of knowing who was alive and who was dead.

In late July came the news that there had been a failed assassination attempt on Hitler. The Nazis were jubilant, broadcasting this news all around. It was a sign, they said, that Hitler was protected by God. That he had a divine mission to fulfil; that no matter how dreadful the news, Germany would emerge victorious. *Grossdeutschland* was destiny; against all odds, it would rise like a phoenix from the ashes.

Later, more details of the assassination came to light. An army officer of Hitler's inner circle, Claus von Stauffenberg, had tried to kill the Führer by placing a briefcase containing a plastic bomb close to his chair during a meeting at the *Wolfsschanze* – the Wolf's Lair – the Führer's secret hideaway near Görlitz, east of Berlin. At the last minute von Stauffenberg was called away by a telephone call, but someone moved the briefcase and, when the bomb detonated, the heavy, solid-oak conference table leg shielded Hitler from the blast; he was only slightly wounded. The plot had failed; von Stauffenberg was, predictably, executed. A Nazi triumph, and a warning.

I remember thinking, thank God Markus had not tried that at Tempelhof. Thank God, he had abandoned the idea of an assassination. Thank God, a thousand times. Thank God, he was safe at Tempelhof. For the time being, at least. As far as we knew, he had not yet left the protection of his stable job.

But then, another letter arrived, and this one was addressed to me – or rather, to Lena Gebhardt. It was from Markus, and the news was the worst possible. It wasn't even in his own handwriting: neither the address nor the handwritten note within it.

It was just one verse, a verse from a song we both loved: the German version of the originally Spanish song 'La Paloma', which we had renamed 'Sailor's Bride' because it has nothing to do with a dove. These lyrics were a far cry from the original song, a story of love. 'Sailor's Bride' told the story of a seaman's love for the sea, for peace, and freedom. A beautiful song. Beautiful, haunting words. But to me, now, utterly chilling.

· · ·

'Sailor's Bride' was a call to freedom:

How blue the sea! How vast the sky! From the crow's nest, I gaze far into the world; forward, for a sailor must never look back. Cape Horn is on lee; now I can only trust in God.

'If ever I flee from Tempelhof... if ever I go underground,' Markus had told me, 'I'll let you know somehow. Look out for "Sailor's Bride".'

And so I knew what those words meant. He had left Tempelhof. His job there was done. He had gone into the underground, and was now a hunted man.

44

MAGDA

And then, out of the blue, I found Markus. Or rather, he found me, but without knowing he'd found me.

One night while I was at home in bed, I woke up shortly after midnight. I had heard a noise, a slight scraping noise. I kept perfectly still. What was it? An intruder? I listened, my heart palpitating at breakneck speed, too loud for comfort. I distinctly heard footsteps in the wooden-floored hallway outside my room. I left the light off, but switched on the torch I always kept by my side at night.

If there was an intruder, I needed a weapon to protect myself. I looked around for one and my eyes fell on a trophy I'd once won at school. Armed with that, I crept to the door and listened. I could distinctly hear footsteps walking past my door, towards the kitchen at the end of the hallway. Once they had passed, I opened my door a crack and peered out. I didn't need my torch; whoever it was had turned on the ceiling lamp. He was walking quite confidently. His back to me. A back jacket that I knew well. It was Markus. Markus had come home! My heart leapt. This was my chance! All I had to do, now, was confront him.

Should I just call out to him? Hallo Markus! Let's talk! What are you up to? *But no.*

I did not want him to know I was here. Not yet. I was unable to confront him. Now that he was right here, I had to think this out.

My mind went into overdrive. What should I do, what role should I play: show myself to him, the sister delighted at seeing him again? How would I find out what his own plans were: should I ask him directly, or try to draw him out? Was he an American spy?

We had not spoken for years; how could I suddenly pop up as if nothing had happened and start questioning him? Persuade him to return to Tempelhof? I was completely unprepared. I was scared, scared for him, scared of him. He had returned my last letter, unopened. He hated me. I remembered how angry he'd been. And now, I was angry with myself. A different person, not the sister he'd known. I felt paralysed with uncertainty. No: I didn't want to talk to him. I didn't want him to see me. Not just yet. I decided to wait and see. To watch. I didn't want to scare him right now. We needed to talk, calmly.

This called for stealth, and secrecy.

But it was too late, surely? Once he saw traces of my presence, he would come looking for me. He would know it was me. Who else had a key, who else would be living at home? And everywhere there were traces of my presence. My jacket hung from a hook in the hall, my boots sat on the shoe-rack. But other jackets hung there, as always, and other shoes sat on the rack. Would he notice mine, amid the clutter? Probably not.

But once he went into the kitchen, he would notice someone lived here. There was a bowl of apples on the table, and half a loaf of bread, wrapped in greaseproof paper, on the countertop. Butter and cheese in the fridge.

But then I breathed a sigh of relief. He did not enter the kitchen; no, he went into his own room, one door before the kitchen door. I tiptoed after him in my bare feet, risking being caught out but too curious to stop myself. His door was ajar, and I could hear him rummaging in there. Drawers opening and closing. Something dragging on the floor. I immediately knew what he was doing: packing. He had pulled out a suitcase from under the bed, and was taking clothes from his chest of drawers. I supposed he didn't have much access to laundry facilities, living underground as he did. And he'd leave again. I was sure of it. I had seen, just from his back, that he was reasonably well-dressed, though a bit bedraggled. A man on the run. My brother.

Slightly calmer now, I took a deep breath. I could just be myself. Walk up to him and explain that I had changed. I could tell him that he was wanted back at Tempelhof. I could try to persuade him... but no. He'd never trust me. He'd think it was a trap. He couldn't know how much I wanted to help.

Yet this was a rare opportunity. I had found him, at last. I could not let him go. But then, a solution dropped into my mind: I knew what I would do.

I returned to my room and closed the door. I was wearing an old nightdress. I quickly pulled it off and replaced it with a jumper and skirt, my everyday wear. Shoes: no time to put on laced boots, but I had a pair of slip-on shoes in my room and I quickly shoved my sockless feet into them. I didn't dare open the door again, not even a crack, because when he left he would be facing in my direction and would notice. So I waited. I waited until I heard the footsteps once more walk in my direction, then past and towards the front door. I put my ear to the bedroom door. Yes, there it was: the click as the front door closed behind him.

I waited a while, and then I was after him. Down the one flight to the entrance hall, hiding in shadows. I peered out the front door. There he was, walking away, down Manfred von Richthofen-Strasse, the street we called Red Baron Street. I sneaked behind him, hiding in doorways, slinking into shadows. The street was empty – he had chosen a good time to come home – but for that reason it was also impossible to stay hidden for long. Yet still I followed him. He seemed nervous, as if aware he was being followed, but the street lights were dim and, because I stayed close to the buildings, he did not see me. At least, he showed no sign of having seen me.

He turned a corner, then another. Several houses behind, I slunk behind him, dark as a shadow. Past a park, but on the far side so that I was still able to hide in doorways, sprinting from house to house. Soon, I found myself in a long street lined with tall terraced houses on both sides. Markus stopped, put his hand in his pocket, pulled out what was obviously a key, pushed it into the door. The door opened. In he slipped. The door closed, and Markus was gone. I walked up to the house, took a note of the number, and walked home.

I went back to bed, but no sleep waited for me. I tossed and turned, trying to put an end to the treacherous thoughts invading my mind. They literally bombarded me. They cut into that armour I'd built around myself; they whispered treasonous ideas into my head. I had reached a crossroads. I had reached THE crossroads, Leah. This was the crossroads of my life. This crossroads would determine everything.

I had to make a decision. I held Markus in the palm of my hand. I had to make a choice. I thought again about him returning to Tempelhof. I loved the idea. Yes, he'd be held under restraint, closely observed and not allowed out. Virtually a prisoner. He'd hate that. But he'd be safe. He was valuable to the Nazi machine; they wouldn't let anything happen to him, much less send him to a camp or kill him. So: the deci-

sion had been made for me, and all I had to do was hand in that note with his address to the Gestapo. My job would be done. Markus would be safe.

But a mutinous idea kept hurling missiles my way. An idea so outlandish, so mad... It destroyed everything I'd lived for the last ten years; everything I'd become, the future I'd built for myself and Germany, that I found myself actually gasping, my stomach in a knot, my heart racing, my lungs refusing to breathe. But so liberating! Oh, so very liberating! I pounded my head with my fists to get those treacherous ideas out of my brain. To no effect.

I could warn Markus.

Warn him that they were seriously after him. That the net was closing in around him, more vicious than ever before.

I could tell him to flee.

I could help him to flee.

And I could flee too. With him.

The entire edifice of Nazism I'd been living so comfortably in – it was crumbling around me. Physically, literally so. Berlin was rubble. It was clearly over. The Allies had won, and I had backed the wrong horse. Markus was right: Nazi ideology was wicked to the very foundation. Markus was the good one. Markus was the brave one, the hero of our story. There would be no future for Markus anyway. No Tempelhof. It was all over.

But here in Berlin, the Nazis still had power, and were more vicious than ever. He was a cornered rat.

We should run, together. My mind worked at a runaway speed, working out a plot for how we would do it.

Has that ever happened to you, Leah? Have you ever had an outlandish idea that grabbed you by the scruff of your neck and catapulted you into a thousand even more outlandish avenues? Took you to a crossroads of destiny so utterly outra-

geous you gasped at your own audacity? Because that's where
I found myself that night.

I would run, with Markus.

I would smuggle him across Germany. I didn't know how
I'd do it, but I would. I'd borrow a car from a colleague; I knew
which colleague. I'd say I was returning to Alsace for a new
story and I'd hide Markus in the boot. I had all my Nazi
papers, my badge, my press card, all the right credentials. I'd
get him into Alsace. I'd bring him to Madame Gauthier. I had
not the least doubt that she would hide him, keep him safe.
And me. Once I let her know I'd saved him, that I had
changed sides, she'd hide me too.

I would escape from this terrible trap I found myself in.
Markus and I would hide at the Chateau Gauthier-Laroche.
We'd be safe until the war was over and we were free. What
would happen then? Well, I couldn't think that far ahead.
Maybe I'd be a hero, for rescuing Markus.

I only knew I wanted to be free. I gave myself up to these
crazy and ridiculous plans. I let myself be swept away on
dreams of a new future, freed from my catastrophic past and
all the terrible mistakes I'd made.

It was possible. I knew it was possible. It was my last and
only hope. But did I have the courage? The courage to save
Markus – and myself?

45

LEAH

In August 1944 an unexpected visitor turned up at the farm. In the middle of the night, I was awakened by a furious banging. I put on my slippers and wrapped a shawl around me and padded downstairs. I opened the door. A bearded young man, his hair long and dishevelled, his clothes smelly and worn, his boots gaping open at the toe, almost fell into the kitchen. I did not recognise him. Not at first.

'Leah!' he said. 'Thank God.'

I didn't even recognise his voice at first.

Then: 'Markus sent me,' he said, and everything clicked.

'Waldi!' I cried.

'Yes, yes. It's me again.'

He took a deep breath before he continued. 'Leah – I've got some bad news. Markus has been arrested. They finally caught him.'

Everything in me turned to ice. 'They – they caught him? Doing what? Where? Where is he?'

I could hardly breathe. I pulled out a chair for Waldi.

'Wait a minute,' I said. 'Let me fetch Helga.'

I ran upstairs and woke Tante Helga, and she followed me

downstairs. She was white as a sheet. I have no doubt that I was, too. I certainly trembled from head to toe, visibly.

'What happened? Where's Markus?' Tante Helga gasped.

I set her down, too, on a chair at the kitchen table, lit the stove and placed a kettle of water on it. Brandy would probably have been more useful than tea, but we had none. My hand trembled so much as I prepared the tea that water splashed out of the kettle's spout, and the teacups clattered on their saucers.

Waldi told us the story. Following the latest assassination attempt, a number of men had been arrested on suspicion of being accomplices – among them, an army officer called Theodore Haubach.

'Haubach was a friend of Markus,' said Waldi. 'They met through Lisa von Berg. Haubach became something of a mentor for Markus. Markus wanted to do something serious. Something big, to rid the world of Hitler. And so, working together with Haubach, he became involved in the plot to kill him. Worse yet... he implemented the assassination attempt.'

'Implemented it? How? How could he possibly...?' My jaw fell open and I hugged myself in panic.

Waldi placed a hand on my arm. It had a calming effect. I stopped trembling. But I could almost hear the pounding of my heart. Surely everyone could hear it? I swallowed, and allowed Waldi to talk.

'It was when he was working at Tempelhof,' he continued. 'He discovered that there was a huge secret bunker beneath the main building...' He stopped, gulped, took a sip of his tea, as if to gather strength, and continued. 'And the bunker was being used for the storage of explosives. By that time Markus had reached a high and trusted position within the complex and somehow learned the security code for the number lock. He also knew someone who worked at reception, responsible for security. Someone on our side. Markus managed to smuggle out some plastic explosives. The theft was traced back to him, just after he quit the job. He's been a wanted man for many months now. A hunted man, a fugitive. And finally, they found him.'

Tante Helga let out a scream. I jumped to my feet and began to pace the room, my face hidden in my hands. 'No, no, no!' I repeated, over and over again.

'Yes,' said Waldi.

I collapsed in a heap on the floor, weeping uncontrollably. My body heaved with sobs.

Waldi crouched down beside me. 'You need to brace yourself, Leah. It's bad. Really bad.'

'I have to go to him!' cried Tante Helga. 'Where is he?'

But Waldi shook his head. 'He's in Plötzensee Prison, in Berlin,' he said. 'It's a high-security prison. We've already checked it out; no visitors allowed. His trial was today. I haven't heard the outcome yet – been travelling all day, to get here. But...'

He didn't need to finish the sentence.

We learned the outcome from the newspapers. Just a small item, on one of the inner pages:

MARKUS BOSCH HAS BEEN EXECUTED BY GUILLOTINE ON 8 AUGUST 1944, FOR HIGH TREASON.

My knees buckled, and in the dizzy whirl that came upon me I was vaguely aware of falling, falling, falling. Arms caught me, I knew not whose. My world turned black.

46

MAGDA

Morning came, and the fantasy of escaping with Markus, of running to the Alsace and safety: it faded with the darkness of night. I knew I would not run, nor would I help Markus to run. It would never work. He was safest back within the walls of Tempelhof.

So yes, Leah. Now you know: I was the one who betrayed Markus. My intentions were all benign, believe me. I believed what I wanted to believe. I wanted to believe that he was this brilliant scientist they were hoping to win back into the fold. That he would work again at Tempelhof, their genius engineer.

After reporting his address to Major Bödigheimer, I expected to be contacted in a day or two. To be congratulated and thanked and to be told that my brother was safe and working once more at Tempelhof. I expected to receive a thank-you from higher up, a pat on the back for putting my country's needs above family loyalty.

But nothing came, and in the end I assumed that Markus had managed to slip between the cracks somehow and evade arrest.

It never once occurred to me that the Gestapo could lie. That there had never been a mysterious American recruiting him for an even grander airport in America. It never occurred to me that all they wanted was him. It never occurred to me that Markus had been plotting to kill Hitler, that he was one of the most hunted men in Germany; that I had been lied to. That I had been used, and was instrumental in the capture and the beheading of my own brother.

I know that my betrayal is inexcusable. I know there's no point in saying sorry; it cannot bring him back. We both loved him; but only I betrayed him.

My beloved brother was dead, and it was my fault. I had led the hunters to the hunted. It was my fault, as surely as if I had dropped that blade upon his neck.

What can I say? There are no words. 'I'm sorry' is so inadequate – a mockery. Yet still, I hope you will keep reading.

PART THREE: AFTERMATH

47

LEAH – BEXHILL-ON-SEA

You're telling me to 'keep reading', Magda? *You?*

You make me want to do the exact opposite. Don't tell me what to do. You've no power over me; you never had that, and, after what's happened, I'm once again inclined to... well, the fire is burning nicely in the hearth and why should I read your 'poor me, look at what I went through' version of history?

You want me to forgive you for sending Markus to the executioner? Because that's what you did. You said it yourself: *as surely as if I had dropped that blade upon his neck.*

I was still digesting Magda's confession when the phone rang. It was Jörg, calling from Norway. I greeted him half-heartedly.

'You sound low,' he said, and added, jokingly, 'Don't tell me you miss me!'

'I do,' I said, 'but it's not that. It's... Magda wrote to me.'

'Magda? What? Oh my gosh! What's she got to say? Are you all right?'

'No, I'm not all right. She's written a kind of confession. It's long – pages and pages, typed. I'm almost finished. It's terrible,

Jörg. Really terrible. Worse than I ever thought. She admits that she betrayed Markus. That she was responsible for his capture.'

'Why on earth does she think she can barge back into your life, after all that? That woman's a demon!'

'It was bad enough back then. But bringing it all back up again, when we've all more or less put it in the past, when we're looking forwards and not backwards – it's just so insensitive! I'm in turmoil, Jörg. This letter – it's like reliving the whole horror all over again. Hearing that he was dead... Oh, Jörg!'

I began to weep. Jörg, sensitive as always, stayed silent, knowing that I had to let it out. All the heartache, once again. When it was over, I said, 'All right. Sorry, I just had to have a little cry.'

'I know.' He paused, then said: 'D'you want me to come home?'

'No, of course not! You've got a few more days to go. I'll be fine. But it's good to talk about it, cry about it.'

'Tell me.'

'It's just too much, Jörg. You can read it when you come home.'

'I miss you.'

'I miss you too.'

48

MAGDA

I could no longer hide from reality. Nobody could. We were losing the war. Leah, you simply cannot imagine the devastating effect this inescapable knowledge had upon me. That we would win the war, win the world – that had been an inviolable gospel for me for many years now. Nazi ideology, Nazi goals, had been for me living truth. I had put all I had into that truth. It had been my entire universe, more sacred to me than God, certainly more sacred than the Catholic faith I had been raised in and which I had rejected even as a young girl.

Then had come my breakdown in Poland, and then Alsace. Since then I had simply played the game, still believing that Germany would win and that I had no choice but to comply. But now, knowing that we would lose, that there would be no miracle victory, that God would not somehow miraculously turn things round at the last moment, it was as if, one day, the sun rose in the west instead of the east. A huge crater opened in the Earth and we were all falling into it. It was the apocalypse, biblical in nature. The four horsemen, the Beast, the end of the world – that was how it all appeared to me, a constant nightmare. And yet I had to pretend all was well and just do *my job, day after day, and never speak aloud what we were all feeling. After everything I'd gone through, the sacrifices and hard decisions I'd made, we were going to lose.*

The Battle of Berlin continued relentlessly well into 1945. The RAF Bomber Command, the USAAF Eighth Air Force and the French Air Force, the Red Air Force: their strategic bombing was laying our great city in ruins. It later turned out that British bombers had dropped 45,517 tons of bombs on Berlin and the Americans 22,090 tons. Berliners were fleeing the city in droves. There was an effort to evacuate children, but their parents refused; it was not possible to evacuate women as they were needed to keep the city running, and they would not send their children away without them. Their men, of course, were all fighting in the thick of things, and falling in droves.

Late that year, I was lucky to escape a bomb that fell just two houses down, flattening the building . All of us were all holed up in the cellar, at the time; but the blast was deafening and every one of us was thinking: will we be the next? Will we be buried under rubble?

The building that housed the Berliner Volkszeitung offices and printing press was bombed one night. After a week of chaos, we all – those of us still alive and willing to work – were evacuated to Munich, where we shared an office and printing press with the Münchener Morgenpost. Instead of a daily newspaper, we became a weekly. Life must go on, even though nobody had the will to live. Time did not stop. We all knew it was over.

I knew. We all knew. We didn't, couldn't, believe it, but we knew. Even the Führer had deserted his people, after telling them to fight until the death. News reached us that he was holed up in the Führerbunker along with his inner circle of top Nazis. That bunker was not like other bunkers; it was basically a luxury underground apartment – as far as luxury could go in those days – with expensive carpets covering the floors and rare artworks on the walls. There he lived with his companion, Eva Braun, right until the end.

While we and other Berliners fled, or were killed in the bombs, thousands of Hitler Youth teenagers were transported to Berlin in early April 1945 to defend the city against that terrifying force – basically, boys in the prime of youth sent to their death; everyone knew that would be their fate. One of those boys was Armin Lehmann, a fiercely loyal sixteen-year-old who was chosen as a courier to run messages between that bunker and the radio room of the Reich Chancellery. Meanwhile, Hitler celebrated his fifty-sixth birthday on 20 April, then on 29 April married Eva Braun in a civil ceremony in which both parties swore they were of pure Aryan blood. On 30 April he watched her commit suicide by swallowing a cyanide pill, and, after that, shot himself.

The radio room communicated the news to us that Hitler was dead.

49

LEAH

That same terrible day, the day we learned of Markus's fate, but after I had calmed down somewhat, Waldi handed me an envelope.

'It's a letter from Markus,' he said. 'He told me, if anything happened to him, to give it to you.'

I read it silently, weeping openly. Waldi turned away, busying himself by making tea. Giving me privacy, yet right there in case I needed support.

If you are reading this, my love, it means I have lost. They have found me, and executed me.

I'm so sorry, my darling. I can only imagine your devastation. I can only imagine your anger at me for not being as careful as I might have been. You wanted me to stay safe. Not to fight. Not to take risks. Your instincts are those of a wife and a mother and they are wholesome and strong instincts. Husbands and fathers should be with their wives and children. That's the way it's supposed to be. I should be at your side, watching our daughter grow, holding her hand when she makes her first steps, catching her when she stumbles, showing her the best way to live. I should be at your side, holding you, helping you when you need help, being helped by you when I need help. I wanted with all my being to be that husband and father. That's my ordained role and I have failed miserably in fulfilling it.

I chose to diverge from that path, to walk along a more narrow and dangerous path, a needle-thin ledge along the Zugspitze, and I have fallen, I have failed. Words cannot convey how sorry I am; not sorry that I chose that path, but that I failed. I failed you and our daughter. I took one risk too many and now you are alone with our baby. Maybe I should not have fought. Maybe even now, you resent me, you're angry with me, for taking that last risk... But you know, I really had no choice. I was catapulted along the road I took almost as if I was an instrument of destiny, and even this abject failure... well. It is as it is, and cannot be reversed.

Leah, you will need all your strength from now on. I cannot be there for you, but my mother can. She thinks of you as a daughter. She will help you, and her granddaughter, precious little Naomi. Please, stay with her, at least until you find your footing in this so unsteady world.

I promise you, one day you will find peace again, and when that day comes I hope you will also find love again. Mourn for me, but do not let your mourning obscure all the good, all the strength that is in you. Please, my darling, find the strength to move on one day, for Naomi's sake and for your own. That is my last wish for you, and my last request.

I wept some more, and then put the letter away and picked up my daughter and went for a walk.

At first, fury with Markus mingled with my devastating grief. Why had he done this thing, and left us to fend for ourselves? Why? Why? Why? I took Naomi to the place we had planned to build our home, and played with her there, and absorbed the peace of nature until something calm came into my being and I knew I would do as Markus said. I would be strong. For Naomi's sake.

If not for Naomi, I suspect I might have died too, to be with Markus. But she kept me going. She saved me. She, and Tante Helga.

Tante Helga arranged for the body to be delivered to the farm. It came in a crate. Neither she nor I could look inside it. She organised a small funeral – a Christian one, of course. I attended it, without Naomi. It was the only way I could say farewell to my beloved and, somehow, it helped.

Waldi stayed with us for the rest of 1944, to help out on the farm and because he had nowhere else to go. He didn't think the Nazis would be looking for him – he had managed to stay undetected, underground, ever since becoming a Wehrmacht deserter in 1939 – they had bigger fish to fry. Still, it was better to keep his head down in this precarious time, when they were lashing out at any and everyone. He had no papers, and no home. Tante Helga offered him a room in the farmhouse, but he insisted on moving into the little room in the attic of the shed. He ate with us in the kitchen, and basically led the life of a farmhand. In early April 1945 he returned to Berlin.

Just a day after we heard of Hitler's suicide I was upstairs putting Naomi to bed when I spotted, through the window, a lone figure riding up the lane on a bicycle.

As the figure drew near and headed round to the back of the house, I gasped, dropped everything, grabbed Naomi and ran downstairs to the kitchen.

'Helga! Helga!' I cried; she had asked me to drop the 'Tante'; I was her daughter-in-law, even if not officially so. 'It's Magda! She's here!'

Helga pushed me out of the kitchen door, into the hall. 'You keep out of the way,' she said. 'I'll deal with this.'

And she did. I don't know what exactly was spoken but I know that Magda never entered the house, that she spent the night in the barn, and that by early the next morning, she was gone.

MAGDA

The first news of Hitler's suicide was radioed to us at the Münchener Morgenpost, as usual, from the Reich Chancellery, which in turn was informed by that young courier, Armin.

I was in the newsroom in Munich when I heard. I cannot even begin to express how I felt: our Führer had killed himself. He, who had instructed his loyal soldiers to fight to the death, had chosen for himself the coward's solution.

My first reaction was a tidal wave of relief. He was gone. It was finally all over. I didn't care how he had died. I didn't care that he had killed his new wife first, by feeding her a cyanide capsule, and then shooting himself. I didn't care about his cowardice. I only cared that he was gone.

Actually, my very first reaction, even before that relief flooded through me, was paralysis. I can barely describe the cold shock that ran through my body as the news came through. You know that expression, my blood froze? That's exactly what it felt like. As if ice water had been poured through my veins, from my brain downwards. Into my heart, into my lungs, so that my breath stopped for a moment and my body struggled for air that would not come. Have you ever felt anything like that, Leah? I suspect you have. With all that you have gone through yourself, and your family, there must have been times when you were paralysed with fear, dread, panic, terror. But then the warm water of relief melted the ice of shock.

Thank goodness! *something in me cried out. It's all over.*

And so: first I froze with shock, and then I relaxed with relief.

My third reaction was naked terror. For myself, and what would come now.

Meanwhile, pandemonium broke out in the office. I sat at my desk, stunned into silence, but everyone else was in a state of panic. Secretaries, screaming and pulling at their hair. Men, slamming their fists into the brick walls and shouting as much with physical as with mental pain. One man pitched his type-writer across the room. Another picked up a chair and hammered it against a desk, yelling, Nein! Nein! Nein!

My mouth was dry as a desert. I stood up to get myself a glass of water. I walked back to my desk, but ended up leaning against the wall. From there, I slid to the floor, my back against the wall, legs sprawled out before me. Collapsed. Waiting for a coherent thought, a viable plan. What was I to do?

That was the fourth reaction: numbness. In spite of that sense of relief, of the nightmare being over, I knew it was far from finished. In fact, the real agony had just begun.

I feel that numbness now, as I write; I've just relived that moment, and need to pause in my writing. I will resume in a day or two, or an hour or two. My fingers fail me, stumble over themselves as I type, and I need a break.

50

LEAH – THE FARM

That year, 1945, brought the finality we'd all been longing for.

Hitler's suicide had been the climax; when Soviet troops conquered Berlin and Germany surrendered, it felt almost like an anticlimax. Before long the free world was rejoicing at the official end of the Second World War in Europe. It was the day Markus and I had lived for, the day when all this was over and we could build a new life, together, with our little family.

'When this is all over,' had been his catchword. But now, with Markus gone – well. I was really just existing, pretending to Naomi that all was well and feigning happiness, for her sake.

Worse was to come. After the initial chaos at the end of the war, people began searching for their missing relatives. The Red Cross was able to find news of our loved ones, and the first report was devastating: Aaron had been sent on a death march from Natzweiler-Struthof to Dachau. There he was executed by an SS firing squad. Dachau, just outside Munich! Bavaria, so close to me! I cannot describe the agony I felt at that news. On top of the loss of Markus, it was hard to bear. But bear it I must, for Naomi's sake. I had to be strong, for her sake. Raise her not in a miasma of grief, but lift myself up and help her to be happy in her innocence.

But then, some good news.

I'd sent out feelers about my two surviving brothers. It turned out that Samuel had found a home with a kind couple in Lewes, East Sussex, while my eldest brother, Mosche, was now an up-and-coming doctor in Boston. And then, the most wonderful news of all: my parents had survived!

They had been hiding in a Charlottenburg house; it had been bombed, but they and the couple who had offered them refuge had survived, in the cellar beneath the house. I was delirious with delight.

After several weeks of waiting, of quivering anxiety, Mother and Father came to join me at Helga's farm. I cannot begin to describe the joy we all felt as we fell into each other's arms – joy soon followed by grief and heartbreaking tears as I told them of Aaron's death. They were devastated – but, Father said, we had to be thankful that only one of our family had died. We had all heard the stories of entire families deliberately executed in those death camps, and we had to be grateful for small mercies. Very soon, my parents moved on to England. Samuel was in England and they'd settle there, at least at first.

Waldi returned to us. He too had suffered losses in his family. He still told us no details of his past, though, and I was too numb to ask questions. I simply took him and his solid presence for granted. I was only grateful that we had a man with us to do the heavier farm work.

On enquiry, we did hear some more good news: Lisa von Berg and Trude had both survived the bombing, as well as most of the members of the Sonnenhof community, and I found strength in correspondence with them. I slowly picked up the pieces of my life.

· · ·

I had decisions to make. Helga said that of course Naomi and I had a home with her, on the farm, for as long as I wanted. She'd be delighted to have us; to watch her granddaughter grow and thrive. I was like a daughter to her, to replace the traitor in her family. Magda had not been a real daughter to her for many years.

I stayed a year with her; or rather, I stayed on the farm while she returned to Berlin to check on the ruin of Kaiserkorso Eins. It turned out not to be quite a ruin; yes, two of the walls had been destroyed, but the trusty old metal lift, built in 1913, by some miracle was still standing. Helga became one of the famous *Trümmerfrauen*, the Women of the Rubble, who proceeded to build back Berlin out of the ruins. I ran the farm in her absence, with Waldi's help, and this gave me time to find my bearings and make my decisions.

I decided I could not stay in Bavaria on the farm, much as I loved it there. I could not stay in the place where Markus and I had started to dream of a future together. I could not even stay in Germany. Who could I ever trust again? Which of the Germans I'd meet on a day-to-day basis would have turned away when I was evicted from my home, refused me entry into their homes, closed their eyes when those trains chugged off to the extermination camps? Yes, everything had come to light after the war, and the reality was worse than we'd ever imagined. How could I stay in this country?

Both Samuel and Mosche invited me to join them in England and the US respectively. Both promised to help me find my feet with my little daughter. Mother and Father had already moved to be with Mosche in Boston, but I chose Samuel, who was closer, in England. I knew that I had to, and wanted to, maintain contact with Helga, for Naomi's sake. Helga was, after all, her grandmother.

And so, after training, in London, as a primary school teacher, I made a new home in the Sussex seaside town of

Bexhill-on-Sea. I raised my daughter as best I could. I corresponded with Helga, and occasionally she came to visit us in Bexhill. I could not bear to set foot in Germany again. And then, years later, Helga too, passed away. Our last connection with Germany was gone.

The years crept by. Sad years, in which my main mission was to raise Naomi and try to keep her safe and happy, and keep her father Markus alive for her. His photo was on the wall by her bed, the first thing she saw when she awoke each day. She came first, and for her sake, I put aside the things that burdened me. But she was by nature a happy child. A brave and adventurous child. I saw so much of Markus in her.

51

MAGDA

I and my colleagues soon recovered from the shock of Hitler's suicide. We had to. Now it was about self-preservation. The war was now unambiguously over and for all of us there was only one course of action: to hide. To save our own skins. I knew I was in big trouble. No one knew of the mental turn-around I had made during the last few years; I had kept it hidden, played the Nazi game as best I could, because that was the only way to keep my head down. Now, in the eyes of the conquering forces, I was nothing but a compliant Nazi, and I knew the punishment would be dire. I had to run.

I knew where I would go. It was obvious. I rushed out, grabbed my bicycle, and pedalled away as fast I could through the streets of Munich. I did not doubt that before long British or French or American or even – God forbid! – Russian soldiers would be crawling through the streets, looking for Nazi collaborators. Of course, I tore off my swastika badge and threw it in the dustbin before leaving the building. I also threw away all my identification papers, the ones I'd once been so proud of. My Party documents. My press card, the one I had so self-importantly flashed when

seeking access to the Reich Chancellery and other prestigious buildings or notable events like speeches by my one-
time heroes Goebbels and Himmler. Papers that now were
not only useless but dangerous, should I be caught with
them.

I did feel a twinge of shame at doing that; it did feel
cowardly. Surely the brave thing to do was confess it all and
take my punishment, whatever it would be. But this was no
time for heroics. The stakes were high. I had become a fugitive.

I knew, of course, exactly where I was headed. Mama
could not deny me refuge in these circumstances. I knew it
could only be a temporary refuge, but it would take time for
whoever was searching for me to find out my links to a remote
farmhouse in Bavaria. In that time I could figure out a more
permanent hiding place.

I pedalled furiously, day and night. The streets both into
and out of Munich were in chaos, with some people apparently
celebrating and others clearly dazed and confused as to what
would happen next. Nobody noticed me weaving through the
traffic and I did not stop to speak to anyone. I barely stopped to
eat or drink – I was used to maintaining myself on very little
sustenance; but when I arrived at the farm at twilight on 1
May, I was not only out of breath but almost falling over with
weakness.

I had not eaten all that day. A single scene, a single goal
drove my pedalling legs: falling into Mama's arms when she
opened the farmhouse door to me. And only one desire filled
my mind: my bed, up in the attic room. The bed I'd slept in as
a child, tucked all warm and cosy under the fluffy eiderdown.
The bed waiting for me. Mama must surely be expecting me.

Oh yes: and before falling into bed, Mama running a warm
bath for me; first half-filling the tub with cold water, and then
boiling several kettles to mix in until the temperature was just
right, me sitting on the side of the tub, dangling my fingers in

the warming water, the two of us chatting away the way we used to. Not one word of war, Hitler, defeat.

And before that: the wooden kitchen table, me blowing on a spoon of one of Mama's famous rabbit stews. Perhaps Oma would be there, a comforting presence, smiling as she encouraged me to have another bowl. I had no idea that Oma had died the previous year.

The only real antidote to the horror of war is the home comforts only a mother can provide. My whole being yearned for those home comforts.

I threw my bike to the ground, rushed to the split back door and pounded on it.

Mama opened the top half. 'You!' she cried. 'What are you doing here?'

Not exactly the welcome I was expecting. I was her daughter! She hadn't seen me for years! What was this? There she stood, not even opening the bottom door to let me in.

'Oh, Mama, come on! Open up and let me in! I'm hungry and tired, been cycling all day! I need food and a bed.'

The door remained closed. 'You can't stay here.'

'What! What do you mean? It's my home!'

'Oh no, it's not your home. It's my home. You decided to leave home, years ago.'

'Oh, come on, Mama! The war's over. You can't just keep me out of my own home!'

'I repeat: this is not your home. I'll give you some food but you can't come in and you'll have to sleep in the barn. Wait here.'

She shut the top door in my face. I could not believe it. I'd always thought that a mother's love was unconditional. I needed to explain to her that over the last two years I had had a serious rethink, that I was no longer the diehard Nazi I had once been – but I had no evidence. My inner remorse had all been in my head, and apart from leaving the Hitler Youth *work, I had nothing to show for it. I had played the game right up to the end. But what else should I have done? Gone underground, like Markus? Got myself executed?*

But even if she saw me as having done wrong, surely, as a mother, she should be all forgiveness, immediate and without question, now that I had come to her for refuge? The story of the prodigal son flashed through my mind. The fatted calf, the joy of the father when the son returned after years of debauched living. That was what I expected from Mama – except I wasn't even back from a decadent life, but a life of dedication and hard work; and, even if I had been deluded, I had meant well. Didn't that count for anything? Surely she could recognise that, at least? Yet here I was, standing at a closed door, so weak I could hardly stop my knees from buckling, and feeling as if I were dying of hunger and thirst.

I lowered myself down on to the doorstep. Mama kept me waiting there for at least fifteen minutes. Eventually she opened the door, bearing a basket hooked over one arm and a ceramic jug in the other. I sprang to my feet to allow her to pass. She resolutely closed the door behind her, as if afraid I'd sprint into the house and hide. So on top of all my other anxieties, there was this: the deep sense of rejection by my own mother. There is nothing worse in the world.

Mama led the way into the barn. Oma had once made a little room at the top of a ladder with a narrow and simple bed, which the occasional farmhand had used for lodgings. Mama handed me the basket and the jug and signalled for me to climb the ladder. I placed basket and jug on the earthen floor of the barn. 'I need the toilet,' I said miserably.

She pointed to the open barn door. 'You know where the outhouse is.'

I did. It was a rickety structure that housed a Plumpsklo. Literally, a dump-toilet, with no flush mechanism and only scraps of newspaper for toilet paper. And no light.

'You need to move on tomorrow,' Mama said, in a voice that brooked no argument. She turned abruptly on her heel and walked away. She didn't even wish me a good night. A filthy lightbulb hung from the barn ceiling and gave out a dim light. I quickly looked through the items in the basket: a closed ceramic vessel with a lid, lifting which I saw contained some hot stew or soup. A mug. A corner of a loaf of bread. A tablespoon, a cup. A torch, and, at the bottom of it all, some folded cloth that turned out to be one of Mama's nightdresses, far too big for me. I had, of course, left all my own clothes in Munich. I had left in such a panic; perhaps I should have gone to my hostel first to pack a suitcase, but I'd been gripped by such terror, such visions of American GIs armed with rifles guarding the door, waiting to arrest me, I had not even stopped to use logic. Now here I was, cursed, it seemed, to wear the same clothes from now until eternity.

Back from the outhouse, I climbed the ladder carefully with the basket and the jug. I sat down on the bed and began to eat. And to drink. And as I did both, I wept. I wept, not only out of remorse but for the collapse of everything I had ever valued in my life. I had also lost Mama, and that, I now realised, was the greatest loss of all.

Basically, I was wallowing in self-pity.

I can best describe my feelings that night as a sense of my entire body having fallen apart into its separate pieces. Like a broken mechanical toy vehicle taken apart by a little boy who was now at a loss as to how to put it back together again. Except I hadn't just fallen apart: I had been torn apart; the little boy had ripped his toy into its components, every last screw, every last spoke in every last wheel. And frankly, I didn't want to be put back together. What was there to live for, now that even Mama, my very last resort, had rejected me? I *had destroyed my life, and I had no idea how to put it back together again.*

I sobbed into my pillow all night. I say this not to garner even a thought of sympathy. There are two kinds of tears, Leah, and only one kind deserves compassion. My tears were of self-pity. They were the crocodile tears of a person whose desires had not been fulfilled. Whose own selfish goals had been defeated. Tears of self-pity are not worthy of compassion and should not be indulged as their source is a mental kink that, if pandered to, can grow into monstrous shape. I am now glad I was alone that night. Thankful for Mama's stern treatment of me. I had multiple lessons to learn, and that first night after my collapse was the start of a recovery that would take years to take effect. The prodigal son had returned in deep repentance; 'I am no longer worthy to be called your son,' he'd said, and only then had there been forgiveness, the fatted calf, and redemption.

Mama came to me early the next morning. I had not slept all night, but had finally fallen asleep at dawn. This time, she'd brought a tray on which was a jug of coffee, a cup, two slices of buttered bread and two slices of cheese. She had somehow managed to climb the ladder with the tray, and now she set it down on the floor beside my bed.

'Magda!'

I heard her voice through my sleep, but only opened my eyes at the third call. I sat up in bed, rubbing my eyes. 'Morning, Mama.'

'Good morning, Magda. Here's some breakfast for you, but you have to leave as soon as possible.'

'Where can I go, Mama?'

'I really don't know. You have friends in high places, I presume.'

My voice broke as I spoke. 'Yes, but...' I let out a loud sob and tried again. 'Do you hate me, Mama?'

She shook her head. 'I don't hate you, Magda, but you have made your bed and now you have to lie in it. It would be wrong to deprive you of that experience.'

'But, Mama, I don't know... I have nowhere, no one...'

'You should have thought of that earlier. I have to go now. Goodbye, Magda. Don't come back.'

'Not ever, Mama? Not ever?'

I thought I saw a softening in her eyes. 'Perhaps one day. If you ever gain wisdom.'

I thought I caught a catch in her voice, and a quivering of her lips, but she turned away then and before I knew it, she was climbing back down the ladder.

'Goodbye, Magda.'

'Mama! Wait! Come back! Please!' All of a sudden I was anxious to tell all, to tell her that I had recanted, that I was no longer the evil monster she thought I was. That I had long been battling my own demons. But any explanations I had were far too late. All I could do was beg for pity, weeping.

'Mama, please!'

I wailed the words, but in vain. She was gone.

There was nothing for it but to return to Munich. This time, I took it slowly. Yesterday's panic had fled, and, on logical consideration, I realised that my capture would not be the first priority for the victors of this cursed war. I should be safe at least for the next few days while Germany's government was juggled, while Munich's new administration sorted itself out. The main thing now was to keep my head down and not be noticed. I knew I was in trouble, but there were bigger fish to catch in the Nazi hierarchy. I was small fry; my crimes were only enormous in my own head.

I returned to the hostel. Most of the other girls had already fled, probably back to their parental homes, just as I had done. I hoped they had found a better welcome than I had. Only one girl was left. Her name was Irmgard, and she had worked in the Munich mayoral office. I found her packing a suitcase.

She swung round as I walked into the dormitory we had all shared, as if she, too, was anxious and feared arrest. But she had nothing to fear. She had not made herself guilty. She had not worked for the Hitler Youth for years, not disseminated lies and propaganda as I had. When she saw it was me, her face relaxed.

'Where are you going?' I asked, without even my usual cheery greeting. No more Hitler salutes either. I felt sharp, edgy, as if barbed wire was coiled within me. No time for niceties now.

'Home,' she said. 'Where else?'

'Will they have you?'

'Of course! Home is home! Why do you ask?'

'My mother threw me out. My own mother!'

'What? How could she? You poor thing! She's not very motherly, is she?!'

Oh, those sympathetic words were balm to my aching soul! I burst into tears and told her how Mama had abandoned me. I wallowed in self-pity. I cried the way I had cried all through the night, but this time my sobs were interspersed with frustrated censure of Mama and anguished cries of 'How could she?'

I sat on my bed, openly sobbing. I had never been a crier, but now I found great relief, especially when Irmgard sat down next to me on the bed and patted my back and kept repeating, 'Oh, you poor thing!'

Finally, she interrupted my sobs. 'Listen, Magda!' she said. 'Why don't you just come with me? You'll like our place.'

I already knew that she was from Austria, and that her parents lived on a farm in the mountains beyond Salzburg, one of the most beautiful regions of what was left of Grossdeutschland.

'Really? They won't mind?'

'I'm sure they won't. Quite the opposite. They're on our side, Magda, and they'll be just as devastated as we are. They'll be welcoming of you, because of the service you gave to our Führer.'

'Don't even speak that word!' I cried.

But she misunderstood. She thought I was reproaching him for committing suicide, for letting us all down.

'I agree,' she said. 'He should not have done that! He should have stayed strong, stayed with us to the end. He should have let them kill him, rather than shoot himself! The coward!'

'I doubt they'd have killed him,' I said. 'They'd have captured him and made him stand trial. Think of the humiliation! He could never have faced that.'

'Hmm,' she said. 'You're right. How awful, to see our great leader in prison, dragged before a court of – of deplorables. I suppose in the end he took the noble way out. I would have been absolutely shattered to see him as a prisoner in the enemy's courtroom. He was thinking of Germany's pride right up to the end.'

She straightened herself, clicked her heels, stuck out her right arm, and cried in defiance: 'Heil Hitler!', obviously expecting me to do the same. I didn't. I sniffed and looked away. I couldn't care less about Hitler right now, I had far more urgent concerns.

'Do you really think your parents would put me up?' I asked again.

'I'm absolutely certain. And it would be wonderful to not only have a companion for the trip, but someone to share the future with. It's all so depressing.'

'Just for a while,' I replied. 'Just till I sort out where I can spend the next few years in hiding.'

'Oh, Magda! Is it really that bad? Years in hiding?'

'Yes, of course. The enemy will count my Hitler Youth

service as a crime, I'm sure of it.'

She nodded. 'Yes, I understand. You'll need to make a new life for yourself. Be a different person. Maybe you can go to Switzerland?'

I shrugged. 'Who knows, Irmgard? Who knows?'

We got a lift with her father, whom she had managed to telephone; he picked us up in his farm truck, with which he brought produce from the family farm to town. One of the industries that had always kept functioning throughout the war was agriculture, and now, my own family farm having failed me, I found a new refuge.

Irmgard's parents, as she had promised, welcomed me with open arms, restoring my faltering faith in mankind. This was what parents were supposed to do, I thought, and happily settled into this new home, with this newfound sister. Our ideologies might not be fully aligned, but at this stage I was grateful for any wisp of human kindness. Irmgard was unlikely to be hunted down, as she had only been a secretary in the town hall. And nobody knew I was with her. I was safe. I slowly built back my personality, and, even when Germany surrendered to the Allies, a new – fractured but resilient – sense of self began to emerge. I was tough. I would overcome. No longer as a servant of Germany, but as an individual struggling to build a life on her own, having acknowledged and regretted her mistakes. My only thought was for survival.

But over the next few weeks my sense of security began to crumble once again.

At first we did not believe it, these reports of death camps – not only far away in Poland, but right here in Bavaria, on Munich's doorstep: Dachau. I mean, I had seen it, at Natzweiler-Struthof, and that had been horrific. But the sheer scale of it as everything came to light. The deliberate extermination of Jews – including my once dear friend, Aaron, as I now discovered. But worse was to come. How could it be? It just could not be true. Yes, the Jews had been identified as the enemy, but surely, surely, no government could be so depraved as to massacre them en masse?

I had of course heard such rumours back when I was working for the Press and Propaganda department. Everyone had. And, like everything else that did not sit well with my own ethical standards, anything that grated against my love of high culture and my belief in Germany's superiority in that regard, I had simply pushed such talk away.

It could not be, and therefore it wasn't. It had been so easy for me to dismiss. I mean, war itself went against all my cultured instincts. As a highborn daughter, I considered all civilisation and the cultivation of rarefied philosophy and ethics to be the epitome of what we should strive for: 'we' being the builders of that magical state we called Grossdeutschland. As a BDM girl, I believed that National Socialism could do no wrong.

But then came Poland; the evacuations. And, after Poland, Alsace. Natzweiler-Struthof. I had seen with my own eyes what was going on behind the scenes. When the camps were liberated, the evidence was out. Photographic evidence, first-hand reports written by non-Nazis. The whole world knew. And summed it up in one word: Auschwitz.

It was worse than I had ever imagined. Worse than Natzweiler-Struthof. You know what happened in those days, Leah. We all saw the photos, the clear evidence. Photographic evidence. Piles of dead, naked Jews. The gas chambers. Freed prisoners as the Allies opened the gates of those despicable camps – living skeletons. Mass graves. First-hand accounts of what had gone on in those camps. Regulated mass murder. That was the epitome of Nazi philosophy. And I had been a handmaiden to it all.

The horror of it burst through the mental shield I had built for myself. The shield that had hitherto protected me, protected my sanity, collapsed into nothing. The horror was right there, in me, alive in my mind. I could not breathe; I could not think. It was too much to bear.

There was only one thing left to do.

I said goodbye to Irmgard's family and thanked them for their hospitality.

'Where are you going?' Irmgard cried in panic as I walked down the stairs and headed for the front door, suitcase in hand. 'What are you doing?'

Her reaction to the horrific evidence had been so shocking, I could not even look at her. 'Well, if it was the only means to the end, so be it!' she'd said, when confronted. 'What do we know, after all? We have to trust our leaders.'

'And if that "means" goes against the very definition of what it means to be human? If it makes of us devils?'

She'd laughed off my concerns. 'Devils? Really, Magda, sometimes you're very overwrought. Only deluded Christians believe in devils – I thought you'd rejected the Church? We have to support our leaders, even in defeat.'

That's when I walked off to pack my suitcase. Now, as I walked out the door, I said, 'I'm doing what I have to do. My duty.'

I would have preferred to go all the way to Berlin, my hometown, but I could not bear to see my beloved city crumbled into rubble and ashes. The following day I presented myself to the new American administration in Munich.

'I have come to confess my crimes,' I said to the man behind the reception desk. 'I request to be arrested and put away forever.'

The handcuffs they locked round my wrists felt like a garland of flowers round my neck. My eyes misted up with relief.

52

LEAH

One day when Naomi was six, a visitor turned up at my Bexhill door, a well-dressed, clean-shaven young man.

'Leah!' he said. 'I— sorry for just turning up like this. I was going to write first but I thought...'

I knew that voice.

'Waldi!' I cried.

He chuckled. 'No. No more code names. I'm not a dissident any more. My name is Hans-Jörg Mühlhause, and...'

I gasped. 'No! I don't believe it! Mühlhause? Then you...'

He smiled and nodded.

'Yes. I used to live in the flat down the hall from you, in Kaiserkorso Eins. Several years older than you so we didn't play as children, but yes, it's me.'

'I'd never have recognised you, when you were Waldi! And even now, I don't see Waldi in you!'

'A scraggly beard makes all the difference, doesn't it?'

'Not just the beard. You're... you're...'

I didn't know how to say it politely. He'd lived with us for six months, back then, and yes, in that time, he'd changed from a painfully skinny vagabond into a physically fit, hard-working farmhand. But he'd kept the beard and kept to himself. We'd hardly spoken beyond practical matters. I'd been grateful for his help, but not inclined to resurrect the close camaraderie we'd had at Sonnenhof. Too many terrible things had happened since then. I'd been enclosed in my private cocoons of pain, and locked him out. It was understandable; I'd been in deep mourning, after all, while trying to keep up the appearance of normality for Naomi. I'd been far too self-absorbed to take an interest in him.

I couldn't tell him that now. And I couldn't tell him how much his new, very dapper appearance, appealed to me. Now, I simply said: 'Come on in! Tell me everything, Hans-Jörg.'

'Just call me Jörg.'

He proceeded to fill me in on the intervening years. He had met up with Helga in Berlin, at Kaiserkorso, when she returned after the war; his parents had fortunately survived, by hiding in the bunkers at Tempelhof, and his brother and sister were also safe. Using his skills as a carpenter and builder, he had taken part in the reconstruction work on the city. He had a good job, a good future. And he had never forgotten me, or Sonnenhof, or Markus.

'There's something that binds us all together,' he said, 'and I just had to check on you. I was the one Markus confided in, the last friend he ever saw. I felt that... well... I just feel this deep connection to you.'

I could see in his eyes what he was really saying. He had been there for me when I needed him. He knew me. He knew Markus. We shared a portion of history. I took his hand.

'I understand,' I said.

He returned to Berlin after that visit, but we corresponded and a year later, he returned. And a year after that, we married. We had a choice as to where we would live: in Kaiserkorso Eins, or here in Bexhill-on-Sea. But I had not forgiven Germany: we chose Bexhill.

53

MAGDA

I spent one year in a local jail before they had the time to review my case. In the end, they decided that I was not guilty of any crime and that my time in jail was exoneration enough for my deeds. I was sent on a de-Nazification course, and then released into the big wide world. To be honest, Leah, I would have preferred a full trial at Nuremberg, a conviction and a harsh sentence. I deserved life imprisonment, locked away from humanity forever. I had forfeited my right to belong to the human family and I wanted the punishment to be appropriate. They let me off with far too much lenience.

The mental armour I'd been wearing to protect myself – the real me, the genuine me who had retreated, cowering, to a distant underground cavity of my mind – collapsed into rubble, just like my home city. That terrible guilt now emerged in full strength and full colour, unsparing and unrelenting. No pause, no respite. Waves and waves of guilt as ugly as the most horrendous monsters from hell.

In fact, I realised there was no such thing as hell as a physical place: this is hell. This mental avalanche of the hideous emotion of guilt, sweeping through my entire being, leaving no space for even the slightest sliver of respite. The terror that one day, the day I died, it would be worse and I'd be thrown head-first into an even greater torment, one that would never end: and the knowledge that I deserved it all.

While incarcerated and awaiting my review, I shared a cell with a female Nazi leader, whose name is irrelevant here. I did not speak to her. All I could do was wail; I only stopped when, in short bursts, I slept. I did try to keep the noise down, and most of the time my wailing could be better described as a feeble but desperate whimper, but sometimes I screamed, loud and carelessly, like a madwoman, hitting my head against the walls.

They removed me and sent me to a mental hospital, where they locked me in a grey stone cell. Some doctors tried to talk to me but I gave no answers. They gave me pills, which I refused. My agony was not merely mental, that much I knew. It was deeper, of a spiritual nature, something locked in the very core of my being.

Then one thing happened that alerted them to the fact that I was still human.

There was a girl there, perhaps sixteen or seventeen years old. Rumour had it that she had been raped by Russian soldiers; she walked about like the living dead and had to be bathed, dressed, fed, put to bed like a baby. For some reason I took a liking to this girl and began to sit next to her in the dayroom. And I started to talk to her, at first just small talk, mostly mocking the stupid attendants who treated us all like dirt. She never responded but I didn't mind. Her name was Greta.

One of the wardens once said to me, smirking, 'Why do you give that girl the time of day? Don't you know she's Jewish? You as an old Nazi should be spitting on her!'

That made me talk to her all the more. And do you know what I started talking to her about, Leah? About you. I told her all about you and how we'd been the best friends ever and how I missed you because you and me, that was special.

The staff continued to mock and tease me and the more they teased me, the more I attached myself to this girl. I began to take over her care. I would lead her around by the hand and spoon-feed her. Of course, the attendants loved that because it meant less work for them, especially when I began to go into her ward (she was in the general ward, unlike me – I had a single room) every morning, get her up, wash her and dress her. I always began the day by telling her, 'Guten Morgen, Greta.'

And then, one morning, she said 'Guten Morgen' back to me. I decided not to make a fuss of it, and just carried on as usual. I asked her if she would like to eat her breakfast herself and she nodded and picked up her slice of buttered bread with jam and ate it.

They didn't like that, the wardens and the doctors. They sent me back to prison, with the diagnosis that I was perfectly healthy and just pretending to be mentally ill. So there I was, in prison again, alone with my guilt and my agony, screaming and yelling to my heart's content. Greta and I had been quietly healing each other. Now, that was over.

I tell you this not to garner sympathy. I was not then looking for sympathy, or any human response. I had to go through this on my own, and something in me knew that it was right. They sent psychologists and doctors to speak to me but I ignored them all and refused to take the pills they gave me.

One day they sent a nun, a laywoman who wore not a habit but a dark blue dress with a white collar. Sister Magdalena – yes, that was her name! – sat herself down on the single wooden chair in my room and smiled at me. It was the first smile I'd seen since long before Hitler's suicide. I did not deserve a smile. I was too wicked for a smile. I deserved to be castigated and mocked. She greeted me by name, remarked on the fact that we both had the same Christian name, then said simply, 'Fräulein Bosch, you can tell me anything you like, whenever you like.' And her face settled into a patient serene expression, and she smiled again, and waited.

This was the first time they'd sent me a woman, and perhaps the fact that she was a woman – and a woman who smiled, in spite of knowing of my Nazi past – touched some hidden chord in me because I found myself, without actually making a decision to do so, downloading the ghastly contents of my guilt on her.

I told her what I had seen. I told her of the Poles I had seen being driven from their homes, how I had watched those wretched people wandering off into nowhere, and done nothing. I'd not written a word of protest, but instead sent cheery photographs of happy Germans arriving to take over their abandoned homes, homes made clean and welcoming by Adelheid's team of willing BDM girls. That I'd sucked up to Adelheid, and had envied her. I told her of my one-time adoration of Hitler, whom I now called the vilest monster of all time, a devil.

'And I'm a monster too!' I cried. 'Everything in me is vile, depraved, black with wickedness!'

Her smile broadened. 'Not everything,' she said. 'There is a spark in you in which you can find forgiveness.'

'There is no forgiveness!' I wailed. 'Not ever! There cannot be, and I don't deserve forgiveness!'

'Perhaps if you should forgive yourself first,' she said mildly.

'Forgive myself? What nonsense! To forgive myself would mean justifying the crimes I have committed! There can be no forgiveness, not from me, not from anybody!'

'Not even from God?'

'There is no God! How could there be a God, when such terrible things can come to pass, when people like me are riddled through and through with malevolence?'

'*There is a spark,*' she said. '*Find it, Fräulein Bosch.*'

She got up to go.

'*Sister Magdalena! Don't go!*' I shrieked the words and grabbed her hand.

She sat back down. I went through the whole process again, telling her all I had seen and done, or not done, sparing her nothing. It was as if I were vomiting up my entire insides into her lap. She said little. I had always disliked the way Catholics preached constantly and acted so superior and goody-goody, but that was not Sister Magdalena. She simply listened and told me to look inside. For forgiveness, that I had to forgive myself. I hated that argument.

'*There aren't two me's,*' I argued, '*a me who is guilty and another me who can forgive the guilty me!*' This was a bit of the old Magda, the one I had been so long ago. Remember the philosophical arguments we used to have, Leah, when we were young? I began to apply them to Sister Magdalena, and she went along with me. She did not preach. She did not try to bring me back into the Catholic fold. She did not invite me to visit the confession cubicle in order to find absolution of my sins. She only listened, and now and again corrected my wording.

'*Let me put that in a different way,*' she said. '*Try to find forgiveness inside yourself. I am sure that it is waiting for you, quite apart from this "me" of yours you are wrestling with. Perhaps you do not need to wrestle at all. Perhaps you only have to ask. Ask and it will be given to you.*'

For some reason, those were the words that destroyed me. '*Ask and it will be given to you*'. I dissolved into another torrent of tears, but this torrent was a different one. There was some element to it that – there are no words to describe it; the nearest word I can find is '*healing*'. Yes, these were healing tears. The beginning of a completely new process.

That process continued for the entire time I was incarcer-

ated, and, when I was released in the summer of 1947, with Sister Magdalena's help I found accommodation in a women's hostel, and work as a cleaner in a hospital, working all hours of the day and night to keep the place spotless. I enjoyed that work. I knew I could never return to writing or any intellectual work ever again. I needed to do the most humble and basic jobs, and wandering around the hospital with a mop and bucket was ideal.

I did not speak to anyone, not the other women in my hostel nor my work colleagues; just Sister Magdalena, whom I visited once a week. I avoided all social contact. I sought silence and solitude. Sometimes I went to a church and simply sat in silence, finding a sweetness and calm there I knew I did not deserve.

I had more or less regained my sanity by now and went out of my way, with the resources available to me, to make investigations into the fates of certain people. I could not find out where you were, but I discovered that Aaron had been sent on a death march from Natzweiler-Struthof to Dachau. I could find nothing about you or your parents. Did this mean you were all alive? I hoped so with all my being. I had already known from Mama's letters that both Mosche and Samuel had escaped to the US and England, and I was glad of that.

While I had not found that spirit of self-forgiveness Sister Magdalena had encouraged me to find, I knew I was making baby steps forward. I was still obsessed with my tremendous guilt, and I knew there was no escape. I was captured in a prison of guilt, yet still there seemed to be a vein of comfort within me, and in times of silence I found that vein and clung to it.

I did the cleaning job for five years, wandering like a ghost back and forth between work and home. I had always been thin but I grew even thinner, gaunt and hollow-cheeked and empty-eyed. At least, I thought I was empty-eyed, but one day

Sister Magdalena said to me, 'Magda' –she now called me by my first name – 'you have such beautifully expressive eyes.'

'How ridiculous,' I scoffed. 'I am dead inside. How could my eyes be expressive?'

'But they are,' she insisted. 'There's a little light in them that wasn't there when I first met you. Then, there was only darkness. Now, something shines through.'

'Huh! Humbug!' I said, and turned away. I could say things like that to Sister Magdalena. A bit of my old Berliner Schnauze had returned to me.

One day, she said to me, 'Magda, how would you like to take a trip with me? A little holiday?'

'Why? Where to?' I had not taken any holiday in all those years, even the ones that were my legal right. I worked on Sundays and bank holidays. I washed floors and scrubbed toilets and mopped up vomit. Clearing away excrement and urine and blood was all in a day's work. Nothing disgusted me. Nothing was worse than my own inner excrement. It was the perfect job for me, as it symbolised everything I was going through internally. Basically, I was cleaning my own soul, and with that understanding and spirit I worked as perfectly as I could. Perfectionism had always been at the heart of all I did, and at this job it was the same. I had always been of an ascetic nature and still now did not afford myself any pleasures in life, did not spend my meagre wage on any special indulgences. Whatever I didn't spend on necessities, I deposited in a savings account.

'To Switzerland,' she replied. 'I'd like you to meet someone.'

I shrugged. 'If you like,' I said, and for the first time ever I took a week off work.

We travelled by train and then by bus. It was summertime, and Switzerland was at its glorious peak – the hills covered in lush green, framed by snow-capped mountains against a bril-

liant blue sky. We arrived at Luzern, from where we took a bus towards the Vierwaldstättersee, and from there another bus to a village called Flüeli. We descended from the bus and walked up a mountain road. We climbed and climbed, speaking little.

Sister Magdalena had still not explained where we were going, or why. I only knew that the higher we climbed, the more an indescribable peace descended on my heart. It was as if the beauty and peace and harmony of nature became a tangible essence that filled me from top to toe. We walked upward along a narrow lane through a mountain forest and the more we walked, the more I felt that peace turn to joy.

I struggled against that sense of ineffable joy. I did not deserve it. I, who had caused such terrible suffering to others, did not deserve even a moment of happiness, ever again. I deserved to crawl along the dark, dank corridors of a dungeon. That was what I wanted for myself; but, despite all my efforts to ban that seeping sense of bliss, it was there. Like a pure stream running through my being.

We came to a clearing, and in the clearing was a small log cabin, typical of the houses around here but much smaller.

Sister Magdalena smiled at me, gestured that I should follow, and rapped with her fist on the wooden door.

The door opened and a man appeared. He had a shaggy salt-and-pepper beard and a thick, longish, salt-and-pepper bush on his head. He wore the typical clothes of Swiss mountain people: worn-out lederhosen held up by braces, a heavy grey shirt. No shoes; on his feet were socks.

'Schwester, dearest Schwester!' he cried when he saw Sister Magdalena, and his face lit up. He took her in his arms in a bear-hug. I wasn't sure if he meant she was his biological sister or if he was referring to her religious rank, but I didn't care because that sensation of joy and peace and simple fullness had completely overtaken my entire being. There was nothing else but that.

Sister Magdalena turned then, and with a beaming smile gestured towards me and I stepped forward and she introduced me.

'This is Brother Jakob,' she said, and with those words a new era in my life opened up.

I won't go into detail here; I have already told you the essence of what was to come. We spent that day with Brother Jakob and before dusk returned to the village, where we had taken a room in a guesthouse. We returned every day for the week. Brother Jakob heard all about me, but I have to say that he wasn't particularly interested in my past and the sins I had committed. He said that all that counted was what I was now. And here. That was what we had to work with. But it wasn't really work at all. It was simply sinking back into nature and knowing that I and nature: we were not two, we were one.

At the end of the week I told Brother Jakob I wanted to return to this place and stay forever. He said I could return; people often came for long-term retreats. He put them up in a small cabin nearby called the Engelshütte, the Angel's Hut. I could not stay there in the winter as it was always snowed in, but I was welcome to stay until snowfall. It had a small cannon stove, and there was ample firewood that he had chopped himself, to last me well into November, should I wish to stay on. What would I do in the winter? I asked. That worried me.

However, Sister Magdalena had a suggestion. There was a hotel in the village that was quiet in the summer but busy in winter, and she got me a part-time winter job there as a cleaner, and a weekend summer job. It was perfect. It meant that I was eligible for the boring practical things such as health insurance and pension contributions. They had in-house staff accommodation and, should I be employed, I could stay in the village during the winter and live in the Angel's Hut in summer, working only at the weekends in the hotel.

Back home, Sister Magdalena and I worked out other details. Since I had spent little money over the years, I had some savings, and with that and my pay as a cleaner, I could maintain myself if I didn't indulge in luxuries – which I didn't. Once I had submitted my excellent job references from the hospital, all was confirmed, and at the end of August, I moved to Flüeli, to the Angel's Hut, to start my new life. I lived between the hut and the hotel for three more years.

I have to admit it wasn't easy. I am not created to be a hermit. Brother Jakob loved silence and, though he was too polite to shut up my incessant chatter, I was sensitive enough to notice when I was being an imposition and learned to shut my mouth, go for a walk, do some cleaning, chop wood.

I did learn a bit of his story, though. I learned that as a young man he had been a flautist in Luzern's Symphony Orchestra but, after reading about the famous sixteenth-century Swiss saint Niklaus von Flüe, he was drawn more and more to Christian mysticism. Eventually he gave up his secular life to become a hermit, and had lived here in the mountains for almost twenty years. His reputation had drawn pilgrims from all over Switzerland as well as abroad. People seeking spiritual healing. People like me.

One of the walls in his cabin was in fact a floor-to-ceiling bookshelf, and it was with Brother Jakob that I finally was able to plunge into the philosophy studies I had once yearned for. Christian mysticism, Vedanta, Sufism, Shuddhadvaita – it was all there, packed into those shelves, and it was wonderful to me to see how well all these systems aligned with each other. The Cloud of Unknowing, The Dark Night of the Soul, Shankaracharya, Lao-Tse, the Bhagavad Gita, the poems of Rumi and Al-Ghazali, Rabia of Basra... In the two years I spent with Brother Jakob I read through all of his books, and though I did not become wise, I at least was on the path to becoming humble.

That first year, I found an old dog in the village whose master had recently died; the villagers were considering putting him down, but I adopted him and he became my dog and my friend and my constant companion. He already answered to the name Fidel, meaning Trust.

Brother Jakob might be a hermit, but he and I had some mutual secular interests and, like me, his one concession to ordinary human pleasures was music. He played the same flute that had been his instrument in his orchestral days, a silver lateral flute that was the only possession he had brought with him from Luzern. One day he presented me with a ticket to a concert in Luzern: Beethoven's Pastorale.

The Pastorale had always been my favourite piece of Beethoven, and no other music (though Vivaldi's Four Seasons was a close second) fitted so perfectly into this new life: not the triumphal heights of the Emperor Symphony nor the majesty of the Ninth, and certainly not my old favourite, Mozart's Requiem. Sitting with Brother Jakob at a gurgling stream, him playing the Pastorale on his flute, became for me the epitome of heaven on earth.

Between the Pastorale and the Four Seasons something like an ineffable peace returned to my heart, a peace that seemed inherent, a visceral part of me. The healing effect of music – good music – is legendary, and it certainly worked on me, together with the beauty of my natural surroundings.

I know what you're thinking, Leah: I did not deserve to find peace. I did not deserve healing. And I would like to respond by saying you should not judge; but then, who am I to judge you and your own conclusions? I feel that never again will I be in a position to stand in judgement over another person or another person's opinion.

But all good things come to an end, and it was not my destiny to become a hermit. After three years, Sister Magdalena returned, bearing a letter for me. My hands trembled as I slit open the envelope, for I recognised the handwriting: Mama.

She wrote:

A lot of water has passed under the bridge, Magda, and I have been in contact with this wonderful Sister Magdalena, who has taken such good care of your pastoral health. She and I have corresponded for some time, and she believes it would be helpful if we met again.

Our last encounter was extremely difficult for both of us, but I would be willing to try again, if you, too, are willing and ready.

I did not need a second invitation. I thanked Brother Jakob and bid him goodbye, with the sense that I would not be returning. I had learned all that I could from him, and it was time to move on. I left the next day for Munich, with Sister Magdalena and Fidel.

I went home alone, on a bicycle, just like the last time, ten years earlier. Alone except for Fidel, trotting faithfully beside me.

Just like the last time, I rapped on the double door of the kitchen. It opened. There was my mother, a half-smile playing on her lips.

'Mama.'

'Magda.'

She opened the bottom half of the door, and I walked through. Her arms opened for me, and in I walked, and they closed around me.

And then at last I cried, and those tears were the most healing of all.

And so, Leah, I have reached the end of my letter. It turned out far longer than I originally planned but that's a good thing. It was good for me to let it all out.

I don't know if it was good for you to read it – if you even read it and did not tear it up. And you must know now why I wrote it. You must feel what I really want to say.

So much time has passed. So much water under the bridge. You know me now, inside out, the best and the worst of me. The worst is terrible. And you know it.

Can you handle it, Leah? Can you handle seeing me again? And, most of all, can you imagine giving me a second chance? I daren't even speak those words – writing them is bad enough. I would love to meet you again, but I know it is presumptuous of me to even entertain the idea. I know you have a daughter, Naomi. My niece. I would so love to meet her, Leah.

And so I will wait, and see if you reply to this.

LEAH – BEXHILL-ON-SEA

It took me a month, but I did reply. A cautious, unsentimental letter saying I was willing to meet her, but she would have to come here, to England, to meet me on my own territory.

The reply came by return of post.

MAGDA

> *Dear Leah,*
>
> *I am so sorry. I cannot come to England. I deliberately did not tell you in my last letter, not wanting to put you under pressure, but now I can say it.*
>
> *I am very ill. I am dying, Leah. I have breast cancer. I have been undergoing treatment for the last year and now it has turned serious. They give me six months to live. I have to go in for treatment at the Munich clinic every few weeks. At present I am in Berlin, wrapping up things here. I am selling the flat.*
>
> *You will never see me again, Leah, after this, and you are well rid of me. I am begging you now to come to Munich. And bring Naomi. I long to meet my niece. Does she look at all like Markus?*

I should tell you that I reconciled with Mama years ago and lived with her on the farm. Mama forgave me once I had made my full confession and told her how contrite I was.

As you know, she died five years ago, and I continued as well as I could. I inherited the farm and all the land around it, and by law it will all go to Naomi when I die, but I have made a will leaving some land to you as well. I have left the will and the deeds with my solicitor. There will be death duties to pay, which is why I'm selling the flat.

But I wanted to see you not for these boring legal matters, but just... well, just to see you. To tell you in person the things I need to tell you.

Will you come, Leah? With Naomi? Please say yes!

If you do reply, please send your letter to the farm. You know the address. I'll be there, waiting, my fingers tightly crossed.

Love, Magda

LEAH – BEXHILL-ON-SEA

The news that Magda was dying changed so much for me. It would truly be over. Perhaps, I thought, I had been too harsh. Perhaps, in her last days, it would be healing not only for her but for me to reach a reconciliation of sorts. Closure. I'd thought I could never, ever forgive her for her betrayal of Markus, but what would Markus have wanted? He was long gone, and presumably, as a Christian who had died a hero, he was in a better place. That's what Helga had told me. And this soreness I felt on his behalf – what good would it do me now? I had my wonderful Jörg, and a better husband, apart from Markus, I could never have found.

Jörg told me that he had always loved me, from the start, when he had winterproofed my cabin on Sonnenhof. He had held both me and Markus in awe. Markus had been his closest friend, and it was mutual.

'Before his last mission,' Jörg told me, 'Markus made me promise to take care of you and Naomi. He knew I loved you and was glad of it; I think he had a premonition that he would die. He begged me in tears. "She'll be devastated," he said, "if something happens to me. And I think it will. Be there for her, and Naomi."'

And he was. And eventually I learned to love him, too.

So why was I bearing this grudge against Magda? All these decades? What good did it do? Would it bring Markus back? No. Would it punish Magda? Would it punish her the way she deserved to be punished?

Yes.

And yet: It seemed even she had found peace within herself, with me being the last, the very last, knot in her heart. I was the only person who could untie that knot and give her resolution. According to her own religion, even God had forgiven her. And if that was the case, was it not the bigger thing for me to forgive her too? The biggest thing?

Was there not a knot in my heart, too – a last knot, that could only be untied with my decision to forgive?

I decided to give her this last chance. She was dying: that changed everything.

We went together, the three of us, Jörg, Naomi, and I. We flew into Munich Airport. The glass door to the arrivals hall slid open. We walked through.

I saw her right away. She had not changed, not a bit. I would have recognised her anywhere. Those features: that stubborn chin, those brilliant blue eyes. But her illness had clearly wrought havoc with her, and there was a pall hanging over her that hadn't been there before. She carried a bunch of flowers and simply stood there. Her bottom lip trembled. She'd been holding the flowers – a bunch of beautiful white roses – to her chest, but as I stood there, just a metre from her, not moving, her hand holding the flowers dropped and she let go of them and they fell at her feet.

I saw that she was crying, silently weeping, silently, her cheeks wet and her nose running. She simply stood there, and so did I.

And then I took a step towards her. Jörg and Naomi both stepped forward with me. Jörg picked up the flowers and Naomi handed her a tissue.

I couldn't hug her. Not yet. But I took her hands in mine. Hers trembled, and were cold as ice, and felt limp and weak. Mine were warm, and closed round hers, strong and confident.

Her whole body began to shake. She was so thin. Barely more than a skeleton. A gust of wind could blow her over. For a split second I saw her as a girl, fourteen years old, before the whole mess started. When she was still innocent. When I still loved her.

How could I hate this wretched living creature?

I then detected the thing I had till now only vaguely been aware of. A kind of nebulous aura around her, of something jittery and dark and nervous, a trembling cloud, a miasma.

Fear. Fear, tremendous, absolute, naked. Just fear. A miasma of fear. She feared me, and my judgement.

Spontaneously, as if driven by an internal force, I stepped through the cloud. I let go of her hands and wrapped my arms round her. Her arms hung loose at her side, as if she had not the strength or energy to return the gesture. Or was too ashamed to do so.

She was still taller than me. Her head bowed slightly down to mine. Her cheeks were wet. As I drew her in, I heard her mutter something into my ear. I couldn't quite make it out, but it sounded like, *'Vergib mir.'* Forgive me.

Only time would tell if I could, if I would. For now, all I felt was pity.

EPILOGUE

About two months after our return to Bexhill, I received a letter and a package. The letter was from Magda's solicitor, informing me that she had passed away. It also contained a copy of her will, detailing, as she had said, her legacy to Naomi and me: the farm to Naomi, and land to me. But there was another legacy.

Magda had written a full account of everything she had seen in Poland and Alsace. It was a draft copy of the book she had always wanted to write, but it was quite different now; written with the wisdom of hindsight, no longer as a proud Nazi but as a contrite reformed soul. It was an untidy, very rough draft. Two hundred typed pages: the original copy and the carbon copy, with hundreds of corrections and crossings-out. Along with two full notebooks of handwritten notes in Magda's own scrawl.

Atrocity on top of atrocity, which she described in full detail. I could not read past the first fifty pages. It was just too terrible to bear. And hundreds of photographs, the ones she had not turned over to the Hitler Youth, instead saving them for this book that she would one day write.

Just as I could not read the book, I could not look at the vast majority of those photographs; so horrific were they. No wonder she had fled to Alsace, but had only found more atrocities there. A codicil in her will passed the copyright of the book, and the photos, to me. All this was now mine, to publish or not, just as I liked.

My first reaction was outrage. What an appalling, ugly legacy to leave to a supposed friend – to a Jew, at that! It was as if she was transferring the concrete evidence of Nazi guilt – the evidence she herself had accumulated – and, in death, cast aside, leaving it to me to deal with. Why had she not finished that book of hers, and had it published during her lifetime, when she could have overseen her notes, put them together, made a coherent document of it all? It was as if she had given up on the project and left it all to me. The goodwill I had been trying hard to gather towards her dissipated in a new outburst of fury.

But in time, my outrage also dissipated, all by itself. I understood. This was Magda's way of saying: *this happened. I was there. I saw this. Please, Leah, make sure it never happens again.* Her legacy was an honour.

And knowing of this last honour she had granted me, slowly but surely the last tendrils of unforgiving melted away. I realised that they were holding me in bondage. I was a prisoner of my own unforgiving, unforgiving of a human being who had found the courage to deeply regret her mistakes. Who had passed through hell, and come out the other side. It was time to do away with unforgiving.

In the end I donated the whole package to the Jewish Museum in Berlin. It was my contribution to the oath that what happened then must never happen again, and it was Magda who had brought me to this point. It was that package that brought me final closure.

And so: goodbye, Magda. I do forgive you. Rest in peace.

A LETTER FROM SHARON

Thank you from the bottom of my heart for choosing to read *The Children of Berlin*. I do hope you enjoyed reading it; that it moved you in the reading of it as much as it moved me in the writing of it. If you did enjoy it and would like to keep up with my latest releases, you can sign up at the following link. Your email address is safe: it will never be shared, and you can unsubscribe at any time.

www.bookouture.com/sharon-maas

I always love to hear from readers, especially if they have been moved or become reflective on reading my novels. You can write me through the contact page on my website, www.sharon-maas.com, or through my Facebook page, www.facebook.com/sharonmaasauthor. If you would like to read my other Second World War books, you'll find info on them on the website.

In particular, if you'd like to know the background to Madame Gauthier– whom Magda meets on her trip to Ribeauvillé – you'll find her in a major role in my Alsace novels, *The Soldier's Girl*, *The Violinmaker's Daughter*, and *Her Darkest Hour*. These three novels all deal with the much-neglected wartime history of Alsace. *Her Darkest Hour* also goes into more detail about the little-known concentration camp Natzweiler-Struthof, the only one the Nazis constructed on

French soil. You'll also find Marie-Claire's full story in *Her Darkest Hour*.

Once again, thank you for reading, and I'd love to hear from you. I promise to do my very best to respond.

www.sharonmaas.com

 twitter.com/sharon_maas

instagram.com/sharonmaaswriter

ACKNOWLEDGMENTS

The Children of Berlin is my fifth Second World War novel, but the only one set in Germany, with an all-German cast of characters; the previous four are all set in France or Asia. This is rather odd considering that I've lived over forty years in Germany and am myself a German citizen. And I have had two fathers-in-law who fought in the Wehrmacht, one of whom was killed in the war. A novel set in wartime Germany seems an obvious subject for me. Yet I always hesitated to write that book.

Perhaps I was just waiting for the right time, the right perspective, and the right book. This is the right book. It is inspired by three German women, all of whom played an essential part in the creation of this particular story. Coincidentally, or maybe not, I met all three of them in India in the seventies. Here's how they influenced my writing.

Uschi was my closest friend for many years, a young woman beautiful in every way. When she was diagnosed with cancer shortly after the birth of her third child, she desperately needed childcare help at home. The year was 1983; I had just finished my degree and had not yet started job-hunting and it was obvious to me that I should move in with her family to help out at home while she underwent treatment.

Uschi lived in what was then West Berlin: a city enclosed in a city, surrounded by a high brick wall. She lived in the building that plays a central role in this novel: Kaiserkorso Eins. Just as in all of my novels, a house, a home, is always the anchor for my characters, and in this book it's Kaiserkorso Eins that pins my people to a location.

Back in the eighties, Uschi recovered from cancer enough to raise her children to adulthood. But cancer is relentless, and it sadly returned with a vengeance, taking her away from us in 2004.

For the research needed for this book, I returned to Berlin in 2022 – now a free, modern, unwalled Berlin – and, at the invitation of her former husband, who still lives there, I stayed once again in Uschi's old Kaiserkorso Eins flat. Nothing seemed to have changed: most especially, the old lift, built in 1913, is still functioning just as described in this book, rattling its way up and down the shaft. Back in Berlin for the first time since 1983, I basked in memories of the best friend I ever had.

That's why Uschi is the first person I'd like to acknowledge here with posthumous thanks. While she had no Second World War material to offer, she offered me the city of Berlin, then and now, so this Berlin-based book is thanks to her. Her former husband, Jörg, once a Berlin taxi driver, was a fantastic host and offered me many Berlin-specific anecdotes. In many of my novels I've 'borrowed' the name of a real person for a character, and in this case, it's Jörg whose name, with his permission, is given to a character. Thank you, Jörg, for everything!

Berlin's Tempelhof Airport, close to Kaiserkorso, plays a huge role in the novel. After the war, the vast airport acquired iconic status as the centre of the Berlin Airlift of 1948–49. During the Cold War, Tempelhof became known as the 'City Airport', offering commuter domestic flights to other German cities and neighbouring countries, and was still functioning during my 1983 Berlin stay. It ceased operating in 2008.

The vast outside spaces are now a city park, while guided tours of the huge buildings are offered daily. I went on one of these tours, and was impressed by the sheer size of the now empty buildings: white elephants, vast, vacant, often incomplete spaces.

Tempelhof's cellars never offered storage space for munitions during the war; at least, not so far as I know. That's one example of creative licence I've taken with this novel; there are other examples, such as the café Zum Zoo and the resistance group *Das Netz* in which Markus was involved. Other resistance groups mentioned in the book, the White Rose and the Baum Group, are, however, real.

The island of Sonnenhof is also fictional. It is however based on a real island; and that's where another close friend, Trudel Elsässer, comes in. Trudel passed away in 2011, aged 102. She *did* live through the war, and, through all the decades I lived in Germany, she was the only person I knew who ever spoke to me of that dreadful time and brought it alive for me. Trudel often spoke of her mother, who was half-Jewish and was thus incarcerated by the Nazis, but lucky enough to survive the Holocaust. Trudel's husband was an engineer who had worked for Siemens in Berlin during the war years; on his retirement the couple built a charming house in the picturesque hills of Alsace, west of Colmar, where I visited her every summer during my student years in close-by Freiburg.

Trudel loved to reminisce. She told me story after story of the war years, often opening her many albums to show me photos of the people she spoke of. Quite apart from the horrors of war – seeking refuge in underground bunkers, seeing dead bodies in the streets – her fondest memories were of an island on the outskirts of the city. A refuge, where as a young woman she'd spend her summers working in her future mother-in-law's garden. The *Sonnenhof* of this novel is based on that island.

The real-life island, called Sun Island by the family, was indeed converted into a sustainable-gardening project in the early 1930s by the famous German landscape architect Leberecht Migge, putting into practice his innovative ideas on ecology and green-city development. It's on that island that Trudel's lifelong love of gardening was instilled, planted there by her beloved mother-in-law, Liesel. Trudel is hinted at in my character Trude, while her mother-in-law inspired the character Lisa von Berg. Trude and Lisa remain entirely fictional.

My last memories of Trudel are of a small, strong woman, the only centenarian I've ever known, white-haired, undefeated, walking along the terraces of her glorious hillside garden, as delighted as ever to show me the flowers she coaxed from the soil.

I was privileged enough to watch a film written and directed by Trudel's son, Thomas Elsässer, a German film historian and professor of film and television studies at the University of Amsterdam, showing original footage from Sun Island and the activities there before and during the war. That film, called *Die Sonneninsel* (2015), was shown on Germany's TV station 3sat in 2018, and is available through Amazon Prime Germany. My thanks to Trudel's daughter, Regina, for sending me the DVD.

My third inspiration for this novel shall go by the letter M. for reasons of privacy. I met M. in 1974 during my very first sojourn in India. M. was an unassuming, middle-aged women who had already lived in India for several years when I first met her. I was a shy, insecure 23-year-old far away from my South American home. M. was most helpful; warm and considerate towards me, she helped me to adjust to the given circumstances and to find my feet in the unfamiliar setting, as well as giving me information about the local culture.

M. lived as a sole European among Indians, often in lodgings that would have counted as extremely deficient in her native Germany. She lived and moved among Hindus, many of whom were orthodox Brahmins who insisted on ritual purity: rules that categorised M. as casteless. Basically, for these purists she was an untouchable, and often treated as such. Yet still, she not only survived but thrived; her aim was inner fulfilment through meditation. She had published a few books on the subject: well-written and authoritative books that inspired and helped many people, including myself.

On learning that M. had once been a high-ranking Nazi, I was amazed. There could not have been a more startling contradiction: she was the very antithesis of a Nazi: open-hearted, understanding, kind. The transformation was undoubtedly authentic. I had not the slightest doubt that she had, in her own private way, atoned for whatever sins she had committed (the Christian concept of 'sin' being understood as 'ignorance' in the philosophy she now adhered to) and transformed herself into a decent human being.

The theme of this book is basically forgiveness. The reader wants to know if Leah can, and should, forgive Magda for the terrible things she has done, not only on the public stage but on a most private and personal level. My own conclusion is yes, she should, but it's a very private decision, not a must. Forgiveness can never be demanded or coerced and is not a human right. Repentance – deep, sincere, repentance – is always a precondition: no forgiveness without contrition, apology, and atonement. It's a deeply personal decision. I have allowed Leah to make that decision to forgive. Repentance and its counterpart forgiveness are matters of the heart, deeply personal, and are only of worth when they are genuine.

And so, my posthumous thanks go to M. for providing me with the bones of this story: the theme of sincere penance, and forgiveness. Magda's story is not M's – it's entirely fictional in every way – but it was certainly inspired by the leap M. made, from worst sort of human to best. Leah, of course, is fictional from start to finish.

Further thanks are due to the wonderful Bookouture team who helped bring this book to fruition, in particular my editor Nina

Winters, whose very insightful comments and criticisms helped make this book the best it can be.

Behind all published books there are the copy-editors, proofreaders, cover designers, as well as marketing and promotional staff who behind the scenes help 'birth' a book. In this case, I'd like to name Jacqui Lewis, Jane Donovan, Hannah Snetsinger, and Claire Simmons, and thank them for their work, as well as the promotional team, Kim Nash, Noelle Horton, and Sarah Hardy who helped bring it to readers.

My thanks go out to the bloggers who also help to bring the book to readers and, last but not least, you, my readers, who have picked up this book and given it your most precious possession, your time. Thank you from the bottom of my heart!

And of course, I'm not forgetting my beloved family members, Miro, Saskia and Tony, all of whom have put up with my rather distracted states of mind while in the midst of writing. I do tend to live in a different world while creating a novel, and thank you for putting up with it all – you know exactly what I mean!